MY
NAME
IS
ONA
JUDGE

BOOKS BY SUZETTE D. HARRISON

The Girl at the Back of the Bus
The Dust Bowl Orphans

This Time Always
Basketball & Ballet
The Birthday Bid
The Art of Love
My Tired Telephone
My Joy
Taffy
When Perfect Ain't Possible
Living on the Edge of Respectability

MY
NAME
IS
ONA
JUDGE

SUZETTE D. HARRISON

bookouture

Published by Bookouture in 2022

An imprint of Storyfire Ltd.
Carmelite House
50 Victoria Embankment
London EC4Y 0DZ

www.bookouture.com

Written by Suzette D. Harrison

ISBN: 978-1-80314-077-3
eBook ISBN: 978-1-80314-076-6

This book is dedicated to
Ona Judge Staines and the ancestors who prepared and paved
the way.
We honor you.
We speak your names.

PROLOGUE

ONA JUDGE

1797, Age 22
Philadelphia, Pennsylvania

The sweet aroma of the jasmine-scented night was lost on me as terror clouded my senses, rendering me barely able to breathe.

I will leave. I will be free!

Heart beating like the drum corps that celebrated Mistress when the General was elected, I rushed through the night, palms sweating, fingers trembling. I clung to the shadows, staying close to the buildings while gripping the hood of my cloak, praying it shielded my face, not merely my head. As a servant from a house of prominence, mine was a familiar face and I could not risk being recognized by anyone I might encounter on those darkened streets. Still, I could not afford to slow my pace and hoped I merely appeared to be a servant dutifully engaged in her owner's bidding.

Mother, help me not to fail. Please be with me.

I'd promised my mother I would accept freedom's hand if

ever it was extended. The chance to escape might never come again. I refused to forfeit it. I *had* to honor my promise and hold on to hope while swiftly, mentally revisiting the hidden clues in Mr. Raitt's elaborate, singsong message. I was to board a ship that night and sail to freedom. But was I really to bypass the blacksmith's shed, the agreed-upon place, and hurry to Sister Vashti's instead? Not knowing the reason for the change in plans, I pushed turbulent thoughts away. I could only pray I'd rightly interpreted Frank's instructions delivered through Mr. Raitt as I rushed towards Sister Vashti's residence in the far, dark distance.

The Creator didn't make me to be someone else's possession.

I bolstered my courage with that simple truth. Tucking my chin closer to my chest, I hurried towards freedom's dream. No person had a right to own me—my spirit, soul, or body. No matter their position in society. Self-important, indifferent persons had erred against my humanity by writing my name in a ledger, same as they did their cattle and sheep. They thought me a commodity to barter and sell; livestock to rule, command, and inventory. But I was invaluably more, and I deserved liberty.

That truth propelled me through the moonless night. It steadied me when a cat shot from the shadows and into my path, nearly tripping me. I lurched backwards and covered my mouth, stifling a scream. Rather than disappear in the dark, it arched its back and hissed as if conveying an otherworldly message. A shiver ran through me; still, I rejected the feline's ominousness and gave it a wide berth. I could not remain in this city of brotherly love and liberty, nor return to Mount Vernon. My right to dignity and freedom wasn't recognized in either place. Heart pounding, I swiftly resumed my uncertain journey, determined to escape fate and living the balance of my life as a slave. I'd been born into slavery where unquestionable loyalty and devotion were demanded, and resistance was violently suppressed. I'd been destined to endure a heinous system and was relegated to a servile position by virtue of the color of my skin. But that night I preferred to stare death in the face or be dragged through Hades than to return to captivity and life with an evil woman who delighted in my being debased. Being given to her as a wedding gift—like fine china or a knitted blanket—was a mortal wound I could not endure or permit.

Hurry, Ona, the ship is waiting!

I obeyed my command as an owl hooted overhead. I glanced upward only to stumble in the process. I righted my step and drew my cloak closer about me despite the tepidness of the evening. The air was thick with warmth, and perhaps my nerve-racking tension. Sweat trickled beneath my arms. My head felt somewhat dizzy, yet I couldn't decrease my pace or abandon the possibility of freedom and fully living. Noticing the slightest change in the atmosphere, my heart galloped with relief. The air had cooled. The brackishness of the water was pronounced. I'd neared the neighborhood adjacent to the waterfront, and my next steps towards destiny.

I must find Sister Vashti's house.

In the dark, things seemed turned about. I needed a moment to calm my racing heart and get my bearings, but time and the sudden clip-clop of horses' hooves behind me allowed no such luxury. I couldn't spare even a moment to turn around and face my possible pursuers or determine if my absence had been discovered and Mistress had sent the authorities to reclaim me. Knowing the slightest delay might mean a return to captivity, I lifted the hem of my dress and ran, the hood of my cloak streaming behind me. Haste was imperative for I was the lady's maid once bound to the President's house, and I had dared to flee. I was the one who'd slipped away unnoticed and was determined to be free. Even if it meant I lost my life while trying.

ONE

TESSA SCOTT

**Current Day
Chincoteague, Virginia**

"It won't take but a minute, baby. I merely want you to see the current state of what you're working with."

It was Friday evening. Sheets of rain and the typical influx of weekenders flocking to the island had turned I-13 into an impossibly wet mess of a logjam. I was behind schedule, at risk of being late, and Dominic—who detested tardiness—expected me back on the mainland. The gentle rebuke I'd earned earlier from my mother had me guilt-tripping over my irregular attendance at family dinners. Even worse, my period was late and my nerves were on edge. Still, I gave Mama Calloway the only response you could give an eighty-four-year-old woman who'd known you all your twenty-nine years and supplied you with abundant love, hugs, homemade cobblers, cakes, cookies, and pies.

"Yes, ma'am."

Damn!

God knew I didn't have time for scoping out an empty, antiquated house in Chincoteague. The house hadn't been lived in in years and had seen better days; yet, it was a gem as far as Mama Calloway was concerned. I should have been northbound, heading in the opposite direction towards Virginia Beach. Instead, I'd left my family's century-old Victorian on the banks of Cape Charles to slowly inch my way south to that island town famous for its wild ponies. All because I couldn't deny Mama Calloway a thing.

"I'll be there as soon as traffic lets up."

"Sounds good to me. I made pecan pralines yesterday. They'll be waiting."

At five foot eight, I weighed one-fifty-five, wore a size ten and considered my weight nicely distributed. My partner, Dominic Daniels IV, didn't wholeheartedly share my opinion and had anointed himself my personal food police. Despite claiming he liked my curves, Dominic constantly treated me to his exercise and fitness sermons, as if I were lazy or ignorant. Dude was anal enough to comment if my breath or kiss held a hint of anything sweet or (in his mind) forbidden. As much as I loved Coni Calloway's delights, I was tired and preferred avoiding a possible argument with Dominic.

"Mama Calloway, my thighs and behind can't afford your confections."

"Tessa Lorraine, with your Coke-bottle physique, you better hush that nonsense! You're beautiful the way God made you. Besides... know what I heard my great-grandbaby, Jade, say the other day?"

I responded evenly despite the tremor that tickled my skin on hearing Jade's name. "No, ma'am. What?"

"Thick thighs save lives."

Laughter burst from me with force enough to exacerbate the pressure behind my eyeballs and my mounting headache.

"Mama Calloway, you're too much." Gingerly, I massaged my temple as she chuckled along.

"Maybe, but I've never heard my husband complain about nothing God gave me. Some women out here buying hips and lips." She sucked her teeth dismissively. "You've never had to swipe your credit card to purchase one curve to my knowledge. So, thank the Creator for what Nature kissed you with. Drive safely and I'll see you and your right-sized thighs real soon."

Responding with another "'yes, ma'am,'" I smiled while depressing the *end call button* on the steering wheel of the Acura MDX I'd gifted myself for my birthday last month, appreciating Mama Calloway's sunshine disposition. She and Dad Calloway had lived in Cape Charles, five doors down from us, since before I was born. Theirs was the go-to house when Mama and Daddy were working and we were too young to be left alone after school. Even when the twins, my big sister Raquel—a.k.a. Rocki—and brother Rico, were old enough that our parents were okay with us being home by ourselves, Mama Calloway was the surrogate grandmother who called to check on us and seemingly saw everything. If we dared to act out or "shame our upbringing," Mama walked in the door from work— thanks to Mama Calloway—already knowing. As a kid I didn't appreciate what I considered snitching. Now? I felt blessed to have grown up in my tightknit African-American community surrounded by people whom I loved and who loved me.

Including B.C.?

"Why the heck am I thinking that?" I leaned into my butter-soft leather seat, frowning at the randomness of my thoughts. Brandon "B.C." Calloway, the grandson of my beloved pecan pralines maker, was my first love and now owned the family's property. Three years older than me, B.C. and Rico were best friends. Throughout childhood he'd treated me like the annoying pest I must have been. Things changed when we found ourselves in a college prep course in high school together, thanks to my being the baby from a family of over-achievers. All my life I've accomplished things at an accelerated pace. According to my parents, I said my first word when I was six months old, took my first steps the next month, and was reading before my second birthday. Clearly, I continued those advanced tendencies and wound up being promoted from sixth grade to eighth, and from eighth grade to the tenth when B.C. was a senior. That's how we simultaneously landed in Honors English and I became more than Rico's snot-nosed, smart-mouthed sister. We had projects together, hung out a little bit. Next thing we knew, we were enmeshed in "first love" shenanigans. Throughout that year we were each other's one and only, married-with-a-picket-fence kind of dreams, until a bitter break-up during my first year in college resulted in intentional distance, dislike, and painful dissolution.

Thinking of B.C.'s nothing more than Mama Calloway's mentioning Jade. And my getting close to Chincoteague.

Jade was B.C.'s daughter by another woman. And Chincoteague was home to that tiny house on the edge of town where B.C. and I gifted one another our virginity.

"God, I'm not interested in skipping down memory lane." I readjusted the rearview mirror, telling myself I had zero time or need for bittersweet memories. Truthfully, lately I had little time or space for much of anything besides managing a growing interior design business, and maintaining an increasingly complicated situationship with Dominic.

Until now I'd enjoyed my romance with a slightly older man, thirty-six to my twenty-nine, established in his career, and whose world seemingly rotated with divine precision. Dominic Daniels was Black bourgeoisie, a highly successful ob-gyn anesthesiologist from old money. Pedantic. Perfectionistic. Driven, outspoken, and laser-focused. Dominic knew what he wanted and how to get it. Including me. He'd wined me, dined me, sent more over-the-top floral arrangements and gifts than I could count; treated me like fine china when parading me as if I were eye-candy in front of his white-tie, yacht-owning, Dom Perignon set. Unfortunately, when beyond the company of his peers, his behavior was less effusive or affectionate. Lately, he was even *less* attentive and showing disturbing signs of selfishness. The shine on our relationship was wearing thin and I was approaching a place where expensive trinkets, exotic getaways, and extravagances were no longer stimulating. Or satisfying. Our romance required too much work, and my energy for it was evaporating. Something was off between us, maybe missing.

Including your period?

I increased the speed of the windshield wipers as if their syncopated rhythm could whisk away worries. Nothing was failproof save abstinence, but experience had taught me to be fastidious about safe sex and self-protection. The idea that Dominic's soldiers might've miraculously stormed the gate had me turning up my sound system to drown disturbing thoughts in the lyrical majesty of Ledisi, Chloe x Halle, and Beyoncé. I needed their sultry, soothing serenades to usher me beyond dread and into willful avoidance.

"As if..."

Denial wasn't an option and, clearly, I lacked subtlety. When stopping by my parents' earlier, with barely enough time to kiss and hug everyone after a meeting with my client ran too long, I'd made the mistake of checking my calendar, for what I can't remember. Staring at blank space where entries for my cycle should've been, I'd gasped for air like a two-ton asthmatic. When Daddy questioned what was wrong, I offered some plausible response and assured him I was fine. My mother eyed me as if she hadn't necessarily believed the lie. But Mama Calloway? That woman was a whole other kind of truth-detector and would know if something was off the moment she saw me. I forced myself deeper into the music, letting it soothe my soul and lift my spirit, rather like a hunter masking her scent to go undetected.

When I get home, I'll deal with it.

Promising myself I'd handle my business like a grown woman, I reached over and changed the temperature settings, increasing the heat to ward off the chill of the November rain. My focus left the road for only a fraction of a second when it was snatched back by an angry symphony of horn blasts.

"Oh, God!"

Heat became a non-thought when confronted by a red sea of taillights blazing brightly, and gridlocked traffic that had stopped abruptly. My furious braking and swerving right were a valiant attempt, but a fail nonetheless. When the front end of my birthday gift to myself connected with the van in front of me, the sound and feel of the impact were nauseating.

"Are. You. *Serious?*"

I let my head sag against the steering wheel while counting to ten to keep from crying like a puny trick-or-treater on Halloween whose candy sack had been snatched by the neighborhood bully.

All through college I'd been carless; had done a happy dance when my parents blessed me with a five-year-old Kia Sportage with slightly under forty-thousand miles as a graduation present. My parents could have easily purchased in cash, brand new off the lot, but they were old school and believed in their children working for what we wanted. Which is what I'd done. I was building my interior design business. I worked. Saved. Until I drove away from an auto auction last month in my birthday gift after my Sportage decided it was finished. My Acura MDX, which Dominic considered "unfeminine," was so new that my vanity license plates hadn't even arrived. I deserved to cry. Instead, I dared to peek into the twilight only to see the driver of the van I'd hit, rain slicker on, trotting in my direction.

He paused where our bumpers met to examine the damage as I pulled my insurance card from the glove compartment and my license from my wallet. I was completely at fault and accepted that.

Rain blew in on an insistent wind, dampening the car interior as I lowered the window slightly. "I'm *so* sorry! Are you okay?"

"Yeah... I guess. Maybe we should pull over," he hollered as drivers honked in annoyance.

"Let's." I followed his lead, forfeiting our place in congested traffic, maneuvering to the side of the road in the descending evening. Grabbing my umbrella, I opened it while stepping into the chilly elements ready to eat crow for my negligence. The other driver had squatted near the back of his van, cell phone in hand—shining its flashlight on the area of impact. I approached, apologizing again, and ensuring his wellbeing. "You're sure you're alright?"

"I should be good," he commented, despite rubbing the back of his neck. "Excuse my language, but with this slow-ass traffic we weren't going all that fast." In close proximity, he appeared to be barely out of high school. And nervous. "I gotta let my boss know what's up. I'm late enough with these deliveries as is."

Glancing at the van, I realized it was a commercial type with wide, double doors in the rear.

Of course I hit something belonging to a business!

Watching Mr. Teenybopper rubbing his neck while calling his boss, my imagination warped into hyperdrive. I saw dollar signs. As in insurance claims, lawsuits for bodily injury, whiplash. I prayed I wasn't dealing with an opportunist while using my phone to snap pictures of the license plate and damage. Thankfully, other than minor paint transfer, the van's bumper appeared to be intact. The damage to my Acura was more extensive, but mostly cosmetic.

"If you don't mind, I'm going to get out of this rain and wait in my car while you finish your conversation. If your manager needs to speak to me, I'm available."

His thumbs-up signaled agreement.

I scurried back to the warmth of my vehicle and, thanking God things weren't worse than they were, called Dominic but got voicemail. "Hey... I had a minor accident. Nothing serious. But I'll probably be late for your father's celebration. Call if you can." I hung up, suddenly tense, annoyed with myself for piling so much on my plate on the same day as Mr. Daniels's sixty-fifth birthday soirée.

It was my typical modus operandi: doing the most and too much all at the same time. According to my mother I was an adrenaline junkie addicted to success who got high from making boss moves and driving too fast. I'd always been high energy, and there was truth in Mama's perspective. Yet, watching the van driver slosh towards me in the rain, I lowered my window, admitting I was tired, that life was beginning to feel imbalanced. Strained. "How'd it go?"

"It's all good. I just need your info and my boss'll be in touch."

I slid a business card from my wallet and gave it to him, proud of the gold embossed logo displaying TLS Interior Design & Renovation—my business, brand, and baby. Moments later, information exchanged, I was back in traffic, moving slightly faster as the rain lessened. I made it to my destination thirty minutes later without further incident, beneath a stormy night sky lacking illumination. Pulling onto the rough, unlit road leading to Mama Calloway's property, I realized I had the driver's details, but nothing pertaining to his employer. Overlooking something as simple as getting the company info or noting any branding on the side of the van could only mean I was off my game. Or perhaps I was plain exhausted.

Either way, make a change.

I promised to follow my own advice while bumping along a road full of potholes that took me deeper into Chincoteague than I cared to be. I should've been at my townhouse in Virginia Beach, showering, dolling up in a little black dress, my grandmother's diamond choker blinging about my neck, five-inch Louboutins on my feet, ready to sashay into Mr. Daniels's party. Instead, I was on this tiny island, the name of which outsiders struggled with. Chincoteague—pronounced "shin-co-teague"— was a land of natural beauty. Serene beaches. Wild ponies. Clam shoals. Oyster beds. Fishermen and fresh catches. A slice of Americana and a tourist destination. I aimed the front of my vehicle at the house Mama Calloway had fought to retain and sat, head beams illuminating the old place, recalling the stories Mama C. told when we were kids of her family's connection to the first president's wife, Martha Washington.

A developer with local ties set his sights on the land a few years back. According to him, he was a descendant of original settlers with rights, accusing Mama Calloway's family of land encroachment. The matter wound up a lengthy legal battle, which my sister, Rocki, ultimately won. Her reputation as a fierce real-estate attorney wasn't fluff-and-foolery. Chick was savage.

Smiling proudly, I looked for Mama Calloway's 1985 vintage Mercedes that she refused to replace, and that her mechanic kept in pristine condition, but didn't see it. I reached for my cell phone to call her nearly in sync with an incoming text.

Waited as long as I could, but had to get back home. Have a pot of beans on stove. Key's under the mat. Pralines are on the kitchen table.

I read Mama Calloway's text, hating that her time had been wasted. She'd come, gone. Now, I was out here in the backwoods. Alone. With nothing but pitch-black. Marsh creatures. And ancestral spirits.

Or maybe ghosts?

Unbuckling my seatbelt, I dismissed those thoughts while responding to Mama Calloway's text. I had a healthy respect for the ancestors. Ghosts and goblins? Not my thing.

"They belong to Halloween."

Still, I hesitated, debating if I should return another time. Preferably in daylight. But my schedule was tight, I was already here, and knew the place well enough. Plus, nothing except the night stood between me and pralines.

I zipped my jacket and left the warmth of my vehicle to rush through the cold, damp dark. Grabbing the house key from underneath the mat, an eerie shiver rolled through me. I straightened immediately, glancing into the night, feeling as if I wasn't alone. As if something or someone was, perhaps, present. Unseen.

"Tessa, you're tripping."

I shook off the weird sensation and hurried to open the front door, glad the head beams of my SUV were still on, dispelling the darkness outdoors. Thankfully, Mama Calloway had left a light on inside.

Stepping into Mama Calloway's inherited home was like stepping back in history. The house had been in the family for generations, nearly two centuries, but hadn't been lived in on a regular basis since Mama Calloway's parents passed away. Instead, it had become the site of family reunions, Christmas, and summer gatherings; a safe haven for displaced relatives experiencing hard times, economically. Now, in keeping with family tradition, the house had been passed on to the firstborn of the firstborn, B.C.

Entering the front room, I felt that little tingle I always felt in old houses with history.

When you enter a dwelling, Tessa, be quiet. Listen. Every

house has a story and a spirit. If you keep your tongue still, they'll tell you how they wanna be handled.

That was wisdom my grandfather—a carpenter who'd built his own business and inspired my father's foray into real estate —taught me. I closed my eyes, sensing this house didn't want to be remodeled or sold. It wanted to be kept in the family.

Parts of the structure had been rebuilt, or added on in prior decades, but certain features had been preserved in their original integrity. Case in point: the huge brick-and-stone fireplace, gaping wide in front of me like a cavernous mouth. Consuming half of a living-room wall, the length, depth, width of that fireplace was vast enough for a body to comfortably sit in. I knew: I'd sat inside it as a kid.

I grinned at a memory of playing with Kimiyah, B.C.'s sister and my bestie, when we were five years old making ash cakes in the fireplace and landing in trouble with Mama Calloway. It took, seemingly, forever for Kimiyah—a.k.a. Mimi—and me to clean the mess we made. Not to mention we ruined our clothing and caught a scolding. Despite all of that, whenever Mama Calloway took us on her trips to dust and air out the house, we made our way to that fireplace as if magically drawn to that cool cavern on hot summer days. After the third incident of our being "hardheaded," Mama Calloway gave up on trying to correct us. Instead, she spread a plastic tarp to protect the hardwood floors adjoining the brick hearth lovingly laid by her great-great-great-grandfather, and made sure we wore old clothing our parents wouldn't mind us ruining.

Maybe the ancestors are playing in that soot and calling to you.

I was too young to understand her words back then. Now? I shivered and felt goosebumps prickling my skin.

"It's freezing in here." I brushed off my reaction and considered grabbing firewood from the rack and lighting it for old times' sake. "Girl, you're here on business. Get with it."

I will as soon as a praline crosses my lips.

Greed led me to the kitchen.

My whole heart smiled seeing that decorative tin on the table. I wasted zero time removing the lid and holding that container beneath my nose. Eyes closed, I inhaled the rich, caramelized fragrance of squares of creamy, nutty goodness. I had a piece in my mouth before my next breath.

"Yesss, Jesus!"

That confection was orgasmic, had me waving my hand like a hat-wearing sister at a Sunday service ready to do a holy dance.

I'd finished one square and was on my second when my cell rang. The ringtone told me it was Dominic. I ignored it. My mouth was full; plus, I couldn't have Mister Hits-the-Gym-Six-Days-a-Week clouding my epicurean experience.

I'll call him back.

Tin of edible treasures in hand, I headed for the living room to start taking photographs. I needed before and after pictures for my portfolio, as well as visual aids to help me brainstorm a redesign concept. After winning their property dispute, Mama Calloway's family was ready to pour some love into the dwelling's aesthetics. Perhaps that lengthy legal battle had heightened their sense of ownership or the property's impor-tance. I was pleased for the family's victory and this redesign opportunity. This was more than adding to my portfolio; I'd be preserving the bricks and mortar of a family's history, and enabling the continuance of a place that factored dearly into my childhood memories. Doing so would be no simple feat. It required not merely creativity, but reverence.

Tessa, make it quick.

I disliked rushing through a project but a sudden ping on my phone was an indicator that Dominic had left a voicemail. No doubt it was a terse reminder that I was behind schedule. That had me stepping up my pace, trying to finish in a flash, when I saw one. Literally. A burst of white light near the fireplace when my camera clicked.

"What the?"

I hadn't engaged the flash. Or maybe I had?

Checking my phone, my heart rate jumped a bit when I saw the flash wasn't on. I examined the photo I'd just taken. Nothing was out of the ordinary, leaving me to conclude I'd been mistaken.

Maybe you hit your head in that fender bender and gave yourself whiplash or an aneurysm.

I might've laughed at my warped humor except a puff of air suddenly tickled my neck, like a breath or as if warm fingers had brushed my skin. I spun around expecting God knows what and found nothing. No one.

"Oh, hell no." I didn't scare easily and loved horror movies. But being alone out there and remembering the ghost stories Mama Calloway liked to frighten us with when we were kids, about the house being the resting place for the spirits of her departed ancestors, I decided to call it quits. As soon as I grabbed my pecan praline tin.

I hurried towards the mantel to snatch it up and, in my haste, inadvertently knocked Aunt Ona off. I knew it was Aunt Ona, and not her counterpart Mama Delphy, because of the smears of pink nail polish marking her base, courtesy of Mimi "decorating" her when we were kids. That caught Mimi a spanking, and if Mama Calloway had been there to hear the unladylike expletive that crossed my lips when Aunt Ona crashed to the hearth, landing heavily on the bricks, I might've caught one too. No matter that I was a grown woman.

Aunt Ona was one-half of a set of oversized candlesticks made of solid silver way back when. Like a century or more ago, long before Mama Calloway was born. And I'd possibly caused her to get damaged. Again.

"Damn."

It took a little effort hefting her solid bulk back atop the mantel. Maybe Dominic was right and I needed to hit the gym or, better told, Aunt Ona was a candle pillar, not merely a stick. Either way, I sighed with relief seeing nothing more than minor scratches on the base that could, hopefully, be buffed out. But the same couldn't be said for the hearth. Brick dust and broken pieces marked the place where Aunt Ona had landed with all of her solidity. Clearly she was crafted for endurance, and this was my night for being chaotically clumsy.

"Dang, girl, you damaged the family's Freedom!"

According to Mama Calloway, her great-great-great-grand-father William Costin—Mama Delphy's husband—had carved the word *freedom* into the hearth after laying its bricks. Doing so was his way of exerting newfound literacy denied him when enslaved, as well as reminding their family of the liberty they'd gained. There was one brick for each crudely formed, block letter. Through the years others had reinforced the message by scraping into the letters, essentially creating a permanent etching. Thanks to my knocking Aunt Ona off the mantel the "O" was demolished. I felt horrible and would have to call my beloved confectioner to apologize.

Reminding myself I needed to hurry my behind back to Virginia Beach, I bent to clean my mess only to notice something beneath the broken brick. Paper? Or perhaps fabric? I could've left with my pralines, but my curiosity was equal to the spookiness experienced moments ago when feeling that breath on my neck. Fine, I was nosey and always had been. Next thing I knew, I had the fireplace poker and was prying up the already destroyed brick that would have to be replaced. My conscience took a hit as I gently lay aside what remained of the letter "O." It came away easily, thanks to Aunt Ona's hit jarring it from its ancient mooring.

"What in the heck is this?"

Squatted on my haunches, I carefully withdrew an object

wrapped in old fabric, the fringes of which literally crumbled in my hands as I began unwinding it. It was shaped like, perhaps, a book and didn't weigh too much. Still, it somehow felt heavy. Portentous. That sensation was heightened by the creaking of the second-story floorboards overhead, followed by the unmistakable sound of slow-moving footsteps when I was supposedly the only one there.

God didn't have to nudge me twice to—as my grandmother would say—get the hell outta Dodge. I grabbed that unearthed object wrapped in musty-smelling, disintegrating cloth and ran-walked my hips towards the front door.

Don't leave the pralines!

"Dang, Tessa, you're greedy."

Owning that fact, I raced back and grabbed my candy tin before whichever of Mama Calloway's ancestors was playing games with my sanity could win. I was out the door, barely pausing to lock it behind me, aiming my fob at my SUV and starting the engine remotely. I ran through the rain, flung open my door, tossed my packages onto the passenger seat, and reversed down the driveway as if it wasn't raining sheets, or pitch-black back there, and the path was pothole-free. I made the mistake of glancing at the house when safely reaching the end of the long drive, only to see what seemed like the glow of a faint light and a shadowy form in an upper window.

I wasn't down for crazy, supernatural encounters and decided that the next time I came out here alone at night would be never. A shudder ran through me as I gunned the engine and headed for the main road leading out of Chincoteague.

TWO

ONA

Spring 1784, Age 10
Mount Vernon, Virginia

"Mother, is it enough?"

My ten-year-old self stood in nervous anticipation while displaying my handiwork for my mother's expert inspection.

She stopped darning the General's hosiery to give the new handkerchief I'd embroidered for Mistress Martha her full attention. She'd assigned me the task to keep me occupied, but I'd finished sooner than expected.

"Let me see it."

She was busy, with little time for distractions, but I wanted to prove myself a student worthy of her tutelage. More importantly, I treasured moments in her presence, as well as her opinion, so I placed the handkerchief in her capable hands and awaited her assessment.

With a slight, tired sigh she held it to the sunlight flowing through the open window of the workhouse. It was often a busy, bustling cabin—greater in length than width, with rows of tables the plantation's carpenter, Isaac, had made, at which sat Mother's apprentices. They had nimble hands and were highly skilled in or learning their craft. Their job was to attend to the matter of clothing the more than three hundred bondspeople belonging to General and Mistress Washington here at Mount Vernon as well as its three farms. But only Mother and her most senior seamstress, Lame Alice, were permitted to manage any clothing worn by the Washingtons.

Watching Mother scrutinize my handiwork made me nervous. I shifted from one bare foot to the other and back again while playing with my fingers and humming the tiniest bit.

"Be still, Ona. Wait with patience."

I stilled myself immediately. I was a restless child by nature —my mother's "black-eyed butterfly," full of energy—but I wanted to prove that I was ready, mature enough to become Mother's newest apprentice. I was in my tenth year of life and had performed small chores for as long as I could recall. Gathering firewood. Collecting eggs and tending chickens. Hauling water to the men and women laboring in the fields. Helping Nanny Moll and others caring for the younger children— including my baby sister, Delphy—throughout the day as their mothers engaged in duties about the plantation. I wasn't much younger than some of those mothers and was in line to receive my work assignment as early as next year. Assignments were based on skill, natural inclination, or as dictated by the plantation's needs and its managers. I had no way of knowing what mine would be until it happened, but I prayed it wouldn't be far from Mother or out in the fields six days a week in whatever weather heaven granted, whether lovely or inclement.

Eustis is my best friend, but I don't wanna work out there with him.

Eustis was only twelve but had worked outdoors the past two years because of his strapping physique. Plantation life demanded that even the young use their abilities for its prosperity, but I didn't want to spend fourteen hours a day in favorable weather, seven or more in winter, bent over in back-breaking labor—pulling weeds, harvesting crops, planting seeds, or the countless other physically demanding tasks fieldwork required. Or be like my older brother, Austin, assigned to multiple tasks in multiple places. I wasn't lazy. But I was afraid of snakes and didn't want to encounter any while working outdoors.

Even worse, I was terrified of being taken from my mother like Dido's son was taken from her. Dido and her son belonged to the General, not Mistress. Perhaps had they been dower slaves like the other eighty-five of us under Mistress's keep, heartbreak would have been avoided, or at least delayed. She'd been in the spinning house weaving when she'd received the news that her thirteen-year-old son had been snatched from the fields and sold along with two other men to settle a debt. That horror happened last year and Dido hadn't yet recovered from her decimating loss. Sometimes I could still hear her blood-chilling, soul-searing screams or see her viciously struggling against the men physically restraining her as the wagon containing her son rolled away from Mount Vernon.

But we're *considered dower slaves.*

Whenever nightmares of Dido's devastation haunted me, I'd remind myself that my mother came to this plantation as the inheritance of Mistress Martha, and that we belonged to her, not General George Washington. A widow when Master Washington met her, Martha Dandridge Custis had been the wife of Daniel Parke Custis. When Mister Custis died, Mistress was granted lifetime use of one-third of the human chattel held by his estate, now considered dower slaves. By law, dower slaves and their offspring could be neither sold nor freed, but were held in trust for her two surviving children, Mistress Patsy and Master Jacky. Mistress Patsy and Master Jacky had lived longer than their brother and sister, Daniel and Frances, who'd died at the age of three and two, respectively. That luck lasted only so long and Mistress Patsy died eleven years ago when barely seventeen. As for Master Jacky, he met his untimely demise three years back, leaving their mother childless and his wife and children without him. Now, we—the dower enslaved—were held in trust as an inheritance for Master Jacky's four offspring.

For as long as I could recall, each new year began with an audit of the estate's holdings. We, the chattel property, were made to line up and give our names which were, subsequently, compared to what was listed in a register that also accounted for livestock and household novelties. I detested having the same classification as a herd of sheep, silver utensils, or heirloom jewelry. But I took consolation in knowing I couldn't be snatched, tossed on a wagon, and taken away. At least not yet. Not until Mistress Martha's grandchildren were of age to claim their inheritance. That didn't make the terror of witnessing General Washington's slaves being bartered or sold any less real.

May heaven grant that I wind up with Nelly, not Evilest Eliza. Eventually.

Ugly notions of living out my latter life with that ill-tempered she-thing had me fidgeting again.

"Ona."

Mother softly speaking my name was enough to cease my agitation. When she beckoned me forward, I immediately closed the distance between us and leaned against her with nervous expectation.

"Remove these stitches here. And here. Make them tighter and neater the way I taught you."

"Yes, ma'am." I plopped onto the hard-packed dirt floor near her bare feet, accepting the handkerchief and the tools of her trade that she handed me. With eager zeal I set to the task of carefully releasing silky threads and re-stitching them, determined they'd be perfect when finished.

I can do this.

I wasn't merely eager for Mother's approval, but for the possibility of remaining in the workhouse with her and the others. If I was to be assigned duties six days a week from "can see to can't," I wanted it to be here in the presence of women who made me feel safe, and with whom I shared a skill, a trade. I wanted to be included in their circle, their stories and gossip, and not just treated as a little girl—like Delphy—and sent elsewhere because I was in the way or too energetic. I had to create beautiful things to prove my suitability and gave my best to repairing the embroidery on that handkerchief in hopes of impressing not just Mother—a former housemaid whose sewing skills eventually moved her into this position—but Mistress.

I was nearly finished when the quiet, sparkling sound of Mother's laughter interrupted and pulled my attention from my task.

I looked up and couldn't help mirroring her smile. "What's funny, Mother?"

"You bite your lower lip when concentrating, same as I do. You can continue..."

It might've been a small comparison, yet it made me feel giddy and I resumed my work with vigor.

I liked the idea of inheriting my mother's traits and not merely her seamstress abilities. Sometimes I wondered if I'd gained my sewing skills from her or Andrew Judge, the indentured English tailor who'd designed General Washington's buff-and-blue ensemble worn to the Continental Congress in 1775, the year after I was born. More than tailoring fancy garments, Mr. Judge had fathered my younger sister, Delphy, and me. Mother never spoke on the nature or constructs of their union, if it was placed on her, or was what she wanted; neither did I know Andrew Judge the way a child does a father. We were of two different castes: we were Negro, he was British. We were enslaved for life because of our color of origin. Whiteness enabled him to work as the General's tailor, resolving whatever his debt. When his term of indentured servitude was completed at Mount Vernon he left for Alexandria, Virginia, and was neither seen nor heard from again. His leaving without looking back—and the fact that he hadn't acknowledged Delphy or me as his, and never attempted to arrange our freedom—led me to believe theirs wasn't an equal fellowship, that my mother had been given to him. Or worse, perhaps she'd been *taken.* Used, like other bondswomen given for the carnal relief of white men residing on the property—be they indentured, employed men, or simply General Washington's guests. Bondswomen such as Mother were treated as consorts. Bed-warmers. Loaned as if human blankets. Yet, used for something so profoundly intimate. I knew such things only because these ears of mine liked listening to conversations not intended for me.

I suppose Mr. Judge's tailoring and Mother's role on the plantation landed the two in close proximity and certainly would have made him aware of her, and may have fostered my sister's and my existence. But, again, Mother wouldn't speak on him or the other men she'd been parceled out to and because of whom she'd borne six children—Delphy, me, Lucinda, Nancy, Tom, and Austin. Perhaps I'd inherited my natural proclivity for sewing from them both, but Mother was the only one who parented me and nurtured such abilities. Now, I sat on the ground, bent over my task, determined that my stitching would live up to her standards as head seamstress.

"There!" I hopped up when finished several minutes later, wearing a satisfied grin. I'd slowed down, taken my time, and was proud of the outcome. "How's this?"

I had to wait until she'd finished a final slip stitch on General Washington's silk hosiery. When she held it up to the light, all I saw was the proof of Mother's magic. The hosiery appeared as if brand new, near perfection. She folded them neatly and placed them in a basket on the table before taking the handkerchief from me. She examined it thoroughly, only to stare at me a long while, straight-faced and not speaking.

I forced myself not to fidget this time, to simply wait, and was rewarded with the twitching of her lips: evidence that she was suppressing a smile.

"Ona, it's... excellent."

I wanted to throw my arms around her in my excitement but caught myself before I did. Instead, I stood proudly composed, pretending I was a more mature individual ready for my official apprenticeship, and not just a freckle-nosed girl with, sometimes, grimy fingernails and wild hair, who couldn't keep still. Pretense didn't curb my grin. "It's enough?"

She stroked my face, fondly. "It is, my black-eyed butterfly. Pretty soon you'll be teaching Delphy."

That made me beam. My five-year-old baby sister was even more active than me, a ball of constant energy. Getting her to be still long enough to even thread a needle would be a feat, but Mother had confidence that I could teach her. I was determined that I would.

"I can do it, Mother. I can teach Delphy everything you taught me. Can we start after supper this evening?"

Mother couldn't respond as we were interrupted by a child running through the cabin's open door. "Mistress is coming!"

The announcement was punctuated by gales of giggles floating on a spring breeze cooled by the nearby Potomac. I detected Miss Nelly's tinkling voice, as well as that of Master Washy, her younger brother. I liked the two, easily enough. Clearly, they liked me. Particularly, Nelly. She was a few months older than my baby sister, and sometimes the two played together. But, whatever her reasons, Nelly preferred my attention to Delphy's. My being five years older than the Washingtons' granddaughter never deterred her from seeking me out whenever possible, demanding my attention and that I be excused from whatever chore was consuming my time just to play with her. Not that I had a choice, but I didn't mind simply because she had a lively spirit and a tolerable disposition.

Unlike that evil thing she calls a sister.

"Everyone. Tidy up!"

Mother's instructions incited a flurry of activity. Fabric scraps, bunting, and spools of yarn, thread, and other sundries were swiftly stored in their proper baskets. Tables were straightened, garments neatly arranged on top of them as I grabbed the whisk broom stored in a corner and swept the dirt floor to make it neat. We worked together so that within moments the workhouse felt pristine. When Mother nodded her approval, we lined up as if soldiers in General Washington's army and were ready—hands clasped, eyes lowered—to greet the mistress of Mount Vernon.

"Oney!"

Nelly and Washy reached the cabin before Mistress did. They burst through the open door and made a beeline for me, using the nickname the Washingtons had elected.

"Oney, we've been looking for you. Come play with us." Nelly grabbed one hand, and Washy, the other. He was a small tike, barely three, and put all his strength into trying to persuade me to do his bidding.

"We can't play just yet, Master Washy. I have to wait for Mistress."

"Well, won't you be delighted that I'm here."

The scent of lavender and lilies preceded Mistress Washington. A diminutive woman, and not one for excessiveness, she entered the workhouse wearing a pale-blue and cream dress, one she'd referred to before as a "simple frock." Bedecked with ribbon and lace, I found the wide skirt and light silk of her everyday finery simply splendid.

If only Mother had such niceties.

I glanced at my mother, unable to resist comparisons. She was a bondswoman without the softer, sweeter things that made life easy. That made her no less lovely in my eyes. I thought her beautiful. She was a mulatto with soft hair, fine features, and fairer skin. But she deemed such traits inconsequential to a person's worth. Her beauty was a natural product of her spirit, her gentleness.

I looked from Mother to the other seamstresses, my head cocking slightly when noticing pronounced similarities I'd never fully recognized before. Like Mother, her apprentices were all fair in complexion, ranging from milky to fresh-churned butter with a touch a honey. Or the sugar cane that Cook roasted to an amber sweetness. Their hair, neatly plaited and pinned beneath kerchiefs, was a texture easily tamed. Not like mine that was wild, bushy. There was something curious about these facts that I wanted to explore but couldn't, due to having to give Mistress my attention.

"Betty, must you line up the girls every time I near the workhouse? You all are standing so stiffly that I feel the need to bark 'at ease' as if I'm General Washington, and back on the front lines." Tale was that during the war that won the nation's independence, Mistress often visited her husband and was of great service to him. She may have been small, but she was strong of mind and very efficient.

"My apologies, ma'am."

Mistress waved Mother's words away with a delicate movement of her hand. "I hope everyone is faring well today?"

"Yes, ma'am," rang out from the women lined up beside me, as if a well-practiced song offered harmoniously.

"That's splendid. It's such a lovely day I couldn't object to accompanying the children or being corralled into their antics. Of course, they had to seek out Oney, and I'm actually glad they've brought me in your direction, Betty. The moths are getting outrageous in their destructiveness. They've even attacked some of my... intimates. I've several items that require mending. Send Oney to get them."

Eyes still lowered, as required in deference, Mother inclined her head. "Yes, ma'am. Ona, do as Mistress instructed."

I immediately hurried for the door, knowing obedience was a fundamental condition of my existence. Not merely obedience to my parent, but to anyone possessing white skin. First and foremost, the Washingtons. They owned Manor House Farm—one of the numerous settlements on the estate—where I'd always lived, as well as more than three hundred bondservants enslaved here at Mount Vernon. They were decent enough, and didn't allow the overseers to get too terribly out of hand mistreating us. Still, even then at the age of ten, I was wholly aware that my life, my time and energy, and my being belonged to them.

Nelly's high-pitched whining suddenly filled the cabin. "But Gram-Gram, we want Oney to play with us. Why does she have to go get some silly intimates?"

Already outdoors, I looked back when Mistress laughed.

"Get on with you, you little scamp." She shooed her granddaughter outside with a wave of a handkerchief extracted from beneath her dress sleeve.

Nelly ran to catch up with me, flinging her arms about my waist when she did. Washy wasn't far behind, his little legs moving as quickly as they could until both children held on to me in defiant protest.

"Oney's ours. She plays with us," Wash decided.

"I can't play with you just yet, Master Washy. Not until I do as Mistress wants." I could deny the child's demands only because I'd been given direct orders from his grandmother. Otherwise, my refusal might have been considered defiance, a punishable offense.

"It's fine, Oney. These two won't rest until they've gotten their way." Mistress's tone was indulgent. A strict disciplinarian, she often made allowances in matters pertaining to her grandchildren. "I'm a wise woman who knows how and when to compromise. Betty, send someone else for the mending basket. Oney may play with these two scallywags." She pulled their ears affectionately.

"And Delphy," the little girl insisted.

"I imagine she's at the nursery with the others?"

"Yes, Mistress," my mother answered.

"Someone go and get her so I may be free of my plaguing granddaughter." With an indulgent smile in Nelly's direction, Mistress turned and headed in the direction of the mansion. "I will take advantage of this free moment to have tea with the General. That is, if he's not occupied elsewhere."

When not engaged in business or entertaining visitors, the General often rode about the estate on horseback to converse with the estate managers and ensure all was well. Whenever he did, I was glad to go unnoticed, as his quiet demeanor and tall stature rendered him rather imposing.

I was only mildly aware of Mother sending her youngest seamstress to handle the task assigned to me and another out back to fetch Delphy as Nelly and Washy—whom the General and Mistress showered with affection—vied for my attention.

"We play army!" Washy had recently received a set of wooden soldiers sent by his mother, who'd remarried and moved away after the death of Master Jacky, her first husband and his father. Thankfully, she'd taken Evilest Eliza and her other daughter, Patty, with her to her new home, sparing me Eliza's unmerited torment. Only Nelly and Washy remained with us. The little boy loved those wooden toys and couldn't get enough of pretending that he was the commander of imaginary wars.

"We played army yesterday. I want to play dolls, or dress-up, or cup and ball." Nelly was a lively sort and her protest was, like her, loud and vivacious.

"I no wanna play girl games." The three-year-old's rebuttal was as fierce as his sister's.

"Well, I'm bigger than you and you have to do as I say."

"Nuh-huh. I'm George Washington Parke Custis, and I'ma be a master when I'm big." Even at his tender age, the child had been made to understand his place in the hierarchy of a human chattel system where some were born free and others in bondage because of something as simple as the color of skin.

"Well, you don't own me. I'm not your slave, so dress-up it is. You have to wear the baby bib."

"I'm no baby!" Washy pushed his sister to punctuate his declaration.

She responded with her own shove and, being bigger and stronger than he, sent him toppling onto the grass. He turned red in the face.

I moved swiftly, knowing tears were next. Mistress hated for her grandchildren to experience distress and I'd catch trouble if any crying reached her ears.

"Master Wash, you're okay." I sat on the grass and pulled him onto my lap, wrapping him in a comforting hug. "I know you're a big boy and not a baby. Big boys know how to keep from crying when their sisters aren't gentle with them." I gave Miss Nelly a pointed look, shaming her for her behavior. "We can play army first, and then a game with your sister. Right, Miss Nelly? I imagine you won't mind waiting. I mean, as you said, you *are* bigger and *much* more mature..."

She made a show of resistance by standing there looking away at nothing, ignoring me. That lasted only so long. Eventually, the young mistress acquiesced by plopping down beside us, knowing that no matter how indulged she might have been, her grandmother did not tolerate their being rough with one another.

"Is there anything you'd like to say to your brother, Miss Nelly?" I prompted the five-year-old, who was acting petulantly.

"Sorry."

"For...?"

"I'm sorry for pushing you, Washy." When she reached over to hug him, he easily returned the gesture, a perfect example of childlike forgiveness.

"It's okay." He hopped up, reaching for our hands, solaced that we were now compliant playmates at his command. "Let's get my soldiers and fight the Red Coats and savages."

Simple as that, all transgressions were pardoned and we set about our play in earnest.

Playtime nearly consumed the day. Delphy joined us, adding her vivaciousness to our number. From army to cup and ball, hunting for leprechauns, jumping rope, and London Bridges that fell flat, we played to their hearts' content. By the time the midday meal was finished and Master Washy went down for his nap, I was nearly exhausted and actually wished I was back in the sewing room with Mother, sitting quietly at her feet or in a corner somewhere, stitching. But Miss Nelly had other plans.

"We must prepare for the ball." She'd crowded a swarm of dolls on chairs flanking a child-sized table brought down from her room and into the yard. We'd already served tea to the plastic-faced, inanimate objects; now, it was time to dress them for a night of imaginary festivities. Tiny dresses of silk and velvet lay at the ready.

"Here, Delphy, you may dress Juliet." She handed my sister a wide-eyed creature with stiff, curly yellow hair. "Oney, take any of the others."

I dressed the doll nearest me, wondering—as I often did when watching Mother handle clothes for Mistress—what it would be like to have such soft material against my flesh. I looked down at my homespun and shapeless shift made of coarse fabric that sometimes troubled my skin. It was plain. Unimaginative. Delphy's was equally unassuming. An odd, agitated feeling sped through me as it always did when realizing we had nothing remotely close to the quality of that owned by Miss Nelly's lifeless dolls. Our rations were distributed at the start of each year. One frock of coarse cloth. A pair of ugly, stiff brogans. Sunbonnet. Kerchief. Undergarments. With the exception of shoes, all were made by the seamstresses. Each item was functional. Nothing was luxurious.

"Hurry up, Oney and Delphy, or the dolls will be late."

"Yes, Miss Nelly." Our responses were automatic, as were our compliant actions.

"Here, let me put them in the carriage." Taking the dolls we'd dressed, she gently placed them onto a toy wagon magically transposed into a fabulous conveyance by sheer dint of imagination. "Negroes aren't allowed to attend, so you two stay here and be ready for us when we return. No! Wait. We need an attendant." She searched a large box of dolls until finding someone suitable. "Here, Oney. You can come after all! You be the chaperone like Mammy Moll."

She placed a ragdoll in my hands that proved vastly different from those on the carriage. This doll had floppy limbs and was the color of pitch with stiff, black, natty hair standing on end. Bulbous eyes and a cavernous, toothy grin had been painted onto its face. Like mine, its frock was plain, save the replicated slices of watermelon decorating the hem.

"Come on, Oney. Get in the carriage."

I looked at Delphy who sat on the grass, her head cocked slightly while eyeing the doll that to me, somehow, felt objectionable. I moved slowly, arrested once again by a curious agitation as I found myself comparing this doll to those bedecked for their fancy evening. She was the opposite of every one of the dolls deemed worthy to attend make-believe festivities, and seemed careless in her construction. Some part of me knew *this* doll had been created intentionally to be the opposite of the others.

"Yes, Miss Nelly..." Whatever energy I had left after a day

of play slowly drained away as my playmate corrected my putting the doll next to hers.

"No, not there. Here!"

The tar-colored ragdoll with her watermelon hem was removed and placed on a ledge at the back of the wagon-cum-carriage—facing outward and away from her ivory-skinned charges. Grabbing the wagon handle, Miss Nelly started forward, declaring with glee, "We're off to the ball of the century!"

I followed, slowly, my steps nearly lethargic. Heavy. When the wagon hit a bump in the grass and the chaperone doll fell off, I didn't inform Miss Nelly or make a sound. Instead, I stepped on that doll and, with my whole weight, pressed her offensive existence against the earth. When Delphy gasped I turned back, put a finger to my lips, and shook my head before making certain Miss Nelly hadn't noticed. Thankfully, she was far ahead, lost in her voyage to grandness.

"That wasn't nice, Ona."

My baby sister's whisper felt like a rebuke and I should've felt ashamed. Instead, I'd been reminded that even in play, there was no escaping this system that would forever relegate us to subservient positions.

"But I don't want Oney to go!"

Night had fallen and, unlike Delphy, I hadn't returned to the workhouse since departing earlier in the day. My mother had made a pretense of coming to the big house to ask Mistress a question. Based on the way she'd watched me as I waited for Miss Nelly to finish supper, I sensed she was worried although I wasn't sure why. I'd given her a reassuring smile despite my fatigue. Now, I stood in Miss Nelly's room witnessing what could become an epic tantrum.

"It's time for bed, my dear. You may play with Oney tomorrow after her other chores have been completed."

The young girl was resistant to her grandmother's pronouncement. "Why does she have to do chores?"

"Such is her station."

"But she's *my* playmate. And since she's my playmate, shouldn't she be with me whenever I say?"

"There will be no more sass from you this evening, Eleanor Parke Custis. Am I clear?"

Tears and sniffles accompanied her contrite response. "Yes, Gram-Gram. But, please, can't Oney just stay tonight... or even always? She'll keep me from under your feet when you have one of your headaches. And she knows how to make Washy and me not fuss with each other and behave. Pretty, *pretty* please. If Oney's here it'll be good for you, not just me."

Mistress laughed despite trying not to. "You are a persuasive little something, aren't you?"

"Does that mean she can stay?"

Eyes lowered, I felt Mistress's attention on me as she called for her maid stationed in the hallway. "Send someone to take word to Betty that Oney's duties are being changed. She is to remain here in the house as a companion to Miss Nelly. Have bedding brought up."

The little girl's delight was obvious in her shrieking with glee while hugging her grandmother before racing towards me.

"Isn't this great, Oney? Now we can play from the time I wake up until I go to bed."

"Yes, ma'am."

She chattered and chirped until her grandmother instructed her to climb into bed. Candles were extinguished and I lay on the pallet that was brought in for me and placed on the floor, alongside Miss Nelly who whispered happy ideas of what we'd do the next day until overtaken by sleep.

I was left to lay in the dark feeling odd, alone, and out of place.

My nights had been spent in the cabin with my mother and sisters—as well as my older brothers before they'd been sent to work elsewhere on the plantation. I'd been in the main house on errands for others, but never like this. I'd often imagined how it might feel to be surrounded by comfort and opulence, but being here like a permanent fixture felt wrong. I wanted the familiar sights and sounds of my family, and shifted on my pallet seeking comfort and ease. Instead, my thoughts skipped back to today's doll game. My mind fastened upon that dark, dusky doll allowed to go to the ball as a chaperone, and I disliked my ill treatment of her when she'd fallen from the wagon.

She's not real. She felt nothing.

I, however, did.

I liked Miss Nelly enough, but I didn't want to be on a bedside pallet in loyal attendance like Mopsey or Truelove— General Washington's beloved dogs. I was a real living and breathing child—neither doll nor dog—with loved ones of my own, but I'd been taken from them at a child's whim. My positioning had suddenly shifted without my consultation or consent. I'd been born a dower slave and had never been free, but a sudden sense of servitude and inequity pressed heavily on me. I couldn't lay a finger on it, but I knew my life—my world— had changed, never to be the same. And, in this, neither my mother nor I had any say.

THREE

TESSA

"You're a damn hour late, Tessa." Such was Dominic's greeting as I entered the venue to find him in the huge rotunda entryway impatiently waiting for me, looking tense and pacing. He kissed my cheek and smiled tightly for the benefit of anyone watching, while whispering against my ear: "Showing up late isn't merely disrespectful, this CPT is ratchet." His hot rebuke accompanied by his hand pressing angrily against my back felt far from good, and wasn't exactly appreciated.

I'd called after leaving Mama Calloway's family homestead, returning his increasingly irritable messages and texts. He was fully aware of the traffic situation, as well as the fender bender that had caused delays. This show of annoyance and his CPT—Colored People Time—disparagement was off-putting but typical. Dominic Daniels was a demanding individual.

"I got here as soon—"

"Showing up for my father's celebration *after* the first course has been served is unacceptable. I expect better, so make this the last time something so inconsiderate happens." He stopped digging his hand painfully against my spine and eased away, allowing me much-needed breathing space. He adjusted his silk bow tie as his eyes roamed over my person. "That's not the dress I'd choose for you, but at least you look good."

I'd opted for a curve-kissing floor-length gown over my little black dress, thinking it more appropriate for this white-tie celebration. My satin ankle-strap stilettos were on point, as was the crystal wrist-cuff and earring set, and my grandmother's string of delicate, floating diamonds draping my neck. I wasn't a vain woman, but my whole look was hitting and I knew it. "'At least?'"

"You know what I meant."

"Maybe I don't, Dominic." I gently wiggled my spine, trying to escape the ache where his fingers had gripped my back far harder than necessary. "Mind explaining that for me? It sounded slightly belittling."

"That's your take on it, not my intention. Stop overreacting."

I took a deep breath and reached for calm. I was tired after the long drive out to Chincoteague and back. Not to mention what had felt like ghostly encounters at Mama Calloway's. I wasn't overreacting, in my opinion, but maybe I was on edge. Still, I didn't appreciate his stank-ass behavior. It felt immature. Insensitive. As if his primary concern was my being punctual and in my proper place, as if I were some necessary but intimate object or accessory. I opened my mouth to articulate my objections only for him to cut me off.

"Let's discontinue this discussion while you fix your face. People are watching, Tessa." He'd expertly masked his displeasure with a charming grin capable of fooling others.

I glanced beyond the entryway and noticed a few eyes on us. I'd been raised right and knew better than to be a public spectacle, but his aggressive response to my tardiness was enough to make me want to push back and hammer this ish out.

Honestly, over the past several months Dominic's behavior had been increasingly—if not aggressive—red flag'ish. Since meeting him at a charity auction the year before, I'd known him to be a focused and driven person who could come off as intense, a bit stiff. He was dogmatically punctual, over-the-top organized, and a fitness freak whose ideas of gender roles sometimes seemed archaic. He liked for me to look and act a certain way, like somebody's brown-skinned Stepford wife kind of chick, but I wasn't Davinia Daniels and couldn't do it. Miss Davinia, Dominic's mother, was a former cotillion queen who—from what I'd heard —had shriveled and shrunk throughout her constrictive marriage to a man who treated her like some pretty little insipid something unworthy to be heard, only seen. Maybe that's how she became an unrecognizable semblance of herself after finding companionship in a bottle. I was fond of Mrs. Daniels, but had no intention of joining some sad, misunderstood sister-hood. I wasn't the silent type and her son's unmerited attack deserved a clapback.

He just wants everything to be perfect for his father's festivities.

That notion calmed me down a bit. Plus, as an anesthesiologist, he had job-related stress. His response to my lateness wasn't what I'd give him had the roles been reversed, but again, this was Dominic. Strait-laced. Exacting. Perfectionistic.

Opposites attract.

My sister, Rocki, too often commented on the differences between Dominic and me, saying we were night and day with my, sometimes quirky, ways and upbeat personality. She even hinted that maybe Dominic was more than I should (not could) handle. Not an ideal fit. But then again, Rocki—not to mention Rico and my parents—didn't exactly connect with him. Not that we spent a lot of time with my family as a couple, but whenever we did my usually warm-hearted, welcoming clan were quiet, cordial at best. I told myself whenever Dominic and I clashed that we were simply different with divergent personalities and that life wasn't pristine. Clashing was one thing. This increased displeasure and running commentary on how I should or shouldn't be, look, or behave was starting to work my nerves and rub rather raw.

I have a daddy.

I wanted a partner and lover, not a micromanager dictating my existence. Sometimes I wondered if our increasing disagreements were attributable to our seven-year age difference. Or perhaps it was a cultural thing. We were both African-American, but I hailed from a family of white- and blue-collar, everyday kind of people who—through hard, painstaking work —had been blessed with success and what some may consider a cushy existence. Yes, we'd climbed the socioeconomic ladder, were well-established, and perhaps privileged, but we came from humble origins. Dominic was from old money. Black bourgeoisie. Five generations of Martha's Vineyard kind of elite.

I bet he's never eaten a chitlin.

That thought was so random and out of nowhere that it left me laughing.

"Is something funny?"

I answered Dominic's heated question by "fixing my face," threading my arm about his, and turning towards the dining room, ready to act the dutiful plus-one, secure enough within herself to hobnob with folks who made my annual earnings in mere weeks.

The sooner this party is over, the sooner I leave.

I was tired, and my period was *still* late—which was enough to put me on edge. That didn't keep me from pushing my shoulders back and stepping forward, one long leg peeking out from the thigh-high slit in my dress. I whispered as I walked, ensuring my voice reached Dominic alone. "I apologize for being late, but I'm here now, so let's do this."

A smile masking my face, I stepped forward with confidence, dodging internal questions about the viability of Dominic's and my relationship.

"Come on, baby. You don't have to stay overnight if you prefer not to. Just come home with me so I can show you my appreciation and take care of you."

The Dominic at the end of the soirée was a completely different being from the beast I'd encountered when arriving. Clearly, the evening had gone to his—and his parents'—satisfaction, and I'd proven myself the perfect little "significant other," intelligent enough to hold my own while providing good eye-candy. Now, he was all horny and magnanimous, trying to get me to his house. Or better said, into his bed.

I considered him, appreciating the tall, handsome, café au lait specimen that he was. His tailor-made tuxedo left him looking magazine-ready. Everything about him was impeccable —from the expertly groomed, low-and-lined hair to the mustache framing his perfect lips. His body was tight and right from religiously hitting the gym and I knew *he* knew how to work it to my satisfaction. Physically he was everything, and I should've been excited about climbing into bed and having my sexual needs met. But lately, even sex had become one-sided, with Dominic dictating everything from our positions to duration and frequency. Lovemaking had become restrictive, unimaginative. Besides, my menstrual cycle was still missing in action. That alone was enough to make me tense, unable to fully relax, and wanting to be temporarily celibate.

"I'm sorry, babe, but I'm exhausted and not at my best. Raincheck?"

We stood in the venue's parking lot beside my vehicle. The rain had stopped and the clouds had released their hold on the night sky so that it was clear, the stars twinkling like faraway diamonds. The autumn air was cool, crisp, causing me to shiver despite Dominic's cashmere coat draped about my shoulders. Removing the coat, I handed it to him while unlocking my door, which he held open as I climbed in.

"The party was magnificent. I hoped your father enjoyed it. I'll call you tomorrow."

He stared at me a moment, a pissy look on his face, before closing my door more forcefully than necessary and stalking off without a "good night" or even a kiss.

"What the hell is his problem?"

The longer we're together the less I understand him.

I watched him march towards the venue, shoulders defensively squared, head proud and lifted. Maybe he was what Rocki accused him of being: a spoiled rich boy unaccustomed to *not* getting whatever he wanted. His stiff, unrelenting body language was enough to make me reconsider declining his invitation. Maybe good sex was what we both needed. I started my engine in order to lower my window and summon Dominic back, only to stop when seeing him approach a woman exiting the building in a short, skintight piece of a dress defining all her bra-less, panty-less business. She had a brickhouse pole-dancer physique with boobs twice the size of mine, incredible legs, a snatched waist, and phat ass that could make a blind man look twice. Her blonde Beyoncé weave flowed down her back. Her make-up was beat. She was sex in a dress, a gorgeous threat. Not to mention Dominic's ex.

Carmel Carter.

Girlfriend sashayed all that "body-ody-ody" towards him, hips undulating like sea grass in a hot, seductive wind. I watched as she hugged him, kissed his cheek, and stood there chatting comfortably until Dominic draped his coat over *her* shoulders and escorted her towards another area of the parking lot, his hand at the small of her back.

A sparkling seductress had my man?

Reversing from my parking space, I drove to the top of the aisle, looking in the direction they'd gone, only to see nothing. As if by magic they'd disappeared, which had me concluding they'd made it to wherever either of their cars were parked and hopped inside. Together. Likely doing something other than talking in the dark.

My imagination took off, gifting me torturous images of the ex and her sexual bag of tricks which, knowing Carmel's reputation, she'd gladly whip open for Dominic.

Spotting his car, I aimed my head beams at it, only to see it was empty. I had no idea what Carmel drove, but turned left, cruising slowly up one aisle and down the next, hoping to find them.

"Girl, what in the whole hot hell're you doing?"

I brought my SUV to an abrupt halt. This foolishness felt stalkerish, the actions of an insecure woman. I'd worked too hard to heal hurts caused by past relationships and told myself to stop this dim-bulb behavior and take a breath. I was better than this. Leaning back in my seat, I followed my advice, closed my eyes, and inhaled deeply, thinking one thing.

Well... damn. Here we go with the m-f'ing infidelity.

Showered, refreshed, and in my favorite, thigh-length Doc McStuffins pajama top, I double-checked that my security system was armed before snatching my praline tin from the kitchen and marching to my bedroom. Seeing my phone charging atop my nightstand, I wanted to call Dominic and cuss him ten ways to Sunday if he wasn't home, where he belonged. Alone.

Shoulda made him install that stalker app same as he did you.

I'd installed some friend-finder app on my phone months ago at his request. I disliked the idea of virtual surveillance taking the place of trust and complied only to end a prolonged argument, and because his rationale seemed somewhat legit. It was for my protection, according to him. I was a single woman often on the road alone—Chincoteague, Cape Charles, Virginia Beach. The island was safe and sleepy, but there were spots where cellphone connection wasn't the greatest and wild terrain where it was easy to get lost at night. When I'd asked if he planned to install the app and share his whereabouts with me, his response had been that he was a man and could protect himself; I had no need to worry.

I was angry, hurt, but also knew I had no idea what, if anything, had occurred between Carmel and Dominic. Or even where they'd gone.

"Maybe they simply sat in her car, chatting, and catching up..."

The only thing Carmel's catching up on is overlooked orgasms.

Telling myself to back away from the ridonculousness, I sighed in defeat, dropped into bed, and sat there staring at nothing. I hated feeling paranoid and insecure, but I'd experienced infidelity before.

But that was then and dished out by a different man...

Dominic and I were in a committed, monogamous relationship. Or was that merely my imagination? Was I the idiot being faithful while he enjoyed other options?

"I'm not doing this."

Not the insecurity or acting like a victim member of Cheateration Nation. I refused to walk that devastating road again. I wasn't down for Dominic manhandling our relationship or dipping his stick in other women, but if that's what he wanted he was welcome to it. He wouldn't, however, find me sitting at home like some dutiful, powerless chick waiting on my turn for his time and attention.

I'd rather be by myself than share a penis.

Pulling back the covers, I eased underneath them and grabbed the novel on my nightstand only to find myself reading and re-reading the same paragraph. It was a Pamela Samuels Young legal thriller that, any other night, would have monopolized my whole attention. My distraction was a clear indicator that Dominic's actions had crawled beneath my skin. I hadn't even opened my praline tin.

"Let me go to sleep."

It was that or give place to a pitiful puddle of tears.

Turning off my bedside lamp, I slid down deep beneath my covers, pulling them up about my neck. The downpour had kicked up again minutes after I'd arrived home. I loved the sound of rain and would have found it soothing any other time, but right then its lyrical lull was lost on me. Even my luxury bed linens suddenly felt scratchy, irritating. My mood was off and comfort was elusive, leaving me lying there staring at a dark ceiling.

Maybe I should meditate.

That was something calming and soothing that I hadn't engaged in much, and certainly not recently. I'd been too busy hustling and grinding out here in these streets growing my business. I was that kid who obsessively decorated and constantly rearranged her dollhouses—painting, staging them—as well as my bedroom. Back then I knew nothing of feng shui or even interior decorating, but I'd parlayed those early interests into a solid business, for which I'd neglected personal time and self-care. Just as I'd neglected my family. I hadn't attended our communal dinners in—as Mama Calloway would say—a heap of Sundays.

Notions of Mama Calloway redirected my thought process.

"Oh my God, that package!"

Turning on the lamp, I hopped out of bed, remembering the cloth-wrapped object I'd unearthed from the fireplace hearth earlier that evening. I'd placed it in one of the plastic containers in which I kept my shoes in order to keep it safe, as well as to keep dust and its ancient cloth from crumbling all over the place. Now, curiosity had me hurrying to the dresser where I'd left it. Retrieving the box, I sat on the edge of my bed and removed the lid only to experience the same sensation I had when out at Mama Calloway's: that someone or something was present. Except this sensation wasn't hair-raising or fear-filled, but oddly pleasant. I shivered with the possibility that I was meant to find whatever this object turned out to be; that I'd been invited into, perhaps, sacred space by the unseen. That had me shivering again and glancing about my room as if expecting some kind of materialization or manifestation.

"Tessa, you need to get your whole mind together." I tried discarding ideas of supernatural forces at play while gently fingering the cloth wrapping, which only seemed to intensify them. "Maybe I should call Mama Calloway."

Or B.C., seeing as how he's the rightful owner of the property.

God knows my nosey self wanted to open that package. Instead, I decided to be respectful, not intrusive. But the longer I sat with that container on my lap the more I wanted to know what mystery lay within the folds of that ancient-looking material. It could be a family heirloom or something equally invaluable, significant. Or some form of treasure, or even something that proved an accused person's innocence.

"You've read too many mysteries." My imagination might've been ramped up, but that didn't resolve the fact that I held a mystery in my lap.

What if I get permission to open it?

I grabbed my phone to check the time. It was after midnight. That was too late to call anyone without causing unnecessary alarm. Besides, if it proved to be nothing more than old socks or handkerchiefs or some other kind of crazy foolishness, I would have interrupted someone's sleep for no reason.

Do you really think anyone would've taken the time to bury something as simple as socks and whatnot?

That thought didn't do a thing except exacerbate the sense of mystery. It left me thoroughly intrigued and determined to know *something*.

"Okay... I'm only going to take a peek. That's it."

I told myself that if the contents proved too personal, I'd stop immediately and simply hand it over to B.C. I was satisfied with that compromise and began the careful unveiling.

There were layers and layers of fabric, and it took several moments to unwind them. I proceeded as gently as I could. Even so, the ancient cloth disintegrated in several places, leaving fragments at the bottom of the container. My hands were coated with dust, thread, and a weird chalky-oily substance. Ignoring the yuckiness, I continued my task, my heartbeat speeding up as I unwound the final layer to reveal an object in a casing that reminded me of the cheesecloth my grandmother used when straining ingredients for her homemade preserves. I removed it cautiously—almost reverently—to reach the object within. It was a leather book or, better said, something like a journal bound by a leather strip and what looked like a satin ribbon, the pages of which were weathered, yellowed.

I felt like a trespasser for merely having it, and downright devious for untying its closures, turning back the front cover, and eyeing its content. The first page was so brittle that it crumbled easily, leaving me to gently brush away its fragments before gingerly continuing. The following page was blank only to give way to one that held slanted penmanship that was small yet somewhat stylized, like script from way, *way* back in the day when writing was accomplished by ink and quill.

Excited and wondering the age of the book, I focused on the

words on the page. Some were smudged and difficult to read, requiring me to lean towards them as if being drawn in. Smudged or not, the power of the script left me feeling immersed; captivated as if by a magical spell.

My name is Ona Judge. Ona Judge Staines, to be precise. I am the one who escaped from the house of George and Martha Washington, the former being the famed army general who became President. I was the favored maid of the latter. The two deemed me a slave and thought me property. Same as they might mules or sheep. They erred in their superior thinking. The Creator made me free, and I am my own woman. As a free woman who has acquired the forbidden joy of literacy, I find myself anxious to tell my own story. The one I lived. Not one artfully, erroneously crafted by someone else for his or her benefit.

Stunned, I leaned even closer to the script and reread that passage twice before sinking back against my headboard in disbelief.

"This has to be a hoax or a joke." Even as protests slipped across my lips, I considered the family's claims that some ancestor somewhere in their lineage had a direct link to the nation's first president. Was this proof of that connection? "Nawww, this is crazy. Somebody made this up and slipped it beneath that hearth."

If it's so farcical and insane, why are your hands shaking?

I grabbed my phone again, wanting to call Mama Calloway. I called Mimi, my BFF, instead only to get voicemail, which left me calling my history-loving big sister.

She answered on the first ring, sounding worried, and as if I'd yanked her from sleep. "What's wrong?"

"Rocki, girl, I found a book!"

Her sigh was irritated yet relieved. "You interrupted my

sleep to celebrate the fact that you're hooked on phonics, baby sis?"

"Chile, hush and listen." I spewed everything from the creepy close encounters at the house in Chincoteague to this painstaking unwrapping that revealed sloping script written by an enslaved woman's hand. Or, rather, a woman who had escaped bondage. "From the house of the freaking first father of this grand old, slave-holding U.S. of A.! That same dude who claimed he couldn't tell a lie after he chopped up his daddy's cherry tree like some little bad-ass urchin."

Rocki chuckled lightly. "That's a lie within a lie. Washington never said that. His biographer made that up in an attempt to make him appear virtuous."

"You know this because?"

"I saw it on a documentary. Anyhow, what's in the book? What does Miss Ona Judge Staines have to say?"

I read the opening passage, falling silent when finished, feeling reverent.

It took Rocki a moment to respond. She audibly exhaled and then whistled softly. "Whew, that gave me goosebumps." Her voice was hushed.

"Right! She's like, 'Hell naw! Y'all ain't fixing to tell some cockamamie bullcrap and write my life all kind of wrong.'"

I heard Lincoln, my brother-in-law, in the background sounding groggy, along with muffled noises as if he was rolling over in bed. "Rocki, what's going on?"

"Nothing, baby. It's just Tessa. Go back to sleep."

"Hey, Linc! And, wow, I'm 'just Tessa' and nothing?"

"Whatever, brat. You know what I meant. So, what're you going to do with this diary?"

I carefully turned several pages to see the same sloping writing. The author hadn't changed. It was still the penmanship of Ona Judge Staines. "That's probably what this is, huh? A diary." That made it all so intimate, and I felt bad for snooping and invading Miss Ona's privacy.

"I hope it doesn't reveal some Sally Hemings-Thomas Jefferson exploitative ish."

I cringed with thoughts of that elicit relationship between the nation's third president and an enslaved teenager housed on his Monticello plantation with whom he'd fathered multiple children. "Big sis, don't make me sick. Oh damn, Rocki, those candlesticks!"

"What candlesticks?" she mumbled through a yawn.

"Mama Delphy and Aunt Ona. The two on Mama C.'s mantel." I'd knocked Aunt Ona from the mantel earlier that evening only for her to crush the brick with the letter "O" on it. She'd landed on the letter of her first name, like some sort of otherworldly guiding force. "Oh, good God, that was her!"

"Who was what?" My sister yawned again—nosey and interested in all of this, same as me, yet clearly sleepy.

"Go back to bed. I'll fill you in if anything progresses."

"Maybe that can be done in person. As in, family dinner..."

Sunday dinner at my parents' had become a tradition, a way of us getting together on a regular basis now that everyone was grown and on their own. I loved sitting on the sprawling veranda of my childhood home overlooking the windy Cape Charles shoreline—eating and laughing with my family. Except I couldn't recall the last time I'd attended, thanks to doing my own thing—mainly working or being somewhere with Dominic.

"Your niece and nephews miss you. I do, too."

Rocki's four-year-old daughter and Rico's six-year-old twins were my heart, but as an aunt I was failing them. "I've been missing in action and need to do better."

"From your mouth to God's ears. I'm going back to sleep. Love you, baby sis."

"Love you."

I disconnected and sat there a moment, telling myself to get my life in check and stop neglecting my loved ones. Chasing success and dollar bills couldn't compete with the support and joy of family and I needed to do better by them.

I will.

Making that promise to myself, I returned to the book, being extra careful. A thick wad of pages near the back were already stuck together and I didn't want to cause further damage. I settled into reading, getting through the first segment detailing Miss Ona's removal from the sewing workhouse, and being reassigned to the mansion. My heart hurt thinking a ten-year-old child could be so easily removed from the life and love she'd known, and that her parent had neither power to prevent it, nor any say. I exhaled so heavily it made me remember what had felt like a warm gush of air against my neck, and the sound of footsteps overhead while at the house in Chincoteague earlier that evening. Not to mention what looked like the glow of a light and the shadowy figure I saw when reversing down the driveway. What if those phenomena were connected to the spirit of Ona Judge, the very same author of this diary?

What if her spirit had actually been there in the house with me?

"Ooo, no ma'am, no sir. I do mysteries, not ghost stories." That had me closing Aunt O's journal and rewrapping it in its decrepit bindings, returning it to the container, and snapping on the lid before jumping out of bed to store it in the closet.

I'd turned off my lamp and was back in bed when nature decided to increase my sense of unease and treat me like both an actress in, and audience to, my own horror movie. Tree branches scraped my windows as rain fell heavily, whipped by a strong wind that was suddenly howling. I told myself it was a normal storm, only to sit straight up when I heard what sounded like the creaking of floorboards. I knew it was nothing more than my townhouse settling, but when lightning flashed and lit the whole room with a pink glow that seemed to vibrate erratically, I hopped out of bed. Again. Grabbing that box from the closet, I hustled down the hallway, storing it beneath the kitchen sink, only to rethink that. Disarming the security system, I went through my laundry room to access the garage and promptly placed that box in the rear cargo space of my SUV.

"You'll be okay out here tonight. Tomorrow you're going to your family."

I hurried back inside and practically ran to my bedroom, closing its door as if it were some impenetrable barrier to phantoms. Washing my hands until they were clean of ancient debris, I grabbed my praline tin, turned on my wall-mounted flatscreen TV and channel-surfed until I landed on *The Golden Girls*. Ten minutes in I was four pralines down, exhausted yet needing Blanche, Rose, Sophia, and Dorothy to distract me from the writings of a former bondswoman and the present-day chaos of Dominic.

My phone vibrated the next morning far too early for a Saturday. Buried deep beneath my covers, half asleep, I reached for it and answered without checking the caller ID. "Yes?"

"How you doing, Tessa?"

My eyes flew open and I rolled onto my back. "Who's this?" It was an idiotic question meant to buy me some time, an act of pretense. Or maybe it was my petty way of letting the caller know I'd moved beyond him.

He merely laughed that low and sexy laugh of his, instead of being offended. "You saying you no longer know my voice, or are we playing games today?"

I started to give a smart-assed comeback only to think better of it. I wasn't stuck in the past, a broken-hearted college freshman dumped by her first love. I could hold a decent conversation like any mature woman living her best life and handling her business. "Why're you calling so early on a Saturday, B.C.? Why're you calling *period*?"

Mama Calloway had been the go-between, enlisting me to renovate the family's property for this very reason: B.C. and I shared too much broken history.

"So, you *do* recognize my voice."

I absolutely did. It was deep, slightly gravelly yet somehow smooth in its sensuality. Unique. Like him. It was enough to trigger memories of what he'd once meant to me. I pushed those errant thoughts away rather aggressively.

"How can I help you, B.C.?" I was so focused on our foolish friction that I forgot to mention last night's find.

"I'm calling about my driver."

"What driver?"

"The one you slammed into last night."

I sat up, frowning, only to remember the fender bender. "Are you serious? That was *your* van?"

"You didn't notice the Jade's Jazz Café logo on the side of it?"

"Of course I did."

"The lies you tell."

I had to laugh. "Okay, I didn't. I was in a hurry and it was raining."

"I'll give you that."

"Wait, why was your van on the island when your closet restaurant's a two-hour drive away in Richmond?"

"Catering an event 'cause I got it like that."

I snorted at his playfulness rather than respond to the pure confidence that in other men would've come across as arrogance. No matter the unfortunate history between us, one thing I knew about B.C. was that he was down to earth, far from narcissistic, and had worked hard for every one of his successes.

"So, Miss Scott, how do we resolve this?"

I grabbed my earbuds from the nightstand and put them in so I could go hands-free and scroll my camera roll. I tapped the pic I'd taken of the van's rear bumper, enlarging it for a better view. "I apologized to your driver last night. I admit full responsibility and apologize to you as well, but I don't see any real damage on these pics of your van. And I hardly *slammed* into anybody." I stopped suddenly. "Wait, did he complain of body aches or injuries this morning?"

"Mitchell's mom had to take him to the ER a couple of hours ago. Apparently, the collision was worse than he realized. The two lowest discs in his back are ruptured and he'll need surgery—"

"*Surgery!* Oh damn." I felt horrible. "I'm so sorry."

"Yeah, well, that's only the beginning. He's looking at extensive physical therapy. Your automobile insurance is up to date, right?"

"Yes."

"Good, 'cause from what I've been told, this claim could run in the high six-digits. Might even hit a million."

"You've got to be kidding! I'm absolutely remorseful about— you said his name is Mitchell?"

"Yes."

I smelled fraud, but chose to be pragmatic versus accusatory. "I hate that Mitchell was injured, but traffic was bottlenecked and we were barely inching along, so I don't completely comprehend how—"

His booming laughter cut me off.

"I'm sorry, Brandon, but do you see something funny that I don't?"

"Tessa, relax. I'm just messing with you. Mitchell's little skinny ass went to a house party last night. I checked on him this morning and the boy's fine."

I pushed off the covers and sat on the side of my bed, irritated. "And you talk about me playing games when you're the one playing with my whole life today?"

"I am."

I couldn't suppress my grin. "What do you want, B.C.?"

"Have dinner with me."

That pumped the brakes on my acting-salty routine.

After breaking up when I finished high school we'd stayed as far apart from one another as life allowed. Intentionally. Which wasn't necessarily easy, seeing as how my BFF was his sister. Still, we managed our delicate dance of avoidance. He went his way; I went mine. He even got with another woman and had a child—a daughter, Jade. Thus, the name of his jazz café that wasn't a café but a five-star restaurant worthy of James Beard awards or high Michelin ratings.

"Thanks, but no thanks. You don't cook all that good."

I smiled as his boisterous laughter filled the phone once more. B.C. had always been jovial, upbeat. Nothing kept him down for long. He was the consummate comeback kid destined and determined to be a success despite life's challenges. Listening to him laugh, his mirth touched me in a way I didn't know I needed to be touched. It was warm, rich. Carefree—and so the opposite of Dominic.

Never compare men. One will inevitably come up shorthanded.

My grandmother's remembered wisdom kept me from sliding down that hazardous hole and revisiting last night's incident that had me scouring a parking lot, looking for a very absent Dominic.

B.C.'s voice brought me completely back to him and our conversation. "Yeah, okay, Tessa. I'ma let you swing by the Richmond café and swallow that lie along with some melt-in-your-mouth red-wine-braised short ribs. Garlic mashed potatoes with gruyère. And maybe some balsamic-glazed Brussel sprouts or asparagus. How 'bout that?"

"You know I'm greedy. You don't play fair."

His tone was suddenly serious. "I'm playing no games. Come on by the café."

"Why?"

"Call it an olive branch if you want, but I think we're both grown enough now to stop avoiding each other like a couple of punk-ass kids. I say we handle our business and squash whatever ish still exists." Silence sat between us until he spoke again, his voice light and playful as before. "Plus, you owe me and I'm cashing in. You know I'm opening a new spot on the island, in Cape Charles, right?"

Our community was only so big, and famous for circulating gossip. "I might've heard something about it."

"Come through and give me some decorating ideas and I'll forget all about last night's accident."

"Oh, so you wanna blackmail a sista?"

"I get it however I can. You coming? Or do I need to make a claim with my insurance company?"

I laughed and stood, stretching one arm overhead and arching my back, reminding myself that more than a decade had passed since our break-up. I wasn't a broken teenager. The life-altering decisions I'd made back then, that had felt so devastating and still had a lingering effect, no longer imprisoned me. Perhaps this was a much-needed opportunity for B.C. and me to bury the past and re-establish ourselves as—if not friends— two cordial adults on an even keel.

I declined the dinner invitation, knowing my dining with my ex would never fly with Dominic. I was, however, open to seeing this new café. That was purely business. "I'll check my calendar and text my availability. How's that?"

"That'll work, TLS."

I smiled at his old habit of running my initials together. "Oh, wait! Lemme tell you about what I found at your Chincoteague property last night—"

"What were you doing out there?"

"Taking pics for renovation concepts."

"What renovation? I have an interested buyer who'll take the property as is."

"Wait. What? Your family has owned that property forever. Rocki just won the case against that speculator, and you're *selling* it?"

He was quiet a moment. "I'm sorry my grandmother brought you into this, but that's family business, TLS."

I couldn't wrap my head around what I considered callousness. Not many African-American families were blessed to have a centuries-old property as part of their legacy. I wanted to tell B.C. he was making a colossal mistake by selling, but that wasn't my place. Plus, my opinion wouldn't do anything except add strain to our already tenuous relationship.

"I need to get off of here and take care of some things. Enjoy your day, girl, and don't eat nothing nasty."

"Bye, B.C." I disconnected, disappointed in his decision.

Shrugging it off, I made a pit stop in the restroom, handling my business before turning my back to the mirror and examining it. It was still sore where Dominic had painfully dug his fingers into my spine when I'd arrived late to the festivities last night. I expected to see bruising. Thankfully, there wasn't any.

You need to tell him something about manhandling you.

Promising myself that I would, I headed for the kitchen, thinking about my Saturday-morning phone call while fixing myself a breakfast of champions. Clearly, Mama Calloway disagreed with her grandson and had enlisted my services of her own volition; but Brandon was the inheritor and it wasn't her decision to make, despite her being a force to reckon with. I'd been pulled into a classic generational clash of opinions and knew my place was to stay out of it.

Surfing social media, I was halfway through my first bowl of Peanut Butter Cap'N Crunch when I came across a pic of B.C. and his daughter, Jade, posted by Cape Charles' community

page announcing the pending opening of his newest establish-
ment. I barely skimmed the text. My focus was on the little girl,
arms wrapped about her father's waist, a huge smile dominating
her beautiful brown face.

You would've had an older sister or brother if...

Unable to finish the thought, I dumped my remaining cereal
down the garbage disposal, wondering if old pains ever truly
went away.

FOUR

ONA

Sometimes I wish I was back in the workhouse.

Spending the past several months as Miss Nelly's playmate hadn't been wholly terrible. Most times it was even pleasant. But it wasn't the same as living my life with family, whom I missed terribly. Especially Delphy. She'd always been my shadow, trailing behind me whenever possible—mimicking the things I did and said with laughable results that amused us all. I often fabricated pretenses, or tried navigating the children in the direction of the workhouse, just to get a glimpse of familiar, comforting quarters and the people I longed for and treasured.

The day after I was assigned to be Miss Nelly's playmate, Mother came to the mansion to return the intimates she'd repaired for Mistress. The delivery could have easily been accomplished by another seamstress, or even Delphy. Knowing my mother had devised a way to see me, my heart bubbled with glee. Outdoors, playing with the children, I'd run to her, throwing my arms about her waist, nearly causing Mother to drop her basket. She hadn't scolded me; she'd returned my embrace.

"Are you well? Are you safe?" She'd held my chin, peered deeply at me, and searched my face.

"Yes, ma'am, but I don't like being away from you." I tried not to cry, but my tears were too quick to prevent.

Mother wiped them with her apron. "Don't cry, my black-eyed butterfly. We may not be together as we have been,"—she placed a hand over my heart—"but I'm always here."

That brought me solace, yet I wanted to be with my sisters, and in Mother's presence—learning my sewing craft under her expert guidance. I missed the songs Mother and the other seam-stresses sometimes sang while focused on their tasks, their voices like soothing whispers from heaven. I even missed helping Nanny Moll with Delphy and the small children whose parents couldn't attend to them while working about the estate —not to mention stealing playtime moments with my friends, Eustis and Callie. Being at Miss Nelly's, and even Master Wash's, beck and call day and night ruptured my childish ideas of who I was and solidified my servile position. Sleeping in the main house on that floor made me painfully aware that I was owned by others, enslaved, a servant. Some nights when Miss Nelly was asleep, I pretended I was back with my beloveds just to ease the knot that sometimes formed in my throat at the thought that I was separated. Alone.

At least I have Sundays to myself.

Or partially.

Just like reading and writing, religion wasn't taught to us on Mount Vernon. Most Sundays the General imbibed wine and indulged in card games with gentlemen visitors. Accordingly, we weren't made to assemble about the main house listening to a hired white preacher spewing holy scripture that reinforced our servitude and commanded obedience, which is what I'd heard occurred on other plantations. Nor did we have our own preacher in the slave quarters other than Caesar, who'd somehow acquired that forbidden fruit of literacy and took to preaching and reading the Bible to anyone wanting to listen. That didn't mean we lacked respect for the Creator, or that some didn't slip away to hush arbors to fellowship, sing, or pray.

I'd gone to those secretive services in the hush arbor a time or two with my big sisters and found them fascinating. Yet, it wasn't the way I wanted to spend my Sundays. I preferred being with Mother, having her wash and plait my hair while her special treat of hoecakes slow-baked in a covered pan buried in hot ashes. Or running carefree with Eustis, Callie, and even little Delphy. I felt like a child again and lost myself in those stolen moments until summoned to the main house by Miss Nelly as evening descended. Then, the cloak of servitude I'd momentarily managed to shake off was put back on and I was Oney once again.

"I didn't have any fun today, Oney, and it's all your fault. Gram-Gram says I'm big enough to keep my own company and entertain myself, but I don't agree with that. You shouldn't stay so long down in the quarters and Manor House Farm on Sundays. I get bored when you're gone."

"Don't you like playing with Master Washy?"

"Sure, but he's a boy, so only for so long. Plus, he's not as fun as you. *And* he doesn't have to do whatever I tell him to."

Mother warned me.

After becoming Miss Nelly's constant playmate and companion I'd been given a few new garments. The General said that my being in the main house necessitated that I be more presentable in the family's presence. Mistress required that I bathe more frequently and eat meals in the kitchen with Cook Hercules and the others, but sometimes Miss Nelly saved portions of her treats to share with me. Even so, Mother had cautioned me against such niceties.

My black-eyed butterfly, don't be seduced by special concessions of clothing, sweets, or sleeping in a fine room. That's theirs, not ours.

My placement may have changed, but my position hadn't. I was still enslaved in bondage. I was ten years of age to Miss Nelly's five, but her casual complaint about playtime with her little brother was a cold, stark reminder that she was in charge of *me*. This five-year-old was the mistress. As Mother warned, I must never forget.

"Yes, ma'am. I understand." Laying on my pallet aside her bed, I responded by rote but my true thoughts were elsewhere.

Did Mother sing tonight for Delphy, Lucinda, and Nancy?

I imagined my sisters in their nightwear, gathered on our pallets. Warm. Safe. Together. Listening to Mother's soft, low—sometimes haunting—melodies drifting through the cabin as she tended to our family's garments, pushed aside until evening when she could get to them. Rising before the sun and stopping her work only when night fell and candles were lit, the day would have been long for her. Tiring. Tedious. My sisters would have helped prepare the evening meal, and once it was consumed and the dishes scrubbed clean in the wash pail, they'd settle down for rest while Mother mended. Austin and Tom lived elsewhere on the estate, but my brothers sometimes snuck down to our quarters in Manor House Farm to ensure that we were faring well. When they did, we'd chat until they had to return to their quarters; and Mother would instruct us to quiet ourselves from the excitement of seeing our siblings. Only then would she sing.

This was my family's routine. It was precious to me, and I missed it and them.

"Guess what, Oney? I'm to start lessons soon. Gram-Gram says that Granddad is hiring a teacher for me. I'm gonna learn all kinds of things like A-B-Cs and numbers and writing. Wanna learn with me?"

A shiver raced through me at the memory of overhearing a hushed conversation between Nanny Moll and Nanny Iris. I was supposed to be working, tending the little ones, but was close enough to hear grown women talk. It was the disgusted tones slipping across their lips, as well as facial expressions as if they'd sipped vinegar, that caught my attention. According to them, a bondsman on a nearby plantation had been savagely subjected to the horror of having two fingers chopped off when a scrap of paper was found near his person. Like most enslaved, he didn't possess reading abilities but at some point in time he'd done the forbidden and learned to write at least one thing: the first letter of his name. When that scrap of paper bearing a letter "M" drawn in a mixture of soot and animal fat was found in the field by the overseer, hell broke loose and the man named Macon paid the price for breaking the laws of slave life.

"Thank you for the invitation, Miss Nelly, but it's not for me to read or write."

"Why ever not?"

"Well, because..." For some reason I didn't want to say the rest, as if keeping ugly things off my lips could make bitter truth nonexistent. I couldn't learn reading, writing, or arithmetic because of being born in colored skin. I was a ten-year-old child who'd never known her alphabet and couldn't spell her name or count beyond a rudimentary level because teaching me was strictly forbidden. Chattel slavery was fraught with such injustice. As a child, I felt it while being forced to work as the Washington's grandchildren played. Or being required to address them as mister and miss despite my being older than they. Or watching them adore then abandon toys often imported from afar while we—when possible—finessed leftover cornhusks into brittle, faceless dolls. Inequities were ingrained within the system and therefore a part of my existence; but now that my days were spent in the main house in the constant presence of whiteness, I possessed a different, deeper comprehension. The injustices of this life were complex, served in a steady diet, woven into the fabric so that it was as natural as breath and to be expected. I couldn't say I liked it. Maybe our being forbidden to read or write was *their* way of elevating themselves while keeping us in an oppressed state. Perhaps it was, as Mother suggested, that they feared our intelligence. Or the black secrets we'd tell if given pen and paper and the ability to express written truths for all to see.

"Pardon, Miss Nelly?" I'd been lost in my thoughts and only caught the tail end of what she'd been saying.

"I said Mother, Eliza, and Patty are coming to visit soon, silly. Weren't you listening?"

"Yes, ma'am."

As she prattled on in the dark, I lay on my pallet, quivering with dread and a touch of anger. I did not wish to keep the company of that ornery Eliza. Miss Nelly's big sister was two years younger than me, but seemingly housed the meanness of someone twice my age. She was much like a storm, fierce and temperamental, not to mention indulged, spoiled. Staying out of her path wouldn't be easy now that I was installed in the mansion as a full-time playmate to Miss Nelly, but I was determined to give her a wide berth, heaven help me.

Turning onto my side, I faced the window, glad for the moonlight peeking through a slight gap where the curtains didn't fully meet. The more Miss Nelly talked, the more I let my mind drift down the stairs and out the door until my thoughts ventured to the safe space of my sisters, and Mother's humming and soothing scent. Nights, when it was quiet and I wasn't busy keeping my charge occupied and content, was when I felt their absence most. Certainly, I knew my family was near enough, but I wasn't *with them*. I was here, surrounded by another's creature comforts and kin.

Eustis once said he wished he worked in the main house instead of sweating and toiling in the fields.

At least he can go to his cabin at night and be himself with people he loves and who look like him.

The niceness of Miss Nelly's room—with its fancy bed and

luxurious linens, the wardrobe overflowing with fine clothes, the dolls in abundance—no longer mattered much. Such niceties were exciting, even eye-widening when I first came into this position. Now? Nothing could replace the love and warmth beyond reach, tucked away in a small, nondescript, sometimes cold and drafty cabin. Missing my mother and sisters, I wiped away a tear, thinking I'd gladly trade places with Eustis just to be closer to them.

The following week the house was in a tizzy. The General was away on business. Visitors were coming and Mistress was in one of her moods and experiencing one of her many ailments. One of the seamstresses once claimed that Mistress was "touched by sorrowful spirits that came and went with the wind" because she'd borne four children and outlived each, as well as buried her first husband. I suppose that's why she doted on and indulged her grandchildren, because they were all she had as proof of children past. I wasn't sure what "mercurial" meant, but it had been used at some point in describing her. Today, there wasn't as much sorrow in her disposition as there was quick-trigger irritability and consummate displeasure.

"Am I to be surrounded and plagued by such useless ineptitude?"

I was in Miss Nelly's room, tucking her in for a nap when I heard Mistress's scream.

"What's the matter with Gram-Gram?" The little girl was half asleep, her voice groggy.

I didn't want my charge getting up and interfering with my time in the servants' kitchen. If Cook was in a good mood and could tolerate my being underfoot, I sometimes helped there when not with the children. It was added work, but I relished the chance to remove the servile mask required in the presence of whites and relax in the company of my people. I could be my truest self, the one created to laugh, think and feel without fear of punishment and simply breathe.

"Take your nap and rest. I'll check on Mistress." I hurried from the room and down the corridor, feeling suddenly inept when approaching Mistress's chambers. Her poor maid stood in the middle of the room, head bowed, eyes trained on the floor, and cheek aflame as if she'd been struck. Tears swam in her eyes and I wished I could intervene, but knew better.

"My one request was that you *bring* me the inkwell, not bathe me in blackness as if I'm some Negress!"

Head lowered, I peeked enough to see several small ink splotches on Mistress's dress. Certainly, they were unsightly and the laundresses might be vexed trying to remove them, if possible, but Mistress hadn't been "bathed" in anything. Even if she had been, did that merit her maid's mistreatment? Clearly, Mistress was in a snit and any bondsperson in her presence would bear the brunt of it.

"Clean this godawful mess!"

"Yes, ma'am."

"I have guests coming in a matter of days and this place *will* be in proper condition to receive them. Oney, why're you standing in the doorway like some shadow of a simpleton? Be useful and help."

"Yes, Mistress."

I scurried into her chambers to grab the water pitcher and bathing bowl to help clean ink splatters from the writing desk only to hear a crash. I froze in place when seeing a crystal inkwell in shards on the floor. Perhaps her hands were shaky with nervousness, but the poor maid had dropped it, and I feared the consequence.

Retribution was swift. The sound of a hand hitting flesh ricocheted about me as I stood like a statue, afraid to move or breathe.

"Go. From. My. *Presence*. You burr-headed ignoramus!"

The words were clipped, low, hissed.

The maid duly responded, rushing from the room, tears streaming down cheeks that were reddened as if blistering.

Afraid I'd receive the same, I made quick work of discarding crystal shards and cleaning ink from the desk as well as the floor. I was nearly finished when startled by the sounds of something being ripped and Mistress's mournful wails. I backed against a wall, stunned by their magnitude and depth.

"It tires me tremendously to merely consider the weight of grief." Winded, she dropped onto the settee, breasts heaving, an old stuffed rabbit in fragmented disarray about her feet. "I long to escape it, yet I can't. Can any of us, Oney?"

I remained silent, afraid to speak and unsure of her reference.

"No... I don't believe any of us can or will." She sat staring into the distance, seemingly less vexed, until a slight sob escaped her lips. Instantly, she muffled it and stood. "I believe I'll take afternoon tea on the piazza. This infernal summer heat is very taxing and I would relish any sweet breezes coming off the Potomac."

I knew that this teatime pronouncement was also a directive. In the absence of her maid, it was for me to ensure that her wishes were obeyed. "Yes, Mistress."

I wanted to flee from the room and escape the heaviness lurking there, but she was closer to the door than I. I allowed her to proceed me into the corridor as was proper. When she stopped suddenly, I did as well.

She turned in my direction. "Loss, Oney. It's the part of life that's inescapable for all. You're somewhat of a bright girl so I assume you understand that completely."

A "yes, ma'am" had barely crossed my lips before she'd turned in her wide, rustling skirt and exited. I hesitated a moment, looking about to make sure there was no evidence of glass fragments or ink spills to spark further displeasure. I was satisfied nothing offensive remained—except the torn and abandoned rabbit. It looked so hapless laying there with fluffy stuffing spilling from its limbs that I felt sorry for it.

"I imagine you were a nice little thing once upon a time." I scooped up its remains to toss in the outdoor rubbish heap only to feel a sharp and jarring sense of sadness, as if Mistress's melancholy had flowed into and possessed this little lifeless object so that it embodied her angst and sorrow. That left me a little shaken and afraid. What if this forsaken toy was home to spirits, embodying other beings like Papa Shinault sometimes did?

Papa Shinault was the oldest slave on the plantation and was stolen from Africa long before I took my first breath. Despite his age he remembered some of the old practices learned back across the waters, not to mention beliefs, and secretly held onto them. Including spirit possession. Others whispered that sometimes on deep, dark nights Papa Shinault slipped away into the woods to sing funny-sounding chants in a language no one else understood, dancing like a young man— growing tall and strong until his stooped posture was erect. Some claimed they'd even seen Papa Shinault dance into the flames of his little fire only to become a woman. My older brother, Austin, swore he'd witnessed this with his own eyes, but Austin was one for teasing so I didn't necessarily believe him.

Shaking off the shivers caused by such fantastical thoughts, I reconsidered discarding the forlorn rabbit.

"It's not your fault Mistress tore you apart, but you have to learn to stay quiet and out of the way when she's in one of her fits so you don't catch a chastening."

Stuffing fuzzy little body parts into my apron pocket, I left the room and raced down the back stairs, outdoors and along the covered walkway leading to the kitchen. The place where Cook's culinary magic was worked wasn't part of the main house, rather it was detached for safety's sake, in case a fire broke out. Not to mention its detached state allowed the main house's occupants to escape the heat generated during cooking and prevented unwanted food smells from permeating the residence. But Cook also whispered that it was just another opportunity to reinforce separation—upstairs folks there, servants here.

Bursting into the building smelling of delicious food for the evening, I announced the need for afternoon tea. Cook and the kitchen staff were so busy bustling about that he barely glanced my way. Muscular but slight in stature with warm, brown skin, Hercules, our famed chef—or Uncle Harkless as the Washingtons referred to him—was prepping for the evening meal, the king of cuisine in his domain.

"Why're you fetching it instead of Simmie?"

I didn't have the heart to say the poor maid had been physically reprimanded, upbraided, and sent from Mistress's presence. "She's busy with something else."

Cook stopped what he was doing to look at me, his shrewd eyes narrowed as if he was thinking. "I have enough to do without concerning myself with who is or isn't carrying a tea tray upstairs." He shook a finger at me. "You be careful, Ona, and take your time. If you drop that porcelain pot—"

"I promise I won't. I'll be *extra* cautious." It was Mistress's favorite and I had no intention of catching a chastening like poor Simmie. I set about the task under his watchful eye, arranging everything as neatly as possible. I even added a dainty saucer full of the cookies Mistress called "biscuits" and seemed to like so much. Slowly lifting the full tray, I carefully navigated towards the stairs only to stop at a thought dancing through my head. "Uncle Hercules, if the British were so bad and we're supposed to hate them so much, why do the Washingtons do afternoon tea and eat biscuits that aren't nothing but cookies, as if they're over in England?"

"I can't account for the whims of upstairs folks," he responded, using the term by which we referred to the Washingtons and other whites. He waved me away. "Go on. Take the tea to Mistress before she gets cranky."

Too late for that, I thought while carefully doing as instructed.

Thankfully, tea was served and received without incident. I stood like a silent shadow against the wall of the piazza until Mistress was finished before swiftly sweeping in to return the no longer needed items to the kitchen.

I'd love to eat a biscuit.

The remnant of a buttery cookie sat on that saucer taunting me with its sweet scent. I wanted to gobble it up and had to fight off temptation.

No one will know.

I'd served the cookies. They hadn't been doled out for me, so no one would know how many Mistress had consumed, or if I'd helped myself to a stolen goodie. My pilfering a leftover piece from the plate wouldn't hurt a thing.

Except Mistress loathes sneaking.

Miss Nelly shared an occasional treat with me, but I often refused because of Mother's caution that I could be accused of being uppity, thinking myself worthy of food not made for me. But taking something without permission—even this broken remnant—might be deemed stealing, and I didn't want the iron mask.

One hard winter when crops harvested in summer ran low, one of the gardeners had snuck into the storehouse and pilfered food for himself, his wife, and five children. When the theft was discovered he and his wife had been made to wear iron masks that were locked over their faces and prevented their eating anything for three days.

Despite the pathway to the kitchen being clear, I left that temptation on the plate, knowing that sometimes things done in secret could come back to haunt you and not wanting to reap a whirlwind.

After cleaning and storing the tea things, I tried helping Cook except he—and his staff, by virtue of his fastidiousness—ran the place so efficiently that I proved little more than a nuisance and was shooed away, told to occupy myself elsewhere. Miss Nelly and Master Washy were both napping and not in need of me. That left me with a mangled rabbit for company.

"We should visit Mama, don't you think?" I put a finger in the decapitated head and nodded it as if a puppet. "What a splendid idea." I smiled at the thought of slipping down the row to Manor House Farm as I often tried to, although sometimes without success. If only for a minute. Just long enough to hug my mother and bundle her warmth inside of me. Perhaps I could even think of an acceptable reason for lingering, helping. Find an inconspicuous place in a corner where I could sit and sew or knit while the women talked freely. I'd fill my ears with their voices and feed my heart's hunger for their presence in that space where I felt most natural.

What if Miss Nelly wakes up looking for you?

My smile faded. If the child awakened without me there and took to whining about that fact, I'd catch trouble. Mistress had calmed herself and enjoyed her tea and the cooling Potomac breeze, but that didn't mean my actions couldn't send her into another fit, easily.

"I'd best stay here and fix you instead."

Mistress didn't favor ostentatiousness, just that things about her be impeccably decent. Knowing this, Mother had gifted me my own sewing implements the day after I was installed in the mansion in case I ever needed to quickly mend my garments. I lived in the main house now and being presentable was imperative.

Tiptoeing into Miss Nelly's room, I found her still napping

—exhausted from play and the hot weather. I quickly, quietly gathered what I needed before easing from the room towards the space where I liked to sit in those rare, stolen moments when no one was around and I wasn't required in constant attendance. It wasn't terribly far away. Hopefully I'd hear my charge if she awakened.

Finding no one in the passageway, I crept towards that magical ladder on silent feet, arriving in the third-floor cupola tower where I wasn't supposed to be, but came just the same. It was the highest part of Mount Vernon's mansion, perched like a small but magical place atop its roof. It was little more than an empty space, but I liked to imagine the cupola as an octagonal jewel box or multi-sided bird cage with its long, vertical windows that—when open—drew hot air up and out of the house while drawing the Potomac breezes into the floors below. I loved looking out of those windows with nothing obstructing the view except the trees in the distance, imagining the world beyond the east and the river that flowed majestically. That flowing water incited me to dream of places I'd never been, and to dream of freedom. But freedom wasn't something an enslaved girl possessed, so I satisfied myself with sitting on the cupola's bare floor, treasuring stolen moments and being alone with my thoughts as I leaned my whole, sometimes weary, self against a wall.

That day, I sat cross-legged and reassembled a rabbit. Laying the pieces on the floor, I arranged them as if a puzzle. Thankfully, they'd merely been ripped apart at their seams, without damage to the actual body, and could, hopefully, be repaired. It was a chance to practice my sewing skills. The tricky part was getting the stuffing back inside where it belonged. Biting my lower lip, I considered the task and landed on the idea of turning the pieces inside out and stitching them slowly to ensure precision until all the parts were reattached, except the head and ears.

"I bet you'd scare Master Washy."

For all his want of playing soldiers and war, the three-year-old was afraid of anything spooky. Pretending it was some monstrous thing from a world of headless creatures, I lifted onto my knees, walking the decapitated bunny about the cupola floor and growling menacingly. I cherished the rare opportunity to play alone, knowing it couldn't be prolonged. I had to finish repairing the rabbit and get back to the second floor before Miss Nelly awakened from her nap. Ending my headless-hare antics, I sat, back pressed to one of the cupola's many walls, and manipulated the fabric until the correct sides were out once again. I pushed its stuffing back into its cloth cavities, sewed the ears to the head and—using the invisible stitch I learned from Mother —put the whole thing together until it was intact.

"Now... what to do with you?"

Mistress had destroyed the little thing in a fit and clearly had no further use for it, but I knew better than to keep it for myself and wanted to avoid questions as to why it was in my possession. The explanation was simple: that I'd wanted to exercise my sewing skills and nothing else. But a misunderstanding and its repercussions were things I didn't dare chance. Still, I was proud of my handiwork and couldn't bear to discard it outright.

"Master Wash might like you now that your head is on."

Happy thoughts of giving the little boy a new toy were interrupted by a sudden commotion below. Jumping up, I peered out of a cupola window to see a carriage entering the west gate and several servants assembling below with the housekeeper as others moved towards the horse-drawn conveyance. Visitors were a common occurrence, somewhat of a holdover from General Washington's days in the Continental Army, but no one was expected today.

Cook would've mentioned it at breakfast.

The fastidious gourmet was a fountain of information,

knowing who was or wasn't coming to meals at the mansion. This arrival hadn't surfaced during morning instructions or conversation, so must have been unexpected.

"Who is it?"

Excitement surged through me at the thought of Uncle Hercules creating something special for whomever was arriving. He was an exceptional cook and culinary craftsman who added even more flare to his dishes in order to impress guests. The praise he was sure to receive would leave him rather generous. If there were leftovers after the upstairs folks dined, he'd sometimes allow the house servants to enjoy a taste of his delectable genius. The mere thought had my mouth watering.

Curiosity and maybe a touch of greed kept me standing at the window in full view until I remembered I shouldn't have been there in the cupola, but busy elsewhere. I quickly ducked down into a squatting position, calming my racing heartbeat, convincing myself I hadn't been seen. Good sense kept me on my haunches, but nosiness and bravery prompted me to peek over the rim of the wooden window casing, determined to see. I watched the carriage pass the wide bowling green to enter the circular driveway of the west entrance to the mansion. I was too high up to clearly see the insignia on the side of the carriage as it came to a stop, but I easily recognized the gale of voices floating through the cupola windows, as well as the sight of two young girls jumping from the carriage with the zest of hopping frogs. A shiver ran through me when I realized it was Miss Nelly's mother and sisters, two whole days early.

"Welcome, devil seed. Goodbye, peace."

I sighed dramatically while stuffing the rabbit and my sewing implements into the huge pockets of my apron, wondering what kind of torment Eliza might devise for me. Moving towards the cupola ladder, I paused to ensure there was no evidence of my having been there. Finding none, I hurried my descent to the second floor and raced towards Miss Nelly's room to wake her from her nap—only to find she wasn't there. I panicked, thinking I'd missed her calling for me in all the commotion. Reversing my direction, I quickly made my way downstairs. Once outdoors, I eased to the back of the line of assembled servants, hoping my late arrival had gone undetected. A quick glance from Cook let me know it hadn't. I'd likely catch a scolding later. Standing, hands folded in front of me, I stared into the distance, stiffly erect like one of the General's soldiers at attention.

The troublesome spirits that had vexed Mistress earlier had clearly departed, and she welcomed her family with joy and open arms. "Eleanor! You're delightfully early." Having doled out effusive kisses on her newly arrived granddaughters, Mistress greeted the woman who used to be Master Jacky's wife before he'd died and she'd remarried.

"I couldn't bear another minute of that infernal heat at Abingdon and the dryness of Fairfax County. Not when the lovely breezes from the Potomac were calling me. And where, pray tell, is our darling General?"

"Away on business, but he should return in time for supper," Mistress assured as her grandchildren, having reunited themselves, scampered up the steps with the energy of lightning bugs.

"May we have ice cream, Gram-Gram?"

"I'm sure Uncle Harkless can arrange for that after supper."

"Of course, ma'am." I was close enough to Cook to detect a veiled hint of annoyance in his tone.

"The day is so hot. I prefer mine now." That Eliza wasn't one to delay satisfaction.

"Of course you do, my dear, but let's save that delight for after supper and indulge in lemonade and biscuits until then." Giving orders for the family's luggage to be brought in, Mistress headed indoors, arm about the mother of her grandchildren.

I breathed a sigh of relief as Master Jacky's offspring

followed behind, chattering loudly.

Evilest Eliza didn't notice me.

Watching the luggage being carted inside and the servants disperse, I mulled over how to keep our interactions at a minimum, only to brighten at a thought. With her sisters present, Miss Nelly might not need my company so much. Perhaps, this visit would allow me to be free and return to the workhouse and my family.

"Ona, run to the icehouse and bring back enough for this dessert I must suddenly make." With the upstairs folks gone, Cook's irritation was openly expressed. He headed for the kitchen walkway, mumbling beneath his breath. "As if I don't already have enough on my plate. Greedy, inconsiderate little urchins."

I hurried to do as told, at least as quickly as the summer heat allowed. It was late June, but hot as August, and would've been more miserable than it was if not for the Potomac. Still, with sweat trickling down my back, and likely making a mess of my simple dress, it was miserable enough. Grabbing the bucket from the hook outside the icehouse door, I couldn't resist standing in its entrance, eyes closed, savoring the coolness for a splendid moment before locating the ice pick dangling from its leather thong on a nail inside the door. I took my time chipping away an adequate amount of ice from the chunks harvested from the river each winter and kept in a wide, brick vat that went down deep below the earth. Eustis, Callie, and I liked to scare each other with stories of a chilly, white monster who lived down there, waiting to snatch children into its icy lair.

"It's just a tale," I reminded myself, while sneaking an ice shard to dab over my face and neck. I even lifted the bonnet I'd been required to wear since coming to the main house and let a piece melt onto my scalp and drip down my plaits, loving the refreshing coolness before exiting the icehouse, task complete.

"This... is... heavy."

I grunted and heaved my way back to the kitchen, missing the coolness I'd just experienced.

"Is this enough, Uncle Hercules?"

Sometimes I called the cook by that more familiar endearment without thinking. He didn't seem to mind, preferring it to that 'Harkless' business doled out by the Washingtons.

"It'll do, Ona. Thank you. Break it into suitable pieces to fit between the bucket and the *sorbetière*. When you finish that, get one of the nicer ice-cream pots. You know how finicky Mistress is, wanting only her best on the table when company's here. If you do a good job, I may just show you how my melt-on-your-tongue magic is made."

My eyes grew big. To be invited into Uncle Hercules's domain was one thing; being taught by him was something altogether more splendid.

If I do a good job maybe, like Mother with her seamstresses, he'll make me an apprentice!

That would mean work that was far more difficult than keeping Miss Nelly and Master Wash out of trouble and entertained. Being an ever-ready playmate was physically tiring, but they wouldn't need me always. Who knew what would happen when they got too big for jumping rope, nine pins, or whirligig? They might find me useless. If such was the case, would I be allowed to return to the workhouse? Or would I be sent to the fields?

I busied myself, chipping away at that ice, while dreaming about working in the kitchen making fancy food and earning something foreign and new: money.

Maybe I'll earn enough for fancy outfits like Cook.

I wasn't sure what flamboyant meant, but these busy ears of mine had heard it in connection with our esteemed chef. Most dinners, particularly when guests were in attendance, Uncle Hercules wore the finery he'd purchased, and of which he seemed rather proud. It wasn't often that we enjoyed leftovers from the marvelous meals prepared for the upstairs folks, because Cook had permission to sell them. He packaged and sold leftover meals to travelers, nearby residents, and the overseers, bosses, and other white tradesmen at Mount Vernon. Sometimes he even sold in the market square on his one afternoon off. Whatever he earned was his to keep, allowing him to acquire clothing that clearly separated and elevated him—at least in appearance—in this human chattel system. I'd been given nicer garments when becoming a house servant compared to the shapeless shifts worn previously, but the idea of splendid dresses and dainty shoes like those Miss Nelly had made my heart pound with excitement.

Make these ice chips a perfect fit.

I attacked my task with sheer determination, only to hold my breath when presenting my finished product for inspection. My smile must have been as bright as the moon hearing Cook's praise.

"Little Ona, you might make a fine gourmet such as myself one day. We'll need cane sugar, cream, and salt. Don't just stand there smiling. Go get them!"

That day in the kitchen was one worthy to be remembered as I learned from Cook, while feeling I was part of the kitchen staff and less isolated. Being allowed to taste the cool confection I'd helped make was such a splendid experience that I didn't mind being asked to help serve supper that evening when one of the kitchen maids took sick.

"But not in that sweat-stained dress!"

I practically ran to the storeroom where my clothing was kept. I might've slept on a pallet in Miss Nelly's chambers, but I wasn't allowed to keep my meager belongings there. I suppose, same as the kitchen being detached from the mansion, it was another instance of separating us from them. As Cook claimed, the reinforcing of hierarchy. A prevention of contamination.

"Oh, no. I still have this!"

I'd begun removing my apron in order to wash up only to feel the weight of the rabbit in my pocket. I needed to return it to Mistress—or rather gift it to her grandson. Whatever I did, it couldn't remain on my person.

"Be quick about it."

My duties waited.

Ona Maria, you will not fidget.

Changed and presentable, I raced for the upstairs chambers, reminding myself to harness my energy and be attentive to whatever tasks Cook gave me. I was nervous, excited, yet ready. My thoughts were on helping in the kitchen, leaving me rather distracted until hearing loud, childish chatter. Immediately, I stopped and lowered my eyes to the floor—as was proper—as Mistress and her family flowed from her chambers and into the upstairs passageway.

"There you are, Oney! Guess what? Mother and my sisters are here." Miss Nelly skipped towards me only to be instructed by Miss Eleanor to walk like a lady.

I didn't have a chance to respond, thanks to her big sister interrupting—her tone sharp, demanding.

"What're you holding?" Evilest Eliza pounced like a cat, snatching the rabbit dangling haplessly from my hand.

Her mother gasped. "Isn't that—?"

"This was my father's!" That evil Eliza's yell was nearly primal. "Why do you have it? Were you stealing it for yourself, you little mongrel?"

I couldn't respond for being ruthlessly shoved and knocked off balance. I fell backwards, slamming my head against the staircase banister. A sharp pain raced through my skull and my eyes smarted with tears as I lay there covering my face while being beat about the head with that rabbit. Mercifully, it was a stuffed creature and didn't hurt much, physically. Still, I was terrified and mortified at being falsely accused as Eliza repeatedly hit me.

"That's enough, Eliza. You'll muss yourself." Her mother moved her away, ending the girl's tirade.

"Give that to me!" Mistress's voice was shrill, commanding. Taking the rabbit from her granddaughter, she marched towards me. Commanding me to stand, she waited as I did before slapping me so violently that I fell yet again. "That rabbit belonged to my son. Return it to my room immediately!"

"Yes, ma'am."

My chest heaved with the effort to swallow my tears as Mistress moved her brood down the stairs. Miss Nelly touched my arm gently in passing. But after the terror that had just transpired, her touch failed to be comforting.

I spent the rest of the evening glum in spirit after that upstairs fiasco. That brouhaha was bitter enough, but arriving downstairs too late to help added to the dismay.

Now I can't prove I'm good enough to work with Cook.

I'd missed my opportunity to change my destiny, and spent the evening in the scullery washing dishes by the light of an oil lamp, sulking and reliving how I'd been abused, chastened.

Stupid rabbit. I should've left you in pieces.

"Ona, you're to go to Mistress."

Glancing up, I found Simmie in the doorway looking miffed.

"Do you know what she wants?" I feared the earlier episode wasn't completely finished.

"I'ma maid, not nobody's tale-carrier. Least I was till you made trouble for me."

"I tried cleaning up that spilled ink as best I could—"

"That ain't my meaning. You—" She stopped abruptly, pulling herself up as if talking to me was a waste of her time and energy. "Just get on up there and see what she needs before you catch the wrath of Cain."

I didn't exactly want to go but knew better than to dillydally and hurried towards the exit, only to be waylaid when Simmie grabbed my arm.

She leaned in, hissing vilely. "Betcha ya thinks ya some kinda special 'cause ya gots better skin." She released my arm as if touching me was worrisome.

Taking a lit candle with me, I hurried off, wondering what skin had to do with this and if it was capable of saving me from the trouble I was surely in.

By the time I reached Mistress's chambers, my bonnet needed repositioning and I was out of breath. I'd forgotten to change my apron and did my best to hide the fact that, thanks to dish duty, it was wet.

"Don't dawdle in the doorway, Oney. Come in."

When things happen that aren't what you want, send your mind to a different place till they're over with.

Mama said that to my older sisters sometimes. I remembered it and tried doing as she'd taught as Mistress ordered me to come forward to where she sat. I thought about Eustis and Callie, and dipping our toes in the Potomac and splashing each other when we were supposed to be helping the fishermen in their catch. I let my mind drift to Mama's hoecakes and honey, and the comforts of my family.

"Oney, did you do this?" Mistress indicated the rabbit on her lap.

Eyes lowered, too afraid to speak, I simply nodded, wishing my mother was nearby and I could run to her safety.

When Mistress lifted my chin, her touch was shockingly gentle and nothing like that raving woman who'd destroyed a possession, abused me, and sent Simmie fleeing in tears.

"You're certain this is *your* work?"

I looked at the rabbit in her lap, wishing it could come alive and help me escape whatever came next. "Yes, Mistress."

I reclaimed a downward gaze when she released my chin

and watched her slowly rotate the stuffed toy in a thorough examination.

"My granddaughter was right in stating that this belonged to my son, Master Jacky. And I was wrong in my mistreatment of it. Sometimes grief overshadows me and is simply too—" She stopped abruptly, as if realizing her position, and that confidences weren't to be shared with a servant. "You are perfectly gifted with the needle, Oney. Your talents mustn't be wasted. I'll assign someone else the task of attending to my grandchildren. Going forward, you will be my personal maid." She smoothed a hand over the rabbit's fluffy tail. "I dare say your intelligence likely outshines hers, but Simmie is knowledgeable when it comes to my preferences and demands. She will train you and teach you what you must know in order to serve me well. Would you like that?"

I pushed shock and trepidation aside to provide the only acceptable reply. "Yes, ma'am."

"Very well. Sleep in Miss Nelly's room tonight as usual. Tomorrow we'll make other arrangements in keeping with your new position."

I murmured in acquiescence before leaving the room, stunned by this turn of events. Becoming a maid to Mistress had never surfaced in my imagination. I'd expected another chastening for taking the rabbit from her room without permission, and feared she'd believed Evilest Eliza's accusations of theft. Slowly padding to Miss Nelly's room, I knew my life had changed. Again. In a mere matter of months I'd gone from being a seamstress-in-training to a child's ever-present playmate. Now, I was being repositioned to become the personal maid for the lady of the plantation. My heart pounded unmercifully.

When laying down to sleep that night, I pleaded with heaven that being in the employ of a kindly but mercurial woman with frequent ailments would miraculously morph into a blessing and not a curse.

FIVE

TESSA

After talking to Brandon that morning, I did a rare thing. I relaxed and read. Tired from the night before, I wound up drifting off and indulging in a nap before finally dragging myself out of bed that afternoon. I should've felt refreshed and, in a way, I did. Even so, I experienced an underlying irritation while getting the mop from the garage, like something was off. Or perhaps missing.

I grabbed the cleaner for the hardwood floors only to stop and stare at nothing in particular. My cycle—like my man—was missing in action and I was afraid of what that meant.

"God, don't let me be pregnant."

Not with Dominic.

I didn't want that kind of permanence. At least, not yet. We hadn't fully examined the possibility of a long-term future together; or better said, I hadn't. Dominic was a five-year-, ten-year-plan kind of man who'd mapped out next steps in his personal life with painstaking precision. His trajectory was marriage in the next two years.

It might not be with me.

Because truthfully? I wasn't ready.

I was still building my brand, my business. I worked six, sometimes seven days a week, including minor holidays. I had goals of financial wealth and positioning myself as one of the top African-American interior designers in the area, if not the entire mid-Atlantic region. I loved being an entrepreneur and was working vigorously towards financial freedom. Thanks to my parents and a partial scholarship, I'd graduated college without student loan debt. That didn't mean I had my finances fully together. I had credit card debt as well as a small business loan incurred as a result of my entrepreneurial venture. I'd purchased my SUV in cash at a wholesale auction to avoid monthly payments, and was able to because my grandparents had gifted me funds—adding to what I'd already saved for that purpose. I had dreams and part of me was enticed by the idea of linking up with Dominic and becoming *that* power couple. Another part of me refused to ride his coattails or misuse his family's position in the community. Building my brand, my business, was *my* dream and responsibility, prayerfully achievable of my own volition and abilities.

Plus, I want autonomy.

Being seven years older, Dominic had a tendency to take over and I too often found myself reminding him that I was his lover, not his project. I wasn't so proud that I couldn't accept help, but I didn't need fixing or manhandling.

"What I *do need* is for my stomach to stop cramping."

I gripped the mop handle and let a pain pass before squirting liquid cleanser on the hardwood floors that had been a hidden treasure. Crazy as it may be, I'd purchased my townhome sight unseen. My parents were seasoned realtors; my brother, Rico, was a mortgage broker. Not to mention my sister, Rocki, was a property lawyer. Scott & Associates, my family's business, represented decades of real-estate acumen and prowess. When Mama mentioned this townhouse that had fallen into foreclosure in Lagomar, one of Virginia Beach's nicest neighborhoods, I snatched it up (once again, at auction) based on her recommendation and the information she provided. I bought it intending to fix it up and flip it, only to fall in love with its bones and structure. I'd tired of apartment living and considered it a perfect opportunity to try homeownership. Finding the original hardwood floors when ripping up a carpet decorated with smelly proof of the prior owner's pet had been a gem that I'd sanded and refinished.

Now, I stood there admiring the smooth surface only for another pain to rip through my midsection so fiercely that I was forced to sit, bent over on the sofa, breathing raggedly until it subsided. When it did, I leaned back, letting the sofa take my weight, concerned about these recurring pains that I usually powered through with the aid of pain relievers and a heating pad. I'd been experiencing them on a monthly basis for a while now. They seemed to be triggered by my cycle and had intensified recently. Except this month my cycle was missing and this particular pain was on a whole other level—harsher and sharper than those experienced previously. Closing my eyes and exhaling raggedly, I had two thoughts.

I need a pregnancy test and an appointment with my gynecologist.

I didn't typically see clients so late on Saturdays, but after I'd designed her office space, Marlene Marshall was interested in having me renovate her home kitchen as well. She traveled frequently as an executive and had already rescheduled twice when unexpected business trips interfered. Accommodating her with a four o'clock appointment was a minor concession compared to the potential outcome. Plus, I considered repeat business the highest compliment and was serious about providing excellent customer service. Thus, my being at Marlene's spacious waterfront condo on a Saturday evening.

"I love your ideas, Tessa. Let's do it!"

My smile was warm and sincere, but inside I was doing a boss woman's happy dance.

"Wonderful! When would you like to begin the project?"

"I'm headed to Colorado tomorrow on business. And who knows? Maybe I'll get a little skiing in. How about next weekend?"

Consulting my calendar, I confirmed my availability without pretending I was swamped with work or too busy.

"I'll have the contract to you by tomorrow and computerized sketches for your review within forty-eight hours after it's signed." We'd discussed concepts and budget. Sketches were where the fun began. Not only did they provide visual renditions of the new space, but they tended to ramp up the excitement and bring even the most hesitant customer fully onboard. "Once you review and approve them, we'll schedule demolition of the existing space as well as a showroom visit to look at sample materials."

I was yet working towards a short-term goal of my own design studio where samples were on hand for client perusal. For now, I had a great working relationship with the manager of a nearby showroom that housed a plethora of materials from flooring to fixtures and more.

"Sounds wonderful. I'm excited."

I laughed at Marlene shimmying her shoulders.

"That makes two of us." I saved my notes to Marlene's client project file before closing my iPad and slipping it into the oversized Coach tote I'd snagged at a seventy-five percent off sale. "Thank you for trusting me with your personal space."

"After slaying my office situation like you did, you were the only designer I thought of when deciding to tackle my outdated kitchen. Which reminds me..." She paused as we both stood. "Do you mind my giving your phone number to a sorority sister who's interested in remodeling her bedroom?"

"Of course not, please do!"

"Perfect. I'll pass your deets on to her. Expect a call from Carmel Carter."

Either I deserved an Oscar, or I'd died for two seconds. Either way, I managed not to react. We hugged and I said my goodbyes before making it to my SUV where I sat a moment catching my breath—and not because of physical exertion. The idea of doing anything with or for Carmel Carter was enough to make a sane sister need oxygen.

We'd met at a business mixer last year but, on a personal level, I didn't know the woman, only her reputation and penchant for relationships with other women's men. Married. In "committed" relationships. Such was her preference. If a man was single, he was safe. Carmel chased the forbidden.

"She *would* wanna bedroom redo. All that illegal man traffic probably broke a bed or two."

Telling myself not to be judgmental, I dialed Mama Calloway hoping to get Miss Ona's journal into her hands. There was no answer and her voicemail box was full, so I started my SUV and headed for the nearest Walgreens. I needed a pregnancy test and a bag of my favorite Pepperidge Farm Milano Mint Chocolate Cookies to deal with whatever the results. Between that and the fact that I hadn't heard from Dominic since he'd stepped to Coochielicious Carmel, his ex, I felt myself being pulled into a negative space—despite having just had a successful consultation. I deserved delicious relief, and to celebrate this most recent success with cookies. Pulling away from the curb, I remembered I had something better: Mama Calloway's pralines.

Sitting on my bathroom floor eating homemade pralines and waiting on a pregnancy test to do its thing wasn't how I'd imagined occupying my time on a Saturday evening. Still, that's precisely what I was doing. I sat massaging my temples, trying to mitigate the beginning of a headache. And waiting.

"I should've done this yesterday. *Immediately*."

As in, when I first realized my period was late. Instead, I'd left my parents', had a fender bender, and wound up at a haunted house in Chincoteague. Not to mention that white-tie affair for Mr. Daniels that ended with me going home alone and my lover God knew where.

Why haven't I heard from him?

I didn't want to be suspicious or accusatory and had kept my tone neutral when leaving a message earlier. But, admittedly, my thoughts were starting to run amuck imagining Dominic and Carmel engaged in all kinds of butt-naked and nasty activities in that tore-up, high-traffic bedroom of hers that needed remodeling.

Maybe you wouldn't be feeling this way if your relationship was straight.

I disliked admitting it, but there were cracks in our relationship that seemed to be growing. Aside from ongoing, increasing demands—needing to know my whereabouts, hinting at how I should dress—Dominic was less attentive and more distracted. Sometimes, even distant. When we first met, we enjoyed hearing about each other's day and the behind-the-scenes intricacies of our professions. Lately, I'd become the sounding board for all his professional woes while he minimized my challenges and concerns, pointing out that at least I wasn't responsible for lives, just color swatches and furniture.

My ringing cell phone yanked me from the ledge of dark ruminations. I smiled, hearing the ringtone assigned to my BFF, and quickly answered, putting the phone in speaker mode. "Hey, Mimi."

"Hey, *chica*. What's popping?"

"Nothing... just sitting here spreading my hips with Mama C.'s pralines."

"Aww, hell naw! Granny made pralines and didn't tell me?"

"Yep." I popped a fragment of goodness in my mouth and smacked loudly. Teasingly. "Obviously, she likes me better than her granddaughter."

"I hope you choke on a nut. And stop chewing like a countrified cow before I conjure up the ghost of the late great *Madame*."

I laughed, knowing Filona Richieux, the executive director of the debutante ball that had introduced us to society, would have whacked our knuckles with a ruler like some old-school, elitist, blue-haired maven for such unladylike behavior. Mimi and I had protested our mothers enrolling us in the program, calling it "some *Gone with the Wind* archaic BS." At least, behind their backs. But our mothers had won and debutantes we were, wearing long white gloves and blindingly white dresses like pristine virgins. Which, incidentally, neither of us had been.

"Let's leave Madame dead wherever she is." I smacked on another tidbit of praline goodness. "I'm not tryna entertain some Marge Simpson aqua-haired phantom. Speaking of... Girl, y'all need to exorcise that homestead." I filled Mimi in on last night's experience, as well as the Ona Judge discovery.

"*Chica*, you're kidding, right?"

"Wrong. This diary may prove your family actually has ties to the first president."

"I gotta see it!"

"I've been trying to reach Mama C. since this morning so I could get it to her, but can't seem to connect."

"Girl, Granny is on a weekend spa trip with my Great Aunt Ruby. She has her cell with her but if the house isn't on fire, she's not answering. Wanna drop it off here? No... scratch that. As the matriarch, Granny should see it first."

"Look at your intrusive behind tryna practice some restraint for a change."

"Right! Aren't you proud of me?" An investigative journalist, my bestie had professional and naturally nosey tendencies. "What's that, and why do you sound like you're in a cave?" she added as the timer on my phone rang.

"My timer. And I'm in the bathroom."

"You've got me on the toilet with you because...?"

"I'm not on the commode. I'm on my freshly mopped floor waiting for pregnancy test results—"

"*What the?* Tessa, you didn't think to start the conversation with that?"

"Stop screaming in my ear. I'm telling you now."

"You are such a ten-teat-having-cow. I hate you."

I laughed nervously while standing and retrieving that little stick of doom. Eyes closed, I said a quick prayer before daring to peek.

"So, what're the results?" Mimi demanded when I remained silent too long.

"Negative." I exhaled loudly, my whole body sagging with extreme relief. For a moment, I almost felt guilty, as if my joy at *not* being pregnant was disloyal to Dominic. Children were part of his five-year, ten-year plans. I liked little people, but didn't want any anytime soon. Besides, choices I'd made in the past sometimes left me conflicted about whether or not I even deserved to conceive again.

"Tessa, heifer, you ain't knocked up. Thank You, *Jesus!*"

I laughed, thinking those were my sentiments, but that I didn't necessarily like hearing them from my BFF who didn't care for Dominic. Still, I agreed. "I'm not ready for anybody's baby so thank God I dodged that bullet."

"Forget a bullet. You might wanna zip it up and dodge that dic—"

"Kimiyah, hush up."

"Okay, okay. Anyhoo... why the test? Did you miss a period?"

Discarding the wand in the trash, I washed my hands. "It's a few days late. I guess I panicked." I'd keep the issue of my ongoing monthly discomfort to myself until I knew what was what.

"I'll take a little panic over a 'little pregnant.' Your birth control's on point, correct?"

"It is, but nothing's one hundred percent fail-proof except abstinence."

"There's that. I say we get into something tonight, T. Let's hang out. Get lit. And celebrate that your hot tail *ain't* pregnant."

Turning off the bathroom light, I headed for the living room that flowed into my kitchen in an open-space concept. I'd knocked down a dividing wall in lieu of spaciousness and loved the enlarged area with its warm earth tones and pops of coral and seafoam blue. "I wish I could, but I have a contract to write up and design specs to work out." I filled her in on my newest assignment while pouring myself a glass of chardonnay.

"I'm not one to hate on another sista's game, but you do realize we've missed four of the past five girls' nights we had planned and haven't hung out in about ten thousand years, right?"

Guilt stabbed me in the gut. "I know, Mimi. I'm sorry. Maybe we can do a weekend getaway when I finish this job for Marlene."

"Wishful thinking," she muttered beneath her breath.

"Meaning?"

"Listen, *chica*, I am not *that* friend... the possessive, jealous one acting all twisted. I support you one hundred. But let me just point out that lately your time and attention are spent on one of two things: either designing or Dominic. I'm trying not to feel some kind of way about that."

I wanted to argue the point, but closed my mouth, realizing I couldn't. Being laser-focused on building my business and brand shouldn't necessitate the neglect of those most important to me. I sipped chardonnay before admitting, "Mama said as much yesterday."

"That's why I love Miss Serenity. We're both women of impeccable taste and good sense."

I snorted. "Mama? Yes. You? That's shady and suspect."

"Whatever, big head. Just go do your little contract."

We shared a laugh.

"On the real, Mimi, I apologize for being MIA and promise to do better."

She was quiet a moment. "You already know I'm holding you to that."

"I expect nothing less." Forever friends since before the days of playing in that huge fireplace on their family's Chincoteague property, our bond was real. Solid. We believed in speaking truth to each other and were painfully honest. Secrets were rare between us.

Except one.

I topped off my chardonnay while pushing away that memory of choices made when I was young.

"Let me get off of here so I can get dressed to hit the club and find a new best friend."

"Mimi, please. Nobody wants you except me."

She laughed loudly. "Oh... *hey*! I hear you're designing Brandon's new restaurant. How'd that happen?"

"I swear nobody keeps anything to themselves around here. And it's not a done deal. B.C. asked, but I haven't answered."

"You will. Now, hang up so I can go live my best life. Love you. Bye."

"Love you, too, boo."

Disconnecting, I leaned against the kitchen counter, sipping chardonnay and thinking I could use some work-life balance. Not to mention an ob-gyn appointment.

Calling me relieved that I wasn't pregnant would be a

wicked understatement. I was ecstatic. That didn't mean I wasn't concerned about whatever was going on with my health. I was. Greatly. Particularly seeing as how my paternal grandmother died six years ago of cervical cancer.

"Don't swing from A to Z."

I knew better than self-diagnosing. That didn't keep me from launching a web browser on my phone and looking up cervical cancer symptoms. I sipped wine, nervously, while reading information on the website of a highly respectable medical foundation. It seemed consistent and in line with what I'd been experiencing. Heavy, longer menstrual periods. Spotting. Dull back aches. I felt myself ramping up and had to decline the desire to visit other sites to compare information, knowing if I did, the details would start solidifying in my mind. Next thing I knew, I'd be calling an estate attorney and writing my obituary. Rather than continue web-surfing and tormenting myself, I opened the app for my HMO and made an appointment with my gynecologist.

"You've taken proper steps. Now, relax."

Knowing myself, distraction was best.

The diary!

If anything could take my mind elsewhere, it was a walk back to the past and the life of a bondswoman who was connected to Brandon, Mimi, Mama C., and family. I headed for the garage where I'd stored the diary in the trunk of my SUV only to pause. Mimi, the nosiest of the nosey, had shown restraint, deferring to Mama Calloway.

"I guess I can do the same..."

Naw!

Reading Miss Ona's diary last night, I'd gotten so caught up in it that I had to make myself stop. Reading of her childhood wasn't easy thanks to that wholly consuming, diabolical backdrop of slavery. I hurt for her when she was taken from her mother and deposited in the big house as a maid to Martha Washington.

"This damn country loves celebrating its founding fathers with all their hypocrisy and holding humans as property." Shaking my head disgustedly, I told myself I'd only read a few more pages. Just to verify its authenticity before turning it over to Mama Calloway or B.C. "Like you're some kind of historical archivist."

I was practically at the garage when the doorbell stopped me. Redirecting my steps, I paused to peek through the front door peephole only to stand there puzzled and irritated when I saw Dominic.

Why is he here?

He hadn't returned my call or responded to my text in that same five-minute response time he demanded from me, leaving me on red. Now, he was on my doorstep?

Don't let his disappearing-act ass in.

Ignoring my own advice, I opened the door to a beautiful floral bouquet that looked as if it cost a pretty grip.

His double-dipping penis can afford it.

"Hey, babe." He cocked his head sideways, genuinely perplexed as I blocked the doorway when he attempted to enter. "Is there a problem?"

"I wouldn't know, Dom, seeing as how we haven't communicated since you rudely walked off last night and got ghost with your ex."

He frowned, looking all confused, as if I'd spoken a language other than English.

I held my ground and didn't relent while waiting for his next action.

He sighed softly when he saw I wasn't budging. "I guess I should've called before dropping by." He eased forward until our bodies met. Lowering his voice, he kissed my temple and poured on the sex appeal. "At least that way I could've added a box of candy to the bouquet, had I known you'd be in your feelings like this."

Wait. What?

No apology. No explanation. Just typical, dismissive Dominic.

One hand at my waist, he pulled me close enough to his gym-hardened body that I could feel all the deliciousness I knew he was working with. When he slowly kissed and savored my neck, I ignored a ping of lust and told myself to stay calm. And strong.

I stepped back, arms folded across my breasts. "I'd rather not play games when this situation merits an explanation."

"What would you like me to explain, baby? That I escorted Carmel to her car as any gentleman would, considering it was dark?" He stroked a finger down my cheek.

I backed up some more, unwilling to play dumb to his distractions. "You walked her to her car in response to my declining your invitation to go home with you, not merely because you're a gentleman. You were being petty. And where precisely was her car parked? I didn't see—" I quickly shut my mouth, refusing to be perceived as pathetic by admitting I'd skulked about the parking lot like a lioness on the hunt and had been unable to find him.

"You didn't see what, Princessa Tessa?" He smiled as if amused when I didn't respond. "Did you go looking for me? If you did, what did you think, that I left my father's celebration with another woman?"

"An ex is a whole"—I drew air quotes—"'another' female kind of category. You've tapped that and might've been tempted to go back." It felt crude saying as much, but it was what it was.

He chuckled while placing one hand on my hip and forcing me backwards away from the doorstep. I didn't resist. Instead, I watched as he placed the bouquet on my entryway table before resuming a position in front of me.

"You can retire the jealousy act, Tessa. Carmel is not a threat."

I ignored his flaccid assurance. "If the roles were reversed, would you not feel some kind of way and just a bit suspicious?"

Darkness flashed across his face and his voice took a dangerous dip as he gripped my forearm. "The roles *won't ever* reverse while I'm your man and you're my woman."

Before I could even respond to the chilliness of his actions, his hands were in the waistband of my lounge pants, pulling them off. He discarded them, as well as my underwear, right there in the entryway before lifting me so that we were face to face, my legs wrapped about his waist.

"I can have Carmel if I want her... but she's not marriage material. You are." He licked his luscious lips. "Plus, what I want right now is what I have right here."

In what felt like seconds, he'd deposited me atop the kitchen counter, lowered his pants, and donned a condom. The heat between us was palpable and foreplay wasn't necessary. He entered me with a heady kind of force that hurt the tiniest bit and made it hard to breathe, leaving me wet and ready.

I stared into his eyes as we moved in harmony and I rode away doubt and the lingering questions I had regarding his temporarily ghosting me.

I wasn't ignorant to the fact that he hadn't completely denied being with his ex or explained his whereabouts. Knowing Dominic, he'd cite being called into work, administering epidurals that eased a birthing woman's pain. Rather than challenge him or launch some long-winded debate, I surrendered to my body and let it lead the way as the luscious feelings pulsing through my flesh had me discounting my common sense.

Tessa, you're ignoring some blood-red flags, girl.

I knew it, but right then my mind was elsewhere. He'd raised my top and clamped his mouth about my nipple with my bra still on. That lacy material added extra fiction that sent rationale out the window and pleasure towards the edge, leaving my focus solely on what was going on between my legs.

I was a helpless mess with one thought.

Jealous, guilty sex is hot as hell.

SIX

ONA

1786, Age 12

I was two years of age when the thirteen colonies declared their independence from Britain and became a nation. A decade had passed since then; and just as in 1776, I remained a bondsperson. The freedom that sparked fireworks and sounds of revelry wasn't for me or mine, but for them; likewise, care for the welfare of my kind wasn't part of the indelible fabric of the Declaration of Independence. We awakened enslaved every July fourth and remained in such a state on July fifth and each subsequent day. I'd recently learned what irony meant. I suppose this was one such bitter instance. Even so, I couldn't help being awed by the colorful lights exploding above the boats on the Potomac and brightening the night sky as the Washingtons and their guests exclaimed over their fiery brilliance.

"I wish the fourth of July was every day." Little Master Washy happily bounced on the lap of the man for whom he was named. "You're the general, Granddad, can't you make that happen?"

I stole a peek at General Washington as laughter rang among the assembled company. He was a tall, serious man, rather imposing. Sometimes, even temperamental and frightening. Yet, he was always hospitable and welcoming towards guests; a devoted husband and grandfather who was absolutely gentle with his grandchildren.

"That would make me God, Washy, and I'm afraid I am not *that* magnificent." The General ruffled the child's hair, affectionately.

"Uncle, that is a matter of too humble an opinion." Miss Fanny's comment incited more mirth. The orphaned daughter of Mistress's deceased sister, Anna Marine, she—like George and Lawrence, the General's orphaned nephews and now his wards—had recently found shelter at Mount Vernon. Not to mention a spouse in another of the General's nephews, George Augustine Washington.

The adults of this expanded family sat on the comfortable Windsor chairs stationed along the east-facing front porch where the Washingtons and their guests had gathered at the end of what had been a long day of celebration. Torches at either end of the piazza provided illumination and warded off pesky insects, keeping the gathered content. Bullfrogs croaked. Fireflies danced about the night sky as Miss Nelly, Evilest Eliza, their sister Patty, George, Lawrence, and children of the families in attendance sprawled about the lawn on quilts enjoying the ice cream and sweets that topped off the splendid spread Cook and his staff had painstakingly prepared for the occasion.

Wouldn't it be wonderful if there's ice cream left after everyone has gone?

The heat of the day had been merciless. The night air was less vicious yet warm enough to cause rivulets of sweat to periodically trickle down my back. It was highly unlikely that any of

Cook's superb confection would remain once the guests had departed, but the idea of cooling my tongue with its sweetness was a worthwhile dream. For now, I was forced to content myself with the occasional breeze.

I wonder what Mother and my family are doing.

I imagined them gathered with the others, way back in the quarters, enjoying a rare evening of relaxation. We knew the celebration of freedom from British rule didn't translate to our liberty. Still, it was an opportunity for food, drink, and community. Perhaps fiddle-playing and even dancing on a night lit by bonfires that provided visibility in addition to warding off dreaded mosquitoes and other insects by burning goldenseal. Songs might be sung. Stories were possibly shared.

Callie and Eustis are there.

I missed my friends and seldom had occasion to be with them. Both worked the fields, while I remained in the main house far from those I loved, in service seven days a week with only Sunday afternoons off. That time was spent down in the slave quarters with family and friends, but it always passed too quickly and never seemed enough.

Even time belongs to them, and is not my companion.

A pang stole across my heart as I stood in the shadows of the porch, a lady's maid in waiting, suddenly longing to be elsewhere.

Two years had passed since I'd repaired the late Master Jacky's rabbit and become a servant dedicated to Mistress's personal care and interests. Simmie had been instructed to train me and did so with veiled, yet immense, resentment. She was wily as a fox, masking her unmerited dislike for me when Mistress was present. Whenever Mistress wasn't, she took delight in doling out harassment. I was pinched. My hair was pulled. She found special pleasure in hiding things that Mistress needed, leaving me to scour her chambers while fervently praying I'd find the missing objects. She'd even blamed me for a figurine that had been broken only for Mistress to state she'd knocked the porcelain lady over herself accidentally. That incident caught Simmie a scolding and an hour of scrubbing the floor on her knees for "lies and false accusations" and brought me respite, if only temporarily. Mistress bringing me into her private sphere as her personal maid-in-training had made Simmie my staunch, persistent enemy.

Despite Simmie's constant torment, the service I provided Mistress wasn't wholly unpleasant, just demanding, tiring. Most days, my duties as her maid remained the same. My morning started long before the sun rose because Mistress and the General were early risers. I had to be awake before them, particularly on cold mornings in order to light the fireplace fire to warm their room before they rose from bed. I remained outside the chambers while General Washington prepared himself with the help of his valet. Once he'd exited to his downstairs office, I brought fresh water for Mistress to wash with before laying out her clothing. I attended to her toilette—her ablutions and bathing—then dressed her for the day, leaving her hair to be combed and styled by Simmie. On rare occasions Mistress requested breakfast be brought to her on a tray, but most mornings she dined downstairs after repeatedly walking the length of the piazza portico for exercise. That's when Simmie and I cleaned her room in tandem.

Of course, Simmie gave me the tasks she abhorred—particularly cleaning ashes from the fireplace and emptying chamber pots used the prior evening when the dark or cold prevented a trip to The Necessary, the outdoor structure where the Washingtons could relieve themselves. When Mistress returned to her room for an hour of morning meditation that was never to be interrupted, I made my way to the kitchen to eat my breakfast. Afterwards, I cleaned and mended Mistress's clothing as needed; managed and organized her belongings. Such were my mornings. Dusting. Sweeping. Cleaning furniture in the bedchamber. Time was not mine, but devoted to another's bene-fit. My days and evenings were equally committed to Mistress's care and wellbeing. I remained in close proximity, unless tasked elsewhere, until she retired to her chambers each evening. Only then, after a day of full servitude, could I collapse in bed. This was life as a servant. Once, I'd been Miss Nelly's constant play-mate, now I was an ever-present attendant at the ready.

Despite Simmie's attempts at sabotage, I'd trained myself to intuit Mistress's needs and did my best to ensure each was met. In part because she was a particular but pleasant enough woman, but more so to avoid her bouts of wrathful vengeance. She was prone to melancholy moods and lashing out on occa-sion. Such bouts of ill spirit had taught me to be silent, unseen, and reserved. In such moments, escaping punishment by being still as a statue, melting into nothingness and shadows was preferable.

"Gram-Gram, may we go down to the quarters to see the darkies dance?"

I stood with other stoic servants behind the long row of high-backed chairs stationed on the piazza in which sat the gentry. Our eyes might've been dutifully trained on the dark distance, but Evilest Eliza's voice had my full attention.

The General responded before Mistress could. "Grand-daughter, we should allow the servants this night to themselves."

Mistress's voice was light as she protested her husband's opinion. "But, dearest, it's a splendid idea, a perfect cap to an evening of merriment."

"*Please*, Granddad."

That evil she-thing scampered onto the porch and took to batting her lashes, a perfect little seductress. Within moments the General caved to her whims, easing from his chair, and standing fully erect. Moving to where the women sat clustered together, he offered an arm to Mistress.

"It seems as if fireworks aren't sufficient entertainment for some of us."

Laughter splashed about as family and guests followed suit, joining the General and Mistress as a male servant hurried ahead, illuminating the way with a lit lantern.

"Simmie, you may come with me. Oney, prepare my bedclothing."

"Yes, Mistress." Simmie and I were seemingly one synchronized person when answering.

As the Washingtons and their guests left the piazza, Simmie followed suit, smiling triumphantly when nearing me. "Do as you're told and be quick about it, little mongrel orphan." She punctuated her whispered venom by stomping on my foot. Hard. Intentionally.

Ooo, I wish I could learn roots from Old Mama Lodie.

Old Mama Lodie was ancient and, like Papa Shinault, she remembered Africa and kept the homeland within her, despite black magic practices being forbidden. She'd preserved and practiced the art of root work learned from her grandmother and knew what herbs and plants could heal and help. And which could hinder. Thankfully for any enemies, she focused on healing. That didn't mean she couldn't dabble and conjure up a solution to adversarial persons or situations when needed.

"If I knew what Old Mama Lodie knows, I'd turn Simmie into a toad."

One of the visiting servants positioned nearest me tittered, overhearing my malicious wish. Tucking my head in embarrassment, I moved aside as the cadre of visiting attendants made their way to the servants' hall erected for the purpose of housing the footmen, valets, maids, and other bondsmen belonging to the Washingtons' guests.

"Why does she hate me so much?"

"Because she's a jealous wretch, not to mention a wench."

Caroline, one of the housemaids, walked alongside me while answering my softly spoken lament.

"But she has no reason for jealousy. I'm the same as she is."

"Mistress likes you and Simmie's scared you gonna replace her. Plus, you have something she don't. A mother."

Simmie wasn't a dower slave inherited by Mistress and held in trust for grandchildren. She'd been purchased by the General and, because of that fact, could just as easily be sold off. The General disliked breaking up families, but Simmie hadn't jumped the broom yet and had no children despite being a good five or six years older than I was. I understood if she felt vulnerable, even hostile. But just then, my head swam with the horrifying root of her contempt. It wasn't uncommon in this human chattel system for someone to not know the source of their origins. The enslaved were property, sold at any age and for any whim—to satisfy a debt, a sporting game gone wrong, when one was deemed useless, unbreakable, or even as a means of discipline. We who were blessed to know a parent were not the norm, rather the exception.

Entering the great hall, Caroline and I faced each other. "But I don't have a father, only the man who sired me." The words felt lame slipping across my lips, like some pitiful proof of our sameness.

"But he left his mark." Reaching out and lifting my arm, Caroline tapped it with her fingertip. I instantly knew what she meant.

Betcha ya thinks ya some kinda special 'cause ya gots better skin.

I was no longer ignorant about Simmie's long-ago bitterly spoken sentiment. Shortly after arriving in the main house as Miss Nelly's playmate, I'd begun to notice differences. Truthfully, I'd noticed before but without fully comprehending. Even that long-ago day in the workhouse when Mistress, Miss Nelly, and Master Wash had visited, pulling me from work to play with them—as the seamstresses stood at attention, I'd noticed. The women, like Mother, were fair in complexion; their hair had a certain soft texture. Their similarities had struck my curiosity but I'd been unable to process the significance. Thanks to Miss Nelly, I no longer struggled in my understanding.

She'd caught me one day, tears streaming while straightening her pile of playthings. I'd hastily wiped my face and denied any sorrow only for her to demand to know what ailed me. I'd quietly admitted missing my family, my friends Eustis and Callie. With ten-year-old wistfulness I'd longingly stated how lovely it would be if my friends could serve in the mansion alongside me.

Eustis and Callie are brown, and brown slaves belong outdoors. Aren't you glad you're not too much darker than us? If you were, you might not be inside, close to me, Oney.

Those words swept away any shadows of misunderstanding and I became painfully clear about the plantation's hierarchy of color and complexion. And it wasn't merely Mount Vernon. The servants who'd arrived with the day's guests were fair of skin, further evidence that such biological markings were a necessity for those allowed in an owner's daily presence and intimate sphere.

I thought about Simmie, her constant pinches, and the pulling of my hair—how she called me a mongrel orphan. I hated such treatment, but standing there with Caroline, I felt inexplicably sympathetic.

"But Simmie's not so dark. And her plaits are even longer than mine."

Caroline leaned forward, whispering in my ear, "Next time you see her, pay attention to her hawkish nose and that hair. Thems the markings that she wasn't sired by a white, but some Injun."

Caroline left to tend to her duties as I made my way upstairs, thinking this whole system confusing, if not outright ignorant. Climbing to the second-floor landing, I paused near a lit wall sconce to examine my hands, my arms.

"None of this makes good sense."

If we were made by the Creator, and the Creator made *all things* well and in His likeness, how could something as essential as the skin I was born in breed contempt?

"*Or* be a means of elevation?"

Sadness and a touch of righteous indignation stung my heart as I headed for the Washingtons' chambers, recalling last year's Independence Day celebration. Hadn't Caesar—the closest thing to a preacher in our community, that anomaly who'd at some place in time learned to read—at General Washington's direction, recited part of the Declaration of Independence for their guests?

We hold these truths to be self-evident, that all men are created equal.

The guests had effusively applauded afterwards, amazed and impressed by Caesar's oratory eloquence. I wasn't. I was too taken with the faces of the other enslaved, finding neither glee nor celebration. Just stoic masks that mirrored my hidden sentiments.

The General is a liar and a hypocrite.

He and his kind held humans in bondage, contradicting their Declaration and its truths that were supposedly "self-evident."

Maybe to them we're not men, children, or women.

Just things. Means of currency. Malleable objects that happened to breathe.

That's enough, Ona. Don't rile yourself up.

Entering the chambers, I set about preparing Mistress's nightclothes, refreshing the water in her wash bowl, and turning back the bedding just to keep my mind from fretting and fuming. I was only twelve. Like others born into this godforsaken system with our kind of skin, I was destined to have nothing save a lifetime of servitude ahead.

Will I never know what freedom is?

That thought left me none too gentle while adjusting the long netting hanging from the bedposts that kept out mosquitoes and other annoying insects. My nose turned up, automatically, as I ensured the chamber pot was empty. My movements were rough, agitated. By the time I finished, Mistress could be heard on the stairs. I tucked away my vexation and hurriedly assumed an appropriate position, eyes downcast, hands clasped as she entered, an air of tired delight about her.

"Oney, your people are simply magnificent. Their singing and dancing were so spirited. But I'm afraid I've overexerted myself and had to leave the others back in the quarters."

"Yes, Mistress. Would you like me to bring tea?"

She sat in the wingchair facing the bed, exhaling wearily. "No, it's too hot a night for tea. I've already sent someone out back to the nursery for a cup of mother's milk. If that doesn't soothe this sudden distress in my head and chest, we'll try some peppermint water or Dr. Craik's bloodsucking leeches." She lifted a foot, indicating I should remove her footwear.

Quickly, I knelt, removing her shoes as well as her silken stockings while thinking about the days I'd spent helping to care for the little ones when I was young. At the end of the workday, many mothers returned from the fields, depleted, the fronts of their dresses sometimes soaked with nourishing mother's milk meant for, but kept from, their infants due to their working the fields.

What will the babies drink if Mistress takes their milk?

"Oney, be quick about helping me prepare for bed. Once I have no further need of you, you may go to the quarters and enjoy whatever remains of the festivities."

I forgot about stolen milk and latched onto the idea of being with my family, Eustis, and Callie.

"Yes, ma'am."

I hid my excitement and forced myself to focus on helping Mistress undress and attending to her nighttime toilette before helping her into bed and settling the netting. Using the candle snuffer, I extinguished the candle closest to her.

"Leave the other so that General Washington has illumination when coming to bed."

"Yes, ma'am."

"Good night, Oney. Enjoy your time this evening, but do not dawdle overly long. Even with guests, we will be about our business as usual come morning."

Offering another obsequious agreement, I walked calmly from the room, down the stairs and out a side door before hurrying over the covered path to the kitchen to hang my apron, nearly knocking over the butter churn in my excitement. The space was empty except for Cook, who sat in a chair, fast asleep, his chin tucked against his chest—clearly exhausted from a long day of work. I was cautious and quiet, so as not to wake him. Lifting the hem of my skirt, I took off running as soon as I cleared the kitchen. My heart raced. A real smile, not the simile displayed for the Washingtons' comfort, spread across my face. The closer I came to the quarters, the larger that smile became, nearly consuming my countenance when I heard merriment in the distance. Joy pranced about my heart as one thought filled my head.

Home.

It was where I belonged, and where I was headed.

Coming upon the vast gathering of the enslaved out in the warm night celebrating, was like plunging into a vat of healing liquid. It soothed and lifted me. Took away the loneliness I sometimes felt, transporting me to the bosom of belonging. Slightly separated from us, the General and his guests clustered near the makeshift stage as the lyrical sounds of fiddle and fife skipped across the night. Rhythmic handclapping seemingly matched the happy cadence of my heartbeat. I pressed beyond the fringes of the gathering, melding into their presence and essence while searching for my family. It was always delicious having moments with them besides what time I was afforded on my Sunday afternoons off. Unfortunately, the crowd prevented me from finding them. Searching, I waded through the sea of humanity while clapping in sync with those around me. I greedily inhaled the sights, sounds, and smells of my familiar. I was suddenly myself again. Temporarily free.

I almost felt a pang of regret when the ditty ended, until I saw someone waving in my peripheral vision.

Callie!

We raced towards each other, embracing as if we'd been apart for years not weeks.

"Ona, I was hoping you'd come!" Callie kissed my cheek. "What took you so long?"

"Thank heaven Mistress took to ailing or I might not even be here now."

"Which one of her sicknesses decided to visit? Never mind. Don't matter. I'll simply thank heaven one of the many did."

I pinched her arm, playfully. "Don't be heathenish. Where's Eustis?"

Callie shrugged. "Probably sniffing 'round Penelope. Find her. You'll likely find him."

I disliked these recent changes: that Eustis preferred spending whatever free time he managed each Sunday with Penelope rather than me and Callie. Similarly, Master Wash no longer followed Miss Nelly around, but took to playing with the slave boys his age. But this thing with Eustis felt different. Like desertion. Callie and I took to looking about as if willing our friend to appear. The gathering was so large, seemingly every living being on the plantation had assembled, making finding Eustis more than difficult.

"Oh, well. He'll turn up."

Callie didn't share my optimism. "But if he does, will he even wanna be with us?"

I linked an arm in hers, glad I wasn't the only one who'd noticed the changes in Eustis. On Sundays, I relished spending time with Mama and my siblings before stealing an hour to share with my two best friends. Except lately, Eustis either didn't show up at our secret place in the garden grove, or came late. And when he did come, he only talked about two things: hating life at Mount Vernon, or the wonders of Penelope. The former made him increasingly sullen, while the latter made Callie and I roll our eyes, tiring of his repetitiveness. But his new practice of cutting our time short so he could go off somewhere with her set our teeth on edge.

"Why he always wanna be 'round her for anyways?" Callie asked.

I leaned in, whispering. "Do you think they spend their time kissing?"

Callie shrieked and leaned away from me as if I'd committed blasphemy. "Don't be a demon, Ona! That's disgusting."

"Maybe. But do they?"

She shrugged again, conveying disinterest. "Race you up that tree!"

She bolted, giving herself an unfair advantage that left me hiking up my hem and pumping my legs. By the time we reached Callie's chosen tree and scrambled up, she on a slightly higher limb, we were breathless yet laughing. We sat, clutching the sturdy branches of the huge sycamore, legs swinging happily as if we were little children. I felt the kind of giddiness that could only come from being with someone I'd known and loved since our days spent in the nursery with the other slave infants—long before Mother became head seamstress.

Our vantage point was wonderful despite not being terribly high in the tree, and I had the sensation of floating—of liberty. I looked about the throng for Mama, my sisters, my brothers; but there were too many bodies crowded down there for me to make them out by torchlight. I contented myself with the thought of finding them once the festivities concluded.

This occurred too soon for me. It seemed as if we'd barely settled ourselves before the music suddenly ended and the air filled with applause and sounds of glee. Callie and I added our hurrahs, which quickly faded as the General moved from the fringes where the upstairs folks had clustered and approached the makeshift stand where the musicians had played. He thanked them before turning to the assembled, wishing everyone a happy Independence Day. He'd barely finished before being interrupted by a young man in the crowd.

"General... sir... excuse us, but might we beg a moment of your—"

He sounded desperate but had no opportunity to finish whatever his plea. He was nearly yanked off his feet by a nearby boss man, an overseer hired to manage workers, who'd stormed towards him as if a bondsman's speaking to the General without invitation was a deadly sin.

"You're not only approaching General Washington out of turn, in front of his guests, but wanting something of him as well?"

Tension was thick, immediate, as the boss hit the younger man with such force that he staggered backwards into the crowd and would have fallen except for others catching him. I stared wide-eyed at Callie and she at me as all the good feelings of the evening vanished on invisible, panic-laden wings.

"Enough, Stilson," the General cautioned his overseer. "Not in front of the women. This is a day for celebration. Not recriminations."

Removing the grimy hat from his head, Stilson bowed to the upstairs women who seemed miffed by this unnecessary bit of unpleasantness.

"Aren't you one of mine?" Lord Fairfax, the visiting master of a neighboring estate and a member of Virginia's gentry, moved towards the young man whose brazen ways had resulted in his being assaulted. "You're Birdie's boy. Correct?"

The man straightened himself, fixing his clothing as if preparing for inspection. "Yessuh. I'se Noble." He looked and sounded a few years older than Eustis, but not as grown as my brother, Austin, who was already courting.

"Why're you here?" Lord Fairfax's tone was no nonsense.

"I'se been given a pass, suh." Noble quickly produced a folded piece of paper from within his shirt which Stilson, none too nicely, snatched from him and handed over to Lord Fairfax.

"Bring some light so I may read." He was close enough to a lit torch stationed in the area, but I suppose Lord Fairfax needed extra on account of his years. A boy I recognized as one of Eustis's friends was quick in complying with his demands, uprooting a torch and bringing it nearer the man.

That had me looking for Eustis again, hoping he was in close proximity to his friend. As far as I could determine from my lofty place in the tree, he wasn't.

"I see my house steward, Trumble, granted you permission to be on General Washington's premises for the evening." Lord Fairfax looked hard at the young man whose head was lowered as required, respectfully. "For what purpose are you here?"

A young woman materialized at Noble's side as if by magic. She was young like him, but older than me, and stood silently, hands protectively splayed across her rounded belly. I gasped and looked at Callie who held a finger to her lips, urging my silence.

"I'se wanting to speak to the General 'bouts me and Mathilda being together."

"It appears to me that togetherness has already happened." Glancing at the cluster of upstairs women, Lord Fairfax stopped himself. "Forgive me, ladies, for speaking on such a delicate subject in your presence."

"I consider it best to disband this gathering." General Washington gave orders that were immediately adhered to: the vast assembly of human property dispersed, returning to their respective lodgings. Except me and Callie. We remained unseen.

I wasn't sure of Callie's reasons for staying put, but I was a lady's maid and didn't want to be seen climbing down from a tree. If Mistress caught word that I'd engaged myself in something so undignified I might catch a chastening. I dreaded that possibility and stayed still as the General gave instructions to two of the housemen to take a torch and escort the upstairs women back to the mansion. He turned to the young couple standing before him.

"It's Noble, correct?"

"Yessuh."

"I believe I've seen you here on the premises. You're the apprentice of my blacksmith, are you not?"

It wasn't uncommon for neighboring plantation owners to loan their servants to one another for specific needs, or even to learn a skill or trade. Noble was an example of such an exchange.

"Why, yes, I suppose it slipped my memory." Lord Fairfax cleared his throat as if hiding embarrassment. "What is this about you and this wench wanting to be united?"

Noble never lifted his eyes, but his shoulders seemed to straighten and he managed to somehow strike that precarious balance of standing taller without exuding arrogance for which he surely would have been viciously disciplined. "Yessuh... Mathilda and me... we'se wanting to jump the broom... make this permanent."

"Is this your pup she's carrying?"

Something inside of me bristled hotly at Lord Fairfax's

referring to the baby growing in Mathilda's belly as something an animal had created.

"Yessuh, this my child. That's even more reason for me and Mathilda wanting to be together."

"Well, General, it appears our plantations are more neighborly than we imagined."

"Indeed. I've no moral objection to the union of these two, but I do take umbrage with the fact that this fraternizing wasn't approved by either of us in advance."

"I agree, General. Not to mention all this godforsaken night-walking..."

"These bucks with wenches on other farms and plantations spend their entire Sundays off with them. That ought to be sufficient. Instead, they lay over until the wee hours of Monday morning before the sun breaks then walk those long miles home. By the time they arrive to work in the fields they're exhausted and it's difficult to get a good day's work out of them. This night-walking is an aggravating practice." General Washington addressed Noble directly. "Whatever time my gracious neighbor has permitted, do not take advantage or inconvenience him. Return to Lord Fairfax's estate—as I tell my Negroes— before the earth warms the sun tomorrow morning."

"Yessuh."

The General and Lord Fairfax turned to leave, only to pause at Noble's gentle throat-clearing.

"Yes, is there something else?" General Washington's voice held a hint of annoyance.

"Suh, just needing to know if'n it be a'right for me and Mathilda to jump the broom and be man and wife?"

It was a kept custom, a holdover from Africa, where a broom was waved above the couple's head to ward off evil spirits that might want to meddle in their new union. That broom was then placed on the ground for the couple to jump over, leaving separate lives behind as they leaped into oneness. Some teased that whichever of the two jumped the highest, he or she would be the decision-maker between them.

Lord Fairfax waved his hand in annoyance. "I've no interest in black magic foolishness such as broom-jumping. Go. Consider yourselves united."

"Yessuh! Thank ya, but may we trouble you only once again?"

Lord Fairfax's irritation was clear, illuminated by torchlight and the moon in the night sky. "Make it quick."

"I'se wanting to use my blacksmithing skills to buy this heah baby's freedom—"

"I am consistent about making rounds on my property and knowing what belongs to me." General Washington's words carried across the night air with unmistakable authority as he focused his attention on Mathilda. "If I'm not mistaken, you belong to Missus Washington, yes?"

The poor girl was so nervous that nodding rapidly was her sole response.

"Then purchasing this offspring isn't a possibility." He returned his attention to Noble. "The dam is a dower slave. So, too, is her issue. All dower slaves and anything they produce are held in trust as part of our grandchildren's future inheritance. You, Mathilda, should know that."

I wanted to reach up and grab Callie's hand at the horrifying bewilderment that seized Noble and Mathilda's countenances.

"You may jump the broom if you wish, but the girl and anything she births will be the property of my grandchildren when they come of age. There will be no buying of either until then. But you may also rejoice that there will be no selling either. Provided you do well in satisfying Lord Fairfax and don't find yourself sent away, you'll be together for many more years."

As the General and his neighbor walked away, Noble's "yassuh" was an automatic but broken whisper wafting mournfully about him and Mathilda like a somber benediction.

"Noble, they can't have our baby! I don't want this child sold from us like you were from your parents."

His voice was stronger now that they were alone. "You heard the General. Our child cain't be sold—"

"Not yet! Not till one of them spoiled, lily-white monsters of theirs grows up and inherits her or him."

I felt guilty, as if intruding as Noble wrapped his arms about Mathilda, trying to comfort a heart already broken.

"Shhh... no more fretting. We'se got only a few more hours together tonight. The good Lord'll help us figure something out."

Callie and I didn't make a sound until the despondent couple disappeared down the lane. Only then did we scramble down from our perch in the tree, grabbing hands almost instinctively.

Callie was first to speak. "What're they gonna do, Ona?"

I shook my head, helplessly. "Maybe they'll be okay with knowing their child can't be taken away..."

My voice trailed off, leaving Callie to finish for me.

"Till then. Till Miss Nelly and her siblings get good and grown." Her voice tremored, nervously. "Maybe they should go see Old Mama Lodie. You know, get some roots and work some hoodoo to make General change his mind."

"I think this whole nation, not just the General, needs changing. Come on. Lemme go see my family before getting to bed."

Hands clasped, we headed in the direction of the Farm House quarters, silent and lost in thought until Callie dared to utter a disturbing possibility.

"Whatcha think'll happen to us once these pasty-faced Custis kids grow up?" Our mothers were both dower slaves. We were their offspring retained for the prosperity of the next slave-holding generation. "What if I wind up with Miss Nelly and you with Master Wash or Miss Patsy or..." She grimaced as if tasting that disgusting quinine tea Mistress made us all line up and drink at the start of every summer season to prevent mosquito-borne illnesses. "That *other* thing."

A year or so ago "That Other Thing," Evilest Eliza, had been visiting, entertaining playmates, when they'd moseyed themselves into the slave quarters. Unfortunately for Callie, she'd been tasked with gathering soiled laundry to cart to the wash house and encountered that gaggle of giggling simpletons up to no good. That Other Thing approached while her cronies stayed a safe distance in the rear, eyes gleaming with excited interest and a smidgeon of fear.

"Turn around so we can see."

"Ma'am?"

Things happened so swiftly that that was all Callie could manage. Before her next breath, she'd been spun about so forcefully that her laundry basket fell. What happened after that left Callie refusing to ever say Evilest Eliza's name again.

"Anabelle, you told a fib! Darkies may be unhuman but they *don't* have tails."

She'd yanked up the hem of Callie's skirt and lowered her bloomers, displaying Callie's private business before pushing her roughly away as if angry that she'd been unable to substantiate her friend's disgusting claim.

Callie had been so distraught and ashamed that she'd cried and cried then cried some more, and didn't eat for two whole days. Now, she hated Evilest Eliza with a vengeance.

"That girl's barely ten and already got enough devil spit in her for a good and grown human. If either of us gets sent to her—"

"Hush, Callie! Don't even say that."

"Heaven knows I don't wish for it, Ona, but it *could* happen."

"I'd rather skip on hot rocks to hell and visit Satan."

"If you do, she'll be there to greet you, seeing as how Satan's her pappy."

Arm in arm, Callie and I headed towards Manor House Farm, quietly laughing.

"Ona!"

Delphy was the first one to see me. She ran through the open door, wrapping her arms and her love about me. I picked her up and swung her around, delighted by her sounds of glee. Placing her on her feet, I wobbled backwards, exaggerating my exhaustion.

"You're getting heavy."

"That's 'cause I'm a big girl not a baby."

The two years that had passed since I'd been assigned to the mansion were evident in her appearance. Her cheeks no longer held their baby-like fullness, and I was slightly taken aback by how tall she'd gotten. Being together once a week on my Sunday afternoons off felt insufficient, I was missing out on too much. My older sisters, Nancy and Lucinda, had the blessing of working in the weaving house close by and returned home every night. Like our brothers assigned to other places on the property, I'd been removed from the bosom of my family. While the spatial distance wasn't massive, separation and absence had still been imposed upon us. It was never our choice to be apart.

"Well, hello, Little Miss Big Girl." I curtsied dramatically. "Pleasure to make your acquaintance."

Grabbing my hand, Delphy pulled me inside, giggling merrily.

My mother and older sisters were already in their nightwear, their coarse cotton shifts hanging from nails in the wall like drab ladies in waiting. I rushed to them, got lost in their embrace. My sisters and I chattered over each other, trying to fill in the missing gaps since our last time together as Mother looked on, a soft smile about her lips. She busied herself, preparing a plate for me, placing it on the rough-hewn table in the center of our cabin atop which sat our single source of illumination, a fat wax candle.

"Here, Ona. Sit. Eat."

Thanking my mother, I sat on the wooden bench, grateful for the plate of roast rabbit and a sweet potato harvested from our small garden plot outside. It was nowhere near as fancy as the meals Uncle Hercules created but, surrounded by family, it tasted like heaven. By the time I finished, I was full of food and loving fellowship.

"Ona, it's getting late..."

A good deal of time had passed since I'd arrived. My sisters had sat at the table with me, chatting. Mother had closed the cabin door and cautioned us to speak quietly. The farm managers were known to pass through the quarters on horseback at night, monitoring activities, as if our being alone without their overseeing presence might lead to misdeeds. Or as if we were children requiring their constant, ominous managing of our beings. We obeyed Mother's caution, not wanting to draw their undesirable attention. Now, with a look of sorrowful regret on her face, Mother reminded me I needed to be elsewhere.

"No, please, Ona can't go yet." Delphy's words were a pitiful whine that mirrored my emotions.

I wasn't ready to leave.

"Can she stay a little longer? We miss our sister."

"I miss Ona as well, Delphy. But Mistress might wake up during the night, needing her."

"But it's not fair! Mistress gets to see her every day, and we only get to spend time with her on Sundays. We need her, too. Ona belongs with us, not them."

"That's enough, Philadelphia." Mother's voice was sharp, stern. Nervously, she glanced at the open squares cut into the cabin walls that served as windows, as if afraid Delphy's complaint might've drifted into the night. "We're *blessed* to be *together*." Mother inhaled deeply, collecting herself. "No matter how brief or unfair it may be."

"Yes, ma'am." Delphy dragged her bare foot back and forth across the cabin's dirt floor, bottom lip poked out, looking forlorn.

I went to her, hugging her tightly. "I miss you more than you miss me."

"No, you don't."

"I do, too. I miss you copying everything I do and being bothersome as some ol' flea. But I especially miss your loud snoring." I made a sound like a horse neighing.

"Take that back!"

I jumped away in time to avoid my sister's playful swat. When she lunged for me, I ran behind Nancy, using our oldest sister like a shield. Delphy wasn't to be outdone and came after me. I dodged her again, pulling Lucinda into our silliness. Next thing I knew, we were doing the unthinkable, playing a game of chase in the cramped confines of our cabin. Mother said nothing. She merely sat on her low-lying bed, her "mean pallet" that was raised on a frame a mere inch above the dirt, a hand covering her mouth as her shoulders shook with laughter. Clearly, the joy of our being together superseded her usual objections to indoor misbehavior. Only the snort of a horse in the not too far distance ended our light-hearted moment.

My sisters and I froze in response to Mother lifting a silencing hand.

"Snuff out that candle!"

Lucinda was closest and obeyed Mother's whispered instructions, plunging us in darkness.

Easily, my eyes adjusted to see that Delphy and Lucinda had crawled onto Mother's pallet and huddled behind her. When she motioned to Nancy and me, we hurried to her side and sat quietly at the sound of a horse whinnying. A deep tension emanated from our mother as she sat, arms spread wide like some majestic bird shielding its precious brood of chicks. There was no need to explain the threat. We understood. A white man was present.

We remained that way, clutching each other and clustered against our mother until we heard noises indicating the unseen rider had reached his destination further down the lane. His voice wobbled drunkenly as he called out for a girl we knew who was somewhere near my older sister, Nancy's, age. For a long time, there was no response, prompting the rider—one of the white men living on the property and tasked with helping manage workers in the fields—to loudly summon her again. She lived in one of the communal buildings with bunk-style beds that housed female help. Her being commanded to appear proved that for us, there was no safety in numbers.

"Don't make me get off this horse and come in there. Show yourself, gal. *Now!*" The man's drunken yell was like a putrid stench contaminating the night.

I peeked through the crevices of our cabin walls where the logs weren't flush together and could detect the movement of the girl being summoned as she exited the communal dwelling. I imagined the trembling fear she must have felt while standing there and being commanded.

"Come on. Let's make this quick. I ain't got all night."

When the man nudged his horse into motion, she followed, her movements slow, hollow. Lifeless.

I watched until their shadowy outlines faded from my limited view only to wrap my arms about my mother's waist and bury my face against her when hearing the girl's cries of distress moments later. I wished I didn't know what was happening but did because Mother had instructed my older sisters and me about the ways of men the year before. I was only eleven when she did and the knowledge felt too heavy, but for us, ignorance was as unaffordable luxury.

In the life of a slave girl, there's no such thing as too early.

I'd been warned, informed. Sitting there in the dark hearing the girl's cries, her pain was like a knife slashing through the night and piercing my heart, my being. I wanted to run out the door and rescue her, do damage to her assailant but knew I was powerless.

"Lay down. All of you." Mother's voice was soft, nearly broken. "Ona, I'll wake you in time to get back in the morning before Mistress knows you're missing. But you'll stay here tonight. No one's leaving."

We didn't gather our pallets, spreading them out on the ground as usual. Rather, Mother made us lie on her mean pallet as she sat on the floor, her back pressed against it, watching the door like a sentinel. We lay listening to the night, fearing any indication that danger might call on us as it had that poor girl. Eventually my sisters and I fell asleep, wrapped about each other despite the hot night, needing each other's comfort.

I was shaken awake just before daybreak.

"Ona, wake up." My mother's whisper pulled me from sleep.

The pleasure I felt when seeing her shadowed face lessened when I remembered why I was still there, why she'd kept me. Extracting myself from my sisters, I eased from the mean pallet and stood. Immediately, my mother's arms clamped about me.

"You be safe. Do as Mistress says. And do *not* take off your bindings."

Last year when teaching my older sisters and me horrid things out of necessity, Mother had taken strips of cloth and tightly bound them about my chest in an attempt to camouflage my newly budding body.

"Yes, Mother." After the horrors of the prior night, I had no desire to gain any man's notice and, in that regard, preferred a shadow life. "Kiss my sisters for me, please."

We walked to the cabin entrance together, but Mother made me wait as she opened the door and stepped outside.

When she'd finished scanning the area surrounding our cabin, she beckoned me forward, hugging me again. "Go. Hurry. I'll be here."

In the early dawn her face seemed haggard, as if she hadn't slept, but maintained her nighttime vigil. Hugging her one last time, I hurried up the lane in the direction of the mansion. I paused several times and glanced over my shoulder only to find she hadn't disappeared, but had stubbornly planted herself like a guardian of my safe passage.

I made it back before the upstairs folks began to stir. They were late in rising, as if the Independence Day celebration had overly taxed them. I went about my duties, tired, lethargic. Mistress even mentioned my slowness. I merely apologized, knowing better than to make excuses for my sluggishness.

She wouldn't understand even if I told her.

She was gentry. Secure. Safe. She would never know what it meant to be snatched by a night rider and forced to surrender her whole self.

I'd helped her bathe and dress and was on my way to the kitchen as she sat for breakfast when the plantation bell rang, causing me to stiffen with alarm. I was outdoors in the passageway that was covered, but not enclosed, that led to the servants' kitchen when I heard the sound of horses' hooves. I wanted to run, remembering last night's rider and his violations, but was frozen by fear. I breathed in relief when the rider sped past me and towards the front of the mansion.

"What's going on?"

Servants poured out of the kitchen into the passage, faces bathed in worried expressions. I couldn't answer the scullery maid's question and simply shrugged as more of us gathered outdoors, curious as to what was occurring.

"That's enough gawking. Back to your business."

Some of us were slower than others in complying with

Cook's instructions, but eventually we returned to the kitchen—resuming duties or eating the morning meal.

"Well, whatever the ruckus is, it can't be good."

"Mind your business, Simmie, and not someone else's."

My nemesis mumbled something under her breath in response to Cook's rebuke, but did as she was told.

I'd just sat down to eat the cold fruit and hot biscuit on my plate when a house servant burst into the kitchen, panting. Breathless.

"Noble and Mathilda are missing."

His words burst into the air like fusillade from a cannon.

Cook stopped what he was doing and rushed towards him. "What do you mean 'missing?'"

"They're gone. Ain't nobody laid eyes on 'em since last night. A rider just came from Lord Fairfax's. Noble never made it back there, and they ain't nowhere on Mount Vernon." He pulled in a huge breath. "They ran away! They escaped."

SEVEN

TESSA

Who thought it was a good idea putting a kindergarten-ready decal on the ceiling?

I'm sure it was meant to be calming but being an adult woman laying on an exam table—legs spread, feet in stirrups with that cold, metal speculum all up in my stuff—I was not comforted by colorful butterflies flitting above a flowery meadow resplendent with honeybees and ladybugs. Concerns about what was going on in my reproductive system left me unfazed by the insect world and its cuteness.

"You're doing great, Tessa. We're almost finished."

Dr. Latimore was the best gynecologist I'd had to date. Her voice was velvety enough for her to be a nighttime smooth jazz radio show deejay, and her bedside manner and care were exceptional. The appointment I'd scheduled via the app was for three weeks out, but when her medical assistant called advising of a cancellation that following Wednesday, I jumped on it. I'd had to push back a client consultation, but fortunately the client was my godsister so rescheduling proved painless.

"Take a deep breath..."

I complied, staring at those daggone insects cavorting

happily overhead as Dr. Latimore carefully extracted that speculum that had to have been invented by a man. The sound alone was enough to make a woman want to jump off the table. Having some long, steel instrument inserted in a private cavity and hearing sounds of said metal being cranked opened was borderline disturbing. I knew it was for my benefit but still, being widened by a mechanical device always made me think of a tire jack.

Flat or faulty, something's wrong with me.

I closed my eyes against a stab of pain as Dr. Latimore examined my abdomen, pressing in various places while manually examining me, internally, with gloved fingers.

"It's tender here." Hers was a confirmation, not a question.

I nodded in response and exhaled my relief when the torture finally ended. I lay there catching my breath as she disposed of her gloves and washed her hands before assisting me into a sitting position.

"The lab results from your pap smear should be available in a few days." Sitting on a wheeled stool, she rolled close to the exam table so that we were inches apart. "I prefer to have conclusive results before offering an opinion..."

"But?"

"I don't think cancer is the issue, Tessa. Based on your symptoms and my examination, I believe what you're experiencing is endometriosis."

I had a basic understanding of the condition and started firing off questions after breathing a sigh of relief, perhaps prematurely, that cancer wasn't the problem.

"Okay, Dr. Latimore, what does this mean? Are we talking surgery? Prescription meds? Is it curable, or is endometriosis something that I need to prepare myself to live with?"

She offered an encouraging smile. "All valid and excellent questions."

I listened attentively as my physician patiently explained

endometriosis—the build-up of endometrial tissue outside of the uterus, typically on other reproductive organs such as the ovaries and fallopian tubes. Every month during a woman's cycle that misplaced tissue responded to hormonal changes and caused bleeding within the pelvis. The result was scarring, inflammation, painful cycles, even fibrous cysts, and swelling.

"Again, we want to wait for the test results from today's exam before drawing conclusions or making a definitive diagnosis. If your labs come back clean, we'll follow that up by scheduling you for an ultrasound. It's less invasive than laparoscopy, but highly effective. Once—rather *if*—my suspicions are proven correct we'll decide next steps as far as treatment options."

"What options would be available to me?"

"That will depend on the extent of the endometriosis."

I watched Dr. Latimore's mouth as she spoke, zoning in on the color of her lipstick as if needing a distraction. It was a matte espresso that beautifully complemented the rich, warm hues of her complexion. She was of Cameroonian descent and, after living in the U.S. for the majority of her life, her accent had all but disappeared. Every now and then a lyrical lilt made an appearance, its musicality making me smile whenever it did. Except today. Right then, I was lost to its charm as concerns wiggled through my conscience.

"You're young and healthy, Tessa." She placed a hand on mine, squeezing gently, as if intuiting my worry. "Those factors will work in your favor."

I silently stared at her a moment before inhaling deeply as if I needed extra breath. "Two last questions... *for today*."

She quietly laughed at my emphasis. "Of course."

"Can I get pregnant? If I want? And did I cause this?"

I'd confided an intimate experience with her when faced with minor gynecological issues, previously; so, she knew to what I alluded.

This time, she laid both hands atop mine and moved even

closer, staring deep into my eyes. "We'll be able to answer the first question once we know what, precisely, this is. As for the second, no, you didn't. Your body isn't being vengeful, Tessa, or making you pay for a choice you had the right to make." She raised her eyebrows as if challenging me to contradict her opinion.

I didn't. I merely nodded in consent. "Thanks. I appreciate that. And just for the record, I lied. I have one final question. What if this *isn't* endometriosis? I mean, my paternal grand-mother... there's family history..." I left that fearful thought unfinished.

She stood and folded her arms beneath her breasts. "We'll cross that bridge, together, if it presents itself."

After exiting Dr. Latimer's office, I didn't leave immediately. I sat in the parking lot, in my SUV—eyes closed, head against the headrest—listening to the sound of rain falling, thinking. I was thankful for being able to get in to see my gynecologist so quickly. That was heaven's favor working. Even so, I was worried about what was happening. I'd never been overly concerned about my health, only because I hadn't had cause to be. The most major issue I'd experienced had been a tonsillec-tomy. Other than that, I'd dealt with the usual ailments. A common cold. The flu. Seasonal allergies. The usual cuts and bruises from playing outdoors, running wild in childhood with friends in Cape Charles or on the banks of Chincoteague. But that was it. Thanks to immunizations, I hadn't even had chick-enpox as a kid. Now, there was this.

Tessa, it's not a death sentence.

Leaning forward, I grabbed the trifold brochure Dr. Latimer had given me from my dashboard. Opening it, I found helpful information about endometriosis, including simple suggestions for alleviating discomfort. Over-the-counter anti-inflammatory medicine. Regular exercise. Use of a hot water bottle or heating pad. Warm baths.

Guess I shouldn't have ignored Dominic's constant badgering and gone to the gym more often.

Regret spooled through me, not merely for my failure to be a faithful gym fixture, but for what I'd done as a college freshman at the age of seventeen. Perhaps, this was the universe's way of clapping back.

Now, my reproductive health is in jeopardy.

Reading that brochure and learning that this disease presented a risk of infertility, all of a sudden I wanted what Dominic wanted: children. A baby.

"Tessa, you're tripping."

I thought about calling him. After all, he was a medical professional. But I didn't want to be bombarded with Dominic's questions and subjected to some strategic plan of action he'd likely orchestrate, telling me what I should do next, when I was still unsure of the magnitude and scope of what I was dealing with.

Let me call my mama instead.

I needed a gentle hand and knew who had my back.

I didn't get the chance as my cell phone rang right then and my sound system announced, "Incoming call from Brandon Calloway."

How eerily apropos.

"Hey, B.C.," I answered, thinking karma really was a wart-nosed witch. Here I was facing the inability to conceive again only to get a call from my first lover and the man I'd conceived a child with.

His family's house on Chincoteague had been our love nest. Most often empty of occupants, it was the perfect place for horny teenagers to hook up. Conception wasn't part of our plan but we didn't use condoms because of my latex allergies, and obviously my application of spermicidal foams was faulty. That summer before we went off to our respective colleges, we spent more time hooking up than we probably should have. Two weeks after moving into my college dorm freshman year, I learned I was pregnant. When I told B.C., he was actually happy and talked about leaving college and getting a job to support us. I didn't want him sacrificing his education and we wound up arguing non-stop. When he attended football camp a few weeks later I took advantage of the fact that our communication would be limited and did what I felt I had to. I had an abortion.

I was too afraid and ashamed to tell my parents for fear of them being disappointed in me, or making me come home from college. With Brandon being her brother, I couldn't even confide in Mimi. Or Rocki. I was out of state, by myself, and shared my condition with no one. That was devastating enough. But when I told B.C. the choice I'd made, he went straight off. Our hour-long screaming match ended with his calling me "narcissistically selfish," getting sloppy drunk at a house party and hooking up with a chick who texted him when she missed her next period. Jade was the result. It was all too much. Our relationship ended in a blaze of bitterness that we had yet to fully extinguish.

"Hey TLS, you rolling through today?"

I threw my head back and exhaled noiselessly. "Of course. Absolutely."

He skipped a beat before challenging me. "You forgot, didn't you?"

Even after all the ish we'd gone through, the deterioration of first love, and the dance of avoidance we'd orchestrated and somehow managed, B.C. still got me in ways that my current man didn't. He'd always been intuitive where I was concerned, plugged in. Spiritually connected. I'd never been good at hiding things from him. Which was why I preferred maintaining our distance.

"It's on my calendar." I offered that truth versus admitting that my agreeing to stop by the new restaurant he was opening had completely slipped my mind courtesy of other more important things, like my health, commanding center stage. "I'm on my way, but I have to drop something off at your grandmother's first."

"That's cool. Tell Granny to send me some of those pralines if there're any left after your greedy self got at 'em."

"I swear Mimi can't hold water. I'm not even sure why that was worth telling, or why you needed to hear it."

"'Ey, that's my baby sister. She looks out for her big brother. See you in a bit."

"Sounds good."

"Yo, T., wait."

"Yes?"

"Do your best not to rear-end anybody on your way over here."

"Whatever, boy. Bye."

His laughter reverberated in my ears even after I'd disconnected, and I found myself smiling. Starting my SUV, I reversed from my parking space, my smile fading. Being cordial on the phone was one thing. I was curious if B.C. and I could remain that way in person.

"Like he said last week, it's time to put away juvenile ish."

I drove off reminding myself I was good and grown, and could handle being in the company of my ex.

"I'm sorry, baby, but I'm still at the hairdresser's. Why don't you head on over to Brandon's and do whatever you need to there? By the time you finish, I should be home."

"Sounds like a plan, Mama Calloway." I disconnected and drove past the turn-off leading to her house, heading for B.C.'s new restaurant without the need for GPS, instead. Having grown up here, I knew the island of Cape Charles, and even Chincoteague further south, like the back of my hand. By the time I reached my destination, the rain had lessened, but not enough to erase the need for an umbrella. The downpour was still steady. And chilly. Stepping from my vehicle, I found that cold island wind proved stronger here than it had been back in Virginia Beach. A wicked gust snatched that umbrella from my grip and sent it spinning across the parking lot like something possessed.

I took off after it, unwittingly sinking my left foot in a puddle that was determined to be the final resting place for the heel of my boot. Trying to wiggle my way free simply sunk me deeper. Despite all my efforts, that hole was relentless. I was the captive of broken asphalt.

"Really, God?"

I was on my way to unzipping my boot and leaving it there just to escape the cold wind and rain when aid arrived in the form of my ex.

"Here! Take this."

He draped a rain slicker over my head which I gladly accepted, ignoring the subtle sexiness of his cologne and an odd flash of something warm caused by his closeness. Instead, I concentrated on his bending to unzip my boot and jerk my foot free.

"Ouch! Dang, B.C., why you gotta be so rough?"

"Your foot is unstuck, right? And you're welcome."

"Thanks." *I guess.*

I stood on one leg as if I'd been birthed by a flamingo while B.C. wiggled my boot back and forth until he could yank it free of its soul-sucking moorings.

"There!" He handed me my knee-high calfskin boot caked in thick mud and debris, it's heel suddenly missing.

"Just wow. You would pick a restaurant with a quicksand parking lot."

He chuckled lightly. "That's so customers never leave and I don't have to worry about them *not* coming back. Hurry up and hold onto me."

"What?"

"Kill the protest, Tessa, and just do it."

"Why?"

"So, we can get inside."

"I'm fine."

"Suit yourself." He turned and trotted off.

The distance to the front door suddenly seemed too far for hopping on one leg like a five-foot-eight-inch human pogo stick; plus, I was already soaked and shivering.

"Okay, okay. Wait! Come back."

He side-eyed me like he didn't have time for nonsense before complying with my request. When he did, I slid an arm about his waist and he did the same around mine.

"You tired of playing Miss Independent games in the rain?"

"Whatever, B.C. Just help me inside already. Wait. My umbrella." I turned at the sound of a big rig blowing its horn only to see my umbrella, whisked onto the roadway by the wind, flattened beneath its wheels. "Well... alrighty then."

"You can put that on my tab."

"Trust me, I will. We can go inside if you don't mind."

I was relieved when we made it indoors. Not just to be out of the wet elements, but to put some distance between us. Just shy of six feet, B.C. was built like a linebacker. Muscular. Solid. He was, for the most part, playful. A jokester. Except when it came to matters of importance, like business or family. Then, he'd morph into a protective pit bull, and—thanks to his size— could seem intimidating or aggressive. Otherwise, he was gentle as the proverbial teddy bear. Lovable. Approachable. And, unlike Dominic, extremely personable.

There you go with the comparisons.

"Sorry about the chill, but the HVAC guy won't get here

until tomorrow to fix the heating system. Here. Put my jacket over yours so you don't get sick."

He positioned his jacket across my shoulders then disappeared through a swinging double door, reemerging with a wad of paper towels that he thrust into my hands before I could protest his jacket-draping, chivalrous kindness.

"Thanks." I patted rain from my face and hair while trying to downplay the impact of his presence, and the warm currents that shot up my arm when his fingers had touched mine. Maybe the attention deficit in my current relationship was more severe than I realized, but B.C.'s helping me in from the rain, tossing a jacket about me, and giving me some rough, off-brand paper towels should *not* have had any kind of effect on me. He was simply being decent. I had no business feeling some sudden, inexplicable, soft vulnerability that I hadn't experienced since we were together. I maneuvered around it with the aid of inane observations. "Lord, my hair's plastered to my head. I probably look like a whole hot mess."

"To another dude, maybe. Me? I like my women wet."

I stared at his lopsided grin while letting the tremor his statement unleashed in my stomach lessen and wondering when he'd become so damn good-looking. He'd always been cute and I'd nursed a crush on him since childhood that continued into high school. But this real-grown man standing across from me—with his smooth cocoa skin, full lips, sexy bedroom eyes, and perfect teeth—was finger-licking delicious.

"Clearly, that's not my business seeing as how I'm not one of your women."

"You could be. Used to be."

Can we make that happen again?

That out-of-order thought hit quick and hard. I jumped away from it, responding in a tone that was tighter than necessary.

"We're going to sidestep traps today, B.C., to avoid falling out and arguing. I prefer to dive into the reason I'm here and stay out of yesterday. What did you have in mind, design-wise?"

"That's on you to decide."

My tone softened. "You're giving me carte blanche to design this space however I deem fit?"

"I'ma stay in my lane and focus on food and let you drop your skills on this place and turn it into something worth looking at." He quickly conveyed his vision. Unlike his five-star restaurants in Richmond and Alexandria, he wanted this location, simply named Jade's, to have a stylish but laidback atmosphere. "All I ask is that you keep it under budget."

His vote of confidence was amazing, standard Brandon Calloway. When he had faith in you it was unwavering.

I stared at him a long moment before slowly turning about, visually assessing my surroundings, noting the floorplan of the front of the house. It wasn't overly large, maybe fifteen to eighteen-hundred square feet of blandness. Old dingy carpet. Faded paint and cracked vinyl booths that looked like something from that vintage TV show *Happy Days*.

I opened my iPad to take pictures of the place just as a call came in. During consultations, I usually silenced my phone out of respect for clients. But my phone was set up so that incoming calls showed on my iPad just in case the call was urgent. I frowned, seeing Dominic's name on the screen.

"Excuse me a moment..." I moved away from B.C. "Hey, babe—"

"I texted you an hour ago. Is there a reason you haven't responded?"

His hostility made my lip curl the slightest bit. I took a deep breath to avoid matching the stank-ass vibe he was giving.

"I'm with a client—"

"Male or female?"

"Pardon me?"

"I didn't stutter, Tessa. But never mind. You answered my

question when you avoided it. Is this payback for my walking Carmel to her car?"

"My consulting with a male client is strictly business. If you don't mind, I'd like to get back to him."

"I'm on my way to an emergency C-section. But you go ahead and try to fit me in if you can once you finish discussing more important things like wallpaper and floor treatments."

That was it. He disconnected.

I closed my eyes and counted backwards from ten.

Girlfriend, if you don't get this man in check!

I inhaled until my chest hurt, thinking I shouldn't have to. I wasn't his mother and there was no need for me to teach a grown man anything. His behavior was *not* my responsibility. Dominic was who and what he was and, positive qualities aside, the negatives were ever growing and glaring.

He's starting to feel like the wrong one for me.

A pain hit the bottom of my stomach. It wasn't the kind of pains I now associated with endometriosis. Rather, it was that "coming to the end of the road" kind of ache and having hard decisions to make.

But not right this minute, today.

I had TLS Interior Design & Renovation business to attend to, so I fixed my professional face, determined to give my client my best.

"My apologies for the interruption. May I see the rest of the place?"

I turned to face B.C. only to find him staring at me in an uber intense way that caused me to freeze momentarily.

"Seeing the place is the only reason why you're here. Right?"

Obviously, he'd overheard part of my conversation. But that wasn't my concern. His almost mournful tone and his searching my face in a way that left me breathless and wanting to offer an explanation was. Before I could, he'd pivoted, motioning for me to follow him without waiting for a response.

I didn't see what I thought I saw. I'm imagining things.

Desire I could deal with. But longing?

It was the only way to describe the look that had consumed his face, telling his business and hinting at some inner turmoil on his part, before he'd turned away.

God, I'm sick of men.

First, Dominic dictating and being dismissive. Now, B.C.'s vibe was suggesting perhaps he wanted something from me.

I followed him further into the building's interior, telling myself I was reading too much into things. There was too much bad blood and bad love between us for B.C. to be anything other than friend material. I told myself I was equally disinterested and turned my attention to our walk-through of the building.

"I can see why you bought this spot."

B.C. had been strategic in showing me the whole of the restaurant before revealing its prize gem. Every space we'd entered was similar to the dining area in its lackluster appearance. But the kitchen? It was a chef's dream. Immaculate. Modern. It was outfitted with state-of-the-art stainless-steel equipment, huge double ovens, and a walk-in freezer. It was easy to visualize B.C. and his crew hustling and bustling, creating culinary magic that enchanted the taste buds.

"This kitchen is outstanding. Why's it so intact when the rest of the place is in need of so much TLC? Was this a remodel gone wrong?"

"Something like that," he confirmed, giving me the back story of three siblings purchasing the restaurant with the intent of going into business without prior restaurant experience. "They couldn't agree on anything except this kitchen and wound up suing each other for all kind of ignorant ish." Their fall-out resulted in B.C.'s getting the property for next to nothing. "This place wasn't about a love for culinary arts. For them, it was an investment and turning a profit." He shrugged those broad, linebacker shoulders. "They pulled out. I pulled in. So, how much time do you need to get the front of the house looking as good as it does back here?"

"What's your projected opening date?" I told myself to remain professional and not twist my lips sideways, give major stank-eye, or call him out his natural black name when he provided a date three weeks away. Instead, I pulled up my calendar on my iPad and consulted it. I had the kitchen renovation for Marlene Marshall—the demolition phase of which would begin this weekend—as well as a possible main bedroom and en-suite bathroom project that was pending a callback from the homeowners to confirm whether or not they were moving forward with it. Marlene's deposit had already been received but until the bedroom-bathroom clients came through with their decision and money, I had availability. While I preferred giving my full attention to one assignment at a time, I'd worked two projects simultaneously before. They had both been small in scale and residential, not commercial. Adding more commercial projects to my portfolio was a goal. That didn't necessarily mean I wanted to take this on despite my schedule being otherwise open.

Why not? You never decline the opportunity for income.

True, but I could think of better ways of earning besides working for my first love.

Telling myself we were mature adults, capable of successfully collaborating despite our problematic past, I returned to the front of the restaurant not merely to examine that space again but because of a sudden need for distance between B.C. and me. Being alone in that kitchen with him—a place where he was chef and king—felt too intimate. I wasn't there for that and needed to focus on business. I had to raise my barriers again and did so by latching my thoughts onto the past and our pain. I was wrong for doing so, but we hadn't been alone in eternity and it was the only tool available to me in that moment. I had to minimize his essence or be punked by God knew what: all kinds of emotions.

Unfortunately, B.C. followed me.

"Tessa, I get it. This situation is last-minute, but that's why I called, 'cause you know how to come through in a clutch. Can't nobody else pull this off."

B.C. mistook my standing there in silence as a sign that I was overwhelmed by the scope of the project and needed encouragement. I wasn't. I was overwhelmed by him and the energy I'd felt the moment he ran outside doing his little rain rescue. I'd downplayed it only to feel it repeatedly during the walk-through, particularly in tight spaces where we wound up in close proximity, our bodies sometimes touching. Standing feet away from him in the front of that rundown restaurant, I felt it more intensely. It was soothing. Magnetic. I suddenly *wanted* to be in the presence of this man who valued and allowed me to be myself without demanding I perform at some elevated, manic level like somebody's trained poodle.

Removing the jacket B.C. had draped across my shoulders, I returned it to him, thinking I shouldn't be there. My concern had been our needing human buffers running interference to prevent our falling out when in fact they were needed to intercept the undeniable energy flowing between us.

"I know time is of the essence, but I'd like to sleep on it, Brandon. Can I get back to you in the next forty-eight hours with a decision?"

He watched me a moment before nodding. "That's cool. I value your time and I'm not tryna press you." His tone was calm, soothing. "I simply have confidence in your skills. Lemme lock up. I gotta bounce to Richmond to pick Jade up from school." B.C. and Jade's mother shared custody, but she lived in

Richmond during the school year, spending summers and holidays in D.C. with her mother.

"How's she doing?" I asked, shivering as we stepped into the cold. At least the rain had stopped.

"Growing like all get out and being bossy."

I laughed. "Sounds about right for a tween."

"I guess." His voice trailed off as his thick eyebrows bunched together as if he was thinking. He snapped his fingers suddenly. "'Ey, wait! Baby sis said you found some book or something proving there's some truth in those old stories. We're linked to the Washingtons?"

"OMG, yes!" I turned towards my SUV, motioning for him to follow. "You gotta see it. Get in so it doesn't get damaged if it starts raining again."

Grabbing the plastic container from the rear, I hopped in the driver's seat and carefully handed him his ancestor's journal. "Be careful. It's fragile."

"I can see that, TLS, but thanks." He read the opening passage only to jerk backwards. *"Whoa! What the hell?"*

"Right! Keep reading." I watched as he did, arrested by the kaleidoscopic emotions parading across his face.

"This is some crazy ish!" He rubbed his forehead before skipping farther ahead in the journal than I'd gone. "This is real?"

"Why wouldn't it be?"

He stared at me. "You think Granny had it made and planted it to keep me from selling the property?"

"Yes, Brandon, I think your grandmother fabricated something to look like a semi-ancient artifact then buried it beneath expertly lifted and replaced centuries-old brick just to get your attention."

He chuckled lightly. "You ain't gotta be facetious, T."

"Not tryna be. So, what do you think? Does it give you pause on selling the place?"

He shook his head. "I'm meeting that interested buyer I mentioned there tomorrow. I do, however, think this book should be analyzed by a museum or some other kind of expert," he stated, placing the journal in the container and sealing the lid.

I hid my disappointment in that interested buyer bit. "Do you want to take it?" I asked, referring to the journal.

"Hell, naw!" He put the box in my lap like a man afraid of holding a newborn. "I don't wanna be responsible for all this."

I laughed. "Fine. I'll go ahead and drop it off at your grand-mother's."

"Yeah, that sounds good and thanks. I'll head over there after I get Jade. I'm interested in hearing Granny's take." Hopping out, he came around to my side and reached in when I lowered the window. "Here. Put your seatbelt on. And drink a hot toddy or something so you don't get sick."

His care hit gently somewhere between my ribs, making me crave his tenderness.

"I will. Thanks again for reaching out on this remodel project. I appreciate it. Especially seeing as how..."

Completing my sentence wasn't necessary. We both knew our hazardous history. Still, that same vulnerability I had felt earlier tried creeping up on me again—had me wanting to lay down the past and repent openly. Or maybe it was this whole journal business that had me taking backwards walks to yester-day. "B.C., I was within my rights... that doesn't mean I handled things the best—"

I quickly shut up when I saw his jaw harden. I mumbled goodbye instead of upchucking my emotional guts, wondering what my problem was.

My problem is him. Brandon.

I blamed my ex and the irrational pull that still existed between us, as well as Dr. Latimore and my faulty reproductive system. I placed blame wherever I could except on Tessa. I wasn't a victim, but I'd only been seventeen when making an adult choice with life-impacting repercussions. Reversing from my parking space, I sped off wishing I had the ability to outrace the conflict that sometimes still haunted me as a result of that long-ago decision.

"Baby, this is *beyond* astounding." Mama Calloway sat in her favorite chair, a towel spread across her lap, some old-school cotton church gloves on like some curator at an art museum.

Why didn't I think to do that?

I'd handled those pages with bare hands. I prayed B.C. and I hadn't marred them with our fingerprints or oils from our skin.

"You found this beneath the hearth?" She asked the question without looking up. Like me, she was entranced by Ona Judge's diary.

"Yes, ma'am."

I watched Mama Calloway slowly, carefully turning pages, pure amazement on her face.

"When we were kids my grandmother used to tell us stories about her great-great Mama Delphy and Auntie Ona. Or was it great-great-*great*? Lord, I forget, but you get the gist. Anyhow, Mama Delphy and Papa Will bought the house on Chincoteague when there wasn't nothing out there except those wild ponies." She read aloud the passage detailing Miss Ona's journey from learning the art of sewing as her mother's apprentice, to being taken and placed in the big house as a maid to Martha Washington.

"Aunt Ona wasn't nothing but a child." Mama Calloway looked at me, brows furrowed, an indignant frown marring her smooth skin. "Can you imagine being taken as a little girl from the bosom of your beloveds to live, day in and day out, serving strangers? 'Cause that's essentially what those folks were. I don't care if they were *the* noble Washingtons! I don't care if they were familiar. They *owned* people." She shivered. "Far as I'm concerned, that makes *them* hostile strangers full of savagery."

I sat in silence as she wiped a tear.

"This is a gift." Closing the diary, she tenderly held it against her breasts. "You know how many of us Black folks long to know who and where we come from? Slavery was one of the biggest atrocities ever inflicted on mankind. It's heinous enough being stolen from your homeland. They added insult to further injury by forbidding us to speak our native language or continue our cultural practices. Those arrogant slaveowners even had the nerve to take our names from us. They were plain *evil* in their need to dominate and dictate." Her eyes fluttered closed and she hummed the slightest bit.

"How you gonna flee persecution in Britain your own white self, come over here and declare yourselves liberated while enslaving and massacring whole nations of God's creation? Just demonic and backwards. Had the nerve to call us lazy while forcing us to build 'their' country on free labor. Called us three-fifths of a human being. Animals. Nothing but property." She shuddered and shook her head. "We won't even touch the physical, sexual horrors inflicted on our women. *And* men." She opened her eyes and looked my way at my sharp inhalation. "It might not be told so much, but yes baby, it sure enough happened. Some of those white masters misused our men's bodies same as they did our women."

Unable to form a word, I sat speechless and close to tears.

Mama Calloway exhaled heavily. "But this here is a *wonderful* gift." Her face brightened. "And I thank you, little nosey girl, for finding it."

I offered a half-smile, unable to laugh as a result of the truths she'd just unloaded.

"I pray that grandson of mine appreciates this journal as much as I do. Has he seen it?"

"Yes, ma'am."

"Good. Maybe he'll rethink that selling business." She reached over and squeezed my hand. "I apologize for pulling you into our disagreement. Brandon has full rights, but I just don't think he ought to sell the place after all the blood, sweat, and tears our family's put into it. We try to help, but I know it's been a lot on him with the upkeep, expenses, property taxes, and such. Plus, he's got Jade and his restaurants to think about, but I sure hope he reconsiders. There's just too much *value* there for all of us."

I agreed, but kept my opinion to myself, remembering B.C. telling me this was a matter for family.

Mama Calloway suddenly leaned towards me, her gaze strong and steady. "I need you to help me find someone to examine this journal for authenticity. Like my granny used to say, I know in my knower it's legitimate. Still, it won't hurt to have a professional confirm that."

"B.C. mentioned it so I'm sure he, or even Mimi, would be the better person to help you with this. Mimi's an investigative journalist—"

"My grandchildren didn't find it, Tessa Lorraine. You did."

I suppressed a shiver at her next words.

"That makes you connected. For whatever the ancestors' reasons, *you* were chosen."

EIGHT

ONA

For all the uproar the upstairs folks were in, we, the enslaved, were woefully silent, voices paralyzed by fear. Two from our community had fled. Now, the upstairs folk were in an agitated, angry state, while every bondsperson on the plantation functioned like shadow people beneath a blanket of dread. We were interviewed, asked countless questions, viewed with suspicion. As if we weren't limited enough, further restrictions were placed upon our movements. Curfews were imposed and we, the descendants of persons forcibly brought here, became pariahs from whom the upstairs folks suddenly needed distance. We were no longer viewed as harmless, imbecilic children; rather, wicked, ungrateful souls capable of independent, heinous decisions.

"I'll be mighty glad when all of this is finished."

Fetching Mistress's breakfast tray, I paused at Uncle Hercules's quiet lament.

"But don't you want Noble and Mathilda to get wherever it is they're headed?"

His words rushed out in a heated hiss. "Of course, I do! I wouldn't wish them back here if God himself asked me to. I'm talking about all this being treated like we have the plague or the pox. Plus..." He glanced about before lowering his voice to a near whisper. "Since those two took off, the General's been demanding I taste everything I serve while he sits there watching to see if I keel over dead. If I planned on poisoning those upstairs folk, don't you think I woulda done it already?"

I nodded despite being shocked at the thought of our beloved chef using his cooking genius to sicken or kill anyone. "Uncle Hercules..." I lowered my voice, matching his volume with mine. "Where do you think they've gone?"

He shrugged. "No idea, but I pray they're following the Drinking Gourd to up north and are far, *far* away from here." That configuration of stars, a guiding light by night, was said to lead runaways to safe territory up north where slavery was frowned upon. "If not that, let's hope they hightailed it to the 'Roons."

I got wide-eyed wondering if the runaways had been so bold as to head to the hills or the Great Dismal Swamp where renegade escapees had established hidden, fiercely guarded maroon communities. The idea of living with wild men and women willing to fight and die to maintain their freedom was baffling yet oddly thrilling.

"Tonight, I'm going to say a prayer for Mathilda and Noble's safe passage," I quietly decided, despite being terrified of possible repercussions for making what upstairs folk would consider such a sacrilegious request of heaven.

"Pray the devil quits riding these pale people while you're at it." Cook moved away, muttering beneath his breath, his face set in anger. "Riding around here terrorizing innocent folks like undignified heathens. Just strung her up and stripped her like a pig carcass."

I winced at his accuracy, glad for Noble and Mathilda's escape but thinking their leaving left the rest of us more vulnerable than usual and at risk of paying penalties. They hadn't been gone but two days and already Mathilda's mother had been mercilessly lashed—hands bound and latched overhead at the whipping post—as if a co-conspirator. Not once, but *twice*! If she knew which way the runaways were headed, she said nothing while taking those beatings that left her unconscious, her back bloody, flesh ripped. After each beating when she was allowed to be cut down, men folk carried her to Old Mama Lodie to wash and treat her wounds with herbal healing. Now, she was at risk of dying or worse: being sold for her silence. Her refusal to aid the Washingtons was an egregious offense that put her future at risk despite her dower slave status. The General was angry enough to ship her off to the West Indies as he often did when encountering difficult, "unbreakable" persons among his bondsmen.

I shuddered at the thought that this kind of trouble didn't go away easily; that we might have more such acts of upstairs folks' brutality soon coming. Disturbed by the notion, I went quietly, quickly about my duties.

I found Simmie busy in Mistress's chambers laying out her clothing for the day when I arrived with the breakfast tray. She seemed to be getting there earlier of late, taking pleasure in being there before me as if we were in some sort of competition for Mistress's approval, perhaps affection. I ignored the smugness on Simmie's mean face and focused on my task.

"Place the tray on the table, Oney. I'll dine at my leisure." Mistress sat in bed, eyeing Simmie and me closely, suspiciously. Since Mathilda and Noble's leaving, she'd been quiet, distant, sullen. Her tone was cold, brittle when addressing us, which she did now only when absolutely necessary, leaving us to skate on the thin edges of her intolerance.

"Yes, ma'am." I followed instructions and placed the tray on a nearby table, ignoring Mistress mumbling to herself.

"I simply do not understand this. Only insufferable ingrates would run away. Oney! Simmie!"

We both whirled when she barked our names.

"Is this family not good and charitable towards you? Do we not clothe and house and feed all of you here at Mount Vernon and on our outlying farms?" Her voice rose and quaked with every word until she was red in the face. I was afraid she was suffering one of her fits. "We are gracious in our duty towards you and ask nothing in return save your loyalty. Is that too much to request?"

Neither Simmie nor I responded.

With a fierce exhalation, Mistress waved a dismissive hand. "Get on with your day. I've no need for mindless, mute Negroes in my presence."

Simmie whirled so swiftly in her attempts to leave that she bumped into the tray table, causing the tea set to rattle noisily.

Mistress clenched her teeth and balled her fists. *"That china was a gift from the General, imported from France, and you dare to nearly break it?"*

She threw back her blankets and practically leaped from bed. Simmie was taller but Mistress seemed to tower over her in the swollen heat of her wrath.

"I no longer have patience for such inane clumsiness, Simmie! Leave. And *never* come back. You'll serve elsewhere far away from me. Now, get!" Mistress waited until Simmie fled the room before easing back into bed. "I'll make do with one lady's maid." Reaching for her Bible, she muttered beneath her breath, "It's just as well, seeing as how there were one too many Negresses here for my current tastes."

A moment later I scurried from the room, unceremoniously dismissed as if a nuisance, but glad to take leave of her sourness. I wanted to escape to the cupola and sit by myself; tensions had been so gumbo-thick since Noble and Mathilda had left.

Not to mention the guests had to depart early as well.

The visitors who'd come for the Independence Day celebration and were to stay the week had taken their leave soon after the runaways were discovered missing, hurrying back to their respective plantations as if the situation was infectious, afraid their enslaved might've absconded. Mistress was immensely displeased that the festivities and her plans had been interrupted, landing her in a snit that she'd been in ever since. I was beginning to feel like Cook, just wanting the whole sordid ordeal over with.

I hope the "pale people" go about their business and just forget all of this.

Descending the stairs and seeing the butler open the front door to a group of men who managed the plantation, I sensed my wish wouldn't happen any time soon. There was a frenetic energy about them that made me stop in my tracks, hoping to avoid their notice. I flattened my back against the stairwell wall and held my breath, eyes downcast.

"Where's the General?"

"General Washington is in his study, sir."

"Well, get him!"

The butler, in his livery, had perfected the art of standing tall while offering an air of servility. "My apologies, but he has sequestered himself with instructions that he is not to be disturbed by anyone without a proper appointment."

From my place in the stairwell, I could practically feel the indignation of the manager who'd appointed himself the group's spokesperson.

"Are you denying our audience with him, blackie?"

I watched the butler, whose eyes were trained in the vicinity of the man's chest, his expression shuttered and masked. "No, sir, I'm simply honoring the General's wishes that no one be allowed in his study without invitation."

"Stop wasting our damn time and go get him, you stupid—"

"What is all of this?" The man's ire was diverted by General Washington himself appearing in the central passage. "Your infernal racket is impeding my ability to conduct business."

The white men—employees of the estate—swiftly removed hats from heads, their behavior suddenly different from that previously displayed. They were tame, subservient.

"Pardon the interruption, General, but we've just returned from Lord Fairfax's estate and came to inform you that the riders and the dogs are ready—"

"The hounds are not to be let off the leash when the runaways are located!" The General's voice was raised, strident. "What Fairfax does with that buck is his business, but the wench is to be returned to me alive, without injury. She's breeding and I won't deny my wife her profit by damaging the bastard whelp that wench is carrying."

"Yessir, General, but—"

"I am intolerant towards ineptitude. Either you're suited for the task at hand or you aren't. Which is it?" He didn't wait on an answer. "Come with me into my study... *gentlemen*." When he spun on his heels, noticing me in the stairwell, General Washington neither paused nor blinked. As in other times when business was discussed or news conveyed over meals while we were in attendance, I was not a threat. I was a nonentity, only a servant.

To them we're nothing save furniture and fixtures. Never be riled up by such arrogance. Use it to your advantage.

My mother told me that not long after I became a lady's maid to Mistress. In her concern for me, Mama had instructed me to keep my eyes and ears open without the upstairs folks realizing it, on the off-chance that something said was important to my welfare or someone else's. To remain mindful of the world in which I lived. I was to stay alert and aware of myself and my surroundings while blending in. The fact that the General hadn't reacted to my presence let me know I'd honed that skill of invisibility and wore well that required cloak of docility regardless of what I may have been feeling.

Hearing the inner door to the General's study close, I

exhaled in relief and hurried down the steps, praying that Mathilda and Noble were safe up north and would never come back. Praying such a lofty prayer gave me a little thrill.

I have a right to want that for them.

Holding an opinion contrary to that of the upstairs folks may've been an act of disloyalty and betrayal—a mortal, unforgiveable sin in their opinion—but I didn't abandon it. That secretive boldness lifted my lips the tiniest bit into a smile that felt freeing and defiant. Sadly, that smile was short-lived.

The moment I stepped from the house onto the passageway leading to the kitchen, a cruel grip latched about my neck, yanking me off my feet. I flew backwards before being slammed face down to the ground as if no better than refuse and rubbish. Someone's full weight landed atop of me. Their chokehold about my neck left me unable to breathe. Panic seized my entire being as I felt myself gasping pitifully.

There're times you fight and times when fighting won't do a thing except hasten your end. If fighting time comes, trust you'll know the difference.

My mother's words floated up from memory as if to serve me. Struggling to breathe, I figured it was my time for fighting and borrowed Mama's strength as if she were present. I swung an elbow backwards, hitting my assailant in the ribs. That allowed me just enough reprieve to flip over onto my back before they recovered and lashed out again.

Simmie!

Who else would be howling like a banshee and clawing at my face as if she wished I was dead?

"Leave me be, Simmie!"

My desperate plea fell on deaf ears. Simmie was lost in her own world of unmerited hatred and violence. I gave everything within me to warding off her blows but, being years older, she was heavier. Stronger. My resistance didn't accomplish much of anything except to make her twice as angry. She stopped screaming crazily only to take up growling like a fang-toothed beast as she went from wildly striking me to wrapping her horrid hands about my throat and squeezing.

I fought desperately, wanting to be free. The more I wrestled, the tighter Simmie's vicious grip became until I felt myself slipping towards darkness. The darkness felt like peace, even more so when my mother suddenly appeared, kneeling beside me, and whispering words I couldn't rightly hear. Her phantom-like presence was enough to make me want to not give up, except something in Mama's face told me to be still, that my struggle was what Simmie needed and craved—that the fight was the "hastening" of my own end. That's when I surrendered and embraced the black blanket spreading over my being. It was sweet. Welcoming. Whisking me to a world where trouble didn't live and all people were free.

"Simmie, stop this hellbent foolishness!"

Blackness broke and my body seemed to jerk itself awake as Caroline snatched my assailant away. Breath rushed into me, violently. I rolled onto my side, choking, gagging, and might have laid there swallowed by swirling relief and rage, but for the sound of horses' hooves pounding the lane that flanked the outdoor passageway.

A gruff shout interrupted any opportunity for my gradual recovery.

"What's going on here?"

I leaned into Caroline as she quickly helped me to my feet, stabilizing myself with her presence and kindness.

"Nothing, sir," Caroline answered when Simmie and I stood there not speaking.

"Looks like plenty mischief to me."

Gaze downcast, I easily recognized the voice of the mounted rider as the one who'd summoned the girl from the communal cabin. Memory of her night-shrouded screams still haunted my sleep, but being close enough to smell the sweat coming off of him and his pawing, restless steed sent a series of tremendous shivers throughout my being. I was unsuccessful in suppressing them and prayed to heaven he hadn't noticed my reaction.

"What ails you, wench?"

Luck was against me and I upbraided myself for gaining his attention, though through no fault of mine. I slowly opened my mouth in response but was pulled back by Caroline as rider and horse moved towards us. I prepared myself for God knew what, only to find his attention wasn't on me but Simmie.

"I'm fine, sir," she said.

"From all the racket you're raising, seemed to me like a bee got in your bonnet." He pointed his riding crop in my direction. "You have a grievance with this wench here?"

"No, sir."

"Why were you scuffling with her, then?"

"We was only playing, sir." The tremulous fear in Simmie's voice hung heavy in the air and, in that moment, I nearly wanted to go to her to offer comfort, strength. Our discord was between us and could be handled privately. Being terrorized by this rider was something I wouldn't wish on anyone. Not even Simmie.

"Playing, huh?"

She nodded rapidly.

"What's your name?"

"Simmie."

Her cap had come off during our tussle, leaving her long, thick plaits untidy and exposed. The man used his riding crop as if it were an extended hand, lifting and playing with her hair.

"Well, Simmie, wouldn't you rather use your energies for the nicer games you and I can play?"

A rider shouting in the distance made Simmie's answer unnecessary. "We're headed back to Fairfax's place. We got a lead on those runaways!"

The night rider straightened in his saddle before issuing his order. "No more roughhousing today, my new friend." That said, he steered his mount back the way he'd come, towards the front of the main house where he fell in with the group of men who'd earlier had an audience with General Washington. They set out like a pack of hungry wolves tearing towards the west gate, heading to Lord Fairfax's.

"*Simmie, what's wrong with you?*" Caroline's voice was more alarmed than angry as she laid a hold on my attacker's shoulders. "You out here stirring up a ruckus. And for what? Now, you and all your antics got that ol' lustful thing's eye on you."

Simmie snatched away. "Get your hands off me!"

"I'm only tryna warn—"

"I don't need no warning or no help. I can handle myself." Her head snapped in my direction. "You, howsomever, best watch how you step. I ain't finished with you yet." She spun around and stomped off before my next breath.

Caroline sighed. "That girl gonna wind up in a heap of mess if she don't fix all that sourness in her soul. How you fairing, Ona?"

Whatever angst I'd been holding back in the presence of that night-riding man decided to free itself. Tears suddenly leaked from my eyes as a broken sob escaped my lips.

"Honey, there, now. We gots enough in life to deal with without letting a mean one like Simmie bring you down." Caroline patted my shoulder. "Go wash your face and fix yourself. Then come on in and get yourself some breakfast." She smiled encouragingly before heading towards the kitchen.

I remained where I was, inhaling deeply and trying to collect myself as Caroline suggested, but it was more difficult than I expected. Perhaps Simmie's attack hurt me deeper than I realized—more in mind than flesh—because I suddenly needed my mother's solace. Hiking up the hem of my skirt, I ignored any need to eat and raced towards safety and wellness.

I didn't mean to startle everyone by bursting through the open workhouse door, but I'm sure I did, not just with all my blubbering, but my unexpected and disheveled appearance.

"*Ona?*" Mother was instantly on her feet, forsaking whatever task she'd been doing.

I rushed into her arms and lay my head against her breasts, bawling like an angry infant. She reacted by holding me away from her, searching my whole self for the source of my distress.

"*What's happened?*" Her gaze was wide, panic-stricken.

"Simmie pummeled me—"

"This is about *Simmie?*" Her worried gaze examined the scratches on my face as the other seamstresses gathered about us. "You weren't... *mishandled* by someone else?"

Shaking my head, I burrowed against her again and felt the immense sigh of relief escaping her chest as she wrapped her arms about my quivering frame.

"That's enough, my black-eyed butterfly. Quiet yourself." She ordered the workers back to their tasks while taking me by the hand and leading me from the workhouse to my family's nondescript dwelling, where she made me sit in order to bathe my face. Her expression was deceptively calm, her anger contained. "That Simmie's gonna wind up on a bed of hurt if she doesn't stop her nonsense."

Clearly, Mother and Caroline held similar sentiments.

"She doesn't like me because of my skin... because Andrew Judge left some whiteness."

My mother reared back as if slapped. "And how did that change your existence? Did that white blood gift you your freedom?" Yanking open the tiny sachet of healing herbs she kept to aid minor ailments, she pulled out a leaf and pounded it in a small bowl, mixing it with animal fat used for various purposes. Her touch was tender when applying the mixture to my wounds; still, I sensed the indignation swirling beneath the surface of her skin.

"It's sheer foolishness," she spoke as if to herself. "All these devilish differences when not one of us is better than the next. If you're dark, stay outdoors. Light, bright? Come in where it's warm." She slammed the pestle she'd been using down on the table. "I don't envy anyone anything. And I can't pretend to know what it means to be someone other than myself. I've only lived in *this* skin." Mother hit the back of her hand for emphasis. "Had I been assigned to the fields, I just might wish to be indoors. But being up close with the upstairs folks puts you in intimate spaces on an everyday basis. Puts you in their notice, at their access. God knows, often times, it's *too* close. And that sure don't make us privileged."

I said nothing when Mother fell silent. Rather, I ingested her wisdom and observations until she spoke again after a lengthy pause.

"Being up under them doesn't make us better, Ona. Or special." Her voice was less strident than it had been, yet insistent. "You know. I know. Being up under their thumbs and at their constant beck and call doesn't make life pleasurable, so never fool yourself with wicked ideas that the closer you are to them, the bigger your greatness. The Creator made us equal. Some folks just choose not to know that."

"Yes, ma'am." I chewed my bottom lip, mulling on my ideas. "That's why Noble and Mathilda ran... so their baby can live like something the Creator created."

She made a humming sound and nodded. "Regardless, when the sun sets, light or dark complexion, we're all sleeping on a bed of bondage." My mother studied me a moment before getting up to close the cabin door. Returning to me, she squatted and grabbed my face in her hands, ensuring she had my entire attention.

"I'll only say this here and now, but don't you *never* forget it." She glanced about as if to ensure no tale-carrying specters were present. "If freedom *ever* knocks on your door same as it did for Mathilda and Noble... *open it!*"

When my eyes grew big, she nodded her head in a hard, affirming way that brooked no argument. That didn't necessarily curb my questions.

"Yes, Mother, but are you saying if we ever get the chance, we—"

"You. Your brothers. Your sisters. Together or alone. *You go!*"

"But you would be there with us... right?"

Her eyelids fluttered shut for a brief moment. "I missed my chance a long time ago. Now, I'm not such a young woman anymore. Most times my body aches more than it did before." She peered at me with extreme intensity. "Youth is with you. If freedom ever reaches out a welcoming hand, take it and don't look back. Tell me you understand what I'm telling you to do, Ona, and that you'll obey."

I frowned, thinking if freedom came for me, I'd accept her invitation only if she extended an invitation to Mother and my siblings. I was old enough to know that if I ever ran away I'd be a fugitive lawbreaker and unable to ever see my family again. Still, I nodded obediently, despite knowing I couldn't go anywhere without my beloveds.

Several days passed with the lazy speed and density of slow-pouring sorghum and molasses. Life and human relationships seemed equally thick. Tense. Sluggish. In addition to the perilous atmosphere caused by the runaways' absence and the ongoing search for them, I could blame a host of reasons. The summer heat. That Evilest Eliza constantly picking at me. Mistress and her sudden, sullen distrust of Negroes who were previously "loved." Add to that the fact that I was constantly on the lookout. I had a new awareness of just how physically vicious Simmie could be and trusted her threat that she wasn't finished with me. That left me nervous, jumpy. I considered fashioning or finding a weapon to defend myself; one effective but small enough to conceal in my apron pocket. Something like one of Mistress's letter openers. Except, my living was already strained. If ever I were found with a weapon, I'd be direly chastened. I abandoned the idea, not wanting to add to the upstairs folks' current opinions that we were nothing save savages. Instead, I consoled myself with the fact that my staunch enemy had been evicted from Mistress's employ and the mansion. Now that she'd been assigned to work in the spinning room, Simmie and I were no longer in close contact.

If I could only get free of Miss Nelly.

As it was summer, she was enjoying a break from daily lessons and had resumed her habit of following me about like a faithful puppy talking my ear off and calling herself "helping." I tried dissuading her company by saying I was too busy with chores to give her the attention she deserved. That merely caused her to pitch in so she'd have my time if I finished faster.

"I can clean Gram-Gram's comb and brush for you. Or I can match up her gloves and line up her shoes."

Miss Nelly meant well but her efforts at helping were minimal and mindless as she chattered, making whatever I was doing worse than if I didn't have her assistance. She'd pair up the shoes incorrectly or put items in the wrong places. I had to fix whatever she mussed, doubling the expense of my energy. Her devotion to me also riled up Evilest Eliza's torment and envy.

The older that one gets, the more she seems to hate the air I breathe.

She was petty, jealous-acting, detesting her younger sister's affection towards me. She might as well have been Simmie—tripping me, pulling my hair. The pinching. Calling me names my mother never gave me. Sending me on constant errands as if I were a dog fetching bones and other useless things. Except, unlike with my arch-enemy Simmie, I couldn't resist, refuse, or raise a hand in self-defense. If I did there would be dire consequences. All I could do was pray the summer season hurried to its end so the devil's little darling could return home where she belonged, miles away from here.

"Miss Nelly, wouldn't you rather be downstairs eating ice cream with Master Washy and your sisters?" I moved around her, needing to lay out Mistress's dress for the evening before doing a light dusting of the furniture.

"I ate too much ice cream yesterday. It gave me a tummy ache. Mother says I have to practice temperance. So, I'm helping you clean Gram-Gram's desk. And practicing not eating." Her smile was triumphant, as if she was proud of herself.

Only, she was more in the way than a help. Handling the items on her grandmother's writing desk with wonderment as if they were new and she hadn't touched them countless times before, she put them all back in the wrong places.

"I should write Frances a letter. She probably misses me terribly."

"But Miss Frances was just here for the Independence Day festivities."

"Yes, but we didn't get to enjoy each other's company as long as we usually do because she had to leave early, thanks to that awful runaway business. Did you know Gram-Gram says we're unique because we can write and read? Apparently, women aren't supposed to know how to do such things."

"Well, aren't you glad you're not a woman?"

"Not yet, but I will be."

I smiled as she dipped a quill in the ink pot and began writing in earnest.

"Please be careful with that ink. Don't get any on your hands or your dress."

"I won't." Focused on her task, she sounded distracted.

I took advantage of her busyness to move on with my chore of dusting.

"*Voilà!* I'm finished."

Her silent concentration hadn't lasted long enough for me to accomplish much of anything.

"You wrote Miss Frances a whole letter that quickly?"

"No, silly. I wrote your name. Come see."

Glancing at that paper and noticing Miss Nelly's large printing, a nervous energy filled my entire being. For someone of my caste, reading and writing were forbidden luxuries, and I hesitated as if the letters on that paper might come alive and devour me. Still, the thrilling notion of seeing my name propelled me forward.

"Do you like my penmanship?"

Staring at the letters on that paper, I merely nodded.

"See. That's your name. O-N-E-Y. Oney."

"Yes, ma'am, but how do you write *Ona*?" I wanted to see the name my mother gave me, not a derivative from the Washingtons.

As if excited by the challenge, that little seven-year-old dipped the quill and bent over the paper again before suddenly pausing. "I bet you could do it yourself, Oney. It's only three letters."

I jumped back as if the flames of hell blazed from her fingertips when she extended that quill in my direction.

"Miss Nelly, that's nothing to play with!"

"It's not playing. It's writing." She shrugged indifferently. "If anyone finds out, I'll tell the truth and say I did it." She waved me forward. "Come on. Don't be such a baby."

I glanced at the doorway to make sure no one had approached without my notice before slowly moving towards the desk, my heart beating terribly fast. When within reach, Miss Nelly took my hand, positioning my fingers about the quill and showing me how best to hold it.

It felt awkward. Foreign.

"The letter 'o' isn't anything except a circle." Her hand about mine, Miss Nelly slowly drew a big, fat sphere that magically transformed into the first letter of my name. "See! Wasn't that easy?"

Delight and wonder spread across my face, but any response from me was instantly tucked away on hearing someone approaching the upstairs landing.

"Nelly! Where are you? We want to play leap frog but—"

The two of us sprang apart at the sound of Evilest Eliza's voice, but evidently not quickly enough to disentangle our deceptive web.

She stomped into the room, eyes narrowed, glancing back and forth between us. "What're you two doing?"

"Nothing."

Clearly, Satan's Seed didn't believe her sister's innocence and maneuvered herself between us, nudging me roughly aside in the process. "Drawing an extra big O isn't 'nothing', Nelly. It's something. That's the same way you wrote when you first started learning. You used to try to teach Washy, but he was so—"

Her gasp left me still as a statue and studying the hardwood floorboards as if my next breath depended on it.

"Let me see this!"

Miss Nelly protested when her sister snatched the paper from the desk, eyeing it thoroughly before releasing it again.

"You weren't teaching *this thing* the alphabet, were you?"

I peeked up in time to notice her eyes had grown wide while staring at that innocent letter resting like an empty world on paper. She grabbed my hands, examining them for evidence of ink. Thankfully, there wasn't any.

"Of course not, Eliza. I was drawing."

I wasn't sure when or how she did it, but Miss Nelly had somehow removed from the desk the paper on which my moniker had been written. Dabbing quill in ink, she drew smaller circles within that large O, followed by half orbs on either side that stuck out like ears before holding up the paper, a broad smile on her lips.

"Isn't she sweet? It's Gram-Gram."

Little Miss Evil as a Boll Weevil snickered dismissively. "You can draw far better than that, Eleanor Parke Custis. Being around darkies all day is making you as lazy and unimpressive as them." Grabbing Miss Nelly's brush from the vanity, she quickly and soundly whacked the backs of my hands before snarling in my face. "That's just in case you ever thought to write a thing." Her tone and ugliness changed magically. "Come on, Nelly. Let's go play leap frog before we have to go in for supper."

"Okay, but first I gotta make sure Gram-Gram's desk is neat."

Her laughter was brisk as I bit my lip to stifle tears.

"You've been gifted a fantastic sense of humor, Nelly. You don't have to tidy anything. That's why we have darkies."

She grabbed her sister's hand, but the younger protested, which resulted in a fussing match that didn't last long, thanks to an unexpected commotion below and beyond the window.

Loud voices. Galloping horses. The sound of a wagon entering the west gate. Noises rushed towards us with the force of a strong gale wind.

"Visitors are coming," the oldest decided excitedly, dashing to the window then out of the room without further hesitation.

"Maybe it's Frances come back to play." Miss Nelly trotted after her sister, the paper she'd written *Oney* on fluttering to the floor for me to retrieve and dispose of properly before following, which I hesitated in doing. Those sounds from outdoors that had rushed towards us with the force of a wind seemed to contain something deeply foreboding within them.

That's no playtime wind or *Miss Frances.*

I fled the room as if compelled by something I could neither understand nor see, only to be caught up by the wave of servants rushing outdoors, assembling as was customary when receiving guests. Silently, I found my place, quickly glancing at the group of riders before tucking away my gaze. Seeing many of the men who'd demanded an audience with the General days before left me swallowing a troubling sense of dismay as some of them removed hats from their heads, whooping and hollering in celebration.

Their rejoicing can only mean one thing.

I stole a peek at the wagon, fully expecting to find the runaways, only to breathe a silent sigh of relief when the wagon appeared empty. But then I heard voices.

"Those black bastards thought they'd outrun us, but we got 'em, General! We got 'em."

Mistress and the General led the phalanx of upstairs folks suddenly swarming the front of the house.

"Bring them here this instant!"

The command had barely left the General's mouth when the sound of more riders could be heard advancing through the west entrance. I never should have dared to peek again, but I did, only for something to crack and crumble inside of me at the sight of four horsemen. The leading two approached at breakneck speed as the latter pulled up the rear, prancing their mounts at a slower cadence, as if to bask in attention. Or perhaps they merely aimed to prolong the humiliation of the man and woman tethered by long ropes and stumbling behind them, wrists bound like the legs of prized hens.

Noble! Mathilda!

My young heart fractured at the sight of them. Not because they were bedraggled and caked in mud and filth; or because

Noble's face bore evidence of chastening and was swollen, his lip split. But because heaven had denied their cries for freedom and overturned their attempts. Five days after daring to seek a world other than that in which they took their first breaths, Mathilda and Noble were captured, enslaved once again.

"Send word to Lord Fairfax that we are in possession of the fugitives."

A rider set off to do the General's bidding as if chased by the hounds of hell. The pounding of his horse's hooves fading in the distance was the only sound for several minutes. Even the birds and insects ceased their noisemaking as if privy to the scene unfolding. Nature's sudden stillness exacerbated an ominous tension as we stood in mournful silence beneath the hot July sun, sorrow binding us servants like chilly river fog.

Even the children seemed subdued until Master Washy moved beside his grandfather, taking his hand, and looking up at him.

"Are those the runaways?"

The General merely nodded.

"What's gonna happen to them?" Miss Nelly's voice trembled the slightest bit.

Her evil older sister's didn't. "Maybe they'll be tarred and feathered, or pulled apart and quartered."

"Eliza, there is no need for excessive grossness."

Her mother's caution might have quieted her, but it didn't keep that child from fidgeting as if possessed by some perverse curiosity or excitement.

"Eleanor, dear, perhaps the children should go indoors." Mistress's face seemed pinched with distress.

"They should remain." Face stoic, body rigid, General Washington contradicted his wife's instructions to the mother of their grandchildren. "The wench is a dower slave, which makes her their inheritance. One of them will eventually own her outright when they come of age."

"Dearest, I do not wish them to be present for any unpleasantness."

"We're privileged planters, Martha. Landed gentry. The children must understand that they have been entrusted with the responsibility of maintaining order and decency while upholding the wellbeing of our community." Not a man of many words, the General paused before continuing. "But, yes, they are young and tender. Because of that fact, I will not allow them to witness anything distasteful. I wish to spare your delicate sensibilities as well, ladies, so neither of you shall be in attendance."

The same did not apply to us.

That evening as the summer sun began to set, the enslaved at Mount Vernon—young and old—were commanded to assemble ourselves and bear witness to Mathilda and Noble's punishment. They'd both been stripped naked and, as I stood there, I felt their demoralization. They were defenseless. I clutched my hands together to still the tremors I felt at this open display that was both terror and deterrent, a way of hobbling the intent of anyone else daring to think on elicit ways of obtaining freedom.

"Is the hole deep enough?"

"Yes, General, and it's padded with hay so the pup isn't injured."

"Very well. Let's get on with this tedious business. Lord Fairfax isn't feeling the best and would like to return home as soon as this is over with. Ten lashes. No more. Because of her condition."

"Yes, sir."

The overseer ordered our attention to where Mathilda lay stretched on the ground, shackled by arms and feet, belly cradled by a hole that had been dug to protect her unborn baby, the Washingtons' property.

"Look on this and understand the repercussions of traitorous actions!" The main overseer's voice was thunderous. "Do not make a sound. Do not avert your gaze. If you do, the buck will receive additional lashes for your insubordination."

"Give the rawhide to the buck." Lord Fairfax was forced to let his hacking cough subside before continuing. He pointed at Noble. "Let *him* deliver her lashes. Every time he looks at her back, he'll know her wounds were his fault and think twice before ever running again."

When the overseer thrust the whip into Noble's hand, he let it to slip to the ground, making no effort to grasp it.

"Pick that up!"

Noble stood mute, eyes focused on the distance as if this world no longer existed. Even when another of the boss men slammed him in the back with such force that he fell to his knees, he refused to touch that instrument with which he was expected to abuse his beloved. Instead, the overseer followed Lord Fairfax's instructions to proceed, unfurling his cowhide whip and slashing it through the air.

Mathilda's scream was soul-stopping. Her mother, who'd been restrained since learning of her daughter's ill-fated return, wailed so loudly that I prayed for a place where sound didn't exist as Noble lurched forward as if to free Mathilda from her bindings. He was struck low again, rendered immobile by two men, his head snatched back by one of the white bosses in an attempt to force him to see his love's violation. Noble screamed and wrestled in an attempt to reach her, not caring that his protests would mean extra lashes for him.

"*Mathilda!*" His bellowing housed the hapless horror of every bondsperson there.

Tears gathered in my eyes, providing a gentle haze to soften and distort the sight of Mathilda being whipped. Yet every time that rawhide sliced air like a sharp whistle in the wind, I heard it. Each dreadful time it landed against her naked flesh, tearing a feral cry from Mathilda, I flinched. And screamed, internally.

I accused heaven of cruel indifference, and wished catastrophe on every merciless white person that was present.

I hope they all burn in hell. The overseers. Lord Fairfax. And especially General Washington.

"Enough. That's ten. Move on to the buck."

When an unconscious Mathilda was unshackled, lifted, and carried away, Noble—tears flooding his face—tried to lunge for her. Perhaps to hold or comfort her, to touch and assure himself that she and their child were still in the land of the living. But he was pinned by men on either side of him, his hands tied to the whipping post as his brutal mistreatment began.

As an indoor servant assembled with other such servants and positioned rather near General Washington, I had the woeful disadvantage of being close enough to feel the reverberation of that whip. There was no unborn child to be cautious of, leaving Noble to bear the full, repercussive weight of his failed escape. My body jerked right along with his whenever that whip landed. I stared at him as commanded, grateful for the tears blurring my vision—allowing me to see through him to the other side of his sorrow while not seeing his nakedness. Yet, the ordeal felt imprinted on the fragile pages of my memory for eternity.

"I wish I could kill every one of 'em."

No one shushed Caroline or scolded her vengeful sentiments the following evening as we sat, spirits downcast, at the communal table.

"They had no business whipping her that way! What's Doll 'posed to tell her grandchild when it's big enough to get to asking questions and wanting answers?"

"The truth," Cook solemnly responded. "That his mother was murdered."

That increased the heavy pall already shrouding us.

As if the beatings weren't horrific enough, Mathilda's going into early labor soon after and bleeding out her life in the birthing cabin was enough to send our souls into a molten abyss.

"If Old Mama Lodie can't fix that child, Doll won't have no need to tell her grandson nothing."

Caroline nodded in agreement with the scullery maid's opinion. "Sukey aided the birth and says he ain't but big as a kitten. Guess ain't a thing we can do but pray his strength in the Almighty."

Prayers were answered in a peculiar way when that tiny baby decided it didn't want to walk this earth without its mother and slipped away to heaven early the next morning.

When a rider delivered a note to the General later that week, we were still feeling low and the typical curiosity an unexpected visitor normally generated was absent. That was until we caught wind of the contents of that missive.

"Uncle Hercules, why would Noble walk into the river with sacks of rocks tied around his waist?" If I thought I'd emptied myself of tears crying over Mathilda and her precious baby, I found more behind Noble's self-inflicted ending.

"Why would he wanna stay here, Ona, when his woman and child are in the grave? It wasn't how they planned it, but looks like freedom came for them a different way."

I thought about my mother urging me to accept the hand of freedom if ever it was extended and could only pray that didn't require death.

"There's one grace in all this."

I looked at Cook, waiting for him to finish.

He did so with a pain-filled sigh and shake of his head. "At least they're together again."

NINE

TESSA

"Of course you *could* opt for granite but have you considered quartz? Quartz countertops provide the same durability and elevated look at a fraction of the cost."

Watching Marlene stroke her manicured hands over the quartz samples on her coffee table, I silently thanked the manager of my favorite showroom for coming through in a crunch. She'd hooked me up with the latest high-quality samples that were now spread before Marlene for her viewing, there in her home.

My client had had a little too much fun on her Colorado business trip earlier that week. Thanks to a bad spill on the slopes, she returned to Virginia modeling one of those medical walking boots as a result of a severe sprain. Days after the incident she was still in extreme pain yet very much committed to moving forward on her kitchen remodel project.

"You're sure you're up to this?" I'd noticed her wince more than once and wondered if handling business so soon after her accident was doing too much.

"I appreciate the concern, but it's nothing a little acetaminophen can't fix." Marlene sat with her injured leg elevated on a stack of pillows atop an ottoman, clearly enjoying her in-home shopping. "I love the marbling in this."

She indicated a creamy-white tile with beautiful gold vein-ing. We'd agreed on a lighter color palette to make her redesigned kitchen appear more expansive, but I had one colorful card up my sleeve that I hoped she'd buy into.

"It's gorgeous," I agreed, arranging gold fixtures alongside the quartz sample she'd selected and ignoring the sound of a text from Dominic. I'd opted for a mental-health break after that ignorant phone conversation at B.C.'s two days back. I needed time and space to analyze this sad situation we called a relation-ship, and determine if it was really what I wanted. In that time he'd gone from being pissed at my not responding to his calls and texts, to sending gifts. I left the Chanel purse in the box to return to him. I did, however, nibble on two or three of the butter toffee pecan cookies from my favorite Black-owned bakery. I wasn't crazy. Dominic was prime real estate. I was simply taking a break from coupledom insanity.

"These cabinet handles and drawer pulls would comple-ment the veining beautifully."

I let her examine them while adding backsplash options for her consideration.

"Subway tiles are definitely in and are a wonderful option. Or backsplash tiles with a raised or beveled effect and design can add texture and dimension to an otherwise flat surface."

"OMG, Tessa, this right here! Done. I'm in love."

We laughed as she pointed out an arched, basketweave backsplash in white and gold.

"You're sure?"

"Darling, yes. I'm excited. Next."

"About those cabinets. I appreciate that you prefer a light and bright palette, but with the ash-blonde hardwood flooring you selected the space could benefit from darker cabinetry. Just to add depth and, again, dimension. I'd like to propose keeping the upper cabinets white while choosing a deeper, contrasting shade for the bottoms."

"Such as?"

She laughed at my, "I'm glad you asked," as I handed her my iPad. I'd entered her chosen materials into a program that offered mock-up renderings of the finished space, granting her a vision of what her remodeled kitchen would look like.

"I suggest navy." I tapped a button and changed the color of the bottom cabinetry. "Or cerulean." I tapped it again. "Or even a pale seafoam."

I sat back, allowing her to toggle through the renderings and mull over my suggestions. Time was money and patience wasn't my super power, but I'd learned not to rush my clients. Doing so typically ended up with them changing their minds, making new decisions not agreed upon because they'd felt pressured or unheard. That could prove costly, as well as cause delays. As much as possible, I preferred to place the client in the center of the project. I valued their desires and what they wanted for their spaces. Simple acts such as showroom visits where they could see and handle materials themselves, or something as painless yet effective as this mock-up generator, tended to give them a sense of power and involvement that resulted in a buy-in.

Time might be money, but agreement is honey.

There was something sweetly satisfying about gelling with a client—getting their vision and trust in my ability to bring it to fruition and signing on to the whole process.

I sat without chattering about the virtues of my suggestions, letting Marlene come to her own decision.

"About these dark bottom cabinets." Eventually, she looked up at me. "I'm here for it."

"Perfect!"

"This cerulean is speaking to my Caribbean heritage.

Thank you for helping me to think outside the box. You're good on your grind, Miss Scott."

My cell phone vibrated, abbreviating my appreciative response. Seeing 'unknown number' displayed, I let the call roll to voicemail and returned my attention to Marlene and finalizing our concepts.

"Will my choosing these cerulean cabinets delay the project? Are they a special-order item?"

I assured Marlene there'd be no delay, while managing not to do a happy dance. My supplier had a set sitting in the warehouse thanks to some other order that had fallen through. I'd need to double-check the specs, and we might have to make minor adjustments, but based on what I recalled, they'd likely fit.

"You're still okay with the demolition starting tomorrow?" I looked pointedly at her leg.

"I know I shouldn't have been on those slopes acting like I'm thirty instead of staring forty-five in the face."

"Forty-five is the new twenty and you rock it with grace."

"If you ever tire of interior design, you might have a life in politics."

We both laughed.

"I'm fine with your demo crew getting in here tomorrow. I'll just exit stage left and hang out at a friend's to avoid the noise and get some rest."

Assuring her I'd be on the premises, we made arrangements for my access.

"Before I forget... your current cabinets are no longer to your liking but they're in excellent condition. Would you be interested in donating them?" Whenever possible, I preferred to repurpose a client's intact materials versus outright demolishing or discarding them. There were charitable builders in the area, like Habitat for Humanity and others, that I liked to gift the items to, not to mention Marlene would receive a donation receipt and could write it off on her taxes.

I returned the sample materials to my wheeled kit and stood, smiling, when she voiced pleasure in the donation idea. "I'll update your portal to reflect today's selections. That way you can view them anytime you choose."

My website was designed with private, personalized pages for clients containing their color boards and design specs. It wasn't merely a visual aid but another way to keep them connected and invested during the transformative process.

"Sounds good. Thanks again, Tessa. I appreciate you."

"Likewise. Take care of that leg."

"And you take care of that congestion."

Despite going home to a hot bath and peppermint tea, I'd caught a case of the sniffles thanks to those unwanted playing-in-the-rain games at B.C.'s restaurant the other day, and obviously hadn't managed to hide them. "Absolutely."

"Oh, wait. Has Carmel contacted you yet?"

Thankfully, she hadn't, and I wouldn't mind if it stayed that way.

After a quick hug I exited, glad Marlene had one of those voice-activated locking mechanisms on her front door and was able to engage it from her position on the sofa. Hearing it click into place, I headed for my SUV while checking my phone for missed calls or texts. I had one of each.

Hi Tessa, it's Mrs. Yancey. Thanks 4 your time, but have 2 postpone until spring. Call me plz.

The text regarding that potential bedroom-bathroom remodel was disappointing and for more reasons than merely messing with my money. I'd told B.C. I'd get back to him on his restaurant remodel, hoping Mrs. Yancey's gig came through so I could deny him with a legitimate reason versus him thinking I was vindictive. Or scared.

You do *have this job with Marlene.*

That was more than plenty to keep a sister busy.

So, why're you even considering this B.C. thing?

"Because..."

One: I was an over-achiever who loved a challenge. Two: it was an opportunity to do a commercial project. Three: it would help me reach my fourth-quarter income goals.

Four and five, you feel obligated and drawn to him.

Renovating his restaurant was a way to do something positive for B.C., as well as allow me to be in his presence.

Telling myself that made zero minus zero sense, I stored my rollaway in the back of my SUV before hopping into the driver's seat and checking my voicemail.

"Hi, Miss Scott, this is Haven, Dr. Latimore's M.A. Can you please return the call as soon as possible? Here's my direct line so you can bypass the receptionist."

I jotted down the medical assistant's number, sensing that this was serious. If it was cancer, I didn't want to face that diagnosis alone, and so I did the only thing I could think of. I headed for Cape Charles and the offices of Scott & Associates.

"Well, look at Jesus! My child lives."

I'd shaved fifteen minutes off my drive time thanks to being a speed freak pressed by anxiety. Entering my mother's office forty minutes after leaving Virginia Beach, I tried smiling at her playful greeting that also held admonishment for my missing family dinner this past Sunday. *Again.* Dominic had slept over after our wild-sex-on-the-kitchen-counter escapade and I'd been caught up with him last Sunday. It had been an unusually warm autumn day and I'd accepted his invitation to go sailing on the Chesapeake Bay. Now, here I was, needing to lean on my mother's strength, feeling ridiculously ignorant and remorseful for all the family time and love I'd forfeited.

"Hey, Mama."

Either my smile wasn't convincing or Serenity Scott's maternal Spidey senses were activated.

"What's wrong, Tessa Lorraine?" Worry erased the joy from my mother's face.

"Where's Daddy?"

"In the conference room with a client. Why?"

Closing the door, I approached my mother, wishing I could curl up on her lap like I did as a child. "I have to call Dr. Latimore."

"Okay..." The word slowly floated from her mouth; her forehead creased in a frown. "Are you here to use my phone? Or do you need moral support?"

One of the many things I adored about my mother was the way she evoked her name. She was constant calm, the peaceful yin to my family's wild yang.

I held up my cell phone. "I have this. But that other part? Yes, ma'am."

Questions revealed themselves clearly in her eyes, but Mama chose not to pry. She simply held my hand as I sat on the corner of her desk. "I'm here, baby girl. Call your gynecologist. We got this."

I loved the "we" and knowing that she'd aligned herself with me without knowing precisely what I was dealing with. As I dialed the number Dr. Latimore's medical assistant had provided, Mama's devotion made my eyes water and I choked up a bit.

Ten minutes later, I couldn't thank God enough for my mother's stabilizing presence. Praise heaven, my tests hadn't revealed cancer. But my gynecologist was certain I had endometriosis—the extent of which remained to be determined.

"What're Tessa's next steps?"

I'd placed the call on speaker phone, allowing Mama to be part of the conversation.

"Tessa, I mentioned conducting an ultrasound at your prior appointment, but if you don't object I'd prefer laparoscopy, not merely to determine the severity of your condition but to be able to mitigate it, if possible, during the procedure."

Your condition. Those words sat on my mind like a five-ton elephant.

"Is that invasive?" Mama questioned.

Dr. Latimore patiently described a procedure involving a tiny incision made in my abdomen allowing a laparoscope—a thin lighted tube with a video camera at one end—to view my uterus and other reproductive organs. It would be an outpatient process with general anesthesia and no hospitalization.

"How long will I be out of commission?" I questioned just as a calendar reminder to contact B.C. pinged on my phone. I barely glanced at it in order to focus. I was the sole source of my income and couldn't afford to be laid up in bed, reneging on Marlene's project.

"That would depend on how everything goes and how you feel. Barring any issues, you should be able to resume normal duties a few days following the procedure." She added several cautions including no carbonated drinks or heavy lifting.

"How soon can she schedule this?" Mama's tone was calm, measured.

My gynecologist answered my mother's inquiry, advising that someone from the surgery department would reach out.

"I know this is a lot to digest, Tessa, but at least we can thank heaven it isn't cancer."

My mother wholeheartedly agreed.

We spoke a minute or so more before disconnecting.

A long silence followed my mother's weighted sigh of relief. "Baby girl, how're you feeling?"

We were seated beside one another on the sofa in the sitting area of her office.

I shook my head, giving myself a moment to collect my thoughts. "If a complete hysterectomy's necessary, I won't be able to have children."

Mama wrapped me in her arms when I leaned against her, her blouse collecting my sudden river of tears. Stroking my hair, Mama encouraged my faith in God without offering false assurances of future outcomes.

"We've faced fires before and came out of every one. We may have emerged a little singed and smelling like smoke, but we survived just the same. This will be no different. Okay?"

I said nothing, wishing I could borrow some of Mama's optimism while wondering if a hysterectomy or infertility would be the consequence of my condition. By nature, I was a fighter, a descendant of a long line of warrior women. Right then I wasn't battle-ready, or worthy of claiming space with the sheroes who'd preceded me, forging a way for me to succeed. I might not have "caused" this endometriosis, per se; still, a deep, empty well inside of me resonated a haunting echo that I couldn't silence or escape.

It's payback and punishment for terminating your baby.

The next morning, I arrived at Marlene's place ready to tackle that project with a vengeance. Being consumed with something I loved and about which I was passionate was always cathartic, the perfect distraction.

After my phone conversation with my gynecologist, I'd declined Dominic's last-minute invitation delivered via text to attend some fundraiser with him, his sister, and her fiancé. Instead, I chose to stay on the island and have dinner at my parents'. It wasn't fancy like a fundraiser, but exactly what my heart needed. Just pizza, salad, bread sticks, Mama's killer homemade salted caramel brownies and family. When the twins, Rocki and Rico, found out I was at Mama and Daddy's, they dropped by, giving me grief, talking about how I hadn't been around in so long that they'd stopped by just to remember what I looked like. What started out as me merely wanting and needing my parents' company wound up being a whole Scott tribe kind of evening. I found myself on the floor roughhousing with my niece and nephews, wanting to kick my own ass at having neglected this love that I wholeheartedly needed to give and receive. I didn't get home until after midnight and fell into bed, blessed but exhausted. Come morning, after a long shower and an extra-large caramel macchiato, I was on site at Marlene's ready to demo.

"Put the goggles and hardhat on." Anthony Whitlow, indisputably one of *the best* general contractors in the area, handed me the safety gear and waited for me to obey his instructions. "And the gloves. Oh yeah... and the face mask."

"Really, Mr. Ant?" We'd met at a home improvement showcase three years ago and struck up a conversation that had led to our ongoing professional relationship. An older gentleman in his late fifties, his workmanship was exceptional and he'd become my go-to contractor who also regularly referred business to me and even brought me in on some of his projects.

"Don't gimme no lip, Miss Tessa. You know the drill..."

I mimicked his voice when finishing with him, "Safety first. Ain't nobody tryna get hurt."

"You're bad as my father with all his overprotectiveness," I teased.

He grinned. "Yeah, well, good birds of a feather flock together. Plus, I can't have you suing me for breaking a nail or inhaling dust or nothing."

I slid on the protective gear and held up my hands. "Am I good?"

He nodded. "Let's go."

Grabbing the handle of the sledgehammer nearest me, I raised it and waited for his customary countdown.

"Three... two... one... hole in the wall, here we come!"

Laughing, I swung that sledgehammer into the dividing wall separating Marlene's kitchen from her family room. Demolishing it would create a larger, more harmonious open-space concept, as well as a better flow of light and energy.

"That's it! Hit it like it did you something."

I laughed again only to flash on yesterday's diagnosis and discussion with my gynecologist. I'd been surprised by the rapid turnaround time when receiving a call from the surgery department late yesterday. The big day had been scheduled and was four weeks away. After time with my family and sleeping on the issue, I was more nervous about the outcome than I was the actual procedure.

Children were in my future.

Hating the possibility of being robbed of the opportunity to create a little person better than me, I swung that heavy sledgehammer, slamming it into that wall as if *it* was endometriosis. It felt good decimating obstacles, and I completely lost myself in what I was doing. By the time that dividing wall was gone and nothing but a memory, I was dripping sweat, breathing heavily.

"Miss Tessa, I may need to hire *you* for my wrecking crew."

I high-fived Mr. Anthony while admiring our destructiveness.

For me, being an interior designer wasn't just about making things pretty. I enjoyed understanding the bones and innards of a home, the sweat equity and getting my hands dirty. I had zero desire to be a general contractor, plumber, or electrician, but my parents had taught me not to overlook knowledge or lessons. To value processes. Understanding a little bit about each aspect diversified my skill set and increased my appreciation for the labor and the laborer as well.

"This is the part I could do without." I reached for a pile of debris only to have Mr. Ant start fussing.

"Leave that alone and let the guys haul the mess to the dumpster."

I moved out of the way, allowing the crew members to remove the pieces of what used to be the wall from the premises.

"Juan and Damon can handle cutting out these non-load bearing beams while we handle those cabinets."

"Don't forget we're only detaching them. They're being donated," I reminded him.

Mr. Anthony narrowed his eyes at me, pretending to be offended. "Do I look decrepit, like I'd just up and forget something like that?"

"No comment."

He chuckled and handed me an electric drill. "Get busy with those cabinets before I sue you for being ageist."

An hour in, my muscles hurt and my stomach was rumbling with hunger but my energy was high. Positive. "I love a naked kitchen."

The area had nearly been stripped down to the floor. It was dusty and dirty, but I had no problem envisioning how it would look once the remodel was finished.

Mr. Anthony was straight-faced when quipping, "You'll love this kitchen even better once we put some clothes on it."

His crew laughed.

"Everybody wash up and get ready for lunch. I'm tired of Miss Tessa's stomach growling like a wild animal. I warned you about not eating breakfast before working on a demo."

"I did eat. I had a caramel macchiato... and a praline."

My favorite contractor shook his head. "Miss T., you're pitiful."

I batted my lashes innocently. "And when it comes to

Mama C.'s pralines, I'm even pathetic. Where do y'all want to eat? My treat." I looked at his crew expectantly.

"Hold that thought," Mr. Ant instructed, ambling towards the front of the house at the sound of several horn blasts. He peered through the open windows before smiling back at us. "Lunch is here. And it's on me."

"What is it?"

"Food from the best caterer in the area. Now, come on here and eat."

Moments later we were cleaned up and out the front door, finding a delicious-smelling meal-on-wheels waiting on us. The construction crew hurried towards the van parked in Marlene's driveway. Seeing "Jade's Jazz Café" on the side of it, I was the only one who hesitated. I was slowed by memories of Miss Ona's diary and wondering about its impact on B.C., not to mention the dynamic presence of the little girl waving at me.

"Hi, Miss Tessa."

I waved back at the eleven-year-old who'd inspired the name of her father's restaurants, needing that moment that I always needed—to breathe and release—whenever we came into contact. She was B.C.'s baby, Mimi's niece—a beautiful brown-skinned girl with a thick, curly afro puff ponytail atop her head, the confidence of a well-loved child, and a sweet spirit.

Seeing Jade always made me consider what might have been; that she would have had a sibling. *If.* But watching her help her father serve the surprise lunch Uncle Ant had ordered, my thoughts shifted.

She should've been ours.

Maybe it was my health predicament, this endometriosis, and the uncertainty of my future reproductive abilities, but watching Jade and her dad work in tandem left me confronting this new, sudden hunger. When B.C. paused and turned in my direction as if sensing my attention, I didn't look away. I held his stare as intense want rolled through me. I told myself my sudden desire was for Jade and redoing the past, not for B.C. I craved the option and ability to roll back time and afford myself other choices and possibilities. Had I chosen differently, perhaps he would have done so as well and chosen me. Watching B.C., I hated experiencing the same sense of confusion and powerlessness as I felt back then. I told myself not to unravel about my edges. I beefed up my resistance by reminding myself of his response to my actions. Rather than stand by me and my decision, he'd gotten with another woman. Jade was the result of *his* unfaithful decisions.

Be a woman about it, Tessa. You can't blame him completely.

I'd done what I'd done without his advance knowledge. In his eyes, it was a mortal betrayal and he'd reacted. Badly, in my opinion. But standing on this side of life with more than a decade between us and then, I was tired of the heaviness separating us and wanted to be free of it.

I was finally ready to forgive.

"Here you go, Miss Tessa. Dad's Swiss turkey mushroom bacon burger without the mushrooms, 'cause Dad said you're allergic."

Why can't Dominic remember that? He repeatedly ordered mushrooms on the Mediterranean flatbread pizzas delivered to his place, leaving me to opt for whatever was in the fridge while he blamed forgetfulness.

"Thank you, Jadie-Boo."

"Really, Miss Tessa? You and Auntie Mimi are the only people still using that baby name. I'ma need you both to quit."

"We will when you're a grown woman."

I chuckled when she smacked her lips and spun away to resume her meal-serving duties.

"And you better not be rolling your eyes, Miss Thang."

She glanced back at me, smiling.

Unwrapping my burger, I sat on Marlene's front steps as B.C. walked up.

"'Ey, Tessa. That burger's making you wish you had two tongues, huh?"

I nearly choked, trying to chew *and* laugh at B.C.'s off-brand joke. "It's *delicious*, but no. My one tongue is more than enough for this and anything else. It gets the job done."

He lowered his chin and raised a brow, looking at me as that same crazy energy I'd experienced the other day zipped back and forth between us with a heat I didn't need.

I stumbled over my words, trying to backtrack. "I-I didn't mean that the way it sounded."

He grinned. "Yeah. Okay." His smile suddenly faded. "I ran into some ish with permits, which means the restaurant renovations are on pause a minute."

I munched on garlic fries so delicious they deserved to live on my thighs as he explained a code violation that the prior owners hadn't disclosed.

"Sounds like you may have grounds for legal action. Call Rocki if you need representation. You know that girl's a pit bull and will go for the jugular."

He grinned that lopsided, lovable grin again. "Yeah, I'ma hit her up."

"Cool. Can I ask you something?" I barged ahead before he could respond. "Do you think this journal discovery is your ancestors' way of asking you to hold on to the property? I mean, for real. It was hiding all this time but suddenly shows up? Why now?"

He looked into the distance, collecting his thoughts. "Could be." He shrugged. "I'm not trying to disrespect my ancestors, my family, or our legacy. It's just a bit much right now. Anyhow... just thought I'd update you on the restaurant reno since I never heard back from you."

"Oh, my goodness." I put my head in my hand, feeling

ridiculous at reneging on my promise to follow up with him within forty-eight hours. I'd silenced that calendar reminder that popped up on my phone during my conversation with Dr. Latimore, telling myself I wouldn't forget. Obviously, I had. My failure was unprofessional, but considering what I'd been dealing with it was understandable. Still, I felt bad. "Brandon, I apologize. I fully—"

A sharp pain in my abdomen ripped away my ability to finish the sentence.

"What's going on, Tessa?" B.C. squatted on his haunches, voice and face tight with concern. "Are you okay? You need a bottle of water or something?"

"I'm fine."

"I don't think you are. I'll get Mr. Anthony—"

I grabbed his arm when he turned to leave. "B.C., I'm good. Really." I didn't feel like being the object of anyone else's inspection.

"You're not, Tessa, and you know it. Your color is rank and you got sweat beads knotting up your hairline."

"Brandon, please. Give me a minute. Okay?"

He gripped my hand as I closed my eyes and slowly breathed in and out until the pain subsided and I could offer a faux smile. "It was just indigestion, so wipe the panic off your face."

"Lies... but okay."

"Whatever, B.C." My smile felt wobbly. "What I was *about to say* is that I fully intended to call you. It was an oversight on my part. I sincerely apologize."

"It's cool. You're busy." He glanced at Marlene's house and released his hold on my hand. "I get it. But I guess it doesn't matter anyhow with all this permit business. Listen, I gotta bounce. You sure you're good?"

"I am. Thanks."

He nodded before calling Jade and swaggering away, but not before I caught the look on his face.

Crumpling my napkin, I tossed it on the disposable food tray, sick of myself and my repeat offenses as he walked off, leaving me sitting there feeling some same old feelings. B.C. and I weren't together in love anymore but obviously that didn't matter. I still experienced what I did and felt immediately defensive.

"My not following up with him wasn't intentional."

God was my witness and could testify on my behalf. That didn't lessen the remorse creeping in as defensiveness melted and truth became clear. Gently massaging my abdomen, one thought repeated itself in my head.

I am sick and tired of disappointing that man.

TEN

ONA

April 1789, Age 15

"Oney, you must hurry! We cannot be late or keep the General waiting."

"Yes, Mistress." Grabbing the shawl that matched her dress the color of cornsilk, I rushed into the room to help her prepare for the evening.

"Is it me, or is it warmer than usual, Oney?" The slight redness and puffiness of her cheeks bore witness to her discomfort. She fanned herself while slipping a foot into the satin shoe I held.

"Would you like me to open the windows, ma'am? There's a nice evening breeze. Perhaps that will alleviate your discomfort."

"No, no." She waved away my suggestion. "That isn't necessary. It's likely all the hustle and bustle of late has interfered with my internal constitution. We've been so inordinately busy since this presidential nomination business began last year. If this electoral college has it way, our busyness will increase to unimaginable degrees." She was quiet a moment before speaking as if to herself. "We've no time for dillydallying but, I must say, even the slightest reprieve would be splendid."

For those of us born into bondage, life was nothing save laborious. A series of inconveniences. Night and day, no matter the season or circumstance, we remained at the ready, in service. We rose early, went to bed late; at times, in order to meet the needs of upstairs folks, we had our sleep interrupted. Neither was there compensation. Unlike the indentured servants, we could not work to pay off our chattel debt, become part of a free society, and weave new lives for ourselves. Without fortuitous events, we were enslaved from cradle to grave. And all that Mount Vernon experienced, we felt. Visitors had always been part of the fabric of the estate, but with talk of the country needing a national leader came a constant influx of guests. Oftentimes, they brought their servants. At others, they didn't. Either way, our work efforts and exertions increased. The upstairs folks weren't the only ones inconvenienced. But such observations would be anathema, not merely impertinent. So I swallowed my tiredness and cosigned her sentiments with an agreeable, "Yes, ma'am."

I'm too young to feel such fatigue.

I was only in my fifteenth year, yet many times I fell into bed at night too weary to even entertain dreams.

Exhausted or not at least I'm still here. Living. Breathing.

Three years had passed since the heart-crushing loss of Noble, Mathilda, and their newborn infant. It took a long while for our community to stop reeling from the immeasurable horror of it; and sometimes at night when the wind whipped through the trees, I still imagined I heard their voices. Crying. Pleading. We weren't permitted to stop and mourn their loss, and we dared not display or convey pain, disgust, or outrage. Our souls were bruised and wounded just the same. Yet, our servile positions required acceptance lest we, too, be dealt inhumane punishment.

Upstairs folks had the luxury of being ignorant to our humanity, blind and deaf to our pain and suffering. But we saw. We knew. Some of us prayed for retribution and vengeance after Mathilda and Noble's deaths. Others, divine deliverance. Perhaps faith in deliverance and otherworldly interference was what enabled some to see what normal sight couldn't. That autumn, when the rainy season began, some folks including my sisters, Delphy and Lucinda, swore whenever the river rose due to heavy downfalls, that the spirit of a woman holding an infant restlessly paced along the riverbank. Some believed these sightings. Others didn't. But last rainy season when Eustis claimed he saw a man emerge from the waters to embrace that spirit woman and child before taking them into the river's depths with him, most of us accepted that it *was them.*

Being in the main house, I didn't encounter her regularly, but before Eustis's river sighting, Callie said Mathilda's brokenhearted mother lived life like a shadow being. After what Eustis claimed, she took to sneaking off to the banks whenever it rained. She was chastened once for forsaking her duties in the fields. That didn't stop her returning every time the rain fell, until her faithfulness was rewarded with the appearance of three ordinary birds descending onto the river's surface only to fly away changed—huge, majestic, and the color of flames. After that, Mathilda's mother remained quiet, with little to say, but she walked differently, her back straight, an odd light in her eyes that made some folks look away.

Those birds were my loved ones stopping by one last time before they flew home to Africa.

That's what Mathilda's mother claimed.

I'd asked my mother if she believed any of it.

Who am I to say what doors grief does or doesn't open?

*Besides, rivers and oceans are magical for folks who were stolen
and brought over on them.*

Mother's words had been enough for me not to be wholly
dismissive.

"Come now, Oney. No daydreaming."

"Yes, Mistress." I snapped to attention, putting away supernatural considerations.

"Oney, do you realize that more than a year has passed since
the General was first approached about this undertaking? And
to think he'd barely retired from the Continental Army. My
husband himself has said he aspires to nothing more than a
humble, happy lot of living and dying a private citizen here at
his beloved Mount Vernon. Now this. And he *never* threw his
hat in the ring. His fellow statesmen did!"

Accustomed to being an audience as Mistress worked out
her thoughts and angst, I merely nodded as she stood to
consider her appearance in the looking glass. Her expression
was pinched, nearly sour.

"I suppose I should be thrilled that my husband is a man of
integrity and deemed worthy of such a laudatory position. But I
must admit that I, even more so than the General, am not
thrilled about the possibility of his leading this nation." She
pinched her cheeks, infusing color into them. "I prefer our
privacy. Being here with the General, Nelly, and Washy. My
family. Not on display for all to see. Yet, I dare say he feels an
obligation to his fellow citizen." She sighed before turning in my
direction. "For now, I will table my discontent. Not only is it
wearying, but it cannot undo whatever it is that these sixty-nine
electors have decided." She lifted her chin in a determined
manner. "I have lived through unimaginable sorrow. I suppose I
shall learn to live with this." Her smile matched her determination. "I *will* be at peace until the outcome is revealed. You will
not need to accompany me this evening, Oney. It's a simple
dinner with dear friends. You may remain here."

That said, she sailed from the room and down the stairs to join the General, who stood outdoors, waiting to help her into their carriage. I followed and, when she was seated, I handed her the shawl and wished her a good evening before stepping back with the others in dutiful attendance. Once the wheeled conveyance exited the west gate, I exhaled audibly.

"Is it safe to say you're looking forward to a Mistress-free evening?"

I shushed Caroline despite giggling. "You will not put your naughty ideas on me. I am innocent of such thinking."

"I know one thing you ain't innocent of?"

"And that is?"

"Hoping you get through the evening without Miss Nelly."

"You are such a miscreant." I grabbed her arm and pulled her indoors behind the others. Caroline was several years older than me and had become like a big sister. We understood one another and had bonded as a result of similar longings of the heart. I lived on the same plantation as my mother and siblings without the blessing of seeing them daily; Caroline, having recently jumped the broom with Bristol, a gardener at Dogue Run, did not have the privilege of living daily with her love.

Dogue Run Farm—like Union, Muddy Hole, and River— comprised the Quarters: farm properties that weren't physically connected to Mount Vernon but belonged to the Washingtons and were part of the estate's wealth and land holdings. Consisting of more than nine hundred acres, Dogue Run Farm was three miles down the road, governed by an overseer, and home to less than fifty enslaved people. Bristol was one of those "night walkers" who perturbed the General so. When finished with his work Saturday evening, he walked the miles to Caroline, heading back to Dogue Run long before the sun rose Monday morning. Whenever he departed, Caroline vacillated between tears and a tender, saturated smile that I didn't fully comprehend but that she assured me I one day would.

She defended herself with a laugh. "I'm a woman of the gospel truth. You would prefer to avoid young miss."

"I'd rather avoid you and your tomfoolery. Not Miss Nelly."

The Washingtons' granddaughter was becoming quite the little lady. She excelled at reading and writing, and music lessons were in her near future. She remained sweet in temperament, but had not outgrown her rambunctiousness or her insistence that we weren't mere owner and slave. Visitors were plentiful. Her siblings. Her friend, Miss Frances. Yet, they weren't there for daily, year-long companionship. Maybe Miss Nelly's attachment to me was a result of planter life, being on a large farm surrounded and served by an enslaved population on a regular basis. Perhaps as time passed and she became an adult, that attachment would dissolve itself naturally. I tolerated, and at times enjoyed, the attachment despite knowing it wasn't lasting. But at the moment, in Miss Nelly's misguided opinion, I was her friend.

"Well, let's hurry on to supper so you can get your reading lesson."

I whirled about to ensure no one else was nearby before pinching Caroline's arm. "That's not funny!" I hissed.

"No, it isn't." Her whisper matched mine. "Who you think gonna be in trouble if it's ever found out? You! Not her. So, stop letting her read to you."

After nearly being caught by Evilest Eliza years ago, Miss Nelly had abandoned the dangerous notion of teaching me to write my name. Instead, she'd taken to reading aloud for my benefit and entertainment. Sometimes I paid attention. Most times I allowed my mind to drift, imagining a free world in which my listening to a little girl read to me wouldn't be cause for alarm or tantamount to sin.

"Caroline, you know how willful Miss Nelly is. But... I promise I'll do something about it."

"You'd better, 'cause..." Caroline's words disappeared in air as we stepped into the passageway leading to the kitchen, encountering a woman with a basket of sundries.

For a brief moment we stood as if locked in a triangle of the past, remembering a time before life changed when she attracted the wrong man's attention thanks to an unholy ruckus. At least, her life had.

I looked past the basket perched on her hip to her distended stomach as she thrust the basket towards Caroline, ignoring me.

"I'm only delivering these for Mistress." She spoke as if needing to justify her presence. "Ain't nothing but new fabrics for her to consider. She asked for 'em."

Caroline pointed over her shoulder. "Go'n in and give 'em to the housekeeper. We're headed to supper."

The basket-bearer nodded. She moved to step around me, pausing when I spoke despite her acrimony.

"Hello, Simmie."

She grunted a passable reply before hurrying towards the main house, a vapor of knotted emotions trailing behind.

I watched her disappear inside, wishing she had something better than what she had. "I think she's sad."

"I think she's just Simmie," Caroline countered somewhat dismissively. "She made an evil bed for herself by fighting you that day. Laying in it ain't easy. Come on 'fore we're late."

I didn't resist as Caroline grabbed my hand and urged me forward as the supper bell rang, but my thoughts were with Simmie. That night rider, plantation boss man had made good on his threat of making her his "new friend." Not only had he taken to calling her out of the communal house where the weavers lived on nights when the devil was riding him, but he was known to show up any time of day, demanding her to abandon her work in the spinning room in order to satisfy himself. He was obsessive. Possessive. I'd heard that sometimes she was required to walk behind him as he rode about the grounds on estate business. Cloaked in humiliation, her life and body had become subject to his whiskey-drenched whims. Now, she was heavy with a second child after having already borne him a daughter.

I disagree with Caroline. Simmie didn't make an evil bed.

This peculiar system had. We were chattel husbandry, invisible non-beings until lusted after or otherwise wanted, needed. Just two years ago at that Constitutional Convention the General attended, we were compromised yet again and deemed three-fifths of a human. As a result of some godawful Three-Fifths Compromise, five slaves would count as three people. And that was only for taxation purposes. Truth be told, they didn't consider us human like them. Not even the same species. How could Simmie, or any of us, control her fate or situation when she was considered a nothing put on earth for their purposes, pleasure, and prosperity? She was—we were—powerless to refuse or resist, or even claim our bodies for ourselves.

If we're beasts of burden, considered animals, then men like Simmie's "suitor" and Andrew Judge are guilty of bestiality. Or perhaps in those times we're magically human'ish.

Such thinking made me nearly stumble into the kitchen with its twisted heaviness. In my soul I knew we weren't invisible beasts seen only at their convenience.

We, too, are human.

"Ona, help yourself to some of my hominy and fish so it can wipe that frown off your face."

It was good seeing Cook smiling again. He'd been so broken after his wife, Lame Alice, passed two years back that Mistress had ordered he be given three bottles of rum as a means of solace.

Serving myself, I pulled my mind from troublesome thoughts and enjoyed the company of others, as well as the delicious fare. After supper, I ran to the cabin to spend time with my mother and sisters. Delphy was nearly a decade old now and too big to sit on my lap, yet she perched herself there just the same. Having already eaten in the kitchen didn't prevent me from snatching bits of the roasted root vegetables Mother made.

"No, Ona, stay!"

I kissed and hugged Delphy, sharing her sentiments that our stolen moment was too brief. With a promise to visit as soon as possible, I made my way back in order to be present when the Washingtons returned.

The sight of fireflies sprinkling the night with their golden glow slowed my steps. I admired their ethereal flight, wondering what it felt like to grace the sky.

The cupola.

Eons had passed since time last allowed a visit to that high point of the mansion, and I suddenly wished to be there. Lifting my skirt, I raced to the house, hoping to avoid an encounter with Miss Nelly just to indulge myself with that splendid respite. If only for a moment.

Heaven was with me as I cautiously entered the mansion and went undetected while pilfering a candle and secreting myself up the cupola ladder. The view was majestic as the night sky greeted me, offering a vantage point that turned fireflies into tiny fallen stars that refused to be extinguished despite their plummet from heaven. I inhaled the night's glory as long as I dared before sitting myself on the cupola floor, nodding off and dreaming I was a firefly, floating and free, until, sometime later, I heard the carriage returning through the west gates. Snuffing out the candle, I hurried down to turn back the linens on the Washingtons' bed and lay out Mistress's nightwear, my dream-like feelings of freedom forgotten.

"This is preposterous. The end of the month is but weeks away! Am I expected to dispense with everything required of me here at Mount Vernon and be in New York by then? That's quite a traveling distance. What of my health, dear husband?"

Days following my firefly enchantment I—having been summoned—stood several feet behind Mistress's chair waiting for instructions as she engaged in what seemed to be troublesome discourse with General Washington. I'd once heard he was a man preferring silent contemplation to gregariousness, due to ill-fitting dentures that affected his speaking, but with Mistress he was vocal. Relaxed.

"Have you not, dearest wife, frequently stated that a change of air is conducive to health?" He sat with one leg crossed over the other, shoulders straight, impeccably and formally dressed as always. His facial expression seemed somewhat sanguine despite what Mistress considered a troublesome topic.

"Yes, but that does not include *New York* air. Need I remind you of the gall bladder disease I contracted there when visiting Senator Schuyler and his wife?"

I focused on a rug in the distance, noting that the General's voice was low, measured when he replied.

"No, wife, you need not. I cannot dismiss ongoing concerns for your health or anything else, yet it bears stating that we are capable of this." He drummed the arm of the chair with his fingertips. "Be assured, I have reservations of my own. I am no longer young as when we met and I am certain there are others better suited, but we were chosen."

"*You* were chosen."

I was unable to view her expression from my position behind her chair but that didn't prevent me from knowing she was distressed. That pale-yellow fan was fluttering in her hand with a rapidity that created a breeze. It left me with an odd, queasy feeling as if a small storm was brewing.

"Consideration of your inestimable qualities was as much a part of this process as anything else," the General insisted. Throughout the many years of the Revolutionary battle to win our independence from Britain, did you not time and again, at my request, meet me on the battlefield in our winter encampments?"

"But *of course* I did."

"You braved smallpox. You boosted the morale of our soldiers as well as raised money for their badly needed supplies and tended to their illnesses, all while being a secretary and supportive confidante to me."

"That was war. This is politics."

I nearly felt the General's long, audible inhalation.

"This is *life*, dearest. You've outlived far too many beloveds and managed your estate after the death of Mr. Custis. You, dear Martha, are more than suited to be the wife of the nation's first elected leader."

"It's too sudden," Mistress contended.

"For months have we not been encouraged by others to believe that the vote would end as it has?"

I found myself shifting from one foot to the other as if embodying Mistress's restless discontent.

"Perhaps," she murmured at length. She sat a long while, wringing her hands in silence before slapping her lap with her fan. "Had I known when that accursed Charles Thomson arrived earlier today that he was the bearer of such news, I would have had him shot on sight."

General Washington chuckled quietly. "The Secretary of Congress was merely the messenger. It is the people who have spoken."

"The people are, indeed, intelligent as is obvious in their unanimously electing you without one dissenting vote. There is no finer man for the position." Mistress stood abruptly. "However, that does not mean I wish to share you, or *us*, with the nation. We have Nelly and Washy. And now Fanny, George, and Lawrence to consider."

"Your niece, Fanny, is fully grown and married. As for my

nephews, they are only semi-permanent residents. You have trained Fanny well and she is capable of watching after the estate in our absence. It is settled, dearest. As I said to Mr. Secretary of Congress, whom you wish to maim, our fellow citizens have honored me and I have no option."

Mistress's hands fluttered like the wings of exasperated birds. "I shall mark today, April fourteenth, as the beginning of the end of the simple solace we have enjoyed at Mount Vernon. Am I to now address you as Mr. President?"

"I won't be sworn in until April thirtieth." Standing, the General bowed gallantly. "But even then, 'Husband' remains sufficient."

"April thirtieth... Washy's birthday. A day that should be one of celebration." Spinning away, Mistress hurried from the room. "Come, Oney. Fetch my camphor tea. I feel a touch bilious."

Calling the days following the General's election as the first president of the nation hectic would be a magnificent understatement. There were visitors aplenty coming and going. Much packing. The indentured tailors who lived and worked on the premises were taxed with ensuring the General's wardrobe was equal to his new position. He was modest yet adamant that the suit worn during his induction ceremony be made of American-made material and ordered that it be constructed with brown broadcloth from the Hartford Woolen Manufactory in Connecticut. When he departed for New York two days later, April sixteenth, the household was sufficiently exhausted. Particularly Mistress, who did not accompany her husband, but remained at Mount Vernon, ostensibly packing up the household.

Those weeks before April thirtieth and beyond, Mistress wavered between weeping tears of pride and sorrow. Her usual ailments increased in magnitude and frequency, as did her temperamental disposition. She was worried, impatient, fretful. I found myself vacillating between administering poultices or tinctures in her drink to alleviate distress, and moving about as quietly as possible to avoid quick and sudden chastening caused by her irascibility. A most decisive individual, she seemed unable to commit to a day for her departure to join the President. Instead, she encountered a series of convenient delays that prolonged her being at Mount Vernon.

"'*Oh, Lady Washington.*'" She suddenly stopped reading the letter she held. "*Lady Washington?* Now I'm to be addressed like the King's nobility? Everyone might as well have stayed in England."

The terseness of Mistress's voice indicated a difficult evening ahead. Still, I stood ready for service as expected.

Miss Fanny, her niece, who'd taken up residence at Mount Vernon, smiled indulgently, unbothered by Mistress's discontent. "Dear Aunt Martha, do continue reading the letter."

"Hmph." Mistress made an indignant sound before complying. "'*Lady Washington, how our hearts soared as Robert Livingston, Chancellor of the State of New York, having administered the oath of office on the balcony of Federal Hall, exclaimed, "Long live George Washington, President of the United States!" Cheers erupted in the overly crowded streets. It was a grand event attended by hundreds. A perfect exposition for such a distinguished gentleman.*'" Seated in the salon, Mistress folded the letter and toyed with the edges of the paper while staring at something in the distance. "John Adams will make a fine vice president." Her tone was petulant.

"Come now, Aunt. I thought you'd made peace with it all?"

"How do you suggest I make peace with the unreasonable restrictions that will be imposed on me now that I'm to become a state prisoner?"

I thanked heaven when Miss Fanny reached for the letter in

Mistress's grasp and hoped her unrest would magically dissipate without that missive in her hand.

"May I?"

With her aunt's nod of consent, Miss Fanny read the remainder of the letter aloud. It was filled with the wonders of the General's inauguration. A military salute and the ringing of church bells that morning. The first presidential address in the Senate chambers after the swearing into office. A divine service at St. Paul's chapel. The General's dining alone at Franklin House, the presidential mansion. The nighttime fireworks that dazzled the skies for an hour.

"Listen to this, Aunt. There was such a plethora of celebrants crowding the streets at the conclusion of the day that dear Uncle and his entourage had to abandon their carriage and return by foot to Franklin House!"

Mistress sniffed and dabbed her eyes with a handkerchief I remembered embroidering. "I imagine we should thank God that the fireworks didn't burn down the town." She retrieved her embroidery hoop from the tea table beside her, working in silence for several minutes before sighing. "I suppose, as my husband stated, it is settled. No matter my opinion. Let us now pray that one day President Washington will shine his favor on us and return to Mount Vernon."

Her nightly prayers were filled with that petition, as if to remind the Creator and all within earshot of her loneliness and the President's absence. It seemed as if her moroseness would last indefinitely until the morning I delivered her breakfast tray and found her rummaging through her clothing.

"Good morning, Mistress."

"Ah, Oney! Your timing is perfect." Sorrow was absent, her smile nearly radiant. "Please send for my trunks and those of the children." She held up a chemise shift while talking to herself. "I must wear frocks made in our nation. Nothing imported. That would be most unpatriotic." She looked at her breakfast tray. "I'm too antsy to eat just now, Oney. Take it back downstairs and ask my niece to come to me if she's up and about. She and I must determine which servants, besides yourself, will accompany me to New York."

That pronouncement left me with a sense of unease and many unnerving questions, but the household had become such a beehive of busyness that I had no one to answer them. I had no knowledge of how far away New York was, or the length of time of our travel. I was nervous and fearful, and had disturbing dreams of being lost in this new place and never returning home again. I suppose my being allowed to have an early dinner with my family before saying farewell that afternoon of May sixteenth was a result of the favor I'd won with Mistress.

Just not favor enough to grant an option.

I wasn't keen on journeying so far away and being separated for heaven knew how long from my family. My one solace was that my many-tasked eldest brother, Austin—a footman, waiter, and postilion—would be a part of Mistress's enslaved entourage. Along with Giles, Nanny Moll, Paris, Christopher, and Will Lee, we would serve in New York as we'd done at Mount Vernon.

"If you ever feel lonesome, look on the moon lighting the night and know I'm watching it too and thinking of you, my black-eyed butterfly."

I drowned myself in my mother's and sisters' joint embrace, kissing each fervently, wanting to take the scent of their hair, the outline of their faces and forms with me. I did my best to imbed them in my memory.

"Keep yourself safe. Here. Take this. And hurry." Mother shoved something into my apron pocket before hugging me once again.

I buried myself in her arms, concerned at how tired she'd been of late, praying she would be okay.

My little sister, Delphy, took my hand, set on accompanying me to the main house where, surely, our traveling party had already assembled.

"Is New York a free place?"

I shook my head. "No, Delphy, it's a slave state."

"Oh. Well, at least you get to go somewhere. Remember everything you see so you can tell us all about it when you get back."

Promising I would, I hugged her once more before taking my place on the wagon that waited behind the carriage transporting Miss Nelly, Master Washy, Mistress, and Mr. Robert Lewis—their escort and the President's nephew.

When the wagon jostled into motion, I waved goodbye to my sister and the others gathered in farewell until we'd left the estate and they were—courtesy of my tears—hazy silhouettes in the distance. I nervously wrung my hands in my lap, willing them to be still only to feel the outline of whatever it was Mother had placed in my pocket. I withdrew it and was delighted by the pear-shaped needle case that also served as a pin cushion and fit splendidly in my palm. Its cloth wasn't as fine as the satin cases Mistress owned, but knowing my mother had embroidered its lovely scene of frolicking red cardinals—so abundant in our state—made it just as beautiful. I secured it in my pocket, grateful to have a piece of home to take to New York.

Eleven days later, after a somewhat trying voyage, we finally arrived at our destination. Our journey could certainly be called adventurous with a broken carriage, wayward horses, and a fearsome ferry crossing troubling us even before leaving Virginia. Even so, it was all new for me which made it enthralling and often frightening, yet thrilling. New sights. New sounds. Even smells seemed different. I was often wide-eyed while soaking in unfamiliar surroundings and experiences and couldn't wait to return home to recount it all to Mother and my sisters. Baltimore. Philadelphia. Shopping and celebrations. All along the way there were parades and receptions, fireworks and gun salutes. Serenades. Church bells rang and citizens flooded the streets, all for "Lady" Washington.

I'd spent so much time since the General's election soothing her distemper—fanning her, draping her forehead with cool compresses, preparing her remedies to be ingested—that I'd nearly forgotten that Mistress was capable of real contentment. I was reminded of that fact when crossing from New Jersey into Elizabethtown where we were met by the President. Her joy at being reunited with him was like the sun appearing after years of inclement weather. Dazzling. Brilliant. Even so, as we crossed on the presidential barge into New York, I wondered if her joy would last in light of her new role.

Equally important, I wondered about the vast changes awaiting we enslaved persons within the new president's household.

And, more importantly, when am I going home?

ELEVEN

TESSA

"Mr. Ant, please tell me you haven't contacted the donation site yet and still have Marlene's cabinets."

I exhaled in relief when he confirmed he hadn't and that they were still in his possession two weeks into the project.

"I'm your favorite designer. Right?"

I couldn't see his expression across the phone, but I was sure it was twisted as he asked what I needed.

"You know how I planned on grabbing those cerulean cabinets from Grayson's? Well, some blockhead didn't remove them from inventory or mark them as 'on hold,' and another customer purchased them. So... we have to reinstall Miss Marlene's cabinets in her kitchen. And add custom niches or open floating shelves so they fit the new design."

I bit my lip, waiting for Mr. Ant's reaction, imagining him kneading the bridge of his nose. I hated asking this of him, but it was an unforeseen complication. One of my design professors had warned our class to always factor in the unexpected, be it a time delay, supply, or budget issue. He'd repeatedly advised we incorporate buffers in our plans to allow for the hazards of our profession.

"Tessa, you know I detest having to redo something already done. You can't get those same cabinets elsewhere?"

I explained that the cabinets were a custom-ordered item. I didn't have time to scour warehouses hoping to find anything remotely similar in color, or wait weeks on a new order to be completed.

"If my crew reinstalls them, then what? Marlene's old cabinets were oak, not some fancy-schmancy blue."

"I'm at the warehouse now doing a paint match based on the pics on my iPad. Marlene's cabinets can be sanded down and repainted at a fraction of the cost of the set at Grayson's." I hushed up, allowing my proposal to sink in.

Mr. Ant mumbled an expletive. "Be sure you get satin or a semi-gloss finish since it's for the kitchen."

I grinned at his instructions.

As if I don't already know that.

"So... you'll reinstall them for me?" We'd worked enough jobs together and developed an amazing rapport. I was banking on that to get what I needed.

"I'm not doing nothing for *you*! It's strictly for Miss Marlene," he teased. "And who's painting these things and building these custom niches or floating shelves? The crew is tied up enough trying to finish the project on your tight timeline. I can't pull 'em off something else—"

"No need to. I'm painting the cabinets. And if there's no time for the niches, floating shelves are a simple fix. We'd only need to measure and mount the planks. I'll paint them as well."

I held my breath in the silence that ensued.

"Fine. We'll reinstall the cabinets once they're repainted and hold off on the flooring until you finish. But I can only give you one day, Ms. T."

"Thanks, Mr. Ant. You're my favorite contractor."

"I know so well."

He disconnected, leaving me laughing. And relieved.

Thankfully I had an account associate at the store who assisted me when purchasing project supplies, and I was in and out of there with gallons of perfectly matched paint in no time.

I'd pulled out of the parking lot and was en route home when my sound system announced a call.

"Incoming call from Mama Calloway."

I answered immediately. "Good morning, Queen of Pralines."

She chuckled heartily. "Grand rising to you, too, baby. B.C. and I've been reading this journal of Aunt Ona's and *ooowee, honey*! It's enough to make your toes curl and your dandruff flare up."

I couldn't help laughing at the colorful response to her ancestor's journal. "I imagine it's an enlightening treasure." I'd never been a history buff. That was Rocki's thing. Still, I valued what little I knew of my family's origins and appreciated genealogy. "It's fascinating, huh?"

"You said a mouthful right there! It's fascinating. Intriguing. Heartbreaking. Liberating. I'm going to pick up wherever you left off and read you some more of it, but first I have an issue."

"Yes, ma'am..."

"My big-mouthed sister, Ardella, went and told her bigger-mouthed daughter, Briana, about the diary when I specifically told my siblings to keep it to themselves until after it's tested. Now, that daggone niece of mine has outsiders in our business, calling B.C. with all their greedy foolishness. Have you heard from that specialist yet?"

I had a sorority sister who was an assistant professor of Anthropology at Cornell. I'd called her asking how to establish the authenticity of historical documents. She'd pointed me in the direction of several agencies, one of which was the American Society of Appraisers in D.C.

"No, ma'am. I imagine they'll reach out to you or B.C. directly versus contacting me."

"Well, I appreciate it. I keep my gloves on, but I suppose I shouldn't even be holding or handling this book before they examine the pages, but it's just so... *amazing*. Now, lemme tell you about that blabbermouth Briana." She wrapped back to her niece, seamlessly. "That nincompoop told her no-good, property-hound of a baby daddy. Now *his* ignoramus behind's working B.C.'s nerves making offers on our land in Chincoteague."

"*Really?*"

"Indeed! And had the nerve to offer a fraction of what it's likely worth. Here he comes with his"—she lowered her voice in a mocking way—"'Miss Coni, I'm interested in preserving the place and turning the house into a bed and breakfast or museum for the benefit of the community.' No, he is *not*! Little lying leprechaun."

I snorted back a laugh and zipped past the bright "Hot Now" sign at Krispy Kreme before the thought of warm, glazed doughnuts could seduce me. "Sounds like he wants to cash in on an opportunity."

"Precisely! He wouldn't do a thing with our land except flip it to some prospector for a bigger profit if this journal is authenticated. Those fools'll have falsifying signs out in the yard talking about 'Come see the house where George Washington's slave was born!' I tell you what. That'll happen when I take up roller skating with Satan. But enough about that. Let me read you some more of this diary..."

The rest of the day proved a godsend. I stopped by Marlene's and was more than pleased with what Mr. Ant and his crew had accomplished. Even with my having to go in and paint cabinets the next day, we were ahead of the game and slated to finish on schedule. Once home, I checked my email only to discover I'd been contacted by a local magazine wanting to include me in a

"Top 30 Under 30" write-up featuring young entrepreneurs and businesspersons of color. I celebrated that honor by surprising Kimiyah, showing up at her place with takeout from her favorite Chinese food restaurant. I missed my girl and her vivaciousness, and felt a weight lift just being in her presence— talking and laughing like we hadn't done in God knew how long. I left her place after a tight hug and promise not to be MIA from our sisterhood ever again.

I capped off the night with a hot bath and a glass of wine, thankful for a blessed day made even better by the absence of pain in my abdominal region. Soaking in the tub, I thought about Mama Calloway reading the journal over the phone to me. I shivered thinking about the words Miss Ona had written. I tried and failed to imagine myself in her position. Taken from family. Uprooted. Traveling to a whole new state. I considered how overwhelmed she must have felt. I went to bed exhausted, yet sanguine, inspired by Miss Ona's courage.

It wasn't until the next morning that my blissful tide turned on me.

In the dark hours of early morning, I got caught up in a disturbing dream. A terrified woman dressed in rags was running for her life, trying to escape a man on horseback in some shadowy, swampy wetland. Despite her desperate attempts to race beyond his grasp, it was as if she was moving backwards in slow motion until her pursuer overtook her. She did her damnedest to fight him off but failed as her captor slid off his horse and wound a rope about her wrists so tightly that blood poured from them. When he forced her onto her knees and commanded she repent for her sin of wanting to escape him, I finally got a glimpse of their faces. She was me. The man, go figure, was Dominic.

Badly shaken, I jerked awake, telling myself it was merely a byproduct of Mama Calloway's wrapping back to read a previous section of Miss Ona's journal to me. That heartrending account involving a pregnant runaway and the father of her unborn child had been traumatizing. That nightmare disturbed me so badly I couldn't stay in bed. Instead, I padded into the family room in my fuzzy slipper-socks to sit in the dark, snuggled beneath a blanket, scavenging the dream for symbolism.

"I don't want to do this."

Still, I did, unable to deny that in some ways my relationship with Dominic was beginning to feel suffocating and, at times, was heavily tinged with a disturbing aura of entrapment.

"But I'm not trying to escape him. Not like *that*. Right?"

I mean, really. On paper he was *everything*. Single. Sexy. Fine as hell. A homeowner. Successful medical professional. No criminal record. Drug-free. Never married. No babies. Old-school Black elite. He had—as my grandmother would say—all the fixings, and might be considered most women's dream. But my grandmother also had another saying.

Baby, you can still be settling even when you settle for someone with seemingly everything.

I guess my temporary mental-health break from calls and texts wasn't merely more satisfying than expected. It was also revelatory. It gave me the opportunity to be truthful about behaviors I should've checked the *first* time they happened, as well as making space for truth and perspective. My mind flashed on that journal and the courage Miss Ona's life required. I had liberties she'd never experienced. That left me facing the fact that I was compromising my freedom and making a bold admission. My truth was I was in a toxic relationship. Point-blank period.

My soul was vexed. I had to confront myself. I could accuse Dominic all day but what about Tessa Lorraine? I wasn't down for victim-blaming, but I wasn't a victim and needed to examine my motives and agenda. I wasn't desperate for a man. Never had been. So why was I willing to sacrifice self-worth and put up with ridiculous amounts of BS just to maintain involvement with an individual who was problematic, condescending, insensitive?

Because I care about him. All relationships have challenges. I'm loyal by nature and I don't quit just because ish gets thick.

"Girl, you're too intelligent for that kinda ignorance. Stop making excuses and admit you're guilty of getting caught up in entanglement traps and exercising poor judgment."

The tenderness, compassion, acceptance of who I was as a woman; the equality, respect—qualities Dominic exhibited in the beginning—were now missing. Being with him had become its own form of emotional captivity, and I needed to set myself free. I was intelligent. Confident, not arrogant. Outgoing and artistic. Kind. Caring. I gave, but the reciprocity was shady and being with Dominic now felt restrictive.

You have an imbalanced mess, not a partnership.

That hurt so badly I couldn't reclaim my sleep. I abandoned my blanket and went into the kitchen to make myself a cup of peppermint tea before returning to the family room to sit in the dark, thinking about this thing with Dominic and, more importantly, the ways *I'd* changed.

Had I really exchanged my values and what I needed for gifts and trips?

I'd been raised to value life, family, God, love. Not things. I felt superficial, shallow realizing I'd dishonored myself, my legacy. My eyes filled with tears that I quickly wiped away as the doorbell rang.

It was barely five a.m. and still dark outside. I eased from the sofa as quietly as possible, contemplating whether or not to go snatch Rico's old baseball bat from beneath my bed, thinking only psychos made house calls before dawn. Peeking through the peephole, I wondered if I'd conjured up an apparition as I slowly disarmed my security system and opened the door to *him*.

"It's early. Is everything okay?"

"Apparently not, seeing that you're in some kind of non-responsive headspace and not feeling me enough to even return a call lately." He walked in wearing scrubs, a stethoscope draped about his neck, ready for his workday. "But don't worry. I won't be in your way. I'm not staying. I have the early shift and thought I'd drop this off on the way in."

I glanced at the garment bag Dominic hung from the frame of my foyer closet, recognizing his petulant pettiness but choosing not to speak on it.

"What's that?"

"Your dress for my brother's engagement party Saturday. It's a size ten." He eyed my hips. "Hopefully it fits."

Perfect example of the jackass he truly is.

I ignored the dig, unable to do much besides stare at him while wondering how much of his madness and bad behavior I'd excused and overlooked this past year. And for what reason? Because he seemingly checked all the extraneous Good Black Man boxes? That didn't give him a license to cruel or vulgar behavior. Neither was it an acceptable excuse or reason enough to continue subjecting myself to his disrespectfulness.

His eyes narrowed a bit and he had the nerve to look genuinely perplexed when I remained silent. "You could be a bit more appreciative, seeing as how I went out of my way so that you look your best and are an appropriate reflection of this relationship."

In the past I would've offered an apology, or expressed appreciation for his efforts in order to salvage his feelings. Right then, after the dark dream I'd had and the contemplative, soul-searching mood I was in, I was highly disinterested in placating or soothing him.

If what I wear reflects this relationship, it'll be some raggedy-ass, bargain-basement-looking disheveled mess.

"I don't need dressing lessons, Dominic."

His face scrunched up as if I'd spoken pig Latin. "What's with all the lip, Tessa? Just say 'thanks' and let it go at that."

Some little cautionary flag waved itself in the back of my mind. His strident tone was uncalled for.

This man has a savior complex.

I never asked him to buy me a dress. He was controlling and it was his way of exerting dominance. Another time I might have been appreciative, but right then I had zero energy for coddling. Instead, I overlooked his jaw tightening, not in an effort to ignore his getting bent out of shape, but because I suddenly didn't care. I was tired. Physically. Emotionally. I had health issues to deal with and in that moment the energy this conversation required was more than I wanted to give. The conversation was ignorant and I was ready for it to end. Still, I made my tone as gentle as possible when responding.

"Like I said, I know how to dress."

Erratic, hostile vibes rolled off him in hot heavy waves as he took a step towards me, altering his voice and slowing his speech as if talking to a mentally challenged person. "This is a *formal* event. Not an opportunity to show your ass."

His behavior was becoming alarming.

"Excuse me?"

"If you plan on wearing anything similar to what you did at Dad's gala, don't." The heat in his voice was off-putting as he continued towards me. "I prefer to avoid a repeat of tits on display and some over-the-top slit nearly reaching your nonexistent panties."

I stepped back the slightest bit as he radiated intense anger and agitation that the conversation didn't merit.

"I'm not some weak punk who needs other men lusting after the woman on my arm to feel good about myself. I'm secure in who I am and I expect my woman to be the same. So, let's ditch the ass advertising and go for tasteful and classy." He stabbed a finger at the garment bag. "Wear the damn dress, and tone down the ho'ishness."

He might as well have slapped me, the bitterness in his words and face were that stunningly harsh. Disturbing.

This is the real Dominic.

Was this hostile, degrading individual the true Dominic Daniels that I managed and restrained by capitulating to his wants and making concessions? Love wasn't blind and ignorance wasn't bliss. Seeing him now was like confronting a threat you'd long been aware of but were afraid to admit or confront. Right then he was exposed, on full display behind something as inconsequential as a dress. Perhaps there was more to the matter, but I didn't make it my business to dig into his mess. His behavior was disturbing enough to cause a seed of fear to crack open inside of me. I needed out of this relationship, but it wasn't the moment to make such pronouncements. I knew I had to proceed cautiously for my safety and focused on getting him out of my house. Immediately.

I stepped past him and held the door open, keeping my tone as neutral as possible. "You should leave so you're not late."

"I'll leave when I'm damn ready." He slammed the door closed and towered over me, chest swollen and angry. "Who're you seeing?"

"What're you talking about?"

"Stop playing games with me, Tessa!" The elevated volume of his voice was startling. Alarming. "You've been dodging my calls. You don't return my texts in the five-minute window I established for us. You haven't been responding to them, *period.* Now, you're acting like an ungrateful bitch." He moved towards me as if he wasn't already close enough. "Only another man could have you acting ignorant. *So, who the hell is he? Huh?*"

I stepped away from him only to feel the door at my back. The situation was ridiculous, yet I had a sudden, frightening sense that it could escalate to a whole other level if prolonged.

I'd never had to navigate this kind of heat from a man and was unsure how to handle it. All I could think to do was keep my voice low and controlled. "I'm not seeing anyone, Dominic."

He suddenly switched up from screaming and acting ignorant to matching the lowered level of my voice as if playing head games he intended to win. "You've changed and I don't like it. What're you hiding?"

Part of me wanted to laugh at the fact that this man couldn't handle my taking a temporary mental-health break. The other part of me knew a temporary hiatus wasn't sufficient. No longer needing the drama or trauma of this relationship, I wanted this thing between us terminated. "I need you to leave, please."

"And I need you to answer my damn question, Tessa! What're you hiding?"

My cell phone chimed before I could reply.

He seized my wrist when I reached for it and thrust his free hand into the pocket of my robe, snatching my phone so violently that the pocket ripped. "Who the hell is texting you at this time of morning! Is it your other man?" Grabbing and spinning me about, he pressed me against the closet door and twisted my arm behind my back so painfully I was afraid it might crack.

I berated myself for not taking the time to grab Rico's bat. "I will call the police if you don't let go of my arm and leave!"

The threat of police involvement creating a blemish on his reputation and that of the great Daniels family was enough to cut through his vile BS.

"Be ready when I pick you up Saturday at seven. CPT is not attractive." He stormed out the door, leaving it wide open.

Hands shaking violently, I locked the door and armed the alarm, feeling cold. Confused. Empty. Pain shot up and down my arm from having been twisted as my heart pounded in the brittle silence Dominic left behind him.

Oh. My. Damn!

I leaned against the door, catching my breath, feeling as if the world were spinning at warp speed and making me nauseous. I wanted to explain away the insanity I'd just experienced, but couldn't. Instead, I retrieved my phone from the foyer table where Dominic had thrown it and, without thinking, started dialing my daddy. When his voicemail came on, I disconnected and called Rico. Getting the same results, I dialed B.C.

"Oh my God, *what am I doing?*" Brandon's natural protector instincts would have him destroying Dominic, beating the ish out of him.

I disconnected, distressed and clearly not thinking straight. For the briefest moment I thought to call the police, but for what? I'd thrown that at Dominic just to get him to leave, but from what little I knew about domestic violence, the police would want a witness to the abuse, or to see visible injuries as proof.

Domestic violence.

Was that what this was?

I suddenly couldn't breathe and felt as if I was hyperventilating. I bent over, putting my head between my knees, focusing on calming my respiration until my heartbeat stopped racing. When it did, I felt dirty and had an immense need to wash away Dominic's touch and to settle my queasy stomach.

I padded towards the kitchen, checking my phone and seeing no incoming text. The chime that had sent him over the edge was simply notification of a daily affirmation. Reading it, I wanted to vomit as I grabbed a bottled water from the fridge. Just twisting off the cap caused additional pain to shoot up my arm. Gently, I flexed it back and forth, ensuring it wasn't broken before heading for the bathroom and downing two ibuprofen.

The hot shower water I stepped beneath minutes later felt entirely good dousing my back, my head, my neck. Steam enveloped me, making me feel as if in the haze of some twisted dream, some insane experience new to me.

He's an abuser!

I could try to outsmart truth if I wanted to, but facts were facts. I was in a relationship with an abusive, self-centered, controlling egomaniac.

That truth hit the bottom of my stomach like a sledgehammer. I braced the shower walls and bowed my head, ashamed. Wounded.

I deserve to live in peace and safety, and be loved like a diamond.

That was the day's affirmation that had arrived on my phone. I repeated it until the words swirled like a river with my tears as they dripped and flowed.

I had Angie Stone, Jill Scott, and Ledisi on rotation, tying myself in their silk-and-satin vocals as if they were warm blankets.

I need to renovate my spirit like Marlene's cabinets.

Making sure my painting supplies were in place, I looked about the kitchen that was a mere shadow of what it would become, appreciating the power of transformation. It was one of the aspects I loved most about my profession: accepting something as it was only to take it through a valley of metamorphosis.

I'm taking myself to butterfly camp.

I was ignoring the pain in my arm and my heart, while opening the paint can nearest me, just as my cell phone rang.

"Hey, *chica.* We're here."

"Cool. I'm coming." I disconnected and made it to the front door in time to see my BFF and her niece exiting Kimiyah's Range Rover.

Two or three inches shorter than me, Mimi was one of those ultra-feminine women. The kind who looked like their stuff was always together. Curvaceous, but petite, she pranced up the walkway in an expensive-looking designer yoga pant-shirt set.

"What kind of painting are you planning on doing in that fit?" I pasted a smile on my face, hoping she wouldn't see through it. "This isn't a sip-and-paint tabletop situation."

"Whatever, *chica*. Just let us in."

"Hey, Miss Tessa, we're here to paint!"

"Whaaat? Jadie-Boo came to help, too?"

"I'm only gonna help if you stop calling me by that crazy baby name. Where's the bathroom? I gotta go bad." Jade followed my directions and took off down the hallway.

"Come on in. The kitchen awaits." I closed the front door expecting Mimi to follow me.

"Tessa... what's wrong?"

I glanced over my shoulder to see she hadn't moved from the doorway. "Nothing. Why?"

She approached slowly until right up on me. "You don't look right. Something's off."

We'd always been connected, not just at the hip, but in spirit and could pick up on each other's inner vibes in a split second.

I opened my mouth to offer more denial but couldn't. My thoughts felt stuck; words wouldn't come. Tears I couldn't suppress suddenly blinded me.

Alarm coated Mimi's voice. "Come on, T., what's up?" She reached a hand in a consoling manner towards my injured arm.

I jerked my arm back, wincing despite the fact that she hadn't made contact. "I'm fine. Let's paint."

"To hell with painting, Tessa!" Her eyes mirrored mine and started watering.

When she gripped my wrist, I clenched my teeth to avoid yelping. That didn't prevent her from sensing what I wanted to remain hidden.

"May I see?"

I wanted to run away, but couldn't. Instead, I stood like a broken remnant of myself as my BFF gently rolled up my sweatshirt sleeve. The marks about my left wrist caused her to gasp. They'd been faint when I'd exited the shower earlier. Now, they were glaringly angry, vivid.

"What the hell happened?"

I could only offer silence.

Mimi started firing off questions then suddenly stopped as her eyes widened. "Did Dominic—"

His name barely crossed her lips before I lost it.

"Auntie Mimi?" Jade's voice floated softly from the hallway. "Is Miss Tessa okay?"

"Baby girl, go in the other room for a minute, please."

Kimiyah's instructions to her niece were essentially lost on me as cries of pain and humiliation poured out of my innermost being. When she wrapped her arms about me, I leaned into her petite frame and let the strength of her love take my wounded weight.

TWELVE

ONA

1790–1795, Age 16–21

I missed home. Dreadfully. I was no vacationer traveling at my leisure with the choice to, once satiated, take my leave. Yet, my homesickness didn't prevent New York from being fascinating. There were food vendors on corners, women in sophisticated fashions. A bustling waterfront and fur traders and trappers. I heard words in languages I didn't comprehend, and felt as if I'd stepped into a world that was slightly foreign. Still, I enjoyed accompanying Mistress on her trips about town. She loved the flower gardens and the abundant orchards with their sweet, juicy offerings, particularly Cherry Garden. The trees were so plentiful and the fruit so succulent that a street had been named for them. It was the street on which sat the presidential mansion.

Samuel and Maria Osgood's residence at 3 Cherry Street was altered and arranged, made fit for a president. The drawing room was expanded. Refurbishments were made. With its mahogany, Hepplewhite and Chippendale effects, Mistress concluded that the New York dwelling was handsomely furnished. It didn't, however, take long for the Washingtons to deem that first presidential residence inconveniently located, not to mention too small for our household and the President's staff. In addition to the Washingtons and we bondspersons who'd come from Mount Vernon, Mr. Tobias Lear—the President's senior secretary—had enlisted an additional fourteen servants. They were white, indentured, and paid. We were not. A mere eight months after we'd arrived in New York, the executive mansion relocated to the larger, better-suited Macomb House at 39 Broadway.

As at 3 Cherry Street, the presidential mansion on Broadway was a busy place with the President hosting a gentlemen's reception each Tuesday, dinner with congressmen the following day, and Friday's levees with Mistress and the vice president's wife, Abigail Adams. Mistress's receptions were amiable affairs well-attended by respectable persons without invitation, offering a less formal atmosphere to interact with the President while refreshing themselves with coffee, tea, lemonade, cake, and ice cream. Despite their dreams of retiring to a simple country life being delayed, the Washingtons adapted to New York and presidential demands—granting themselves moments for church attendance, walks in Battery Park, and plays at the John Street Theater. Yet, Mistress often pined for the comforts of Mount Vernon. She was dutiful but granted herself much-needed refreshment with simple pleasures like carriage rides and strolls in the park. I accompanied her, in faithful servitude, seeing the city and discovering that some aspects of New York were too similar to Virginia. Mainly, slavery.

Servants in homes. Workers along the East River, loading and unloading ships. Enslaved persons peddling goods, or selling hot edibles on the streets for their owners' gain. Even the

Meal Market—the human auction at the foot of Wall Street—where bondsmen were bid on, bought, traded, and sold as if wares and products served a bitter taste of home. Just the same, we settled into life in this new place only to be uprooted once again when the government moved the nation's capital to Philadelphia, Pennsylvania in November of the following year.

For the Washingtons, Philadelphia was presidential duties, hosting visitors, museum visits, church attendance, and plays. I enjoyed the city for my special reason: every time the word was said, I heard my sister's name. I'd never been away so long and was thankful for Mistress's periodic trips to Mount Vernon that allowed me to visit family. I loved recounting my journeys so that Mother and my sisters felt as if they'd been there. I even offered animated reenactments that often left them laughing and did my best to provide vivid details. Their laughter, awe, and interest would fill the cabin, binding us together as if absence had never happened. Those visits provided relief from the homesickness that sometimes enveloped me.

The following spring, the homesickness seemed not to last as long and became more tolerable thanks to new experiences and Uncle Hercules. He'd been brought to the presidential residence to wield his culinary magic and, often with him as chaperone, I ventured into a living that I never knew existed.

"You won't believe it unless you see it." Uncles Hercules led our small group through the Philadelphia streets as we made our way to the circus. "This'll be my second time and I guarantee you I'll still have trouble believing my eyes."

Mistress was so taken by the acrobatics of a traveling circus —particularly its tumbling feats—that she'd allowed us the evening off before the circus moved on, knowing the staff of fifteen indentured servants employed at the presidential mansion would meet their needs while we were gone. Such new experiences were a lifetime away from Mount Vernon, and I was like a wide-eyed, giddy child, filled with restless excitement. I could barely contain myself and thanked her profusely when she doled to me a minute amount of money as she occasionally did since our relocation here.

We're no longer in the countryside, Oney. This is a city and you shall enjoy the occasional night at the theater, outing, or treat.

It was merely enough to purchase my entrance and perhaps one small refreshment; still, that coin felt so majestic and magnificent that I clenched it in my gloved hand all the way there.

I love my gloves. They're exquisite.

My residence had changed. My appearance had as well. As a highly visible servant of the President's household, I was doled finer quality clothing to supplement the standard issue brought from Mount Vernon. When I accompanied Mistress on her visits and outings or ran errands for the household, I was a reflection of Mistress and it was imperative that I emulate her status. I'd never owned such finery and treasured the new frocks, gloves, bonnets, shoes, and stockings now in my possession.

"How much farther, Uncle Hercules?" I adored my new shoes, but they weren't suitable for walking long distance.

"We're nearly there. Maybe one or two minutes."

I smiled in acknowledgment and looked about as the others in our group chatted, happily. I'd come to enjoy the new sights, sounds, and foods experienced here, and found the streets of Philadelphia striking, not because of manmade monuments but because of its free Black community. All about us, Negroes born free or who'd acquired their liberty, flowed as part of the river of humanity. Officially, it was a slave state, yet Pennsylvania's political landscape had undergone many changes, positioning it as a place of justice with a strong Quaker, abolitionist presence that enabled a vibrant and growing free Negro community that I found completely fascinating.

"Find seats at the back."

Arriving at the venue and paying the entrance fee, I experienced a delicious excitement as we followed instructions to the rear where Negroes were required to sit, whether free or bondsmen. I was too thrilled to care about segregationist practices and settled in for the entertainment. It proved wildly wonderful with daring acrobatics and physical feats that left me so breathless that, when it ended, I didn't want to leave. I chattered incessantly, feeling like the restlessly energetic little girl I'd once been.

"Did you see the human tower they made? They were stacked on top of each other's shoulders"—I raised a hand overhead—"three men high!"

"We sure did see 'em, Ona. We were there." Nanny Moll's response brought laughter from our small entourage.

"And the tumblers were magnificent!" I'd never witnessed human beings tumbling, twirling, leaping with such synchronized force and speed.

Uncle Hercules turned to respond only to pause and smile broadly at something behind me. "Good evening, Brother Joshua!"

"Good evening, Brother Hercules." A tall man the color of sundried tobacco leaves approached and shook Cook's hand. "Ladies." He tipped his hat brim before addressing the men in our group that included my brother, Austin.

Mister Joshua's was a fine hat, but nowhere near as fancy as Cook's. Still selling meals and earning pocket money even here in Philadelphia, Uncle Hercules's taste for the fine, colorful clothing he treated himself to hadn't lessened any.

"How's Sister Emma and the new baby?"

"Just fine, thank the Lord. You remember my sons, Philando and Frank Staines."

Uncle Hercules shook the boys' hands before introducing

them to us. I nodded at the older one named Frank, finding something in his sunny smile that reminded me of Delphy.

"Will you be attending the meeting tomorrow evening, Brother Hercules? We'll be taking up that matter of Sister Vashti's husband."

"Of course."

I glanced at Uncle Hercules while pleasantries and good-byes were said, wondering how he could possibly be at a meeting tomorrow evening when it wasn't his regular night off. As we walked home and the others pulled slightly ahead, I dared to ask.

He slowed his pace, allowing the others greater distance. "Little Miss Nosey, I'm only telling you this because, who knows?" He shrugged. "One day you might benefit from it. You know I sometimes make meal deliveries after dinner's served and the Washingtons dismiss me for the night, right?" He lowered his voice when I nodded. "I don't always return right away. Sometimes I attend FAS meetings."

I gave him a puzzled look. "What's that?"

"The Free African Society."

"Which is?"

I listened attentively, intrigued by this benevolent mutual aid organization founded by Negro preachers, Absalom Jones and Richard Allen. It had religious origins and undertones, but provided more than mere charitable acts for widows, orphans, or others in need. The Free African Society built churches, cemeteries, as well as schools—promoting access to education and apprenticeships for free persons of African descent throughout the city.

"You mean they teach reading and writing to Negro children?"

He looked about, furtively, before continuing. "Children. Adults. And not just free Negroes. It's a lot more difficult to do on account of the laws... but we can learn, too. If we want."

I gasped and placed a hand over my mouth.

"Don't be dramatic, Ona." He pulled my hand down. "And don't draw attention to yourself. You're from the President's household. If somebody goes back and tells Mistress you seemed disturbed on the street, you'll have to answer to something."

Banishing shock from my face, I resumed a casual appearance and sent my thoughts elsewhere. "What's wrong with Miss Vashti's husband? Mister Joshua said it's a matter of discussion..."

Cook's voice was suddenly tight with rage. "Slave-catchers rolled into town and snatched him off the streets claiming he fit the description of a runaway they were paid to recapture. They took him to Georgia. Only problem is, he was born free and was never nobody's slave. Now, the greedy fool of a plantation master—who, by the way admits Sister Vashti's husband is the wrong man—won't release him until he's compensated for the cost of the idiot slave-catchers and the price of his runaway."

Cook gripped my elbow when I nearly stumbled from thinking this system incredibly unjust and evil.

"What's going to happen?"

Cook shrugged as we waited for a carriage to pass before crossing the street. "Won't know until I attend the meeting, but last time there was talk of everyone pooling in and raising the money if possible."

"And if they can't?"

He lowered his voice. "They may have to go over state lines and steal him back."

"But that's dangerous!"

Uncle Hercules nodded. "Most worthwhile things have risks, Ona. Question is, are they worth it?"

. . .

"Oney, I hope you enjoyed the circus as much as we did when we attended."

I smiled at Miss Nelly's exuberance. At twelve years of age, she was becoming an accomplished young lady with her French lessons, needlepoint, harpsichord playing, and all manner of intellectual and artistic pursuits and abilities, including painting. She'd begun taking classes with other young ladies of genteel station and sometimes brought them home for tea—particularly Genevieve Browning and Elizabeth Langdon. Despite such niceties, she still bore shadows of being her grandmother's "wild little creature"—high-spirited and talkative.

"Thank you, Miss Nelly. I did."

She launched into a recounting of her family's circus visit with vivid imagery that made me feel as if I had also attended. "I must admit enjoying the equestrian act even more than that rope walker." She leaned towards me, whispering, "Don't tell Gram-Gram, but I liked the clown far better than those tumblers. Which performance was your favorite?" She patted her bed, inviting me to sit.

She was still Miss Nelly, insisting on time spent together and shared confidences while disregarding the impropriety of such intimacies. I was Oney, her faithful childhood friend; not someone bound to her by virtue of a slave-master relationship. It wasn't that she didn't understand the vagaries of this system defining our existence. She was a very bright young lady. Just strong-headed. And persistent. She'd even managed to manipulate my sleeping arrangement to her advantage. While the other enslaved house members slept on the third floor or in the attic, she'd convinced Mistress that my sleeping in her room was for her grandmother's convenience.

My room is right next to yours and Granddad's. Just think, if Oney sleeps in my room she'll be nearby should you need her any hour of the early morning or night.

Miss Nelly got her way. My pallet was moved into her

room. As always, it remained up to me to navigate her ongoing wants in a way that kept me safe.

"I can't just sit and do nothing yet, Miss Nelly. Mistress may need me."

I wasn't Miss Frances or Miss Elizabeth, friends on equal footing who could lollygag and chitchat, be carefree or take liberties. We weren't girls playing dolls or equals to sit in simple conversation. I had to retain the propriety of my position.

"Gram-Gram retired shortly after you left. I'm certain she's in dreamland."

When returning, I'd come up the back stairs, reaching Miss Nelly's room first. She'd immediately begun peppering me with questions about the evening before I could check in on Mistress.

"Thank you for letting me know, but I really should see for myself."

"Oh, bother. Be quick about it." Dressed in her nightwear, her back against her headboard, she shooed me from the room.

I left only to return within moments after confirming that her grandparents were, indeed, slumbering peacefully.

When she patted her bed again, I grabbed the comb and brush from her dresser instead. "Miss Nelly, your hair is a fright. We should braid it and put on your bonnet."

She carelessly fingered the brown tangles atop her head. "I despise sleeping bonnets. They're so provincial."

"Wearing them makes for easier hair-combing in the mornings."

"But I don't comb my own hair. My maid does, so why bother?"

I failed to answer before an evil wind in the form of her older sister blew in.

"Nelly, which of these gowns should I wear to Frances's for tea tomorrow?" she queried.

I froze at the visiting Hurricane Eliza entering the room, only to remember to offer a quick bobbing curtsy.

"Oh, Oney, don't do that." Miss Nelly's distaste showed clearly.

"It's what I require of and deserve from darkies, so why shouldn't she?"

"Because this isn't England, dear sister, and you're not His Majesty."

"Perhaps not,"—Evilest Eliza waved a hand as if swatting away her sister's response—"but I'm certainly worthy of displays of utmost respect and fealty. Now, which should I wear to tea? The yellow or the green?"

"They're rather elaborate for afternoon tea, don't you think?"

"I think no such thing. I'm no peasant."

I waited silently as the sisters went back and forth until they made a decision on which gown should be worn the following day to the home of their family friend who was in town for the season and hosting a teatime soirée.

"You're quite right, Nelly. The green is best suited for my coloring." Mistress's oldest surviving grandchild held the dress against her frame, admiring herself in the looking glass. "Oh, fudge! The hem is dreadfully ripped. I must've snagged it the last time it was worn without being aware of it. Here, Oney. Have it properly repaired by morning."

I took the dress she thrust at me. "Yes, ma'am."

"Oney was about to braid my hair."

Evilest Eliza, who prided herself on being more ladylike now that she was fifteen, delicately shrugged her shoulders and responded to her sister's protest quietly. "There's no reason why she can't do both. She did nothing today except attend the circus and couldn't possibly be exhausted. Besides, her kind never wearies of serving. Did you enjoy the circus, Oney?"

I longed for permission and power to recount all the unpaid "nothing" I provided this family on a daily basis, from before sunrise to beyond moonlight. Though it wasn't always easy, I worked hard, doing my best to perform efficiently and with as much dignity as allowed to someone in my position. And, heaven was my witness, most often it was wearying.

Knowing upstairs folks need not concern themselves with any of that, I simply said, "Yes, ma'am."

She moved towards me, smiling brightly. Having learned over the years that her mirth hid fangs, I lowered my gaze.

"I heard that when the circus returns next year, they'll have acts featuring exotic creatures from around the world. Nelly, do you suppose they'll include some of Oney's bestial ancestors from Africa? If so, she can reunite with them."

"Don't be droll, Eliza."

I shielded my face with a blank expression as she ignored her sister and slowly walked a circle about me. My body tensed, unsure of what she was doing. When she stopped behind me, I had flashes of Callie's bloomers being pulled down so others could search for a tail. She wasn't that same girl, and may have prided herself on her maturity, but over time Miss Evil as a Boll Weevil's pettiness and cruelty had also increased.

"Eliza, what're you doing?"

She was silent a bit longer before responding to Miss Nelly. "These mongrels are so *fascinating*. Oney has freckles and her skin isn't as dreadfully dark as some." She moved in front of me and lifted my chin before snatching the bonnet from my head. "Those fairer qualities might've worked to her advantage and even made her attractive, but for this vulgar, bush-woman hair."

With lightning-quick speed she grabbed the scissors from my darning basket and hacked off one of my plaits before I could finish my next breath.

"Eleanor Parke Custis, stop that!" Her sister sprang out of bed, placing herself between us and yanking the scissors from that wicked wonder's hand.

"I was merely trying to improve her appearance. But nothing probably can." She flung the plait in my face, shuddering and wrinkling her nose as if all things pertaining to me were offensive.

"Good night, dearest Nelly. Enjoy sleeping with your darkie."

Replacing the scissors in my darning basket, Miss Nelly patted my shoulder while handing me my fallen bonnet. "Don't mind her, Oney. Eliza has always been mischievous."

I inhaled, exhaled slowly, staunching angry tears. *Mischievous* was Master Washy putting a frog in someone's shoe. This cretin was disgustingly maniacal and I couldn't wait for her visit to end.

Oh, how I wish she'd fall head first off a mischievous *cliff!*

It wasn't until after Miss Nelly had fallen asleep that I had a chance to view myself in the looking glass. The tiniest measure of hair remained in place of my missing plait. My hair was thick enough to camouflage the area easily, but that didn't lessen the sting of being carelessly violated by someone for whom there was no punishment—unless Miss Nelly reported the incident to Mistress. I certainly couldn't. And even if she did, that evil thing might catch a scolding, but nothing that would infringe on her freedoms or alter her the way she'd altered and abused me and my dignity.

Gathering that green dress, I sat on my pallet near the window soothing my jagged feelings but not suppressing my tears. I let them flow, praying they'd cleanse away all bitterness so that my heart wouldn't be black like hers.

Remember Mother said whenever faced with hardness in life try to send your thoughts somewhere pleasant.

My thoughts turned impish, leaving me digging my nails into my palms to prevent gales of laughter at an image of a chamber pot being dumped over that evil thing's head. Clearly, fantasy was my only satisfaction. Besides, after a lifetime of enduring this creature's visits, I knew she was incapable of anything save cruelty and vileness. Instead, I allowed the act of mending by candlelight to soothe my spirit.

I wonder how many times I'll have to redo this hem?

I'd mended items for Evilest Eliza in the past only for her to abhor my workmanship. She once even took a knife to a dress, claiming my "inept butchering" had ruined it. Examining the elaborately decorated hem, I found the damage quite extensive. Repair was possible but would likely prove a slow, steady process. Bent over, working by candlelight, my eyes strained from fatigue at the end of a long, eventful day, I embraced the work and the quiet. The mere act of mending made me feel as if my mother was present, or I was a little girl again, in the work-house learning my craft.

I miss you, Mother. Sisters. Brother.

Pushing aside the drapes, I paused to consider the moon and remember that my mother had promised to think of me whenever its silvery light bathed the night.

"I'm thinking of you, too." I blew my whispered words through the open window, willing them to float across the distance and softly land on my mother's bosom. Then I smiled as I remembered a trip home to Mount Vernon was imminent.

Since moving to Philadelphia, the Washingtons made the return voyage often. Our visits were a godsend, allowing me to see my family, Eustis and Callie; but their frequency sometimes made me think perhaps the Washingtons disliked Philadelphia. It often seemed just as we got settled, we were heading back to Virginia. Sometimes with the President, but mostly with Mistress. The voyage by wagon was long, sometimes tedious, but at its end was a reunion with my beloveds so I happily endured it.

"Ouch!" Daydreaming of family, I'd been unfocused just long enough to prick my finger accidentally. I sucked a tiny pearl of blood from my fingertip before it could mar Evilest Eliza's dress. "Ona Judge, pay attention."

I rolled my shoulders and stretched the kinks from my neck before resuming my task. I'd threaded several needles from the pouch Mother gifted me and had lined them up so that when one length of thread was finished another was instantly at the ready. I would have preferred to be sleeping, the moon's silver softness kissing me, but couldn't tuck away on my pallet until the gown was repaired and delivered to its ornery owner who would, no doubt, inspect it at great length as if anticipating flaws.

If my work is so shoddy, why task me with this?

We both knew my needlework was beyond reproach. I'd been taught by my mother, the estate's primary seamstress, and my workmanship was deemed superior even by Mistress. Her granddaughter was critical and contemptuous simply because that was her nasty nature. Still, I took extra time and care to ensure the repair was flawless, despite it taking longer than anticipated as I had to undo several layers of crinoline and lace and reattach them after repairing the lace itself. My humming, the soft light of the moon, and magical memories of the circus kept me company until I finished with the faintest hint of dawn in the distance. My back ached. My fingers were stiff, my eyes were bleary, and I was utterly exhausted. Yet, I examined my finished work with objective scrutiny, determining that the dress appeared as if the damage had never happened. Standing, stretching, I gathered the gown and quietly eased from the room so as not to awaken Miss Nelly.

I entered the guest room where Evilest Eliza was staying, soundlessly placing the gown on an armchair so that she would see it upon awakening. Turning to leave, I froze when she rolled over in bed, mumbling in sleep before stirring. She raised her head ever so slightly.

"Who's there?"

"It's me, miss, delivering your dress." Fatigue and propriety prevented the disgust I felt for her from manifesting in my voice.

She lay back down. "No need. I'll be wearing my blue gown instead. You may toss that green monstrosity on the rubbish heap."

Taken aback, I hesitated the slightest moment, glad no candles were lit to illuminate my ire. "Yes, miss."

Rather than return to my pallet in Miss Nelly's room, I headed downstairs to the kitchen where Uncle Hercules was already bustling about as if the sun had risen.

"Well, don't you look like a slow dance with death! Why the long face, and why're you still in the same clothes you wore yesterday?"

"I haven't been to bed," I complained, informing him about the dress before pulling the bonnet from my head to show him Eliza's latest.

He fingered my scalp while shaking his head in commiseration. "Lord, sometimes I think that girl was either birthed feet first in an acid bath, or head first in a briar patch. Either way, she's pricklier than a pig around a plate of bacon."

That caused me to smile for the first time since being molested by scissors last night. I plopped down at the long, rough-hewn table where we took our meals, yawning and rubbing my fatigued eyes, too tired to laugh. "Wouldn't it be something, wearing beautiful gowns like this?" I sat back, fingering the dress destined for the garbage.

"What would be even more wonderful is you making and selling them."

My eyes rounded. "I couldn't!"

"Why ever not? I sell my cooking with the Washingtons' permission."

I stared at him, not wanting to hurt his feelings by saying one meal didn't require days of intense labor, only to realize that sometimes—as in holidays and celebrations—it did.

Cook looked over his shoulder before lowering his voice to a near whisper. "Attend tonight's FAS meeting with me so you can hear about how free Blacks are making progress in the community."

I often marveled at the ability of the city's free Black population to come and go freely, and in my mind they possessed a certain dignity that I was deprived of exuding. My attire may have improved so as not to bring shame on the house of the nation's leader, but I still donned a bonnet and apron when moving throughout the city, like badges of servitude. And while my status as Martha Washington's maid allowed me a modicum of prestige, I wasn't free. We, the enslaved of the President's house, were amongst the minority in this city where a Negro was more likely to be emancipated or born free than enslaved. It wasn't that free women didn't wear aprons and bonnets similar to mine. Some did. Yet I noticed something different that had nothing to do with garments. The difference was in their carriage. The lift of their shoulders, how they didn't avert their gaze in deference to upstairs folks. Free Blacks looked upstairs folks in the eye most times, even exchanged greetings or engaged in conversation. And when free women were seen about in aprons or domestic-looking attire it was because they were engaged in enterprise, selling foodstuffs or even wares for or with their husbands. Most in their population were literate. Or actively learning. Free Blacks felt different from me. They felt *separate*.

"Thank you, Uncle Hercules, but I shouldn't." Toying with the fabric of the dress and wishing I could keep it for myself, I didn't offer an explanation for declining his invitation and, thankfully, he didn't ask for any.

He simply nodded and offered a quiet, "Whenever you're ready."

I watched him move about the kitchen while considering my condition. With great care I performed all the duties of a lady's maid and, according to Mistress, she relied on and "couldn't do" without me. She was one for simple elegance, but exacting. In many ways, demanding. I'd been physically chastised a time or two when she was in one of her dour moods. But I wasn't treated poorly and hadn't experienced—like Simmie— some of the horrors known by many females in my position. Indeed, Mistress often patted my hand while praising my work or calling me a godsend.

Miss Nelly and Master Washy were still as pleasant as when small children. Even their frequent friends Miss Frances and Miss Elizabeth were kind-hearted towards me.

Why would you need the FAS when you have these things?

The sudden chiming of a house bell jolted me from my chair, forcing me to realize I'd nodded off while entertaining such thoughts.

I followed Uncle Hercules's gaze to the far wall.

"You'd best get going. Mistress is awake."

Reminding myself to be grateful for all blessings, I hurried from the kitchen, unable to escape a niggling question.

You may have attained certain questionable liberties, but are you free? As long as you're a bondswoman, Ona, you're someone else's property.

Within weeks of the circus, we were once again packed and bound for Mount Vernon. Seated on the back of the wagon with my fellow bondservants, I could barely contain my excitement at the thought of traveling home to see my beloveds. Uncle Hercules, however, looked as if he'd been forced to eat multiple bushels of the sourest lemons.

"Cheer up before you scare all this sunshine away making that ugly, ten-mile-long face."

Everyone laughed at Giles's teasing. Except Uncle Hercules.

Like my oldest brother, Austin, Giles was a postilion. Seeing as how Austin was up ahead manning Mistress's carriage, Giles was with us, the gold buttons on his uniform sparkling magnificently in the sun. He playfully nudged the cook's shoe with his own when he failed to respond.

Cook snatched his foot back, clearly in no mood for playfulness.

Nanny Moll tried a softer approach. "We know things ain't been the same since Alice passed, but you gots other kin waiting on you when we get—"

"This ain't got nothing to do with Alice!" His voice was low, seething. "It got everything to do with these conniving, double-faced Washingtons."

An immediate hush fell over us and was only broken when Giles raised up in the wagon to peer at the road ahead. He dropped back onto his bottom, brows knitted as if afraid.

"What's wrong with you, Herc! You can't be talking like that." His voice was a violent hiss. "You best be glad the carriage is far enough ahead that Mistress and Mr. Lewis can't hear."

"I don't care one damn about them hearing. I should be *free*! State law says *all of us* should be."

I felt sick to my stomach hearing Cook explain some Gradual Abolition Law passed in 1780. Not wanting to isolate or anger its existing slaveowners, the state of Pennsylvania had opted to abolish slavery over time, gradually. Enslaved persons owned or purchased prior to the passing of the law would remain enslaved. However, this Gradual Abolition Law prevented importation of new bondsmen into the state and freed babies born there after the law was passed when they reached the age of twenty-eight. It also forbade slaveholders from intentionally taking a pregnant woman across state lines so that her child would not be born in a slave state. Additionally, spouses could no longer be separated, nor children from their parents. The state allowed slaveholders to maintain their human property only if they were registered annually, like declared articles of possession. Failing to do so would result in manumission.

"What's that got to do with any of us? We wasn't born here, and we ain't expectant women," Giles challenged.

"Anybody wonder why we headed to Mount Vernon again when we were just there a short time back?" Cook's eyes snapped fire as he slowly looked at each of us. "'Cause one day more in this state and we would've been free men and women!"

A cold sensation slithered through my entire being as Cook continued, his words hot as Hades.

Although the presidential house was located in the state, officially the Washingtons were residents of Virginia, not Pennsylvania. Under the Gradual Abolition Law, non-residents of Pennsylvania were prohibited from keeping enslaved persons in the state for more than six months. Doing so would provide emancipation instantly and automatically. To prevent our being set free, the Washingtons merely had to remove us across state lines even for one day to void our Pennsylvania residency. Rotating us in and out of the state to prevent our freedom was an illegal loophole President Washington exploited.

"Who told you all this?" Nanny Moll questioned.

Uncle Hercules lowered his voice as if sharing a confidence. "I attended the FAS meeting last night. When I told Brother Joshua I'd miss the next few on account of us heading back to Virginia, he commented that it seemed like we'd just visited home not long ago. That started up a conversation that led to Brother Absalom mentioning this law. Folks in the state ain't even allowed to build or contribute materials for ships used in the slave trade." He pounded a fist against the wagon floorboard. "Yet, here we sit as the Washingtons' slaves!" His chest heaved angrily. "All we gotta do is step *one foot* outside of state borders before that six-month clock runs out and our status as slaves is maintained. These Washingtons're so slick they don't got us just stepping outside of Pennsylvania. They got us high-tailing it all the way back to Mount Vernon—"

"Just so it looks like some legitimate trip. Like they abiding by the law and can maintain they good name," Giles concluded, when Cook ran out of steam.

"So *that's* what he and Tobias Lear was talking about that day I took a calling card into his office." His jaw spasmed as Frank Lee, the butler, looked off into the distance. "I came in on the tail end and had to wait while they finished. The President seemed to think he was above something on account of his position, but Mr. Tobias said the attorney general 'lost all of his when waiting past the six-month mark' and President Washington shouldn't chance losing his property as well. The President took some time to reply but when he did, he told Mr. Tobias to do it in a way that 'they and the public are deceived.' No one was to know except them two and Lady Washington." Frank Lee angrily spat over the side of the wagon. "Looks like we're the 'they' in question."

"When did you hear all that?" Cook asked.

"Last year... a week or so before that first trip from here to Mount Vernon."

"Lord, it's been six months since the *last* trip." Cook rocked slowly back and forth, angry and dejected. "Looks like we'll be stepping outside the state at least twice a year, so keep your traveling shoes ready."

My cheeks were suddenly hot. I fiddled with my fingers. My foot bobbed back and forth. I was angry and agitated by the President's unlawful subterfuge, attributing his heartlessness to being a landowning master and man. But Mistress? She would knowingly allow us to be rotated in and out of the state like breathing chess pieces for her continued comfort and gain? All of her kind pats on the hand, her praise for my seamstress skills, her claiming my care indispensable, and the recent generosity of providing me coins for treats suddenly meant nothing to me. Hot tears burned my cheeks as I realized that doling out money was Mistress's way of appeasing her conscience, a distraction from what was truly happening. I drew up my knees and buried my head in my lap to weep in peace.

I'd been betrayed. Deceived.

Nanny Moll's hand against my back was gentle, soothing, as Uncle Hercules quietly warned, "Always know your enemy."

Knowing our captors was often key to the survival of a bondsperson. We didn't possess the power to prevent atrocities, still we studied upstairs folks to know their ways and, when possible, to keep ourselves safe.

When we'd reached Mount Vernon, I'd fallen on my mother's bosom, weeping, lamenting how I'd been lulled to sleep by new prestige and niceties.

"I feel misused. And ignorant!" I was so caught in my misery that I barely noticed the increased fatigue cloaking her like a shawl.

"Ona, slavery is a longstanding web of trickery. You're not but one person, and barely a woman. You're not the first of us to be deceived by upstairs folks, so hush your crying." Mother held me away in order to see my face once my sobs quieted. "These Washingtons may be more decent than most, but they're still owners of *people*. And owners won't never consider us above themselves. Now..." She smoothed my hair away from my face. "Remember what you promised me? That if freedom ever comes for you, you'll go wherever she leads?"

I nodded, sniffling.

"Good. All of us may not have outsmarted this ugly system yet, but that don't mean you can't." She kissed my head. "*I* may die a slave, but I'll die happy knowing some of my blood made it off this plantation."

. . .

I was there, on that plantation where I was born, when my childhood friend, Eustis, jumped the broom with Penelope. I was present when Miss Sukey, the midwife, delivered Simmie's fourth baby, and even took Simmie a small basket of yarn to help with the knitting all birthing mothers were required to contribute during their three or four weeks of recovery. I spent golden moments with family and Callie when not attending to Mistress.

I never revealed what I knew about how she and the President moved the presidential mansion staff in and out of Pennsylvania like game pieces. My knowing wouldn't have made a difference in their conscience or decisions. More importantly, any mention from me would've amounted to impudence and exacted some form of punishment. Instead, I performed my duties as always and kept that knowledge to myself while vowing to never be anesthetized by powdery words, coins for sweets, or genteel deviousness again. Recalling Cook's admonishment to know our enemy, it was more important to me to know *myself* even better than I had.

In the shadows of the Washingtons' trickery, I wrestled with its sting. Their deceit was a wound that cut deeply; yet I could never respond to it openly. Rather, unrest quietly gnawed at me, causing a subtle shifting, an internal unfurling. I cloaked it masterfully, yet was without relief until we returned to Philadelphia and I attended my first Free African Society meeting at the Quaker African School House with Uncle Hercules.

It had been an uncommonly quiet night in the presidential mansion, and when Uncle Hercules asked Mistress if I might aid him in delivering the meals he sold, she'd consented.

"I feel a mite fatigued, and might benefit from one of my elixirs. Oney, assist me in turning in early and you may help Uncle Harkless."

When the last meal had been delivered and he steered us away from the presidential mansion, I learned the true reason for his invitation. He wished me to attend an FAS meeting.

"You've seemed a bit sad, different, since learning about that out-of-state rotation. I feel you could benefit by experiencing this for yourself. But the choice is yours, Ona. Come with me, or go back home to the Washingtons."

I stood there in the early evening, torn in my decision and afraid of the consequences if Mistress awakened and I wasn't there if needed.

"She took a sleeping draft," he offered as if privy to my thoughts. "She won't awaken before morning."

Concern made me hesitate, but a more compelling something inside of me made me want the experience.

"What if someone recognizes me?"

"Someone may, but if that happens, this is a safe place. Who attends is never an outsider's business."

It felt like the most daring thing I'd ever considered in life. Still, I pulled the hood of my cloak over my head to conceal my identity before following where Uncle Hercules led.

Now, hands clasped in my lap, I sat in awe of the fountain of humanity that flowed about us that evening. Negroes of every hue, economic station, and position filled the edifice. Hymns were sung and prayers prayed before Reverend Absalom Jones spoke from the pulpit. His was a powerful, magnetic spirit that drew me in. My heart tingled with his passionate prose. My spirit thrilled. It felt wonderfully subversive being exposed to new ideas. Heaven had more for me than mere enlightenment. That glorious gathering offered fellowship and friendship. When Brother Joshua's son, Frank, and others about my age welcomed me into their circle without hesitation, it felt divinely delicious.

Their friendship helped sustain me three years later when my brother Austin died in Harford, Maryland on a trip back from Mount Vernon. It wasn't clear if his horse threw him or if he fell from the saddle while crossing a troublesome river, or perhaps was knocked unconscious and drowned, but he was found in a water-filled ditch after a terrible storm, face down. My family was devastated, but none more so than Austin's wife, Charlotte, and their five children who were marked as Master Washy's inheritance when he came of age.

A year after my brother's death I was busy making a chemise for Mistress when the housekeeper summoned me. "Oney, Lady Washington is requesting your presence."

"Yes, ma'am." Placing the chemise in my sewing basket, I went to the salon where I knew Mistress to typically be at that time of day.

"You may enter, Oney," she instructed before I'd even knocked on the door that I found open on my arrival. She sat, face marred by distress, a folded letter on her lap.

Staring at that letter, my heart began to beat unmercifully. I'd been extremely cautious when I attended meetings, disguising myself by wearing my old clothes from Mount Vernon, but perhaps it hadn't been enough.

Someone must've recognized me and wrote to inform her of my FAS involvement!

I hovered near the door, afraid to enter. "Yes, Mistress. You needed me?"

She reached out a hand in a gentle fashion. "Come, child..."

I hesitated the slightest bit before obeying.

"I've just received a missive from Mount Vernon." She reached for my hand and held it tightly. "Dearest child, it pains me to inform you that Betty has passed away."

A moment lapsed before those abysmal words pierced my comprehension. When they did, anguish ripped a scream from my lips. The room swayed. I clawed at my hair, unable to save myself from the horrid words reverberating in my head. When nothingness enveloped me, plunging my world into blackness, I welcomed its embrace, glad to escape the horrifying news that my mother was dead.

It was night when I awakened on my pallet. I had no recollection of ascending the stairs. Clearly, I'd been carried there. No candles were lit, leaving me to lay alone in abject darkness. Sorrow and devastation left me light-headed, and my chest burned beneath an intense weight of grief so crushing that I felt lifeless.

Forgive me, Mother. I wasn't there. I was here. With them!

My being absent when my mother passed left a hole in my soul that felt as if it would never be filled. I'd noticed Mother's fatigue on our recent trips home, but she'd dismissed my concerns and assured me she was well. Still, I was unprepared for this loss, and I'd blacked out before Mistress provided details. I could only pray that my mother's departure had been painless. Fifty-seven wasn't ancient, but there was never a good age to leave a child motherless. Wrapping my arms about myself, I rocked back and forth as molten tears flowed like a rushing river, wishing I was home at Mount Vernon. I needed my brother. My sisters.

Delphy!

She was a sensitive soul and my heart broke even more imagining my baby sister's pain-filled bewilderment.

A noise behind me intruded on my mourning, causing me to stifle my sobs and sit up suddenly. I turned expecting to see Miss Nelly but instead found her older sister, a candle illuminating her visage.

I moved to stand, but she waved a halting hand.

"It's terribly sad to hear about Betty. She was a fantastic seamstress and an even better slave. Her workmanship will be sorely missed." She sighed as if tasked with the impossible burden of finding my mother's replacement. "Cheer up, Oney.

If there's a darkie heaven, hopefully your mammy made it in." That said, she exited as quietly as she had come, without my requisite 'yes, ma'am.'

My heart burned with indignation at her failed attempt at kindness and her arrogant insensitivity. Religious instruction had never been a large part of my life, but I'd risk my soul by hurling stones at any god wicked enough to bar my mother from eternal rest because of the color of her skin.

Turning my back to the door, I lay down again, shattered and weeping for my motherless condition, and boldly admitting that, with everything within me, I hated Eliza Parke Custis.

THIRTEEN

TESSA

Painting Marlene's cabinets with Jade and Mimi last week was the best fun I'd had in forever. It pulled me away from the raw emotions unleashed by my crying jag, the shoulda, woulda, couldas of my relationship with Dominic, and all the things I'd willingly overlooked that left me questioning my intelligence. I'd had other relationships and never been desperate, or a gold-digger. I believed in my self-worth and didn't need his prestige. Still, I'd elected to excuse Dominic's off-brand behavior for whatever my reasons. I was artistic, but also analytical, and felt the need to uncover the roots of my missteps by doing a deep dive into my soul, my spirit. But that cabinet-painting day, Mimi had summed it up in such a simple, succinct way that I was able to move forward.

We're fallible humans and sometimes we simply get with the wrong person.

That was an in-a-nutshell mouthful. Belittling, demanding, anal, and controlling, Dominic was the wrong person for any woman.

And this feels all wrong as well.

Seated in Mama Calloway's living room, I eyed the developer spieling okey doke better than a snake oil salesman. Thanks to Mama Calloway's "big-mouthed" niece, Briana, she and B.C. had been contacted by several entities expressing interest in the family's property in Chincoteague despite B.C.'s electing not to move forward with a sale until the diary had been examined. Today's visitor wanted to turn the house into an inn. B.C., unfortunately, had an emergency at his Richmond restaurant and couldn't be in attendance.

"Well, you've certainly given us a lot to consider..."

I grinned at Mama Calloway, watching her squinting and extending the business card today's visitor had given her at arm's length before moving it inches from her nose trying to find the right focus.

"... Mr. Sakowski. We'll be in touch." She waited until Mimi had shown the man out the door before adding a sarcastic, "Maybe."

Her exaggerated grimace of distaste had me grinning. "You didn't like him, Mama C.?"

"No! His breath smelled like dirty baby diapers and that sideways toupee wasn't impressive." She folded her hands in prayer and looked towards the ceiling as Mimi and I fell out laughing. "Lord, forgive me. Seriously, babies, these folks must think I'm some old crazy Colored lady they can smart-talk outta anything. I appreciate you sitting in on this visit today 'cause I sure dislike them approaching me with all this foolishness."

She'd been contacted by two other land developers besides Briana's baby daddy and was more than a little annoyed by, in her words, the vulture-ism.

"Granny, going forward, make sure B.C.'s here, or Grandpa's home during any appointments, 'cause you know they'll go rogue," Mimi joked.

"I'm not bailing neither of them outta jail for pointing your granddaddy's rifle at some poacher!" Mama Calloway sucked her teeth indignantly. "Lord, let these folks go somewhere and leave us be. We haven't heard from that conservator in D.C. yet, and the buzzards are already circling."

B.C. had arranged for the safe delivery of Miss Ona's diary to the conservator for analysis. It would be forwarded to a curator or appraiser if the outcome merited it. Prior to shipping it, Mama Calloway had photographed its interior, not only to ensure nothing was compromised or altered, but so she could continue reading her ancestor's writings. Again, I felt honored that she included me by calling and reading the journal entries like divine, historical bedtime stories.

"Well, I have top dibs on this newsworthy story if Aunt Ona's journal proves legit. Matter of fact, I'm already on it." Mimi's investigative journalist antennae had gone up the moment she learned of the diary that might lend credence to family lore passed down for generations. They'd always spoken of a connection between themselves and the Washingtons, but no proof ever existed and—other than a few failed attempts before the age of personal computers—it wasn't something they poured excess energy into. As with many Black families, their legacy story was simply accepted, like those candlesticks—something that always existed. With or without external validation. Part of the legacy fabric.

African-Americans are descendants of people for whom oral history was everything. We didn't always have literacy, so sometimes we forget about the importance of written accounts or archival research. Plus, with the way the dominant excluded us or skewed history to their advantage, we don't always trust their renditions of facts. Not to mention, until now we didn't know Aunt Ona's surname. I guess I should've been curious enough before this to just dive in and look for myself.

Mimi expressed those sentiments ashamedly, as if she'd failed her family by not exercising her professional acumen. Now, chick relentlessly haunted the internet and countless websites housing information on her ancestor, the country's first president, and Mount Vernon.

"Baby girl, you have *all the dibs* on this," her grandmother affirmed with a wink. "Until we know what's what, from here on out we're gonna do our darndest to keep things hush-hush. Now, lemme pick up where I left off."

Mimi and I had dubbed Mama Calloway's calling and reading the photographed pages of the diary to us the "Aunt Ona's Reading Time Regime." Seated there in person, we glanced at each other, grinning and listening as her grandmother read a passage detailing a move to New York. I hadn't known that the Big Apple was the nation's first capital and had allowed slavery.

I'm loving the history I'm learning.

Frowning when an incoming call broke my focus, I checked my phone only to see an unknown number. Instinctively, I felt it was Dominic and massaged my arm unconsciously, as if he were still violently twisting it. I'd deleted and blocked his contact. He'd resorted to either using a different phone or blocking his number on his end to prevent my knowing it was him. Either way, our relationship was finished, and I had no need to ever share air with him. Yet, I couldn't keep my mind from revisiting the idiotic aftermath of that horrifying incident.

Why am I standing outside waiting? Open the door and hurry up before we're late! And did you find my cufflink?

The fact that he'd gone to my home expecting compliance after being physically abusive was a picture-perfect example of his arrogance and delusion. He'd phoned from my front porch last Saturday after that abusive encounter as if my attending his brother's engagement party with him was even a possibility. I'd intentionally chosen not to be home. It wasn't about cowardice, but self-protection. Grateful I'd never given him a key—and knowing he'd show up as if everything was fine—for safety's sake I'd gone to Mimi's.

I'd kept my voice level, emotionless. "You'll be attending the event without me, Dominic. This relationship is finished."

"Listen, if you dislike the dress I gave you, put on something else. Just make it quick. I'm standing outside your door and the fundraiser starts in twenty minutes."

"I can't play ignorant games with you, Dominic. You know who and what you are so I won't waste my breath telling you about yourself, except to say you need help—"

"What the hell're you talking about?"

"You understood me perfectly." My mind had flashed on Miss Ona's diary. I thought about her leaving the extravagance of a presidential residence, preferring her freedom. I felt an uncanny sense of connection, and chose to do without the posh offerings of an abusive man. This was *my* flight to freedom. I took a deep cleansing breath and stated my truth. "You're not what I want or need. I choose not to be with you."

"I know you're not trying to ghost me." He'd laughed heartily before cursing up a hot storm, seasoned with expletives when he realized he was the only one laughing. "Do you know who the hell you're screwing with? I'm Dominic Daniels IV, you ungrateful bitch! My family has connections, and I will use every one of them to ensure your business dries up. I can and will make your life more than miserable! That's no threat. It's a promise. Do you understand what I'm saying?"

"Absolutely." I paused a beat. "But if I feel I misunderstood anything, I'll listen to this conversation, seeing as how it's being recorded."

I'm not ashamed to admit that some triumphant kind of thing glittered in me as I paused my phone's memo-recording app to replay part of the conversation for his benefit. It had been Mimi's suggestion, one I wholeheartedly agreed with, and it proved the insurance I needed.

Tense silence enveloped us when I paused the recording in

the middle of his cursing like an evil, drunken sailor. Knowing he wasn't finished, I resumed recording.

"You conniving bitch." His voice was a hot hiss.

"You're entitled to that opinion, but what you're *not* going to do is come for me or my business. Should you choose to, I will use this however I deem fit to protect myself, even if it means involving law enforcement or going public and embarrassing you and your family. Are we clear about *that*?"

"You're a waste of my energy and time."

"And you, mine. I need never hear from you again. Enjoy your life, Dominic."

I'd returned home the next day and gathered up everything he'd ever given me. No amount of designer shoes, purses, or other trinkets could atone for being brutalized and disrespected by someone who should've been caring. I'd dumped all that ish in a huge plastic bin and scheduled a donation pick-up with a local women's shelter. I didn't need material substitutes for being treated with kindness and decency.

The sound of an incoming text pulled me back to the present. I quickly read the message only to realize the unknown number *was* Dominic. It wasn't an apology or acknowledgment of his cruelty, but idiotic drivel and a plea for me to search for some tired-ass cufflink.

> *I wore them to my dad's birthday bash and haven't seen one of them since. Those cufflinks are a custom-made one-of-a-kind heirloom passed down from my great-grandfather, so it's important.*

His text offered a detailed description as if I'd never laid eyes on that twenty-four-carat gold mess. I had, but didn't care. The same way I'd ignored the earlier calls, I deleted this text and focused on Mama C.'s reading, until she stopped suddenly at what sounded like a motorcycle revving in the driveway.

"Lord Jesus, I *know* that boy didn't keep that thing!"

Mimi got up and looked out the front window before opening it and hollering, "Ooo, you're in trouble, B.C.!"

I chose to ignore the warm sensations rolling through me as Mama C. ambled over and snatched the front door open.

"Brandon Thelonius Calloway, did we not agree that you were selling that Harley?"

Mimi scampered out the door behind Mama C. like a mischievous five-year-old thrilled at her big brother's scolding.

Feeling doofus, knowing I wasn't doing a thing except attracting attention to my obvious avoidance, I got up a few moments later intending to head outdoors. I stalled slightly as a text came in. Reading it made my mouth twist. It was Carmel Carter advising she'd been referred by Marlene and would be in touch soon to discuss her needs. I suppressed a naughty thought that her needs likely included a treatment for STDs and went outside to find Mama Calloway perched on the back of a dope-ass Harley, her arms wrapped tightly about her grandson's waist.

"Hurry up and snap the picture, Kimiyah, so I can brag at my next bridge game."

I glanced away from her smiling face to B.C. in jeans, a tee stretched across his wide muscular chest, and aviator shades.

Damn, that man is sexy all day every day.

"'Ey, Tessa, what's poppin'?"

"Not much. When'd you get a hog?"

"I've had it a quick minute but certain people"—he hooked a thumb towards his grandmother—"act like they're about to catch a coronary if I don't get rid of it."

Mama Calloway popped the back of his head playfully. "I told you I'm not scraping my great-grandbaby off nobody's highway."

"Oh, so you're only concerned about Jade, not me?"

"Exactly," she teased. "Now, help me off this thing."

B.C. steadied the bike while Mimi and I helped Mama C. dismount.

She fanned herself with a hand. "That's enough excitement for the day. That thing had my heart racing and we weren't even moving."

"Lightweight," B.C. teased as his grandmother headed towards the house.

"I heard that, little boy. And put your helmet on!"

"So, you're selling it?" Mimi questioned.

"It's sold. I'm meeting the buyer tomorrow."

"Aww, poor baby. Guess you'll have to find a new thrill, like jumping off bridges." Mimi laughed at her joke. "I'm going inside. It's cold."

"'Ey." His palm was rough, yet his touch tender when he reached for my hand as I turned to follow his sister. "Come on, Miss Speed Freak, take my last spin with me. Or are you all soft and sedate in your old age?"

"The shade!" I snatched up the helmet from the back of the bike and put it on before better sense could kick in. Gripping his shoulders, I mounted behind him and settled myself against his broad back. "Hurry up, *old man*, before your grandmother comes out here with a switch."

I actually squealed when he made a U-turn in the wide driveway and took off like the wind.

Decades ago, a children's book author made Chincoteague's wild ponies and the island famous when one her books was adapted for film. Now, thousands of visitors flocked here to see the pony swim and penning each year. Owned by the Chincoteague Volunteer Fire Company, the foals are auctioned annually to maintain population control of these stocky, shaggy creatures with thick manes and round bellies. Seated on the riverbank at the back of his family's property, B.C. and I watched the herd in the distance living their best lives, grazing, cavorting. Penned in on the other side of a shoal, their once abundant numbers were limited to one hundred and fifty, intentionally, but even the smaller herd was awe-inspiring proof of nature's majesty.

"When we were kids, my great grandmother used to tell stories of our ancestors arriving on this island with nothing except a talent for sewing and an affinity with those ponies. The story is that one or more of our ancestors had mad needle skills and was the go-to seamstress on the island way back when. Black folks in Chincoteague are less than half a percent, so I'm still curious how we even got here."

B.C.'s tone was quiet, reverent, after our wild ride from Cape Charles that had me feeling as if I was flying. Carefree. I suddenly didn't have the burden of a failed relationship, or a pending surgery wrapped about my neck. Just the company of my first lover who could perhaps become a friend again.

"Remember when we were in high school how this island used to annoy the hell outta me? It was slow and time-warped, and you couldn't get into anything. Now? When my schedule allows, I ride out here to sit and do nothing but think."

I nodded, understanding. Virginia Tech had an excellent interior design program, but I'd elected to attend Savannah College of Art and Design in Georgia, not merely because it was one of the top design schools in the country, but to see something other than Cape Charles and Chincoteague. Like Brandon, I'd come to appreciate this slow, idyllic place; but I hadn't taken time lately to simply sit and let it speak to me. I'd been too busy building TLS and managing that dysfunctional mess with Dominic. I deeply inhaled the tranquility of my surroundings, determined not to let my disturbing choices depress or shame me.

"It's peaceful out here, B.C." I eyed the dance of marsh grasses swaying in a gentle breeze, and the waters slowly lapping the bank. Their motion was nearly hypnotic, causing my mind to drift until my thoughts fell on Miss Ona. Mama Calloway's ongoing reading of the journal had brought her ancestor to life for me. It was as if she'd morphed from some nebulous phantom figure, to a real *woman*. Each time Miss Ona's journal was read, I was drawn deeper into her life, her story, and felt invested in her wellbeing. I could've easily surfed the internet to uncover what I could myself, but I valued the rare gem that journal presented and preferred being swept up by its content. "What if the diary is authenticated and confirms your family's link to the Washingtons?"

He shrugged indifferently. "I don't necessarily care about confirming some connection with famous white folks, but if that journal's legit then it's like an artifact or something belonging in a museum."

"For real. If it is legit, you'll probably want to get another land evaluation before selling," I gently suggested, wanting to get a glimpse into his headspace.

He rubbed a hand over his face. "My grandmother and her siblings are upset with me and don't agree with my selling the homestead. Like I said before, I'm not tryna be disrespectful. It's just..." He sighed heavily. "The food industry ain't no joke. I'm doing good enough now, but I've bottomed out before. The house probably wouldn't appraise for much and might be better razed than renovated, but the land is worth something. I'm tryna make sure Jade has money for college, and I can take care of my parents and grandparents, plus have a little something to give whenever relatives need help." Leaning forward, he scratched his head before looking at me. "I guess this isn't like selling a Harley. I'd be selling my ancestors' heartaches, triumphs, dreams, and history."

I allowed his sentiments to settle before asking, "Did you read the journal?"

"Not in its entirety. You?"

"Your grandmother is reading it to me." It was mesmerizing. Inspiring. Hearing Miss Ona's struggles made me want to be a better me. "She's shared enough of it for me to gather that your ancestors were all about family."

"What's your takeaway?"

I paused, not wanting to come off as intrusive or preachy. "They likely would've done whatever was necessary to preserve their legacy."

"Yeah... probably." For the longest time he stared at the shoreline before slamming me with, "Why'd you go without me?"

That took me totally off guard. Not merely because of the naked vulnerability in his tone, but because it was unexpected territory we hadn't accessed before. We'd done the volcanic shouting matches, the wild cussing and tearful accusations, and every bitter emotion imaginable at the painful end of what could've been a forever relationship. It seemed as if life and Spirit had gifted us grace and maturity enough to finally *hear* one another. This gentle question wasn't one I'd ever considered. It disarmed my defenses. Still, I took a deep breath and held it to make sure I responded without acrimony.

"I didn't want to be pregnant, B.C. Not then." I listed the things he already knew. I was seventeen. A college freshman. I couldn't disappoint my parents or sabotage my future. Didn't have a job. "You were in college, too." We weren't ready to be parents and couldn't support a child. Plus, I was pure-D petrified.

He took it all in, again, before sitting silently for a minute.

"Listen, I wasn't tryna infringe on your rights or tell you what to do with your body, but it took the two of us to conceive a child, TLS." He held up a hand, stalling my intended protests. "You know I can be slow on the uptake when it comes to processing important things." He exhaled wearily before turning to look at the landscape. "All I'm saying is, I might not've agreed with your decision immediately... but I could've understood eventually and been there for you, if given the chance." His voice broke the tiniest bit. "I hate that you went through that process by yourself."

His confession rolled through me like a sweet summer breeze. It left me speechless, touched by his humility.

"I felt like less of a man for not supporting you, and I regret doing what I did afterwards. But Jade was the result and I wouldn't trade that girl for anything... still, forgive me."

"She's a blessed young lady. You and her mom have done a boss job co-parenting." I surprised myself by reaching over and taking his hand. "You're forgiven. I wish we would've cleared the air and had this conversation a long time ago."

"Yeah, well, obviously neither of us was ready until now. Don't tell her I told you, but Jade started her... you know... cycle last year. Her mom did good in educating her about that stuff, but I had to get up in her space and talk to her from a male perspective. I told that girl she couldn't date until she was forty, and if I found some little punk sniffing around her before then I was going to jail."

I tossed my head back and laughed.

"I'm serious! Jade's gonna be the world's next forty-year-old virgin. Watch and see." He chuckled before quieting. "On the real, those talks with my daughter—making sure she understood she has power and choice and that her body belongs to her— helped me view what happened between us differently. So, yeah, having a daughter's a good thing. The *best* thing."

I squeezed his hand before releasing it, feeling peace instead of the usual sadness that haunted me when considering what could have been.

We're not there anymore. We're here.

We quietly sat, lost in our thoughts until a swift breeze elicited a shiver from me.

"You cold?"

I looked over my shoulder at the house behind us. "That, or Aunt Ona's watching."

He laughed. "I don't do ghosts, so let's just keep it at you're cold."

When he stretched an arm behind me, inviting me to snuggle up against him for warmth, I didn't hesitate. His hug was warm syrup on buttery hotcakes. Grits and shrimp and cornbread. I lay my head on his shoulder and sucked up all that nourishment like a hungry woman coming home to a place where she always should have been and where she was wanted.

FOURTEEN

ONA

March–May 21, 1796, Age 22

"Miss Ona, my split stitch doesn't look like yours. Yours are perfect. Mine are pathetic."

I smiled at Naomi's exaggeration. "They are not pathetic, young lady. They're..." I searched for a description that wouldn't hurt her feelings. "In progress."

The other girls of our sewing circle seated about me, in a room offered by Mother Bethel African Methodist Episcopal church, tittered merrily.

"Now, girls." I wagged an admonishing finger, causing them to tuck their heads and return to their tasks with furtive grins. "Come, Naomi. I'll show you the stitch again."

As she stood beside me, watching in earnest, I had a memory of standing at my mother's side, learning.

I miss you dreadfully.

Going home to Mount Vernon after her passing stripped my spirit bare. I'd learned that the fatigue I'd glimpsed in her was far more pronounced than she'd let on. Her energy had greatly waned, and she often had coughing fits. Her health, like so many others, had been compromised by the demands of endless servitude and dwelling in a drafty cabin. I'd visited Mother's gravesite with my siblings and found myself kneeling in the moist Virginia soil at the foot of her grave weeping inconsolably. Since then, whenever grief hit like a merciless avalanche, I tried soothing myself with the knowledge that, unlike many enslaved children, I'd been blessed to live my life in the light of my mother's love. For that, I was thankful, but it didn't necessarily ease grief. In many ways, Mother's absence left me feeling unbearably incomplete.

"Miss Ona, why're you crying?"

Naomi's soft inquiry caused me to sit up straight and recollect myself.

"I wasn't aware that I was."

Before I could whisk my tears away, Naomi did, her touch tender, innocent.

"Why're you sad?"

Her huge brown eyes were so filled with care that I didn't conceal the truth.

"I miss my mother. She's no longer here."

Another of my sewing circle pupils gasped. "Was she sold? Or stolen?"

Instantly, my class of seven gathered about me with worried countenances.

"No, sweet ones. My mother wasn't stolen or sold. She passed away."

"Oh... we're sorry. I bet she misses you, too, Miss Ona. Guess what? Reverend Allen preaches that the Bible promises a reunion in heaven. That means you'll see your mother again."

When Naomi wrapped her slender arms about me her fellow classmates followed suit, securing me in the center of their sweet consolation.

I am thankful for the FAS granting me such beautiful experiences.

I greatly yearned for my mother after her passing, and was often overcome by sadness. A month after our return, a fortuitous visit from Mistress Abigail Adams, wife of the vice president, resulted in a blessing that helped alleviate that by providing divine distraction.

"Philadelphia's free Negro population is steadily increasing." Mistress sniffed delicately as she, Mistress Adams, and several wives of prominent Philadelphians sat at tea. "It would behoove the city to ensure there is neither idleness nor vagrancy."

"Lady Washington, I wholeheartedly agree. Freedom is no excuse to lollygag or become a public nuisance. They must stay especially busy. Particularly the young."

Standing ready in service to Mistress as always, I listened as Mistress Adams highlighted the virtues of keeping Negro youth busy and, thus, the city safe from "shiftlessness."

"The boys should be engaged in manual labor. Their girls should be trained in skills that aid the genteel women of our community. Such as cooking. Or sewing."

"My Oney is an impeccable seamstress."

I tucked my head even lower at Mistress's compliment.

"I'd consider this new generation fortunate if they possessed even half her skills. I wonder if..."

My hands seemed to clutch tighter together as her voice trailed off the slightest bit.

"I might be able to prevail upon Reverend Osgood's wife to organize a virtuous endeavor such as a sewing circle for free Negro girls. I suppose their dams have taught them the basics, but Oney's skills are nothing short of superior. If she aided Mrs. Osgood the outcome would be exceptional."

Mistress Adams gasped. "But aren't the Osgoods abolitionists? And how ever would you manage without the constant attentions of your maid?"

I peeked up in time to see Mistress lifting her head in a manner that conveyed bravery. "I would suggest that the circle be held no more than an hour or two each week. The President and I must be good examples of charity. Even if my maid's two-hour absence proves a hardship, I will endure for the greater good of our community." Her shoulders gently rose and fell as she continued. "As for abolition, our servants are family. I have no fear of abolitionist heresy poisoning Oney."

As Mistress's concept came to fruition, I found myself delighting in being a help to Mistress Osgood. Not merely for the time away from my duties that it provided, but for the dear-hearted girls whom I instructed. Our circle began with five, but had tripled in size these past few months so that Mistress Osgood determined it best to split the class in half. She taught the older girls in another room, and I this precious crew. Their beautiful spirits softened the ragged void Mother's absence created. This small room at the rear of the church provided a place where I felt safe. Loved. Wanted. Not just needed for requisite acts of servitude sealed with abject obedience. Here, I mattered and belonged, was seen and valued as human.

Mistress Osgood's being an abolitionist worked in other ways, to my advantage. Unbeknownst to Mistress, after the first hour of our sewing circles the reverend's wife invited my girls to join her for Bible lessons, leaving me free to attend the FAS meeting. Our classes were strategically scheduled on the same night as the Free African Society gatherings that Cook had long ago invited me to and that he covertly attended. Now, I was part of such fellowship.

"Come now, girls. I treasure your sweetness, but we must clean up and prepare for your Bible lessons."

"Yes, Miss Ona."

"Don't worry if we take too long and you're late, Miss Ona. I'm sure my mother saved you a seat."

I smiled at Naomi's confidence, thankful, yet again, for the ability to come to her mother, Sister Vashti's, aid the second week of my involvement. In a hurry to a FAS meeting, she'd accidentally snagged and ripped her bodice on a nail head protruding from a hitching post near the church. She'd rushed indoors nearly in tears, clutching her torn garment, trying to escape embarrassment. Several women, myself included, escorted her to a back room where, with the help of the items in my ever-present needle pouch, I'd mended her dress. Her thanks had been effusive, and while she had little, she'd refused to let me go uncompensated. Her giving despite her meager conditions had inspired the parents of my other students to act in kind. The joy of earning even a small sum was great, and I disclosed those earnings to Mistress only because Evilest Eliza was known for snooping in places she had no business. To Mistress's credit, she didn't demand the lion's share as other masters of working bondspersons plying their skills most often did. She allowed me to keep it—same as Uncle Hercules— simply requiring that she count it upon my return to ensure its accuracy.

The blessing of the occasional earning couldn't compare to knowing that I was teaching skills learned from my mother, or the generosity of spirit by which I was surrounded. The Free African Society exceeded my needs when welcoming me with open arms. Admittedly, I was initially hesitant and lingered on the fringes thinking my status as a bondswoman might cause me to be shunned or looked down upon. Instead, I found friendship as sweet as that experienced with Eustis and Callie. In the presence of my new community, I wasn't Oney. Or Mistress's maid. I was Ona Maria Judge. Simply me. Merely one of many who came weekly to hear the truths espoused from the pulpit by Reverend Allen.

Leading Mistress to believe I attended Bible lessons, not FAS meetings, wasn't a complete untruth. Objecting to Negroes being segregated and forced to sit in the balcony at St. George Episcopal, Reverend Allen, a former bondsman, had founded Mother Bethel African Methodist Episcopal church. In that hallowed sanctuary where meetings were now held due to increased membership, I learned of a Creator who wasn't a respecter of persons and tenderly cared for Negroes, not just whites. My heart opened to a message of God's all-encompassing embrace and I encountered peace not previously known. Yet, when Bible lessons concluded I attended the FAS meetings that might have been considered political, revolutionary in tone. But even that couldn't compare to the particular risks I took before each meeting ended.

I promised my mother I'd accept Freedom's hand.

"I doubt she meant that."

"Pardon, Miss Ona?"

"Nothing, Naomi. I was thinking to myself."

"Your thoughts are kind of loud."

I laughed and herded my sewing circle from the room and into the sanctuary like a mother hen with her chicks, remaining at the back as they joined their parents, knowing it would be easier for me to slip away at the appointed time without disturbing others. With great interest, I listened to the news about ongoing work to recover Sister Vashti's husband before seeing Frank Staines excuse himself.

That's my cue.

I waited several minutes before following suit.

Quietly, without drawing attention to myself, I eased from the sanctuary and hurried along a corridor until reaching a rear exit to find Frank seated on a step with a stub of a candle, paper, and a stick of charcoal.

"Let's hurry before the meeting ends. What letter did we leave off on?"

"J," I proudly answered, reciting then writing the letters of the alphabet Frank had taught me thus far. While the FAS offered reading and writing lessons, I was a bondsperson and a resident of Virginia for whom such learning was forbidden. If ever the President or Mistress caught wind of my activities, I never wanted the FAS to suffer because of me. Yet, being around Philadelphia's free Colored population had stirred a hunger in me for mental liberty. My hunger for such freedom was answered when Frank offered to secretly teach me.

Frank had become a dear friend since meeting him and his father, Brother Joshua, the night of the circus that seemed so long ago. With that sunny smile like Delphy's, he was full of encouragement and applauded when I recited and printed my letters with minimal error.

"Ona Judge, soon you'll be writing sonnets."

I laughed, knowing about sonnets because of Miss Nelly's having to learn them. "I doubt that, but there is something I would like to write more than anything. Will you teach me to write my name, please?"

"We haven't reached two of those letters yet, but you're smart as a whip so let's try it."

Moments later when sounds from indoors signaled the meeting was nearing an end, Frank quickly gathered our materials, offering me his handkerchief to clean the charcoal from my hands.

"Thank you, Frank Staines, for believing in me." I hugged him quickly before hurrying back inside ahead of him, as was our routine, before finding Uncle Hercules. I smiled through the after-meeting fellowship complete with refreshments, and all the way home—barely hearing half of Cook's conversation—thanks to the three wonderful letters dancing nonstop in my head.

O-n-a. O-n-a. O-n-a.

"Ona Judge, I doubt you've heard a thing I've said."

I laughed as we neared the presidential mansion. "I apologize, Uncle Hercules. I'm slightly distracted."

"I can see that! Does all this distraction have anything to do with Frank? Don't think I haven't noticed your... affiliation."

I blushed at Cook's inference. "There's no affiliation. At least nothing romantic. I promise," I insisted at his skeptical expression.

"Mmm-hmm, we'll see," he murmured as we entered the residence at Sixth and Market.

I hurried ahead of Uncle Hercules to avoid further interrogation, knowing there wasn't anything remotely romantic about my relationship with Frank, yet curious if my life would ever allow such splendor.

"Thomas Law is twenty years her senior!"

The sound of Mistress's voice coming from the President's study startled me not simply because she should have retired by now, but because her dismay was highly evident.

"And dare I mention this English *gentleman* brings with him his half-caste sons sired with some woman in India? Eliza simply cannot marry him."

I approached the study to see Mistress seated, wringing her hands, and the President pacing.

The President stopped abruptly on noticing me waiting at the entrance. "Yes, Oney?"

"Good evening, sir, I wanted to inform Mistress of my return."

"Why yes... I see. Thank you, Oney." Mistress seemed somewhat distracted when instructing, "Please prepare my nightwear. I'll be up shortly."

"Yes, ma'am." I turned to leave, but not before hearing Mistress voice a fear that perhaps Mr. Law would want to return to his homeland.

"I've lost so much in this world, dear George, that I cannot bear to have my granddaughter living on the other side of the globe."

I mounted the stairs thinking how much nicer life would be without Evilest Eliza's occasional visits. Though her courtship with Mr. Law had been brief that didn't prevent my praying.

Dearest Lord, please let Evil Miss marry Mr. Law and move to England.

My prayer was answered when, despite her grandparents' objections, Elizabeth "Eliza" Parke Custis wed Thomas Law that spring. The months prior to the wedding were tense, filled with Mistress's objections and laments. Understanding how it felt to lose someone precious, I took great pains to show care and compassion.

"Oney, you are forever an indispensable comfort to me. If I've failed over the years to tell you how delightfully helpful you are, I am remiss. You have solaced me on many occasions, and your value is without question. I am appreciative."

Her kind words had been so genuinely spoken that I'd reassured her I was pleased to be of service.

But two months later, like specters in the night, her words boomeranged with haunting hypocrisy that left me distraught, empty.

Unable to attend the March wedding, the Washingtons had invited the newlyweds to honeymoon in Philadelphia that May. Evil Missus Newlywed was too consumed with her new husband to indulge in her usual torment, which left me greatly relieved until I overheard a conversation not meant for my ears one evening.

Mistress had been oddly quiet that afternoon, pensive and moody. Now that night had fallen, she sat at needlepoint with her granddaughters in the salon while the men communed elsewhere. I approached, wanting to know what she wished to wear on our trip home in three days, but froze outside the parlor door when I heard news that terrorized my entire being.

"I still say it's unfair. I wanted Oney for myself!" Miss Nelly's tone was strident, petulant.

"I'm the oldest surviving grandchild, Nelly, and the first to marry. It's only fitting."

"Eliza is correct, dear. She has first rights."

"But Gram-Gram, you're gifting Eliza eighty slaves from her inheritance now while you're living versus after you're deceased. She doesn't need Oney as well."

I pressed myself against the wall, body trembling, breathing jaggedly as understanding cruelly dawned on me. I was to be Evilest Eliza's property?

No, Heavenly One, please!

"But, dear Nelly, she does have need of Oney. Your sister has had a difficult time adjusting to married life and being an instant mother to stepchildren. Oney is a steadfast servant who's capable, efficient, and understands your sister's temperament. She will be of great benefit."

"Gram-Gram, can't you gift Eliza someone else?"

"Nelly, enough protest," Mistress sternly cautioned. "I, too, will miss Oney dearly. She's been of great service to me, but I must share her magnificence now that she is needed elsewhere."

"What if Mr. Law doesn't care for her?"

"My husband, and I quote, thinks her a 'fetching wench and a boon' to me, his beloved."

"And that, Eleanor Custis," Nelly's grandmother concluded, "is the end of this discussion."

I was so discombobulated by what I'd overhead that I forgot my purpose for approaching the salon and fled in the opposite direction.

Heaven, don't let this happen!

Not only would my soul not survive servitude with Evilest Eliza, but I was terrorized by the fact that her husband had fathered children out of wedlock while working in India and would become my master.

Will he use me the same way, for carnal relief?

I managed to reach the rear garden before regurgitating. I heaved, unable to breathe as a molten puddle of tears seared my face and I begged divine intervention to prevent this atrocity from befalling me.

"Ona, what're you gonna do?"

"I don't know, Frank, *but I refuse to be* her *slave!*" My sleep had been restless, riddled with tormenting nightmares. A life of servitude had taken me from the workhouse to Mount Vernon's mansion, to New York and now Philadelphia. My consent was neither needed nor granted. All had transpired without my consideration: enslavement made me obligated. Now, my life was to be uprooted again in ways beyond my comprehension. Desperate to distance myself from the shattering news, the next morning I'd rushed through my errands in town, needing to see my friend.

"How could Mistress discard me so readily? She *knows* her granddaughter's vile distemper, yet she'd pass me on like some wedding gift and make me subject to her heathenish disposition?" All of her praise and claiming I was a comfort was a bunch of hollow nothings. I was unprotected. I hurled a rock at a fence lining the back of the blacksmith shed owned by Joshua Staines, Frank's father, before breaking into jagged weeping.

Frank smelled of sweat and metal from his workday, yet I welcomed his comforting embrace as he led me to a wide tree stump where we sat until I'd collected myself.

"Are you leaving with the Evil One immediately?"

I shook my head while drying my eyes with the heels of my hands. "No. She and her mister are visiting friends before meeting us at Mount Vernon." The Washingtons were yet rotating us out of the state every six months to prevent our freedom under Pennsylvania law. Our packing was nearly finished for our impending departure to summer in Virginia. I shuddered, imagining the mistreatment I'd be subjected to without Miss Nelly or Mistress as buffers between the Evil One and me.

And then there's the husband...

"I can't do it, Frank!"

He waited for another crying jag to end before softly asking, "Is your own packing finished?"

"Nearly."

"Send your belongings here."

I stared at him, strangely. "For what reason?"

"Ona, we both know you can't stay with a woman who relishes treating you as if you're subhuman. You have to leave. You *have* to be free. Get yourself somewhere the Washingtons can't find you. When you leave, you'll need your clothing and other sundries."

I stared at Frank, not in shock, but admiringly. My night had been a tug-of-war between nightmares and sleeplessness during which I'd fantasized about freedom, but never considered I could obtain it. Now, Frank had boldly articulated my longings. His words were a fantastical lift that buoyed me.

"I have to leave..."

He nodded. "It's dangerous but it's either leave or live the rest of your life with tyrants. I've never been involved in something so risky, but my parents can help." He lowered his voice. "They both escaped slavery."

My heart seemingly stopped momentarily, only to gallop into a frenzy as a sweet dream of freedom settled over me. With it came dread. And peace. Still, the idea of fleeing someone as powerful as the President felt doomed, ludicrous. What would happen if I failed?

What will happen if you succeed?

Remembering my promise to my mother and hearing her voice, as if in answer to my fears, I gazed at Frank while silently responding to the question.

I will be free.

Frank and I quickly formulated a plan for hiding my belongings within the free Black community. I divided my personal effects into separate rubbish sacks, tying each with black string before placing them at the back of the presidential residence to be gathered and tossed onto Mr. Raitt's wagon during his normal garbage collection. Not only was he loquacious to the point of distraction, Mr. Raitt was a staunch abolitionist whose wagon housed a false bottom that had helped transport enslaved persons to freedom. Now, it was being used to prevent my belongings being lost or contaminated by the city's refuse as Mr. Raitt went along his normal route.

"Ever sailed a ship, Chef Hercules?"

"No sir, Mr. Raitt, I can't say I have."

"I can't claim to have been captain of anything as grand as the *Mayflower*, but I've sailed a small dinghy or three." He tossed the rubbish sacks onto the wagon, including mine designated with black string. "Being out there on God's waters gives such a sense of *freedom* and wellbeing."

Wanting to be present during the rubbish pick-up to ensure my bags made it onto the wagon, I'd brought rugs from Mistress's room outdoors and made a pretense of beating the dust from them. Unfortunately, Uncle Hercules had chosen to gather herbs for dinner from his small garden. Now, he was entangled with Mr. Raitt.

"In fact, I'm sailing tonight... oh, around eight. Come accompany me, Chef Hercules. God's waters beneath the moon are a majestic sight indeed." He climbed onto the wagon seat with the ease of someone half his age. "Malachi, my fellow congregant who lives not far from the blacksmith, is no longer able to go. That leaves room for one passenger."

Uncle Hercules laughed. "Mr. Raitt, you are kind, sir, but I'm a bondsman who can't come and go as I please."

Mr. Raitt's face reddened. "Pardon my insensitivity. I must be going. My customers need my service and I must always be at the ready, unlike Queen Esther."

"I believe you mean Queen Vashti, sir. She rejected the king's summons to appear. Queen Esther didn't," Uncle Hercules gently corrected, referring to that biblical queen whose actions helped rescue her people from a wicked man's intended slaughter.

"Yes... you are correct. Queen Vashti it was. I take my leave," he sang in conclusion, "for tonight my ship sails with room for one passenger with me." Humming, he stomped his boot in a rhythmic sequence before moving on without once looking my way.

Uncle Hercules waited until he'd gone before chuckling. "Mr. Raitt's a good one, but he's a strange pigeon."

Busy eyeing that wagon retreating in the distance, I didn't respond.

"Ona, you okay?"

I turned in his direction, nodding as he placed a hand on my shoulder.

"There now. Don't fret. Life with that woman ain't never gonna be easy, but you're strong. You'll make it. If it's any solace, by staying in the family you'll have visits to Mount Vernon." He patted my arm before walking away, mistaking my pensiveness for dismay.

I waited until he was indoors before clutching my chest.

That was a message from Frank!

We'd devised a rhythmic code of *one, one, one-two-three*, the same way Mr. Raitt had stomped the floor of his wagon at the end of his little ditty. It was our seal or confirmation when conveying information.

My heart raced as I revisited Mr. Raitt's ramblings, extracting his emphasis and nuances until light and clarity bloomed in me. Tonight, a ship with room for one passenger would be sailing at eight, and I was to go to Sister Vashti's, not the blacksmith shed and Frank's family.

I shivered beneath the warm May sun. This was my choice, my chance. My life, my dignity depended on my next actions, but freedom had come and extended her hand.

"Oney, there are a few more pieces I've decided to take for our summer in Mount Vernon. They're on my bed. Please pack them before you go to dinner. And make sure you're packed yourself. Tomorrow we depart at first light and don't want delays."

"Yes, ma'am."

I walked with Mistress to the dining room and waited until she was properly seated and the family had fully assembled. When I turned to leave, Mistress waylaid me.

"Oney, wait. Please bring my shawl. It's a little cool this evening."

"Yes, Mistress." I hurried from the room, ostensibly to do as instructed, and mounted the stairs as calmly as I could, despite my heart pounding like a drum corp.

Ona, it's now or never!

This was my time and I couldn't risk it by running back and forth fulfilling errands all evening. I'd never defied an order, but I *had* to leave. Bypassing Mistress's room, I hurried along the second-story passage to descend the rear staircase without sentiment for any fond memories I might be leaving. I couldn't weight myself with such things. I had to focus on safely escaping into the new life

I'd be living. Yet, the thought of disappearing without one final farewell with Cook and the others was disheartening. As quietly as I could, I stole along the back corridors until I reached the rear entry where I'd stashed my old hooded cloak to conceal myself from being recognized on the streets. Noiselessly, I slipped from the rear of the house, ten thousand bees swarming in my belly.

Do not look back. This is your only chance.

I was a raw jumble of nerves as I neared the rear alley, only to scream when a hand clamped about my mouth and I was pulled into the shadows.

"*Shh*, Ona! It's me."

I spun about to find Uncle Hercules.

He stared at me incredulously and slowly shook his head. "I couldn't figure it out, but I knew something was off this morning with Mr. Raitt." His voice lowered to a whisper. "You're going?"

Throat tight with emotions, it hurt to speak. "*Please don't say—*"

"I'd rather eat my own tongue than tell these upstairs folks anything."

"Mistress will be looking for me when I don't return with her shawl."

"Don't worry." He laughed, drolly. "I'll do something sacrilegious like burn the rest of dinner to sidetrack them."

Swallowing tears, I laid a hand on his cheek. "I'll never forget you, and will be forever grateful if you'd tell my family I love them for eternity."

He nodded and grabbed me in a crushing hug. We clung together as he whispered in my ear, "Go with God."

FIFTEEN

TESSA

Mr. Ant was a beast. Even with that cabinet-painting situation, he and his crew finished the kitchen renovation in three weeks as projected. The walk-through was complete, Marlene was ecstatic with the end results and had signed off on the project. With the final payment received, I treated Rocki and Mimi to a celebratory lunch before heading home to prepare for tomorrow's surgery. Now, I was on the phone with my mother, discussing last-minute kind of things.

"What time should I pick you up in the morning?"

"Mama, I appreciate that, but it's not necessary. I can take Uber or Lyft—"

"What you can do is be quiet. No child of mine is taking rent-a-ride to the hospital. Hold on, your daddy's interrupting." Mama muted her phone a quick moment before resuming our conversation. "Your father said he can cancel his morning appointment and drive us both."

"Tell Daddy I love him to pieces, but this is female and feminine. I prefer no testosterone, if you know what I mean."

Mama conveyed the message and came back giggling. "He said he likes you least of all his children."

I cracked up laughing. "Lies! I'm his baby and his favorite. I appreciate you offering to drive." Admittedly, I was nervous and could use Serenity Scott's calming presence. "Can you be here by eight?"

"Of course. I'll bring an overnight bag."

"Mama, it's an outpatient procedure."

"I'm aware of that, Tessa Lorraine. If it's alright by the Queen of Everything, I plan to stay overnight just to make sure you're fine."

"Yes, ma'am. Since you'll be here, will you make me some red beans and rice?"

"Little girl, you're getting chicken broth and saltines."

"Come on, Mommy. *Puhleeez.*"

"*Mommy?* You're laying it on thick." She hesitated. "I'll think about it. But if I do, those beans are going in the freezer until Dr. Latimore says you can have solid food. See you in the morning. Love you."

"Love you, too, best mother ever." Disconnecting and daydreaming of red beans, I ignored an incoming call from an unknown number thinking it might've been my ex with whom I hadn't exchanged communication other than to confirm what he already knew: that we were *finit.* Yesterday's history.

That was two weeks ago and, thankfully, I hadn't heard from him since. Still, every now and again, random 'unknown number' calls rolled in. Initially, I'd had concerns that this could become some kind of obsessive, stalking situation. I couldn't take my safety for granted, and always had my mace or pepper spray when out and about in case of a confrontation—and was even open to, if need be, filing for a restraining order. Fortunately, nothing further occurred. Perhaps, other than these stupid calls from unrecognizable phones, he meant what he said when he called me a waste of his energy.

"All he wants is that damn missing cufflink."

I'd searched my room but hadn't found it yet. And if I did I wasn't sure if I'd return it or donate it to an unhoused person to pawn and put a little sumpin'-sumpin' in the pocket.

Grinning at the idea, I resumed a task I'd meant to accomplish before my mother called.

Honey, when the devil gets to acting up and you wanna run his ugly behind outta your house, burn some sage.

I turned on some ambient chakra music Mimi was into before lighting a bundle of sage purchased at one those holistic crystal places. The smoke had me coughing, but I persisted in going room to room, purging my dwelling of Dominic and his demons. More than purging *him*, I was clearing the path to reconnecting to me again.

I'd sacrificed common sense and willingly ignored the universe and her kind nudges to pay attention. To not devalue myself. And for what? Because he was from old money, an upper echelon family that possessed power in our community? Because I looked good on his arm, and he was fine next to me? The lavish trips, and being "prized" by an older man as if I had some absentee daddy complex when I had a loving father who adored me? Waving my bundle of exorcising herb, I was aware that some might argue I didn't fit the profile of a woman "targeted" by an abuser. I wasn't exactly submissive, had decent enough esteem, financial independence, and came from an intact family. I had, however, allowed myself to become isolated from people I love, and been totally immersed in Dominic's kingdom. Perhaps that right *there*—the profiling and classifying —was the danger and the lesson. I understood the value of identifiers, but I was a prime example of someone who'd excused herself, or who might be overlooked for failing to check off all the "abused woman" boxes. I didn't *feel* like a victim, had never phoned law enforcement during Dominic's tirades, yet I'd lived and survived abusive situations.

Well, damn.

A tear escaped as I allowed that truth before recommitting

to family, journaling, self-awareness, and finding a life coach who could help me rediscover Tessa.

Sorry, Nana, but this sage is giving me a headache.

Extinguishing the smoking bundle, I tossed an oversized pillow on the floor, intending to do as Mimi recommended: sit in a lotus pose and center myself. Thank God, the doorbell rang before I could twist my uncoordinated self into a knot of pain. Grabbing my pepper spray, just in case, I headed for the door, squinted through the peephole, and wound up smiling.

"Hey, B.C. Why're you here?"

"I'm good, thanks, T. You inviting me in?"

I grinned and stood aside so he could enter. Since our motorcycle ride the week before, we were easing into friendship. We called. Texted. I enjoyed being open with him again, but we weren't on the road to romantic. He was a busy girl dad with restaurants demanding his time. For me, that was fine. After Dominic, I needed to tend to Tessa.

That doesn't mean I don't have eyes.

I did, and the man was sexy fiyah and fine!

"'Ey, I can't stay. Just wanted to drop this off real quick." He handed me a rectangular gift-wrapped box and coughed. "Dang, girl, whatchu smoking up in here?"

"I was burning sage."

"It smells like Eau de Snoop Dogg air spray."

"Whatever, B.C. What's this?"

"A gift."

"I can see that." Remembering how trinkets from my ex had allowed me to compromise my authentic self, I decided I wouldn't accept whatever was inside, but then I opened the box and discovered a pair of fuchsia work gloves with black velvet trim and thick black suede palms. They were adorable, but my logo embroidered in gold metallic thread was the absolute business. "Oh, my gawd! Where'd you get these? Fuchsia is my favorite color."

"I know, and I don't reveal my sources. I peeped those ugly-ass, old-man gloves you had hooked at your waistband the day I fed your crew. I was like, 'Naw, man, your girl needs some help right around the hands. Those *ain't* the business.'"

I laughed so hard I snorted.

"That was ladylike, TLS."

"I know, huh? Hold this." I gave him the box and tried on the gloves. The fit was perfect. "I refuse to use these for demolition. They're too ca-*ute!*" I kissed his cheek. "Thanks, B.C."

"You're welcome. Thought I'd give them to you today... just in case."

He was aware of my pending procedure without knowing the nature of it. "In case I don't make it?"

"That's not funny, T., so quit playing. I wanted you to have them so you know work and good things are waiting on you."

"Including you?"

He grinned that sexy, lopsided grin that used to make my stomach flip—and still did. "I'll check on you in a day or two. Just know I got you." He pressed his hands together and bowed his head in a gesture of prayer before turning and exiting.

Locking the door behind him, I lifted my gloved hands in admiration, finding them one-thousand percent sweeter than anything received from my ex. It wasn't fair, but there was *zero* comparison.

"God, thank You for giving me back my friend."

I was cheesing like a clown when a text arrived.

Here're my boudoir pics. I'd like a remodel estimate by tomorrow.

"Carmel Carter..."

No "hello, negro." Just straight to what she wanted.

Marlene had given her my number. Now, she was texting pics of a bedroom that looked like a cheetah convention. Headboard. Linens. Lampshades. Throw rug and pillows. You name it: cheetah print was on it.

"Lawd, even the nightstands?" I zoomed into a nightstand featuring leather animal print drawers and a black lacquer top. "That's just... *wrong*."

That room needed an intervention, but I wasn't the woman for it. All money wasn't good money, and I had a feeling working with Carmel would be far from satisfying. I was about to send a preformatted message declining the job when something shiny atop the nightstand caught my eye. I zoomed in again to see a gold cufflink with an imprinted D.D.

I wore them to my dad's birthday bash and haven't seen one of them since.

"Whoop, there it is."

That missing cufflink, bearing the initials of all the Dominic Daniels since my ex's great-grandfather, provided proof that Dominic *had* gone home with Sex in a Dress that night. Whether or not Carmel staged the pic so I'd see it didn't matter. The truth was, he'd been there.

"Girl, you're welcome to him."

Sending my preformatted decline text, I deleted Carmel's message and added her to the blocked number cache, preventing further communication. It wasn't unprofessional. It was a move to protect my peace, and I deserved that.

My procedure revealed stage two, or mild, endometriosis with a build-up of scar tissue. Thankfully, Dr. Latimore was able to remove the damaged tissue as well as a cyst in its infancy and send it to pathology. I was in and out of surgery and back home that evening, bloated from the gas that had been inserted into my abdomen to aid the camera's view, and a bit achy and slightly loopy—but otherwise good.

"Tessa, are you ready for soup?"

"No, ma'am. I'm ready for ribs, fried chicken, and candied yams." On doctor's orders, I'd been unable to eat twenty-four hours before surgery. Now, I was sprawled on the sofa, an ice pack on my abdomen, starving. "Oh, and collard greens and hot water cornbread."

Mama laughed. "You're restricted to a liquid diet for the next two days, so soup it is."

The doorbell rang as Mama headed for the kitchen. When she opened the door, a herd of happiness rushed in. Mimi, Jade, Rocki, and her daughter, my four-year-old niece Kennedy, came in bearing balloons, a huge teddy bear, and sleeping bags.

"Auntie Tessa, we're here!" Kennedy raced towards me, stopping only when Rocki reminded her to be careful not to hurt my "owie." She gave me a tender hug and kiss filled with all the love she could give.

"What's all this?" I asked, eyeing my sunshine regime.

"It's a sleepover," Kennedy sang. "We came to keep you company."

"Hi, Ms. Tessa. Daddy sent this." Jade walked over with a large pot in a cardboard box. "It's his homemade chicken soup."

"Yass, huntee! I need a bowl like yesterday."

"*Now* you suddenly want soup?" Mama had her hands on her hips, playing indignant.

I gave my mother wide, innocent eyes like that cat from *Shrek*.

She pursed her lips. "Come on, Miss Jade, let's take that into the kitchen."

Minutes later, surrounded by my best women, I greedily devoured soup seasoned with gourmet love—appreciating the company and camaraderie as we watched animated movies. I pouted as everyone else munched popcorn and Mama's triple chocolate chunk cookies. I offered Kennedy and Jade twenty dollars to sneak me a cookie, but those little traitors outed me instead of accepting the money. I laughed at Mama's fussing that I was devious for trying to hoodwink the innocent, knowing I was loved. Cherished.

As the night progressed and the kids fell asleep and we switched to PG-rated movies, I felt the sweetest contentment and wellbeing surrounded by loved ones by choice and blood.

I wonder if Miss Ona felt this kind of inclusive peace when connecting with Philadelphia's free Black community?

Mama Calloway's including me in the story-sharing meant a lot to me, and I found Miss Ona's journal an invaluable treasure offering indescribably intimate glimpses of the past that shouldn't be forgotten. I was inspired and humbled by their young, enslaved ancestor who'd endured and overcome more in life than anyone ever should and I ever would. I studied my wrist, remembering the bruises. I would never be so arrogant as to compare my story to hers, but I recognized similar abuse in my issue with Dominic and Miss Ona's relationship with the Washingtons. Particularly Martha and Eliza. It was physical. Tangible. She'd dared to flee that, and the scarring that slavery inflicted on her soul and psyche.

Miss Ona, if I have your courage when I grow up, I'ma be real good.

I glanced at Mimi, my BFF since the days of sitting in fireplaces, and knew she hated being sworn to secrecy. But if Daddy, Rico, B.C., or my herd of male cousins found out about how I'd been treated, my ex's pic would be on the back of a milk carton. She didn't agree with my silence, but she supported me. In time, perhaps I'd share with Mama and Rocki. Right then, I chose to sunbathe in the light of all this love. For the first time since getting with my ex, I felt balanced. Free. And completely like me.

SIXTEEN

ONA

1796–1799, Age 22–25

The night I escaped is forever etched in my memory. It was terrifying and I constantly feared discovery, severe punishment, or being sold for absconding. Still, I fled, fueled forward by the bitter reality of the bondage behind me.

Keeping to the shadows, jumping at every sound, I followed Frank's coded message and swiftly made my way to Sister Vashti's to find him and Brother Staines waiting. Without her husband present to help provide a living, Sister Vashti and Naomi existed in a tiny, damp rented room near the dock. As Naomi was part of the sewing circle, if I was seen there my presence wouldn't seem suspicious. As Naomi slept, we four adults clasped hands while Joshua Staines quietly yet fervently prayed for my safe passage to freedom.

Our goodbyes were tearful. My heart ached leaving loved ones behind once again, but I couldn't reverse my decision. Nor did I desire to. "Thank you all for your kindness. Heaven be with you."

With one final hug I slipped into the night with only Brother Joshua.

Frank had begged to accompany us, but his father had been adamant.

"Son, if you're ever questioned you may honestly answer you've no knowledge where Miss Ona went. You were born free. I'm a man who escaped slavery. Let me take the risk and any consequences."

It was dark and a short distance from Sister Vashti's home to the docks, yet it felt as if an eternity passed with Brother Joshua taking a circuitous route to confuse others and escape notice. Lying flat in the blacksmith's wagon, hidden beneath strewn hay, barely able to breathe, I prayed every inch of that journey until the wagon halted behind a series of buildings. I remained where I was as instructed while he quickly retrieved a carpetbag someone had donated to carry my belongings and that had been hidden on the docks in advance.

"Your passage has been paid." Brother Joshua aided my descent and pressed a ticket into my hand.

He refused when I attempted to reimburse him from the sewing-circle earnings I'd saved and stashed inside my needle pouch, now sewn in the hem of my dress so it could not be lost.

"I'm a free man because others helped me. The FAS purchased your ticket. My brother, Jack Staines, is aboard this ship and will help you from here. Go in peace."

His was the last familiar face I saw before being rushed aboard the *Nancy*, a ship captained by John Bowles and bound for Portsmouth, New Hampshire. I was instantly approached by a sailor aboard the ship and rushed so swiftly below deck that I was breathless. Locked in an unlit tiny cupboard of a space, I clutched that carpetbag against my chest, afraid to breathe as if breath itself might betray me and my hiding place. I rocked back and forth, fearful I'd been seen or that Mistress had already noticed my absence and had begun searching for me. What would happen if such was the case? Would an alarm be raised and the city searched? Would those who'd aided me be faced with dreadful penalties?

The mere thought of others suffering caused me to regret not giving more thought to my escape, for planning with such haste. How I wished I could have done as Joseph's brothers had in the Bible days when selling him *into* slavery. They'd ripped and stained his precious robe of many colors with animal blood, claiming he'd been lost to wild beasts in order to cover their heinous actions. I'd left no such diversions, and prayed Uncle Hercules had managed a mighty distraction.

Mother, help me, please!

I pressed my face into my carpetbag to prevent my weeping from being heard on deck. I was a stowaway, an escaped slave, and could not draw attention to myself. Yet the sudden ocean of loneliness and fear threatening to drown me pulled body-racking sobs from my chest.

Quiet yourself, my sweet black-eyed butterfly.

Hearing my mother's voice, my head sprang up. I sensed her presence so keenly that I peered about the darkness expecting her to appear. Instead, her calming spirit fell on me like soft Virginia snow, and I was no longer alone. The nearness of Mother's spirit soothed my soul, decreased my distress, and I found myself giving thanks mere moments later when the ship lurched into motion. I sorely wished for a window through which to watch the Philadelphia shoreline fade into the distance but could only call upon my imagination as the ship set sail, leaving my captors behind, and taking me on a voyage towards life.

I am uncertain how much time passed, but I drifted off and was jarred awake by the sound of the door being unlocked. I sprang to my feet, squeezing that carpetbag like a weapon as a man entered. In the dark, his silhouette was tall, formidable.

"Grace and peace, miss." His voice was hushed, secretive. "Come with me, please."

My movements awkward, stiff after my tight confines, I struggled to match his long stride while following him to a ladder leading upward.

"May I?" He extended a hand towards my carpetbag.

With a shake of my head, I declined. Apart from my needle pouch, all my remaining worldly possessions were in that bag. Unable to part with it for even one second, I awkwardly climbed the ladder with it in my grasp until I reached the top deck, only to pause when greeted by the faintest hints of dawn.

I stood a long moment taking in the salty ocean air and the pale-pink hues on the horizon of my first morning of freedom.

"I imagine you're hungry or perhaps need the privy, Miss Ona?"

I spun about, alarmed. I'd agreed with Brother Joshua's sound advice to conceal my identity aboard the ship, yet this man knew me.

"No need to be afraid. I'm Frank's uncle, Joshua's younger brother, Jack Staines."

My body relaxed, yet I seemed unable to stop staring at Mr. Jack. He was tall and solid with the sturdiness of a man often at sea. Just the same, he was the most beautiful Colored man I'd ever laid eyes on and I quickly looked down, embarrassed for staring. I was silent as he showed me to the place where I could relieve myself before inviting me to sit with him in a small alcove where I was served gruel and smoked fish for breakfast. There was nothing fancy in such fare, but my first meal in freedom was a feast I'll always remember.

I looked up when he laughed.

"That's likely a far cry from what you're accustomed to at

the presidential palace, but you sure made good on it. Would you like more?"

I smiled at my empty bowl. "Yes, please."

He returned a moment later with more for himself as well. Thanking him, I resumed eating, realizing I hadn't had supper the day before. I'd been consumed with fleeing. Now, I was aboard a ship to liberty. Soft contentment drifted over me, and I looked up only to find myself lost in the stare of the man with me.

He leaned towards me. "That smile there could light the night."

I blushed at his observation and looked away. "Where are we?"

"We've cleared the Delaware and are on the Atlantic Ocean. Portsmouth is several days ahead, but we have bright skies and a good wind. We'll make it without incident. Are you cold? Would you like a wrap or blanket?"

"I'm fine, thank you." Closing my eyes and lifting my face towards the early-morning sky, I inhaled the salty scent of the ocean, remembering what my mother once said about bodies of water being magical for those who were stolen and brought over on them. Now, this vast ocean buoyed my journey to freedom. "I would have been up for hours by now, busy preparing for the day, in the President's house."

"What was it like, being in service to the Washingtons?"

I looked at him and intuited only concern, not itching ears for gossip or salacious knowledge. Perhaps his apparent kindness and the fact that I was barely emerging from a harrowing experience prompted my divulging to him the past I'd fled.

We talked for what felt like years. I not only told him my story, I asked for his. I learned that he'd purchased his freedom years before and had been sailing with Captain Bowles ever since.

"Miss Ona, looks like the crew is up and moving."

I looked about, noticing others for the first time since coming on deck. "I've kept you from your duties. I apologize."

"I can't think of a better way to have been kept. Let's get you to your lodgings," he quickly offered when I lowered my head bashfully. "It's better than where you were last night, but not by much. At least there's a bed so you can get some real rest."

"On a voyage of freedom, even a brick will sleep like a dream."

Something tingled softly within me when he laughed, causing me to blush as I followed him to the small holding that would be my cabin.

"It's intentionally away from the others. You're free to move about as you wish, but be cautious. Remember to keep your identity to yourself to prevent opportunistic people from ruthlessly misusing that knowledge to their advantage. We'll be stopping at several ports along the way. When we do, it may be best for you stay in your cabin."

"I understand, Jack. In case there are slave-catchers looking for me."

He nodded gravely.

Placing my carpetbag on the floor near a narrow slip of a bed, I smiled up at him. "Thank you for helping me, and for your companionship."

Touching the brim of his cap, he departed, leaving me to my unadorned accommodations.

Sitting on the hard, narrow bed, I considered my cramped surroundings. The cabin was a far cry from the comforts of the presidential mansion, but this was the first place I'd ever had to myself, and that alone made it splendid. Folding my hands in prayer, I asked wellness over my family and gave thanks for all who'd aided me—including Captain Bowles and Jack Staines, a kind, sweet-eyed sailor who'd shown himself friendly and was no longer a stranger.

. . .

Arriving in Portsmouth, New Hampshire was akin to entering heaven by virtue of it being the first place my feet landed as a free woman. The old streets and markets felt fresh, exciting, and I approached wide-eyed, having thanked Captain Bowles and vowed to never betray his name before disembarking with Jack Staines.

"Ona, please remember caution is key."

New England was largely hostile towards the human chattel system and home to many abolitionists. Slavery had been legally abolished in New Hampshire several years back, but that did not mean its residents were fully favorable towards Blacks. Additionally, there was the Fugitive Slave Act of 1793— which allowed the seizure and return of runaway slaves—to contend with.

"I'll be careful, Jack," I promised as he prepared to leave the residence of Elmer and Prudence Kraft, a free Black family offering sanctuary. They were abolitionists with rifles for protection and the utmost discretion; but it was Mrs. Prudence's mannerisms, so like my mother's, that made me feel secure.

"Frank will correspond with you when safe to do so. I mean no offense, but can you read?"

I tucked my head shyly. "Frank was teaching me."

Placing a finger beneath my chin, he lifted it. "Let Mrs. Prudence help you and you'll be reading like the wind. I have to hurry back to the *Nancy*. We're sailing for Vermont shortly. I'll call on you when we return. With your permission, of course."

"I'd like that. A lot."

When he kissed my hand and departed, something tightly coiled inside of me gently opened and dared to bloom and breathe.

. . .

Life in New Hampshire proved pleasantly uneventful, but to me it was exciting, invigorating. I was never lazy; labor had been ingrained in me. Still, I slept in well past dawn just because I could, and experienced a little thrill whenever I did. Earning my board and keep by aiding Mrs. Prudence about the house and taking in sewing or doing domestic work elsewhere, I quietly made friendships within Portsmouth's small, free Black community, and even attended church services where I accepted Christianity. But my favorite pastime was sitting with Mrs. Prudence as she taught me to read and write.

I've never tasted anything as sweet as freedom.

I retired to bed one evening with that delicious thought informing my dreams only to encounter the beginnings of a nightmare the next day.

"Ona, this is for you."

I paused my darning to find Mrs. Prudence extending a small envelope. I was puzzled until I remembered Jack saying Frank would be corresponding.

"The outer envelope was addressed to me for safety's sake. Please let me know if you require help with any of the words."

"Yes, ma'am." Joy raced through me as I rushed to my room and ripped the envelope open to find a letter from Frank as expected. I read slowly, sounding out unknown words to the best of my ability. There were several beyond my comprehension, yet I understood the overall missive. "Advertisements were placed in the *Daily Advertiser* and *Philadelphia Gazette* two days after I left?"

It was reported that I'd absconded without provocation, perhaps enticed away by a Frenchman. Physical descriptions of me as "slender and delicately formed with very black eyes and bushy black hair" had been provided and it was warned that, because of the quality of my clothing, I might be passing as a free woman. Reportedly, the President was livid and Mistress couldn't fathom why I'd possibly leave when I was treated like a beloved daughter and not a slave. I was insulted to read that there was a ten-dollar reward for my return.

Is that my worth?

I'd served the Washingtons since my earliest days of gathering kindling, carting water, and helping in the nursery, and was unable to list the innumerable chores and tasks I'd performed since. Anger coursed through me until reading that while there was no evidence, Uncle Hercules had been suspected of aiding me and knowing my whereabouts. His protests of innocence fell on deaf ears and he was severely beaten. That left me crying molten tears.

Fearing someone would recognize me and wish to claim the reward on my head, I limited my ventures outdoors after that, feeling like a desperately hunted animal. I continued my lessons with Mrs. Prudence and didn't breathe easily again until Jack returned several weeks later and came to dinner. There was something remarkable, solid, and steady in him that lured me to a soft place of security that I couldn't recall feeling since I was a child too young to understand the life I was meant to live. He was handsome. Honest. Kind and charming. More importantly, he was a free man fiercely devoted to protecting his liberty, and now mine. He instructed me on safe houses in and beyond the city that I could escape to if ever there was a need. I was saddened when he set sail again, but thrilled when he didn't kiss my hand in farewell, rather my cheek.

God is with me.

Such was my daily mantra. And one I believed, only to have my faith tried once more when I heard my name called one day, two months later, on the streets.

"Oney?"

Pure terror shot from my head to my feet, knowing that was a name only upstairs folks used when addressing me. Rather than search for whomever had hailed me, I turned and ran, grateful for the crowded street, finding shelter in a tight space between two buildings. Pressing myself in the shadows, my heart thundered as I heard the party nearing.

"I swear before heaven that was Oney! It had to be."

"Come along, dear, we've lost her and can't do anything save inform Lady Washington."

Recognizing the voice of the first woman, I remained in my hiding place the longest time, thankful to have escaped Miss Elizabeth Langdon, Miss Nelly's classmate and friend.

Not long after, I learned the woman with Miss Elizabeth had, indeed, made good on her promise.

"This way to Mr. Whipple."

"Yes, ma'am." Nervously, I followed Joseph Whipple's housekeeper as she led me to his study, hoping he would find me suitable for employment. I'd made my willingness to work known to others in my community and considered Mr. Whipple's summons to interview with him a blessing.

"Come in, child. Don't linger by the door."

Doing as instructed, I proceeded into a study that seemed somehow neat yet cluttered with a plethora of objects, large and small.

"I understand you're in need of a position?"

"Yes, sir."

"What experience have you to offer?"

"I was—" I caught myself before blurting my past enslavement. "I can clean, sew, and I've been a lady's maid."

"That's why you're here. As we are both aware, my wife is in need of a maidservant. Was your service as a lady's maid rendered here in New Hampshire?"

"No, sir... elsewhere."

"Would I be able to obtain a reference?"

I shifted nervously and had to still my hands from fluttering. "I fear not, sir. My lady and I have lost contact."

"I see." He toyed with a paperweight atop his desk while peering intensely at me. "I gather by your accent that you are not from New Hampshire. Is that correct?"

I nodded.

"How long have you been here and where are you from? Do you have family? A beau? Or husband? Are you married?"

A subtle unrest prevented me from responding and I lapsed into silence at the insistent, increasing intimacy of his inquiry.

He sipped from the teacup on his desk. "Were you born a free woman? Or did you acquire freedom through other means?" His inquiries were too personal in nature and had nothing to do with the position. Each rolled from his lips with a forcefulness that made me suspicious. "Have you ever resided in Philadelphia? Or Virginia? Have you ever entertained a French suitor?"

The walls of the room seemingly pushed towards me, squeezing, suffocating. I couldn't respond for falling into a terrorized silence. This Mr. Whipple had not summoned me to interview. His was the interrogation of someone seeking to confirm my identity. My heart galloped painfully as he lay aside the paperweight he'd been fiddling with and lifted a sheet of paper from which he began to read what I already knew to have been reported.

"Very black eyes... delicately formed... she abandoned the President's house, perhaps been abducted by a Frenchman..."

When he stopped suddenly and peered at me, I cast my eyes downward in fear.

"Are you the Oney Judge of whom this speaks?"

I wanted to turn and flee, to wail for my being duped into appearing before this man of ulterior motives, but I knew my actions would be futile. I was a fugitive, a bondswoman. Power wasn't mine, but his. Yet, despite the fear-filled darkness wishing to consume me, I managed the courage to quietly speak. "My name is Ona Judge. Not Oney."

"Indeed. We now know each other's identities, but are you aware that I am a customs collector and that my services have been enlisted by the President?"

I clasped my hands in front of me to still their quaking, but said nothing.

"I've been asked to collect and return *you* to Mount Vernon."

My whole body shivered with dread, and I suddenly longed for Jack.

"However... I wish to assist you."

My amazement was supreme on hearing of Mr. Whipple's eagerness to help gain my emancipation from the Washingtons. *Eventually.* "They are both irate and devastated by this inconceivable deception, but I will do all within my power to negotiate your freedom. It is such a delicate matter that I must ask you to show goodwill by returning with me to Mount Vernon."

I was suddenly nauseous, knowing that returning to Virginia would never be in my best interests. Still, Mr. Whipple persisted with countless pleas and persuasion.

"I want this to be neither difficult nor physical."

With Portsmouth being home to many abolitionists, and possessing abolitionist tendencies himself, Mr. Whipple refused to use force, fearing the backlash and embarrassment such an abduction might cause himself and the President. Short of carrying me bodily, he did everything in his power to convince me to meet him at the docks and board the next ship bound for Philadelphia.

The situation was wholly exhausting. I felt heavy beneath the weight of my vulnerability and knew I could not ward off recapture if imposed on me, bodily. I could only pray Mr. Whipple was an honorable man of his word and would not force me to leave. Yet, he was in service to the President and would not cease in his persistence.

The truth of my vulnerability fell on me. I knew I could never return to Mount Vernon, yet in that instance I was hard-pressed to find a solution. All I could think to do was compromise, even if it was a lie, simply to bring the torturous interview to an end. "I will return only if they promise to free me upon their demise. Otherwise..." I inhaled deeply and shook my head, knowing I'd never do as he or the President wanted. I simply needed time to think, to find a way to escape this new predicament. I preferred death over slavery or being *given* to *any other* person.

Thoughts of Jack and the love I was forfeiting filled my mind as Mr. Whipple instructed me on what day and at what time to meet him at the dock. When he finished, I rushed from his residence, stumbling into the streets, my steps laden and uncertain. Arriving at the home of the Krafts, I hastily packed my carpetbag and was shortly headed elsewhere to *my* destination.

I cannot, will not go back.

When Mr. Whipple arrived on the docks on the designated day and time, he did not find me there. I'd defied the orders of upstairs folks for only the second time in my life and chosen myself and my wellbeing. I took refuge at another safe house and stayed there until certain the threat had passed. My actions that day birthed in me a wondrous boldness that was delightfully shocking, liberating.

Know your enemy.

Cook said that long ago. It haunted and helped me then. I knew the Washingtons. They would not allow themselves to be bested by a Negro wench, and I accepted that my life might be a series of flights and risks. Freedom might require my being constantly alert and overly cautious, but that was a small price to pay when compared with the alternative. I would do whatever was necessary to never be in bondage again—to keep my present from reconnecting with my past.

Daily, I thanked heaven for grace and cautiously lived my life as a free woman. It was not without trials and tribulations. I remained in Portsmouth at the home of the Krafts, taking in sewing as well as hiring myself out as a maid to earn my living. I aided Mrs. Kraft in her domestic chores to reduce my lodging expenses. I often fell asleep at night more exhausted than I'd ever been. Yet, if offered a fine bed in bondage I'd decline for the fatigue found in freedom. My life was simple, yet complex. My safety was a constant care, as was my longing for my beloveds. Still, I found myself laughing freely and embracing my new existence and even discovering love with Jack Staines.

He was a kind-hearted man who helped me laugh and dream, and encouraged me to bravely embrace my new liberty. In his presence I felt safe, protected, and I missed him dreadfully when he was gone at sea, relishing his every return, not to the mention the flowers and sweets he never failed to bring. I loved walking along the wharf with him, my hand snuggled in the crook of his arm as we shared confidences, or merely enjoyed the sweetness of each other's silence. He was companion, friend, and the man I discovered love with. When he asked for my hand in marriage, I ecstatically accepted and we exchanged vows that following January. But even our becoming man and wife was not without obstacles.

Our application for a marriage certificate encountered innumerable delays in the hands of Portsmouth's clerk. After many attempts at resolution, we learned of Mr. Whipple's interference. Having caught wind of our pending nuptials, the collector had disclosed to the town's clerk my true identity. The clerk was unwilling to offend the nation's leader by aiding us in any way, and created so many barriers and hindrances that our license became impossible to obtain. Determined to have a legal union, Jack and I journeyed to the neighboring town of Greenland and obtained our certificate so that we might be joined together, properly, in the sight of God and man.

I never imagined the bliss of loving a man so freely. Our union did not require a master's permission, merely our mutual desire and divine connection. He carried me across the threshold the day we were wed, allowing us to enter a dynamic oneness that was so sweet it put my teeth on edge. I'd sometimes awaken at night to ensure Jack wasn't a dream, only to settle myself by running my hands over his hard planes as he slumbered beside me. I was my beloved's. He was mine. We shared a union blessed by heaven.

Ours was a small dwelling that I took great pains to keep clean and tidy. I loved picking wildflowers from a nearby field and arranging them in a glass on our small mantel to add colorful cheer. I was no great cook like Uncle Hercules, but I'd managed to learn enough from Mrs. Kraft that our meals were satisfyingly delicious. We leased the spare room at the back to a boarder to generate income, and so that I'd have company during those seasons when Jack was gone. It wasn't stately like the mansions I'd lived in while enslaved by the Washingtons, yet I put every energy into making it a sweet place for us. Each time Jack returned from sea, I made sure he was greeted with delicious meals and generous love.

"Were there any incidents while I was away?" he would always ask. Since that encounter with Mr. Whipple, he worried that something might happen to me in his absence.

"No, love. There weren't."

"You remember where to go if anyone comes for you?"

I rattled off the locations of the safe houses he'd drilled into me, ending with, "Or Nancy Jack up in Greenland." I liked the idea of going to her if the need ever arose simply because her name combined my ship of freedom and my husband.

Jack nodded, pleased. "There's another place I want you to consider. It's a tiny island, Chincoteague in Virginia—"

"*Virginia!* Why in heaven's name would I go *back* to Virginia to escape? That's the last place I'd want to be."

"Precisely! No one would expect you to return to a place of enslavement and hide in plain view. But only as a last resort, and just long enough to throw off any pursuers." He quietly described the island he'd learned about on his voyages. "It's a wild strip of an island overlapping Maryland and Virginia. It's not used for much besides livestock grazing and wild ponies, and not much inhabited. Anyone there is more interested in those ponies than your past." That had benefited runaways who'd camped there long enough to throw off their captors. "There're other safe houses closer to here. Just keep that one in the back of your bonnet."

"I will. Jack Staines?"

"Ma'am?"

"Do you love me more than you do the sea?"

We were sitting on the low end of the dock, barefooted, our feet trailing lazily in the water as we admired the sun setting in the distance. We often came to this place, this port where I first landed as a new, free woman. Even when Jack was away at sea, I'd sit there occasionally, imagining him wherever he was and wishing him back to me.

"Jack?"

He slowly rubbed his chin. "Hold on. I'm thinking..."

I socked his shoulder before playfully pouting. "You're terrible, Jack Staines!"

He gathered me against his strong chest and kissed my neck. "I suppose I love you best. The sea smells a little bit." His grip tightened about me when I tried to stand and flounce off. "Be still, little missy. You can't get away from me."

"Neither do I want to," I admitted, lying my head against his chest over the place where, when enslaved, he'd been burned with a searing-hot branding iron bearing his former master's crest. At night when we lay in bed, I often rubbed the raised, black skin wanting to soothe any trauma it might have retained. "Thank you, love, for my candlesticks. They're gorgeous."

He'd returned from his most recent voyage bearing two candlesticks of solid silver.

He shrugged, as was his custom whenever I gushed over anything he'd given me. "Just wanted you to have something special to light the room while you practice your penmanship."

"I can't believe how much I've learned! Mrs. Prudence is a spectacular teacher."

His lips were soft against my temple. "You're a spectacular student. You should write your story."

I pulled away in order to see his face. "What're you talking about, Jack Staines? I don't write that well, and I certainly can't think of any books by Negroes."

"Who mentioned a book? I'm talking about you recording your memories."

"Is that why you gifted me that leather-bound journal?"

He nodded.

"My story's no different from countless other enslaved persons'. No one wants to read that."

"It's not about who outside of this family does or doesn't care to know what you have to say, Ona Judge Staines. You were a bondsperson owned by the most powerful man in this country. And *you* escaped! Do you understand the monumental courage and strength required to do what you did? *Those* virtues are important to the legacy of our children. Record your stories for *them*."

I sat silently a while. "I'll consider it." If any part of my experience could benefit our children, then so be it. Both of their parents had been enslaved. But they would be born free. Perhaps, the telling of those stories *was* a gift worth sharing.

"Do you suppose our children will love to read?"

He chuckled quietly. "They'll have no choice with you as their mother."

"Nor with you as their father." Reaching over and taking his hand, I placed it on my belly. I pressed gently, willing him to feel the living dream safely cradled inside of me. "If I teach this little one to read, you must teach him or her to write, because your penmanship is far better than mine."

He sat open-mouthed and tongue-tied for the longest time before urgently whispering, *"Are you expecting?"*

I smiled shyly and nodded.

He stared at me before cupping my face with a touch so full of love and tenderness that I wanted to weep. "Whatever we need to do to maintain our freedom, *we do it.*" His voice overflowed with emotion. "This child *will* be born free and never know a day of bondage."

Without a care for public propriety, he kissed me deeply and I him.

When he released me, I blushed and fanned my face. "My love, you're simply scandalous."

He tossed his head back and laughed that huge laugh of his. "I beg to differ." He gently rubbed my belly. "Am I not your sweet-eyed sailor?"

"You are."

"Then, considering this blessed news, I cannot be reprimanded for kissing my wife."

I gently stroked his jaw. "Kiss me again so I flutter like your black-eyed butterfly."

EPILOGUE

TESSA

Seven Months Later

"Miss Tessa, you finished with the purple thread yet?"

"Jade, that's the fifth time you've asked and my answer hasn't changed. No. Find another color, chick."

"GiGi, Miss Serenity, tell Miss Tessa to quit hogging the purple thread already."

I laughed at Mama Calloway, Jade's GiGi, as she scolded me. "Tessa Lorraine, stop tormenting those babies and act your age."

Mama simply cut her eyes at me.

I tossed the thread to Jade and stuck my tongue out at her when she grinned. "Little snitch."

She batted her lashes. "Just one of my many talents."

Smiling, I reached for a different skein of embroidery thread and sat back to take in the full effect of the beautiful females seated at numerous tables arranged on the grassy back side of the family's Chincoteague property. I was humbled that Mama

Calloway had invited Mama, Rocki, Kennedy, and me to join their tribe in a living celebration, a sewing circle gathered in honor of Aunt Ona and Mama Delphy. Unlike Mama Calloway and her sisters, the majority had limited, even pitiful sewing skills. That didn't prevent us from designing colorful squares that would be assembled in a huge homage quilt.

God, I'm blessed.

Seated there surrounded by love and grace, I leaned back my head and let the summer sun sprinkling through the leafy canopy of trees overhead bathe my face. I had so much to be grateful for. The cyst removed during my procedure was benign, thank God. My post-surgery recovery had been smooth and, in Dr. Latimore's opinion, I shouldn't experience problems conceiving if and when desired.

Business was real good. I had so many upcoming projects that I was considering hiring a part-time assistant.

He either ignored or evil-eyed me when our paths crossed at various events, but I'd otherwise had no further interactions with Dominic. He was back with Carmel now. Chick had the nerve to post negative reviews of my business on social media. I'd attended a "Sis, Be Fierce" forum sponsored by a local African-American sorority a few months ago and sat in on a panel session featuring abuse survivors. Remembering one sister saying, "When you move forward, don't go back, not even to vindicate yourself," I laughed at Carmel's attempts to throw shade, did a block and delete, and kept moving. I'd escaped a dark path and my present and future were more important than playing sandbox games with dimwits from my past.

There was, however, a part of the past that I considered a precious treasure.

Miss Ona's journal had been rigorously tested, appraised, analyzed, and cross-referenced. It was fully authenticated, despite some sources arguing that Ona Judge Staines never existed, or objecting to the nation's first president being "outed as a slave master."

The dominant never wanna own their ish, or admit they benefited by keeping others in deficits. You can love the founding fathers, reenact the Civil War as if the outcome will change, and wear red, white, and blue all day every day. That's your prerogative. But what we're not gonna do is sit up here erasing facts. George and Martha Washington owned people. My people! Hashtag facts. Now, deal with it.

That was B.C.'s response to a caller who'd phoned a local radio show he was a guest on, claiming the family was unpatriotic and dishonoring the Washingtons, despite it being well documented that the Washingtons had indentured servants and owned enslaved persons of African descent. In true B.C. style, he shut that down with the quickness.

Interviews were part of the new terrain the family navigated after the media got wind of Miss Ona's diary. It created a frenzy, complete with kooks and crooks coming out of the woodwork claiming family ties or making outlandish offers to purchase the property. Mimi's investigative write-ups had been serialized into newspaper and magazine articles, and she was a guest on several podcasts. Some family members were featured on local talk shows as well as national televised news outlets and programs. For the most part, B.C. declined and ignored the blitz and glitz and focused on preserving his family's legacy. A family trust had been created, the state was funding the restoration and preservation of the house, and the homestead had been approved as a historical landmark.

And to think he wanted to sell this place.

Now, he was its protector. All because of Miss Ona's journal. Its discovery and presence had shifted things for B.C. He saw it as the gift that it was, valued its heritage and legacy. Clearly, Miss Ona had faith that sharing her story would one

day impact her descendants and somehow uplift the generations. And it did.

I still wasn't sure why I'd found the diary, why—as Mama
Calloway claimed—I'd been chosen when I wasn't blood-
related.

*We come from communal societies that had nothing to do
with blood ties. We've gotten away from that. Maybe Aunt Ona's
journal is a reminder to get back to living like we're inter-
connected.*

I accepted Mama C.'s wisdom. Still, I found it humbling
that I'd unearthed such treasure.

Tessa means "harvester; or to reap, to gather."

Jade had some school project about name origins a few
months back and had looked up my name.

*Miss Tessa, that kinda makes sense, like how you harvested
the journal and helped my dad and GiGi gather together and get
on the same page about the family property. That's pretty dope.
You're living like your name.*

Out of the mouths of babes.

"Miss Tessa, you can have the purple back if you still
need it."

I held up my embroidery square. "Nope, I'm on to my next
great color: aqua. My masterpiece calls for it."

Jade twisted her mouth sideways before cracking, "Too bad
Aunt Ona's needle case is being preserved like an artifact. You
could've benefited from her magic."

A needle case decorated with cardinals had been found,
pressed within those clumped-together pages at the back of
Miss Ona's journal. It was crazy enough finding the diary, but
touching something she'd used, perhaps on a daily basis, was
amazing and, like Jade said, magical.

"Whatever, *Jadie-Boo.* Stop hating on my skills."

"Yo, TLS, what's this?"

I glanced over my shoulder to see B.C., chef apron on,

studying something on his phone while heading in my direction.

"What's what, Brandon?"

"This, baby!" He turned his phone so I could see the estimate for his restaurant renovation. It had taken Rocki's legal genius to finally resolve the matter of code violations and undisclosed issues the previous owners had concealed. It took a minute, but now that the matter was handled and issues corrected, we could move forward on the renovations.

The project had me excited. I wanted to knock out part of the wall separating the kitchen from the dining area so that diners could see the food preparation, creating an interactive experience while highlighting B.C.'s culinary genius in action.

"Ten dollars and ninety-eight cents for an umbrella, Tessa. What umbrella?" He looked thoroughly confused.

I suppressed a laugh. "That's for the umbrella that blew away that day I stopped by the restaurant in the rain. You told me to put it on your tab, so I did."

"Really, T.? And this two hundred and sixty-eight dollars for a pair of boots is because?"

"You broke my heel off snatching my boot out of that quicksand deathtrap you call a parking lot."

"I could've left your fine behind out there in the rain."

"But you didn't, did you?" I stretched my neck back when I felt him standing behind me and got the kiss he leaned down to give.

"That was *one* boot, TLS, so cut the cost in half." His eyebrows were all bunched up as if I was committing highway robbery. "And why're you even putting it on the renovation estimate? You could've just said something."

I stared at him a long, hard moment before laughing. "It's a joke, B.C. The legitimate estimate is the second attachment."

"Oh... Naw, I'm fixin' to CashApp you for that five-cent umbrella and that dollar-ninety-nine broke-down boot."

I waited until he'd turned away before jumping up and hopping on his back. "You gonna pay me what you owe me, Black man!"

Laughing, he walked off, taking us towards the water's edge with me still clinging to him, piggy-back style.

"Why're you over here, infiltrating our sewing-circle business? Aren't you supposed to be barbecuing with the men?"

"Maybe I missed you."

"Maybe you didn't. You just wanted to sweat me about the family trip to Mount Vernon."

A weekend trip to visit the Washington estate at Mount Vernon was three weeks away and I had yet to respond to his invitation. We'd spent the past several months mending our relationship, ensuring that it was founded on trust, mutual respect, honesty, and friendship. Only recently romance had slipped into the mix, and I loved falling in love with this grown and sexy version of the first man I'd ever given my heart to. But we hadn't been physically intimate yet and I didn't consider a family trip ideal for sexual explorations.

"Separate rooms, boo," he suggested as if intuiting my thoughts. "I'm not tryna get with you with my family in the next room. If I remember correctly, you get a little vocal when the getting gets good."

I squealed when he dropped down into some bump-and-grind routine. "Quit, before you drop me!"

Chuckling, he straightened and wrapped his arms about my thighs, anchoring me.

"Do you think we'll feel them there, B.C.?"

"Who?"

"Aunt Ona and Mama Delphy?"

"Mount Vernon wasn't their final resting place, but it was a large part of their lives, so maybe."

I started to respond but was completely sidetracked by a

kaleidoscope of colorful butterflies swarming a clump of flowers blooming near the bank of the bay. "Oh my God, baby, look!"

B.C. turned in the direction I was pointing. "What?"

"Those butterflies!"

"Yeah... what about them?"

"Look again! See it?"

He nodded when he did. "Didn't Aunt Ona write that her mother called her black butterfly?"

"Black-eyed butterfly to be exact," I added, enchanted by the sight of a singular black butterfly in the center of a riot of color.

"That's dope."

"I agree."

My life used to feel heavy. I was moving and shaking, hustling and grinding out here in these streets, trying to make a name for myself while ignoring the warning signs of an abusive relationship. I'd forsaken my family, sacrificing them in the name of satisfying a man. I'd compromised myself, put up with treatment I never should have. I'd been imbalanced. Finding Miss Ona's journal and reading her story was a lesson in dignity. She'd been a person *owned* by other persons. Yet, when faced with the reality of being "gifted" to yet another master, she knew enough about herself and her inherent worth to know she deserved freedom, and risked life and limb to get it.

She was barely grown but dared to face an unknown world with all its hostilities, uncertainties, and risks because she believed she deserved to be free. Hers is not a household name, yet she's a personal treasure who inspires me daily, enabling me to face any self-doubt and challenges knowing that I have the strength of the ancients. I am the answer to the fervent prayers for freedom that they prayed. I am their future and I'm here because of forebears like Ona Judge Staines. I may have more material, more access than she ever did, but she survived with far less than I have. She taught me to appreciate freedom, rights, liberty, and to embrace every breath.

Watching that dazzling black butterfly flit and cavort on graceful wings, my heart overflowed with gratitude for Miss Ona's journal, and that she'd chosen me.

* * *

ONA

My niece many generations removed, Constance "Coni" Calloway, is correct in saying we come from a long line of communal people for whom blood ties are not our sole bond. Even before those who were forced to take the voyage were placed on slave ships, we were separated, not allowed to be in close proximity with others from our tribes or villages. The power of our unity and language were feared; enslavers couldn't risk our plotting rebellion. So, we were kept apart, placed with others who looked similar but did not speak the same language. Tossed into a world of strangers, we crossed tribal and language divides and blended our cultures to create family with one another. That's why it offended me greatly that Martha Washington thought she'd treated me like a darling daughter and couldn't comprehend why I chose to escape. Being forced to serve another with every waking breath wasn't familial love. It was bondage.

It wasn't the love for a darling daughter that led the Washingtons to pursue me relentlessly. It was the pride, outrage, and arrogance that comes with playing God and exalting one's self as a rightful captor of humans. Mr. Whipple's failure to secure my return didn't stop the President. He simply enlisted his wife's nephew, Burwell Bassett. While in Portsmouth on a business trip, the man searched me out, promising that the Washingtons would emancipate me upon my return to Mount

Vernon. I instantly smelled the vile lie. The Washingtons had repeatedly broken the law by rotating us in and out of Pennsylvania and I had no reason to trust them. I informed Mr. Bassett that I was already free and chose to remain that way. That was in 1799, three years after I'd escaped, when my courage was broader, increased.

My response did not sit well with Mr. Bassett or the President, and when Bassett returned a second time, he was determined to take me back to Mount Vernon and slavery, by force if necessary. When Mr. Bassett bragged of his intent while dining in the home of his host, state senator John Langdon, heaven was gracious. Though a staunch southerner, Senator Langdon—father of Miss Elizabeth—had recently manumitted his bondsmen, rehiring them as paid servants, and was sympathetic. Secretly, he sent word to me of Bassett's plans, warning that I should leave that very evening. Jack was at sea, so I bundled our precious one-year-old Eliza (named for Jack's mother, *not* that evil thing) and fled to Nancy Jack in Greenland. That was the last time the Washingtons pursued me, for the President died of a throat infection in December of that same year. It wasn't until then that I seemingly took my first full, unhindered breath since my voyage to freedom began.

In his will, the President instructed that his slaves were to be emancipated after his wife's death. Fearing for her safety and the possibility of a slave uprising when a suspicious fire broke out at Mount Vernon, she set them free in 1801, a year *before* her passing. That preemptive freedom did not, however, apply to the dower slaves held in trust for her grandchildren—only those owned by the President. Oh, how I wished it had, for my beloved Delphy would not have met with the fate I escaped and been given to that wretched Evilest Eliza. Many nights, I tossed and wept, imagining how monstrously my baby sister must have been treated. The blessing was that while in that evil thing's household, she was allowed to marry her love, William Costin.

I think it not strange that John Law and Evilest Eliza's union proved faulty and tense. Maybe that—and the fact that he'd sired half-caste children and was perhaps sympathetic—led Mr. Law to emancipate William in 1802 and Delphy five years later. My Jack, being a free man and sailor, was able to travel to various ports and destinations, and move among other Negros—free or enslaved. He was a conduit of information and was able to get word of Chincoteague, the place the Natives once called Gingoteague, to Will and Delphy. Together, my sister and her husband worked and purchased that plot of land and built a house there for themselves and their children, before moving to Washington D.C. Having fallen in love with those wild ponies, they labored to maintain that home on the island, visiting it often. A housekeeper lived there year-round, and it was made available to persons needing lodging, or as a safe place for runaways who dared to cross the wild island in their journey to elsewhere. I like imagining that Uncle Hercules passed that way as well.

In 1796, the year I escaped, during one of the return visits to Mount Vernon, Uncle Hercules was chastised for an infraction his son, Richmond, committed. When the young man was accused of theft, not only were both he and Uncle Hercules severely beaten, but our dazzling cook was stripped of his culinary duties and position and assigned hard labor in the fields. It was an injustice he could not overlook and that following February, on the President's birthday as the President prepared to return to Philadelphia, Uncle Hercules absconded, never to be recaptured. At times I wonder if my successful escape inspired him to do the same, and smile fondly at the notion of him cooking as a free man, satisfying no one's tastes and hungers save his own.

My hunger for authenticity and truth prevailed upon me to keep reading and writing. The lessons I'd begun with my husband's nephew, Frank, and continued with Mrs. Prudence

Kraft, I furthered after fleeing to Greenland to escape Mr. Bassett. I studied at every opportunity when not caring for my young family. I wrote my recollections as my beloved Jack suggested, compiling them in that leather-bound journal he'd gifted. But I was never able to complete it after choosing to put that journal in Delphy's safekeeping.

I was at market one day, selling the goods I sewed by hand, when I overheard in conversation the news that a grand-daughter of the famed deceased president, Eliza Parke Custis Law, was visiting the vicinity. Reliving her cruelty with light-ning-quick clarity, I feared she'd come to succeed where her grandparents had failed, by recapturing me. Unable to bear the thought of my children living even one second as her slaves, I hid with them for several days. Thankfully, it proved errant information and a false threat; but that incident propelled me to ship my journal and those candlesticks to Delphy. Before doing so, I affixed the needle pouch in the back of the journal. If ever I was separated from them, I wanted my little ones to have some-thing to hold that not only I, but my mother—their grandmother —had touched as well. As if it were a conduit and tangible connection, I prayed they'd sense a strength of ages, and the power of my unending affection. The candlesticks I sent so that Delphy might sell them if Jack or I weren't here and our chil-dren had need of provision. My heart rejoices that those beloved items remain in the possession of my beloveds, and I thank heaven for Tessa.

I didn't mean to frighten her that night she came to Delphy's. I merely exhaled on her neck to get her attention away from those pralines. My sister's house is a festive place, usually noisy with family and life, and quiet moments are infre-quent. Tessa was there alone, in stillness, snapping photos for what she thought would be *her* project. But it was *ours*. I didn't demand her attention merely for my sake. She'd begun a slip-pery voyage into bondage, and her spirit was breaking but she didn't know it. As a woman who'd existed for the first two decades of life enslaved, I recognized her captivity and was grateful she accidentally knocked my candlestick onto that brick and uncovered my writing. She wasn't a mere cog to get my family moving in unity. That precious daughter's soul needed renovating. And if my journal aided that process, then I consider myself even more blessed.

Now, she's opened herself to tenderness and healing, and I rejoice seeing her loving and being loved by my nephew many generations down my line. She and Brandon are proof that restoration happens in her own season and time.

It's my season for release. Through the years, I've lived to the best of my ability, to show my Creator that I am thankful for being free. Life was imperfect and I endured great loss, yet I wouldn't trade a day of my existence in exchange for perfection. Like Tessa I, too, now know the meaning of my name: *God was gracious.*

God was. God is.

The Creator's graciousness is wholly evident in this lovely sight before me. What a glorious assembly, these free women. Out here on a sweet summer day gathered on my baby sister's property fellowshipping, quilting, sewing—honoring we who preceded them, who sustained ourselves by giving love through needle and thread. Yes, some of their stitches could use a little nudge in a better direction, but I've learned that much beauty is found in imperfection. Every stitch is a link, a connection. A whisper of their inheritance. Whenever they stitch and laugh and admire the beauty of rare black butterflies waltzing on air, I will sit in my completion and watch and admire them. Now, I'll take my rest knowing my struggles weren't in vain, and my name won't be forgotten.

A LETTER FROM SUZETTE

Dear Reader,

Thank you so much for choosing *My Name is Ona Judge*. I hope you thoroughly enjoyed it! If you did and would like to keep up to date with all my latest releases, just sign up at the following link. Your email address will never be shared, and you can unsubscribe at any time.

www.bookouture.com/suzette-d-harrison

Also, if you enjoyed Miss Ona's and Tessa's journey in *My Name is Ona Judge* I'd be very grateful if you could write a review. I'd love to hear what you think, and it makes such a difference helping new readers to discover my work as well. If you're using an e-reader the app lets you post a review when finishing the book. How cool and convenient is that? So, please take a minute to share your perspective. Your review can be as brief as a sentence, but it has tremendous impact. And by all means, please tell a friend!

I love hearing from my readers—you can get in touch on my Facebook page, through Twitter, Goodreads, or my website.

Blessings until next time,

Suzette

KEEP IN TOUCH WITH SUZETTE

www.sdhbooks.com

 facebook.com/sdhbooks

twitter.com/Sdhbooks

instagram.com/suzetteharrison2200

AUTHOR'S NOTE

Dear Readers,

My Name is Ona Judge is without a doubt the hardest book I've ever written. Not merely because of the horrific landscape of slavery in which it unfolds, but because Miss Ona was a real person. My intent from the beginning was to honor her life, and to let her truth and existence breathe on these pages with the greatest possible authenticity. I prayed. I meditated. I called on Spirit, Miss Ona, *and* the ancestors. They helped me, guided me. The result is this story.

Melding the life of a real person with fiction requires tenacity, a little bit of crazy, and a whole lot of research. I cannot tell you the number of browser tabs I had open throughout the process, the articles I devoured, videos I watched, or the constant fact-checking, spreadsheets, and notes that went into this. It was intimidating, humbling. It was a true labor of love, but presenting Ona Judge to a wider audience makes every effort worthwhile. To my knowledge she is not a well-known heroine or figure, despite having bravely escaped enslavement in the house of our nation's first president. Yet, this bold soul deserves our notice.

Like Martha Washington, Ona Judge experienced heartbreaking tragedies. Six years after marrying Jack Staines, her beloved husband passed away. As a young widow, she raised their three children—Eliza, Nancy, and Will—and was often hounded by poverty. She shared a home with Nancy Jack, the woman who'd once provided a safe haven, and was considered a pauper, receiving aid from Rockingham County. It's been said that in some ways life as a widowed mother was even more physically demanding than what she'd experienced while enslaved by the Washingtons. Yet, when twice interviewed in her latter years by newspaper reporters, she still preferred freedom. She survived devastation yet again when, in the 1830s, both her daughters preceded her in death. It is believed that her son, Will, likely became a sailor and followed in his father's footsteps. As a fugitive from slavery, it is also possible that she never returned to Virginia or saw her surviving siblings again. On February 25, 1848 Ona Judge Staines passed away in Greenland, New Hampshire.

Stepping into the life of Ona Judge Staines has been nothing short of breathtaking and amazing, daunting and humbling. I thank you for joining this journey into the life of a courageous woman who didn't wait for liberty to be handed to her. She took it. Bravely. Like Tessa Scott, I too am honored that Miss Ona chose me.